THOROUGHFARE OF STONES

THOROUGHFARE OF STONES

Richard Haley

HEADLINE

First published in 1995
by HEADLINE BOOK PUBLISHING

10 9 8 7 6 5 4 3 2 1

Haley, Richard
    Thoroughfare of Stones
    I. Title
    823.914 [F]

ISBN 0-7472-1491-3

Typeset by
Letterpart Limited, Reigate, Surrey

Printed and bound in Great Britain by
Mackays of Chatham PLC, Chatham, Kent

HEADLINE BOOK PUBLISHING
A division of Hodder Headline PLC
338 Euston Road
London NW1 3BH

For Gary and Elizabeth

One

She lived on The Hill. Most of residential Beckford was built on hills, but there was only one hill that counted. I drove up into the heart of Daisy Edge on a fine sunny morning in July.

The house, like most of those on The Hill, was large and square, and set well back from a tree-shrouded drive. It had rosemary tiling and stone-mullioned windows. As I walked through the garden, a little old man was in the final stages of giving an immense lawn an immaculate wash-board effect with a sort of Rolls-Royce of the power-mower world. All you could hear was his false teeth clicking.

I rang the bell of a panelled-oak door – soft chimes distantly sounded. A thin-faced woman in a green smock opened it.

'John Goss,' I told her. 'I have an appointment with Mrs Rainger.'

'Please come in . . .'

I followed her across a large sunny hall and into a large sunny drawing-room. She went off; I glanced round. Chinese rugs, landscape paintings, inlaid walnut tables, Berlin woolwork and a marble fireplace, its opening concealed behind a flowered tapestry screen. The

1

house keeper would light real fires in its dog-basket, come October, of sweet-smelling logs. The Daisy Edgers had never really taken to designer flames.

Beyond the french windows, a balustraded terrace gave to a rear garden screened by ornamental trees. To the right, on a turning-circle, stood about sixty thousand pounds' worth of Porsche coupé, which the little old man had probably waxed earlier this morning to psych himself up to the right pitch of artistic frenzy for wreaking a terrible beauty on the front lawn.

'Good morning, Mr Goss.'

She was smallish, late thirtyish, and had smooth, short, dark hair and a slightly olive skin. She had a good unobtrusive figure and good unobtrusive clothes – the sort of shoes and cotton dress that titled cameramen photographed for up-market magazines against trees and an out-of-focus country house. She was very attractive if you'd nothing against the older woman. I hadn't, not a thing.

'Thank you for coming here,' she said.

As if there'd been any choice. The wealthy didn't come to your place, you went to theirs. The lateness of their cheques didn't do much for your cash flow either, but the good news was that they never bounced.

'I have a task that should take about a week,' she said. 'How much would that cost me?'

It was only ever middling people who pussy-footed about money talk. The poor and the rich invariably gave it top billing.

I sighed inwardly and began the old, old spiel.

'Private investigators don't work like that, Mrs Rainger. We work at different things at the same time – credit checks, legal work, missing persons and so on. I'd need to fit your assignment in with other work and charge it to you on an actual time basis.'

'I'd need total commitment,' she said flatly.

'That would be expensive. I'd have to farm out . . .'

'How expensive?'

As I said, the wealthy didn't prat about. I thought of a number.

'A thousand a week plus expenses.'

'That's a great deal of money.'

'Not, I think, much out of line with what the others have quoted.'

'What makes you think there were others?'

'Keen businesswomen shop around.'

'You're a very astute person.'

'That's what makes me such a good investigator.'

She watched me for several seconds in silence, with brown eyes that had a bird-like intensity. 'I believe you,' she said finally. 'In any case you are marginally cheaper than the others I spoke to, apart from the ones who gave no impression of competence.'

'Good. I'd hate you to select me simply because I was the best.'

'Do sit down.'

I did so, on a couch that stood at right angles to the left side of the great fireplace. She sat on another that stood opposite. The Daisy Edgers didn't go in much for three-piece suites either. Getting her to grant me even the faintest smile was becoming something of a challenge.

'Perhaps you'd like something to drink,' she said, and hesitated for the first time. 'Coffee . . . or something stronger if you prefer.' She glanced towards a half-moon table on the back wall, banked with decanters on a silver tray.

'Mrs Rainger,' I said gently, 'do try and forget the old films. I don't smoke cigarettes, I don't wear a trilby hat and I never drink Scotch at eleven a.m.'

She considered this impassively. I'd found it easier getting a smile out of a Halifax traffic-warden. During this new silence she must have touched a concealed bell-push. There was a knock at the door and the woman in the green smock came in, her expression as neutral as that of her mistress. Perhaps they practised on each other.

'Mrs Chalmers . . . would you be so kind . . . coffee and biscuits . . . thank you so much . . .'

She turned back to me when the door closed. 'I want you to maintain round-the-clock surveillance on my husband.'

So that was why she didn't smile. I sighed inwardly. Not very long ago I'd sworn I'd never get involved in another matrimonial dogfight. Husbands – it was always husbands – could get very difficult when they found out who'd done the leg-work on the leg-over. Last month a man had come to my office anxious to rearrange my face, and had only been persuaded against it when I pointed out that I was bigger than him, worked out twice a week and wasn't servicing two women simultaneously. But I could do without all the time it wasted, not to mention the shouting, which Norma complained did her head in.

On the other hand, there was a thousand pounds on the table for a few days' relaxing obbo on summer streets. In my business it constituted a week's paid holiday.

There was another knock and then the housekeeper brought in a tray which contained about twenty-two

4

pieces of bone china. When she'd gone I said carefully: 'If you're looking to obtain a divorce it's completely unnecessary these days to provide any proof of your husband's infidelity. All you need to do . . .'

'I know exactly what I'd need to do, Mr Goss, if I were looking to obtain a divorce.'

She poured coffee. Coffee that had been freshly made from freshly ground beans. The aroma seemed to fill the mind with indefinable desires. She handed me a cup, indicated ten kinds of biscuit, arranged like nouvelle cuisine on an oval plate. She watched me intently over her own cup.

'Divorce doesn't enter into it,' she said. 'And never will.'

'But you suspect there is another woman?'

'That's what I'm retaining you to find out.'

'You just need to know?'

'I . . . must know.'

Women who had to know. I hated it. Because they never did. Want to know. What they really wanted was for you, the neutral professional, to return and assure them they'd got it all wrong. Yes, he *had* started taking rather long lunches, but it was all to do with client entertaining and nothing to do with leg-over and chips.

And it was the sort of news I'd rarely been able to bring. I'd found from bitter experience that if the wife had begun to have suspicions about the new secretary with the honey-coloured hair and the freckled arms, the affair would be at least three months old. The husband would have lulled himself into such a sense of security that he'd even have begun to leave his car outside his girlfriend's house, instead of parking it in a side street a quarter of a mile away and homing warily in on a

5

circuitous route, wearing dark glasses and a tweed fishing hat.

When you went back to the wives and confirmed what they already knew they despised you for it. For that kind of money they wanted a lot more than the truth. They could get the truth for nothing. Sending them a bill served only to add insult to injury.

No, I didn't like it, even when it meant a nice easy week.

'Are you quite sure . . . you want to know?'

'Quite sure.'

I felt the first moment of genuine unease then. There was altogether too much self-possession going on here. She wasn't the only middle-class woman I'd done this for – it was usually only middle-class women who could find the money to retain me – and well-bred as they might be, they had all shared a common trait, an embarrassed sadness, an inability to look you easily in the eye.

There was a cold objectivity about her search for the truth that would only have made sense if she was going to take him for his shirt in a carefully prepared separation.

I said: 'Have you a good recent photograph of your husband?'

'No. There's no picture of him since we were married. He has an aversion to being photographed. He's not very much interested in the past or what he once looked like. He quotes someone called Barthes and says he can see little point in looking at old dead selves.'

Yes, well, that all sounded very elegant and literary, but I'd known many a Jack the Lad, and the one thing they all had in common was an intense dislike of the

happy snap. People could do things with photographs –
ex-mistresses could blackmail you, husbands of
ex-mistresses could find them and put you in the casualty
ward, wives could show them to private investigators.

It looked very much as if Mrs Rainger's husband had
been playing the field, and for some considerable time.
If that was the case how could she have missed it for so
long? And if she'd known about it for so long why was
she only wanting her worst fears confirmed at this late
stage? It was beginning to seem very messy and odd, and
my instinct was to back out.

If only I had.

'Perhaps you could give me his car and office details
then?'

'There could be a problem. He has very dark glass in
his motors which makes it difficult to see him clearly.'

Especially at the hour of leg-over and chips.

'I could watch him getting out in the car-park –
through field-glasses.'

She shook her head. 'The car-park's beneath the
office. It can only be entered by keying a code into an
instrument that raises a grille. Pedestrians can only get
into it from the inside by using another key-pad in the
door that leads from the hallway.'

'He must go out at lunch-time . . .'

'The trouble is they often lend one another their cars
to save time. The first cars in are often difficult to
manoeuvre out because of the later ones . . . If you
followed the car with his number you might be following
the wrong person . . .'

The man who had taught me so much about my
business had once told me that unfaithful husbands
swapping cars with colleagues at lunch-time went back to

the time of Henry Ford the First.

She looked past me, her eyes unfocused, as if she were thinking. I wondered how she knew so much about his routines. It was all very odd. I had half a mind to ring her later and tell her I didn't want to know. Her cool glance came back to mine.

'You have a dinner-jacket, of course . . .'

I shook my head. 'They've never been mandatory at Pizza Hut.'

She sighed audibly. 'I suppose you'd better hire one then. Rather that than have you following the wrong man for half the week at these sorts of prices.'

I wondered if someone had done exactly that, spent two or three days tailing the car driven by Rainger's best friend, while the car containing Rainger rocked gently on some deserted strip of moorland. I wondered if I was the last in a line of private men to be hired to find the truth she was determined to know. She'd obviously begun to realise what an elusive man he could be, and a man who took such meticulous care of his anonymity had to be sharing himself out. It gave the case a bit of genuine professional challenge, I supposed, if nothing else, though the man hadn't been born I couldn't get the story on.

She said: 'In two days a friend of mine is having a party at home, just along the drive. There'll be a great many people there including my husband and me. I'll arrange for you to be included in the guest list. Perhaps you could bring a female companion.'

'I'll make a start on my black book as soon as I'm back at the office.'

'It'll give you a good chance to observe him properly. Apart from that, the woman he . . . may or may not be

going about with might also be there. It's unlikely but
your trained eye might detect any significant nuances of
behaviour, bearing in mind that my husband is in any
case charming to all women.'

That I could well believe. I took my notebook out and
wrote down the first details of the Rainger file. She gave
me all the information I asked for in her clear, precise
tone, but when I wanted date of birth and schools
attended she said sharply: 'I'm asking you to follow him,
Mr Goss, not write his biography.'

'Take my word,' I said, 'you can't imagine how
valuable these details can sometimes be.'

She raised an eyebrow but she provided them. I rose
to go. 'I'll make a start right away.'

'Just as you wish,' she said, 'but the actual fee is
payable from seven-thirty on the evening of the party.'

'I hope you didn't think I'd be pressing the stop-watch
the minute I left the house, Mrs Rainger.'

We crossed the hall with its lyre-backs and its cabinets
and its bands of well-bred Daisy Edge sunlight. I said: 'I
sincerely hope your fears are unfounded.'

I sincerely meant it, and I couldn't honestly say why,
because it seemed that whatever the outcome she'd be
able to handle it; no one I'd ever dealt with in similar
circumstances before had been so calmly in control, so
keen to receive value for money. And yet I dreaded
having to tell her what I was almost certain was going to
be the truth.

She was a little behind me, and I turned round to her.
Perhaps the movement was unexpected; all at once I
caught her with the mask off. I had a glimpse, so brief as
to be almost subliminal, of a look that seemed to contain
both anguish and an almost desperate unhappiness. At

9

the same time, I felt a peculiar chill in the hall. It was a hot sunny day, one of the french windows had stood ajar in the drawing-room on swells of heat that smelt of grass and carnations. No doubt the cold air came from a kitchen conditioned by a portable unit, but it made me think uneasily of those drops in temperature that are said to occur in houses with a dark history.

Our eyes met – it was as if the old controlled elegance had never been away.

'Until Wednesday then, Mr Goss.'

Perhaps not, I thought, as I walked back along the garden, practically certain by now that I was going to trust my instincts and give her the elbow. But then I passed the gardener and he said 'Goodbye, sir', and touched his forehead, as if I were an acceptable professional, like a lawyer or a banker, or the man from the Equitable Life who only dealt with clients with more than a liquid million to invest.

Looking back, I sometimes think that little old man swung it.

Two

The George was the oldest pub in Beckford. It would have been pulled down in the Sixties, when they were pulling everything else down, except that it was part of a listed public building, with the same lancet windows and Venetian Gothic pinnacles. If I wasn't too busy I always tried to get in there some time between six and seven.

'There you go, pal,' Kev said, placing a gin and tonic clinking with ice before me at the same moment I reached the bar. 'Your friend's down the bottom end.'

I took my glass and picked my way through the crowd. Fenlon sat on a stool, morosely drinking bitter and chewing peanuts. The peanuts were a displacement activity for smoking, a battle not yet decisively won.

He shook his head. 'This place is in a time-warp. We're reliving the Fifties again, when Beckford was a wool town and Market Street was still cobbled and there were dance-halls with live orchestras.'

'*The Cruel Sea* playing at the Tivoli . . .'

'Bitter one and a penny a pint . . .'

'Alma Cogan top of the charts . . .'

'Four farms within three miles of the town-hall clock . . .'

I smiled sadly. 'Dad loved it here. Liked exactly that

11

kind of talk with Kev and Tom and Irene. I suppose it reminds me of him. He had all Alma Cogan's records. *And* Michael Holliday's, whoever he was.'

Fenlon sighed. 'They must have had a nicer class of crime in those days too. Can you imagine it without drugs and joy-riding and a burglary every twelve seconds?'

I shrugged. 'Still no picnic, according to Dad. He'd get home drained. There wasn't as much crime but the force was smaller and they hadn't the technology.'

He nodded. 'My old man says much the same. *Plus ça change . . .*'

'But neither of them wanted to retire, did they? Dad died because he'd nothing to live for. His idea of heaven would have been starting all over again, with new villains and new gear and a tape of *The Bill* to watch when he finally got home.'

Fenlon gave me a wry smile. I sensed he was thinking more of me than my father.

'How are things in your game?'

I shrugged. 'I'm making a living. How about you? You have the appearance of a man on the verge of lighting a high-tar Benson and Hedges.'

He pushed the peanut dish away irritably. 'We're getting nowhere. Heroin. A lot of it, good quality, even cut and cut again. It's everywhere. We can nail the pushers, no problem, but we can't turn the tap off. They get it from some guy on the street, and they don't know his name, of course, and even if we nailed *that* guy he'd be getting it from some *other* guy on the street.'

'Heroin.' I frowned. 'I thought it was a bit passé these days. I thought it was crack now.'

'That's only partly true. There *is* crack around but it's

expensive and even the kids are a bit leery about what it can do to you. Heroin's almost the *acceptable* kick these days, like pot used to be. A lot of crack users tick over on heroin between rocks. There really is a lot of it about and the Chief wants something done about it. Like within a week.'

'I thought the pressure must be on,' I said, glancing at the hand which again hovered over the peanuts.

'Oh, sod it!'

He strode across to the cigarette machine and began feeding it pound coins. He came back distributing the packets about his already bulging jacket.

'You're well out of it, John,' he said. 'You don't get made up if you don't get results, and they let you know that once a day.'

The moment he'd said the words he wished he hadn't. He gave me another wry smile. 'Let's have another,' he said.

He had to go after that, but I lingered on for a further fifteen minutes, listening to elderly wool men reminiscing, half-wistful for a city I'd never known, with its smoke-blackened buildings and its dance-halls and its vertical-process mills, where bales of grease wool went in at one end and fine suitings came out the other. All I'd known were wide roads and curtain walling and discos, and I didn't think I'd be looking back in middle age with quite the same degree of nostalgia.

I tried to reach a decision about the Rainger case. I couldn't really afford to be too picky. My fees might seem high but I had the overheads of a well-run agency, a decent office suite, a hard-working motor, a woman to look after the paper, faxes, PCs, a mobile phone – none of it came cheap. If I didn't take the job, some other

13

investigator would, and the thousand pounds, plus commission I'd get on routine work I could farm out, would keep us nicely ahead during the slack holiday weeks. And all I had to do was find out where Miles Rainger was currently parking his dong. A bagatelle, despite his motor-swapping, his smoked glass and his high-tech basement car-park.

I thought of the gardener respectfully touching his forehead to me. Mrs Rainger might be the bridge to other wealthy people. She might not like the answers I'd almost certainly come up with, but if those answers were presented to her in a meticulously documented manner she might at least pass my name on to her friends as being a reliable professional. The problems of the very rich were varied and endless. They needed advice on making their houses completely secure, they tended to draw up complex wills in which obscure beneficiaries had to be traced before the rest could get their hands on the loot, their daughters often took up with men whose backgrounds rewarded scrutiny, forsaken wives needed pointing towards the lawyer who specialised in creative divorce settlements. There was a lot of really good quality work available to a man they could trust.

On the other hand, the fact that Rainger was wealthy and probably powerful might mean, if he found out about my involvement in his exposure, that he might go on the revenge tack and pull every string he could to break me, small beer as my operation might be in his scale of things. That might have been the half-formed thought that lay behind the strong instinct I'd had to let the job go.

'Anyone in there?' Kev said. 'I was asking if I could get you another drink . . .'

14

'Sorry, Kev, I was miles away. I was just trying to imagine what it was like dancing in your best worsted suit to a real live orchestra.'

'Tell you what, pal. It has the edge on dressing in rags and jumping up and down in a cellar while some guy with a beard and rimless glasses plays gramophone records.'

The Beckford location of Brit-Chem PLC was housed on three floors of a modern office block called Hanover House, on Shilling Street, just off the York Road roundabout. I went there in the late morning of the following day to get the feel of the place. I knew I was working in my own time until Wednesday evening but then, as my self-employed grandfather used to say, you can't do enough for a good boss. That was his joke. He only had the one.

The entrance hall contained a great deal of marble and bronze and tinted glass. An old man in a commission-aire's uniform crouched near the door with the brooding look of someone who'd just been told his car was starting to go underneath.

I gave him a card. 'Key-pads for the garage,' I said. 'Routine inspection.'

'I *told* them,' he said, staring at me through glasses that enlarged his watery eyes. 'I *knew* they'd be nothing but trouble, them number things. It's me they come to, don't you see, when they won't work.' His quavery voice rose. 'And then I have to get the master out and open them that way. Wherever I am, whatever I'm doing, I have to get this lot out and run down yonder. You could be having a pee . . .'

Part of his generally misshapen appearance had been due to a large bulge near his thigh. He pawed at his pocket and pulled out a ring with what looked to be a hundred keys on it. My card lay on his desk, unscrutinised.

'Where's Andy?' he said fretfully. 'He was never away last month.'

'Nervous trouble,' I said. 'Hanover House was one set of key-pads too many. You wouldn't have the combination, would you, only I've left my pack in the van.'

'Oh, don't ask me,' he said, rummaging about in a cluttered drawer. 'I got the key, I never bother with them numbers. Here, is this it?' He handed me a plastic bubble with a card sealed inside, on which was printed in large red letters: KEEP THIS CARD ON YOUR PERSON AT ALL TIMES. REPORT ITS LOSS TO THE MANAGEMENT IMMEDIATELY.

'That seems to be it,' I said casually, committing its five-figure code to memory.

'Nervous trouble,' he muttered darkly. 'Don't talk to me about nervous trouble. Think I'd've been doing this kind of work all me life if it hadn't been for me nerves. I trained as a wool sorter. I was in the war, don't you see – Pioneer Corps. The things I seen . . . don't get me going about the war . . .'

I didn't.

The number operated both the basement key-pads – the one on the door that led from the entrance hall and the one that enabled you to raise the grille to drive your car in from the street.

I was now sure of a parking spot – the principle would be that possession of the number meant you'd been cleared to use the car-park. And that was important – the Shilling Street area was covered in unbroken yellows. Parking, especially when you were on obbo,

16

was the investigator's nightmare.

I could put the car downstairs in a nice dark corner and always be ready for Rainger's comings and goings. It wouldn't matter if the commissionaire saw me because I would keep altering my appearance with the glasses and wigs. Not that he'd remember anyway. He didn't seem the type who remembered anything very much, apart from the adverse effect on his nervous system of the Second World War.

Reception for the Brit-Chem suite was on the second floor. I walked up. You could get a lot together from a receptionist or an office manager. You said you were Detective Constable Maddox, investigating persistent weekend thefts in the building and had Brit-Chem had any incidents they might not have reported.

You were rarely asked for identification. The girl in reception would think it was the office manager's job and the office manager would think she'd already done it. If anyone ever did ask it was quite sufficient to flash the official-looking all-purpose card with the passport photo attached that you kept in a worn-looking leather holder.

You then got the office manager going about starting and finishing times, lunch breaks, who stayed in, who went out, and who worked late. In ten minutes you had a useful profile of staff comings and goings in general and executive movements in particular. It all helped towards getting your act together for the tail work.

I opened the door and stepped on to about five hundred square feet of dark-green Wilton. Cleverly angled lamps gave an added richness to fabrics and wall-coverings and white net curtains shimmered over picture windows. The air-conditioning provided a welcome coolness after the summer heat outside. The receptionist just provided coolness.

I knew instantly I was dealing with the genuine article. This was no scrubber whose switchboard only partially concealed a half-eaten Cornish pasty and a paper cup covered in lipstick.

She had longish hair that seemed almost black but was a very dark brown, and green eyes set fractionally too far apart. It was the sort of flaw – if it could even be called that – that seemed, like the flaws of so many attractive women, only to enhance the rest of her features, the high cheekbones and the full mouth. The effect of the eyes was slightly feline and slightly Slavonic, and totally riveting. She was slender and shapely and wore a sleeveless yellow dress that looked new.

'Can I help you?'

She gave me a smile so brief that if you blinked you missed it.

To her right was a VDU, which I could glimpse scrolling through complex-looking data; in front of her was a narrow electronic switchboard with touch-sensitive keys. On a side table stood a flask on a heated stand, with half a dozen cups and saucers of delicate floral design – coffee would be offered to important customers if it looked as though they might have to wait longer than sixty seconds.

A company that spent that kind of money on a reception area would not have failed to train the receptionist in how to get shot of people claiming to be DC Maddox. I made an immediate decision to make my excuses and leave.

I smiled hesitantly. 'I'm sorry to trouble you, but I can't find the commissionaire. I'm trying to locate the

Acme Insurance Company. It's not on the board in the hall but this is the address I was given.'

'It's usually Acme-something,' she said evenly.

'Sorry?'

'People trying to find which photocopiers we use – they usually start by asking about some company with a name like Acme or Apex. Falcon's quite a favourite too. I believe you call it the oblique approach.'

I was right, they hadn't skimped on the front desk.

I gave her my warmest smile. 'I should have realised I was dealing with a pro.'

'It would have saved time. And whatever you're trying to sell, from word-processors to plant-watering, we've got it. Perhaps you'd also make a mental note that the office manager never sees anyone without an appointment.'

The voice went with the figure and the looks, it had depth and timbre and was so perfectly modulated it might almost have been trained. Perhaps it had. Her tone held a faultless mix of frigid and impeccable politeness.

'How about a coffee then?' I said, making the smile go faintly Jack the Lad. 'Before I go on searching for the firm that *hasn't* got everything.'

It sometimes worked, the cheeky grin, the ready word, the refusal to be put down, the hint of how attractive you found them.

'That won't be possible,' she said, with no change of tone. 'And may I ask you to leave now – I'm expecting visitors in a few minutes.'

She was already studying the scrolling lines of data. Nothing worked quite like indifference. Irritation, impatience, or even temper you could regard as a challenge; it meant that at least they were reacting to you. But when you were regarded simply as a waste of space there was nowhere else to go.

The electronic switchboard made a noise like an upper-class cricket. She picked up the hand-set, put a hand briefly over the mouthpiece and said pointedly in my direction: 'Goodbye.'

But she had to return to the phone, from which I could just detect impatient hellos. I continued to stand there, smiling vaguely.

'Yes, Mr Rainger,' she said hurriedly, 'there *was* a message – Mr Keynes, he'll be in the office till one. Nothing else.' She listened for a few seconds, then made a note on her pad. '. . . London . . . Friday all day. Will you be contactable? No . . . I see. Shall I book you on the Executive? No. Are you sure? They often book up; there are only two first class coaches . . . No. Very well.'

She put down the phone with what, even beneath the polished manner, seemed like anger. She didn't like Mr Rainger. Her coolness with me didn't begin to compare with her clipped glacial correctness with him.

I was in luck. I now knew that my quarry was going to London but didn't want any reservations. Why? So that he could keep his movements flexible for fitting in a flying visit to some discreet *pied-à-terre* in Knights-bridge? I could be ready in advance for a day out in the Smoke.

It was a useful start. I wondered if I should try once more with this cool, pretty woman who knew all the answers.

'I don't suppose I could ask you to lunch,' I said, 'to make up for wasting your valuable time.'

'I've got my foot on a pad beneath this desk,' she said

20

calmly, 'and if you haven't gone in ten seconds and I have to press it, two very large men from Production Planning will arrive to carry you out.'

'Just as long as it's not the commissionaire,' I said. 'I don't think his nerves would stand it. He had a dodgy experience in the last war, you know . . .'

But having made certain I was on my way to the door she was immersed once more in her VDU.

I decided to have lunch anyway. I was hungry by now, as living alone I'd never really got to grips with breakfast. They said going without breakfast was very bad for you, and if you leapt out of bed ten minutes before setting off for the office they threw their hands in the air – didn't you realise that the majority of heart attacks happened within two hours of getting up, to people who'd stepped from the bed to the car? And if you did it on a *Monday*, after a Sunday of wine and roses, they just didn't want to know. I wondered if I'd make it to fifty.

I went to a small Italian café-restaurant in Town Hall Square, the sort of place where you could have a coffee, a sandwich or a full meal. It was efficient and inexpensive, and as none of the staff was English they didn't regard waiting at table as being beneath their dignity. It was almost full, but I was shown a table for two near the window. I took off my jacket and sat in shirt-sleeves. The town baked in a July heatwave and light flashed off the metalwork of cars. Young men from the offices sauntered the pavements eyeing brown-limbed women who wore bright minimal dresses, and the square seemed filled with an almost palpable sense of desire.

I'd almost finished my tagliatelle when the receptionist from Brit-Chem came in. She glanced around. The restaurant seemed completely full now. She was tallish and looked even more striking standing up. One of the waiters touched her arm. She followed him to the only table with a spare setting. Mine.

She looked down at me, unsmiling.

'Is there nothing else, Gino?' she said. 'I think I'll wait for one of the banquettes.'

'It could be ten, fifteen minutes, signorina.' He displayed a keyboard of white teeth. 'The sun – she bring everyone out, yes . . .'

'You've nothing to fear,' I said. 'I give you my word I'll not try to sell you anything.'

She frowned, looked at her watch and glanced through the window to confirm its accuracy on the clock tower of the town hall. 'Oh, all right,' she said reluctantly. She seemed to bring some of the cold air of Brit-Chem's reception with her. 'Just a tuna salad sandwich, Gino, and a coffee.'

'A pleasure, signorina . . .'

'Small world,' I said.

'How did you know to come here? Have you been following me?' Her green eyes, gleaming with reflected light, rested on mine with cold suspicion.

'I . . . don't see how I could be following you if I got here first . . .'

I spend my life talking to people and, like a comic working the clubs, I've learnt to be quick on my feet; but she'd thrown me. When I'd left Brit-Chem I'd accepted she was too sharp to be fooled and, apart from that, didn't fancy me. All, I had decided, was square.

'You could have followed me yesterday,' she said.

'But how could I be sure we'd end up at the same table?'

22

'You'd find a way.' She glanced at the smiling Gino as he put down her sandwich and coffee, her expression unaltered, as if he too might have been part of a dark plot to bring us together. 'It's happened before, you know. Car salesmen keen to get the fleet – they seem to think I've got the inside track to the Area Manager.'

She began to eat. She seemed to bring a certain artistry to that too, breaking small pieces from the sandwich and moving her lips almost imperceptibly. It was oddly compelling, it was as if even eating was part of that poised and sophisticated picture she presented, the picture itself a study that was endlessly refined. She had good hands too. I'd always looked at hands ever since an artist acquaintance had told me that very few women had really good hands, however otherwise attractive. They were either too stubby or too thin.

Her hands were near-perfect, supple, well-proportioned and with long tapering fingers.

'Please take my word that I'm not following you around,' I said, 'much as I'd like to.'

The compliment was ignored. 'But you *are* selling something . . .'

'Life Insurance. I'd hoped to get hold of the office manager. I'll write in.'

'But you'd thought if you took me to lunch . . .'

'No,' I said simply. 'I invited you to lunch because I wanted to take you out.'

The look of suspicion shaded into faint but noticeable contempt. It hurt. It seemed to indicate I was out of my tree even thinking I was the type of man she'd find remotely interesting. Either that or she put insurance salesmen one up from lavatory attendants.

I finished my coffee, anxious now to tiptoe away from

23

the mound of ego-damage. I moved around a lot and I talked to many women – they were far more reliable than men at providing information. They had a healthier curiosity and a better eye for detail, and they tended to be more helpful. I was single, unattached, and if the vibes seemed right I would sometimes ask one of those women for a date. Some said yes, a lot said no. But even if they said no they almost always looked pleased to be asked. Sometimes they even apologised for already having a partner.

This woman seemed not to think she needed that kind of grace.

I got up. With complete indifference she opened her shoulder-bag and took out a diary – one of those long thin leather ones sold by the more thrusting of the women's magazines – and began studying its densely covered pages.

I'm not sure why I did what I did then. Perhaps it was part of the discipline of my work, which dictated that I should always try to get along with people, however difficult they were, because people were contacts, people had memories. Ill-will in my business was an expensive luxury. There was also the fact that Mrs Rainger's friend's party was just over a day away and I still had no one to go with, though if push came to shove I could always take Norma along and pay her overtime.

But it was more than that. In the end I suppose it was just pride. It was an attempt to show I wasn't a total nobody, that I had friends in highish places who threw parties where men wore dinner-jackets and the women dressed like Mrs Rainger.

'Why don't we make a new start?' I said, smiling down at her soft wavy hair. 'I've got a friend on Daisy Edge

Drive who's having a party tomorrow night. It's rather formal and the men will be in black tie but I should think you might enjoy it.'

She put down the diary, her eyes slowly coming up to rest on mine. The earlier suspicion was back.

'Daisy Edge Drive . . .?' she said at last.

'Seven-thirty for eight . . .'

'Do you *live* on Daisy Edge Drive?'

'Not yet.'

'This isn't some kind of joke . . .?'

'I never joke about Daisy Edge Drive,' I said, my face beginning to ache slightly with the effort of keeping the smile in place.

She turned back to the diary and looked carefully at tomorrow's half-page and the items written on it. She ordered her life, this one.

'Very well,' she said finally. 'If I rearrange my evening I can find the time.'

'Good. I'll pick you up at seven-fifteen if you'd like to give me your address. I'm John, by the way, John Goss.'

'Fernande,' she said, 'Dumont.'

As I went off into the city heat I suddenly wished she'd stayed all of a piece and turned me down. Her cynical agreement to go out with me because of what was on the table was an even worse blow to my pride.

But I'd asked for it.

Three

On Wednesday morning, very early, I was on The Hill again. At the rear of the houses on the lower side of Daisy Edge Drive, of which the Raingers' place was one, a substantial plot of tree-lined land sloped gently, to separate the drive from any other group of houses. A thrusting Seventies builder had tried to acquire this strip of land for development. The Daisy Edgers, with the usual reluctance of the Yorkshire wealthy to spend money, had decided to buy the land themselves and maintain their cordon sanitaire exactly as it was. Their bid was derisively topped by the builder, and their next. With land in that area he couldn't lose. So then the Daisy Edgers took him quietly aside and told him that if he went ahead, not only would he not be invited to join the Masons, not only would he never achieve a knighthood, whatever he did for the party, but when his membership of the Daisy Edge Golf Club came up for renewal, they'd ensure it wasn't. Outer darkness from the golf club clinched it.

This incident, and the power of the Daisy Edgers, passed through my mind as I moved cautiously up through the trees to the wall of the Raingers' back garden. I let myself in through the gate, concealed from view of the house by dense foliage, first checking that it wasn't wired in to an intruder alarm, as the gates of the wealthy increasingly were, and then I found a spot in the middle of the trees and shrubs where I had a clear view of the rear of the house, the terrace, the turning-circle to my left and the stone-built double garage.

I'd already asked myself why I was doing this when I'd be able to see Rainger easily and in comfort at the party tonight, especially when I was still working in my own time.

I settled myself behind foliage in which I'd arranged a little window, took out my camera and checked the battery level. It was small, modern, lightweight, and could do anything from reading the light level to refocusing continually on someone walking towards it. It joined the fax and the car-phone as items I could never see how I'd managed without.

I set it to automatic zoom and waited. This would be the first picture in the file. Sometimes they insisted on seeing photos of the mistress, sometimes they couldn't bear to. I'd never forgotten the way one woman had looked when I'd had to show her pictures of not just one mistress but two.

I'd decided that if Rainger was one of the craftier wife cheaters the sooner I started the better. Why wait until this evening when he might be taking the girlfriend for a spin at lunch-time? The sooner I could establish the infidelity pattern – and all these types had one, even the smoked-glass-and-car-swapping brigade – the sooner I could tick over on the case, fit in other work, draw a nice cheque for minimal effort.

None of this was the exact truth. It had touched me on the raw to realise that even though she'd decided I was

an 'astute person' she still felt I needed to see him as a
sitting target to be certain I was following the right man.
It hadn't done much for my professional pride, I
suppose. It seems silly but it was the way I was.

I had been at the house at half-past six. I'd found from
long experience that provincial businessmen fell into
three groups when it came to starting a day's work –
those who started very early, those who started exactly
on time, and those, usually fathers' sons, who started
about ten, when the mail had been sorted, and, if they
had a good PA, half of it dealt with.

Rainger, rather surprisingly, was an early starter. At
seven-thirty, one of the french windows opened and he
came out on the terrace, where he spread his hands on
the low ornamental wall and gazed at his immaculate
lawns and flower-beds with a faint smile of what seemed
satisfaction.

'Gotcha! As they say in all the best tabloids,' I
murmured, taking three rapid shots, the soft whirring of
the film-advance mechanism lost among the gathering
bird-song.

He wore the trousers, perfectly cut, of a dark-blue
suit, a blue-and-white-striped shirt, a plain blue tie. The
suit's jacket hung over his arm; the day was already hot
and sunny. He was about five foot ten, with a compact
physique, blue eyes, regular features and dark-gold hair.
What did you give a man who had everything? I was
certain Mrs Rainger's suspicions were well founded –
somewhere, some pretty young thing would be trying to
put together the best package of grooming, flattery and
physical co-ordination that would provide that little
something extra.

I knew I'd not need a week to find out who she was.

29

He glanced at his watch, looked back towards the open french window as if half-expecting to see his wife standing there to wave him off. I knew she'd not be around, could have told him that once a woman suspected a man of being unfaithful she immediately concentrated on making the best of herself. By now, Mrs Rainger would have started on that process of intense grooming that would leave her looking as elegantly attractive as the morning I'd met her. Not for her the relaxed start to the day of dressing-gowns and mules and tumbled hair.

Rainger walked down the steps from the terrace then, and across to the garage, where a remote-control device attached to his car key-ring made the doors slide quietly upwards automatically, to reveal the Porsche coupé and the Mercedes, a picture of which I also took. I heard it cough softly into life, watched him back out, turn and set off up the drive to the front entrance.

I walked slowly down through the copse and along to the distant quiet crescent where I'd left my own car. I'd not been able to follow him from his own house, but the point at this stage had been simply to clock him. As he was going to London on Friday, I could assume he probably wasn't going anywhere today until he'd checked in at the office. In any case, senior executives didn't do much routine fieldwork; their job was to organise and administer.

I wished I could shake off the feeling of unease, could forget about The Builder's Tale. I wondered if it was wise to mess with people seriously wealthy enough to draw up their own rules. There was still time to pull out.

I checked the Hanover House car-park – the Mercedes was standing there. I waited until ten, but he didn't show, and so I felt it safe to assume he'd be there until lunch-time. I was back at noon – at half-past he came into the car-park – with three other men. They all got into one car – not his – and drove to a pub just beyond Clifford Park, where they had a simple lunch and a couple of drinks, and were back at their desks by a quarter to two.

I returned at four. Tonight was party night and he'd probably want to be off in reasonable time to change. I was certain I'd not see anything resembling a mistress there. The single trait nearly all men having affairs had in common was to keep one life firmly separated from the other – sleeping with a friend's wife could mean the possible loss of a valuable business contact and golfing partner, let alone half the house and pension rights.

At five, I followed Rainger's Mercedes, which definitely contained Rainger, out of the city and along Beckford Road, but at the point where I'd expected him to take a left in the direction of The Hill, he kept on going. Beckford's urban sprawl, on its north-western side, rapidly gives way to open green-belt land, and several miles further on he turned left, and I followed him, from two cars back, up a steadily climbing route that at its peak gave panoramic views of the Aire Valley. A car-park, fringed by broad-leaf trees, had been built specially to enable sightseers to admire the view from their car windows, and at this time of the day there was invariably a handful of cars standing there, in which people, who'd probably been penned up in offices all day, simply sat, gazing and unwinding.

Rainger swung off into this car-park. I smiled, drove on, parked over the brow of the hill. Was this where his *petite amie* got out of her own car, nipped discreetly into

31

his, and was whisked off to some more private spot for a quick game of doctors and nurses? I'd put a week's takings on it. I grabbed my camera, darted back to the parking spot and concealed myself once more among trees. The Mercedes was parked strategically to the rear of the shady tarmac. The usual handful of cars stood at the extreme edge of the park, where the land fell sharply away, their owners drinking in the view. There was no car near Rainger's, and no car at the front that contained a woman on her own. Was she late? Could she not make it? I couldn't believe either, not with a catch like Rainger. I glanced at my watch – five-thirty. Wasn't he in any case cutting things fine? He'd need an hour at least to get from here to the secluded spot, do the business, return her. He'd then need a further twenty minutes to get back to The Hill.

I stood, camera at the ready, for fifteen minutes, becoming more and more puzzled. He seemed just to be sitting there, not near enough the edge to admire the view, not taking a mistress on board.

I heard the click of a car door opening. A man in suit trousers and a white shirt got out, went to a wire waste-container at the edge of the car-park, jettisoned rubbish – copies of the *FT*, paper cups, wadded envelopes. Like me, he probably almost lived in his car. He went back to it, reversed, drove off.

Nothing happened for another fifteen minutes, with Rainger simply sitting there, his outline dimly visible through the darkened glass. It was all very odd. The cars at the far end came and went, as drivers completed their mantras. Over the half hour, I dare say all the original drivers had been replaced.

At last I heard Rainger's car cough into discreet life.

He himself drove to the waste-bin, got out, began disposing of rubbish of his own, though, as he was close-parked and had his back to me, it wasn't possible to see exactly what it was. He was now wearing the jacket of his blue suit, despite the heat. But the suit was probably lightweight and the Mercedes air-conditioned. Perhaps he'd had so much on his mind he'd forgotten to take it off. And perhaps he'd simply come to this place to get away from phones, stress and business worries, like all the others, and a man cleaning out his car had prompted him to do the same. The trouble with my line of work was that it became difficult to accept obvious explanations for people's apparent oddities of behaviour.

Yet why dump his rubbish here? When there was a housekeeper he could simply hand it to, or the little old man who gardened and washed the cars? Rainger reversed away from the waste-basket, turned and swung out on to the road.

I let him go. I didn't see how there could be time now for even the quickest of quickies, not if he had to be on parade at the neighbours' at seven-thirty for eight. Having a look in the waste-basket might quite easily prove to be the more valuable option. There might just be a screwed-up note there, or even the pieces of one, that he couldn't trust to the office waste-paper bin. It would go with smoked glass and motor swapping.

I retrieved my own car, drove it into the car-park and drew up close to the waste-basket. I had no problem in finding debris of my own to get rid of. I put it carefully in the basket, which must have been cleared earlier in the day as it contained only a few inches of waste. I checked rapidly through the last layer. It seemed to consist exclusively of back numbers of *Shooting Times* and *Yachting Monthly*.

I glanced surreptitiously at myself in the immense mirror with its ornate gilded frame. I only rarely wore a dinner-jacket, and the last time I'd worn one I'd thought I detected a slight resemblance to the earlier Paul Newman. I'd been wrong. Looking beyond my own image, I caught sight of Mrs Rainger's, on the other side of the wide room, her expression briefly unguarded. The person she was looking at was out of mirror range, but I knew it would be her husband.

I remembered the mask slipping on Monday morning, in the hallway of her own house, when for part of a second she'd looked so desperately unhappy. This look couldn't have been more different, this look seemed to be simple adoration. The eyes were gentle, the lips parted in a tender smile, as she gazed to where I knew Rainger was standing, at the foot of the room. This evening the lady seemed mad about the boy.

The look was almost as fleeting as the earlier one had been. Both emotions had seemed extreme. Maybe it was her pampered life-style. She didn't need to work and even the work of the house and garden was taken care of. Maybe she had too much time to brood. I felt another flicker of the unease that was beginning to dog me about this case.

I tried to shrug it off. I was merely the hired hand. Why not try to relax and enjoy the do? It wasn't hard. Fernande had taken a great deal of care with her appearance. Her hair had been drawn back into what I believe is known as a french pleat, and she wore a dark-green clinging dress, in a classic style with a rounded neckline. Her only jewellery was a fine gold chain, and it was this simplicity that seemed to bring out the cut and fall of the material and the slenderness of her neck.

Her face was fascinating in its attractive oddness, the spacing that gave that look, part cat-like, part Slavonic, to the eyes.

She was glancing around with obvious approval at the Venetian crystal chandeliers, the oil-paintings of grouse moors, the hired waiters with their trays of drinks, and the other guests, who gave off that aura of luxury that was like a fine golden haze.

I'd picked her up from a large, solid house below Clifford Park that had probably once belonged to a wool merchant. It had been converted into flats, with most of its lengthy front garden flagged over to provide parking space for the five or six tenants. It was occupied mainly by young professional couples who, for one reason or another, wanted a good address and a short lease, and it looked as impersonal and as cared for as a well-run hotel.

I pressed the bell next to the name-card saying F. Dumont, wondering if she really was of French origin – she'd pronounced her Christian name in the French manner.

'Hello.'

'John Goss.'

'I'll press the release. You have to open the door before the buzzer stops otherwise we'll have to begin again.'

Undistracted by her physical presence, I realised even more sharply how well she used her voice. It had total precision and yet a sort of unhurried gliding quality.

I wondered if her Brit-Chem salary was enough to

cover the cost of her accommodation. She was on the top floor in what was obviously a flat for one squeezed into the attic area. The door stood ajar, and as I knocked I could see that one of the walls was reduced by the pitch of the roof, but the room itself was light and airy, with views over the roof-tops of smaller houses to the trees of Clifford Park.

'Come in, John Goss . . .'

She was smiling. It was a smile that seemed to compare with yesterday's as the sun compares with a sixty-watt bulb. It was almost possible to overlook that she'd only agreed to go out with me because of the party, not for myself. Her rapid glance seemed to take in every aspect of my appearance, from my freshly barbered hair to my gleaming funeral-and-wedding shoes.

'You look well in formal clothes.'

'You look tremendous.'

It wasn't hyperbole. A good deal of effort had gone into the way she looked. I'd rarely seen make-up applied so artfully, seeming to be a barely perceptible enhancing of her natural healthy colouring, yet giving a remarkable intensity to her green eyes, which I'd already noticed had a propensity for shining with reflected light.

She accepted the compliment with a slight widening of those eyes, a minute forward shrug. She knew she looked good, knew that compliments were her right. She wasn't the kind who was going to say she was glad I thought so.

'Nice place,' I said.

'Madly expensive, but that's the price of an address on the right side of the park.'

She glanced round the sunny room, her expression

clouding slightly, as if cash flow might be a problem.

I said: '*Are* you of French descent, by the way?'

'My grandfather was French. He was in textiles. He came to Beckford between the wars.'

'It must have been a great help with your French O-levels.'

She smiled, nodded. 'I'll get my bag and then I'm ready.'

There was a slight delay while she was in the bedroom, no doubt she'd be putting a final unnecessary touch to that already impeccable appearance. I wondered why she was only a receptionist. Why not a PA or an administrator or a saleswoman – all jobs it seemed she had the confidence to handle? I glanced round the living-room. Modern furniture, framed prints of theatre and ballet scenes, a stereo system, books and magazines in a recessed wall unit, elegant table lamps. It was all more or less standard working girl, but working girl surely on a career path. The reception desk didn't seem to fit in at all.

I smiled wryly. What had it got to do with *me*? Our paths had only crossed because I was wearing a dinner-jacket and taking her to Daisy Edge. She was a *date*, for God's sake, not a case, not someone I was investigating. As I may have said, investigation work tended to develop certain hang-ups.

She came back with a narrow embroidered bag in her hand, and we went down the many stairs and out to my car. It was a Sierra. She glanced at it with an expression that gave the faintest indication that she felt it would simply have to do. I wished it could have been something sleek and sexy then, with a convertible top. I could imagine the wistfulness and envy we'd have aroused, driving in an open car through the evening traffic in slanting sunlight.

Even so, it was the high spot of what had been a relatively humdrum year, to cruise with this fragrant and attractive woman along the park's perimeter road. We could hear the thock of tennis balls against nylon through the open windows and, in the distance at the side of the lake, could see old men bowling as shadows lengthened over greens that seemed as smooth and artificial as freshly ironed table-cloths.

Then I drove upwards on to the hill known simply as The Hill and off to the right along the lengthy drive known simply as The Drive. I was aware of her glancing to both sides of the road, at the great houses at the end of vast lawns, which could only be glimpsed fleetingly through arched stone gateways, screened as they were by tall, dense hedges and the forest trees whose branches met and intertwined above The Drive itself.

'A fine and private place . . .' I found myself murmuring involuntarily the words that had come into my head on Monday when I'd called on Mrs Rainger.

She glanced at me. 'I thought that was supposed to be the grave.'

I smiled. 'I was thinking aloud. But it fits, don't you think? There'll be people in those gardens playing croquet and tennis and sipping their sundowners, but you can't see them from here.'

'I see what you mean. They do seem able to afford a very fine kind of privacy.'

There was approval in her tone but not, somehow, envy, as if she were more interested in the money the houses represented than the life-style.

I parked my car among the Jaguars, Mercedes and

BMWs, and we walked past the usual perfection of lawn and teeming border, and through a front door that stood open. A tall, rather languid woman with very pale looks and yellowish hair came across to us. I was beginning to gather that despite the leisure these women had for sitting in the sun, acquiring a tan was something that was decidedly not the sort of thing they did, not wanting, I supposed, ever to be mistaken for the sort of people who'd just returned from a fortnight in Benidorm.

'Mr Goss, how nice to see you. And this is . . .'

'Miss Dumont . . . Fernande . . .'

'Do come this way . . .'

She didn't know me from a central-heating engineer, but she carried it off beautifully, taking us about half-way down a cavernous reception room, introducing us to a handful of adjacent people, making sure we had drinks, and then more or less leaving us to it.

As we sipped our drinks, I reached a compromise with myself. Fernande was simply here because of this, and I had to stop trying to let myself believe that the warmth of her welcome might be a sign I had the slightest shred of intrinsic attraction; it could only lead to disappointment. Best just to make the most of the evening and then forget her, as she'd almost certainly forget me, as soon as she'd confirmed what she possibly already suspected, that what she saw was what she got, a Sierra man to whom for some reason the Jaguar men had tossed a bone.

'Ah, Mr Goss, how nice to see you again.'

It was Mrs Rainger, in chiffon and pearls, playing a straight bat. She glanced at the glass of Chivas Regal I was reverently putting away and said: 'So you do drink after all.'

'Only after seven,' I said. 'Who was it said that those people who don't drink, when they get up in the morning that's as good as they're going to feel all day?'

Impassive as before, her brown eyes rested on mine with the usual intentness. Perhaps it was the way I told them. I introduced her to Fernande. I'd been worried they might already have met. It was only after the spur-of-the-moment decision to invite Fernande that I'd realised Mrs Rainger wouldn't like me bringing a receptionist from her husband's company; she might think I was going to use her as an informant. Which was true, of course, if I got the chance. But they seemed not to have met.

She smiled encouragingly at Fernande, like the Queen slipping an old lady a Maundy shilling. 'What a lovely dress, my dear.'

'Thank you, I'm rather fond of it myself.'

I'd suspected the dress didn't come from Debenham's. Mrs Rainger's expert scrutiny, which probably priced it within a pound, placed it well on a par with the dresses of the other women, any one of which would be the likely equivalent of five of my suits – though don't run away with the idea that I actually *own* five suits.

Mrs Rainger turned back to me with the slightest look of interrogation. Had I got the fix on her old man? I inclined my head a fraction. She'd arrived ten minutes after the kick-off on Rainger's arm, had looked casually round the room till our glances met. Then she'd left him near the door with a group of men while she circulated. As he'd tended to stay at the bottom of the now very crowded room, there hadn't been the problem of him seeing Fernande, though I'd have known how to handle it had the contingency arisen.

So it wasn't all cakes and ale; I was still working behind the costly booze and the hired threads. But it was nice work if you could get it.

'Champagne, madam,' the man in the white jacket murmured. 'And Chivas for you, sir, I believe . . .'

'That memory could get you on *Mastermind*.'

He inclined his head suavely and passed on.

Fernande smiled at me. She was smiling a lot this evening. 'This is tremendous fun,' she said. 'Thanks for asking me.'

A certain respect was entering that low, agreeable voice.

'The pleasure's all mine,' I said. Truthfully.

An expensive flat, a very expensive dress – she seemed not even to belong in offices. I wondered why she wasn't in antiques or riding stables or Cordon Bleu cookery.

'If only you'd said you were a financial adviser yesterday morning,' she said, her shapely hand on my arm again, 'I could have got Peter to see you. He'll only see people with decent credentials.'

We both knew it was a lie, but she did it very well.

'I should have done some advance soundings. I usually do. But someone had cancelled an appointment and I had an hour to spare. You looked so formidable behind all that technology I didn't think I stood a chance.'

'But you must have so many contacts . . .' she glanced round the room.

'Not . . . so far in the bigger companies. I've tended to concentrate on what they call the old money. The lawyers and the brokers, the family firms . . .'

She now accepted my cover completely. People in our part of the room had quite taken to us, especially when the women had clocked her dress. Her voice, her assured manner and her ready smile were a great help.

These people sensed we weren't in their league, but the fact that we were there at all carried weight. I think they'd decided that if we could fork out for a dress like that we must be the coming people. I may have hinted before that the very rich were not really into etiquette; if they wanted to know about you they just went right ahead and asked.

'And what's your business, young man?' one of the grandees had demanded, and when I'd told him financial adviser had run completely true to Yorkshire form and tried to get a great deal of free financial advice.

But it was a cover I'd used many times before and I'd mugged up on it all – the insurances, the bonds, the annuities, the trusts, the PEPs, the AVCs; you name it.

I knew how to tell a wealthy man his best tax-effective options, and the things I told him must have been what he'd already done or was considering because he nodded his head in cautious agreement once or twice, anxious to dispel the slightest impression he really had got a few bob to one side, apart from the little he'd scraped together to help with the grandchildren's school fees.

In the end I could feel myself basking in Fernande's open admiration, as more people drifted towards us, like sharks picking up the scent of blood, the men hooked on those words so close to their hearts, such as flotation and tax-shelter and off-shore investment, the women keen to get an exact costing on Fernande's dress.

'Not forgetting Betterwear,' I said. 'Shares up a hundred and forty-two per cent last year and forecast to rise by the same again this. There aren't too many firms can show ten million *cash* as a balance-sheet item. An essential part of the portfolio I'd have thought, for anyone', I added prudently, 'who had any spare money.'

'That's just it, John, do you see, we've all taken a bit of a bath with the recession. I only wish I could lay my hands on a few thousand . . .'

Other heads sagely nodded, as rapid eye movements hinted at brains speedily evaluating the recent discussion.

The games people played. As the sun set over the topiary and the summer houses and the ornamental pools, they pretended to be cleaned out and we pretended to be their sort of people. Because Fernande was pretending too. I was just a working boy, reasonably skilled in the art of dissembling, keen to get myself across for professional reasons. But she was coming on as if these were her own kind of people. I'm not sure how I became aware she was acting – perhaps it took one to know one – but she seemed to be selling herself too, in the dress the Brit-Chem salary couldn't possibly have paid for; and to me the charm and the easy chat and the frank acceptance of the admiring glances of men who mentally undressed her, was a performance that came on marginally too strong, class act though it was.

Oddly enough, there was one other person, apart from Fernande and me, who didn't appear to make an entirely seamless fit into that gathering – Miles Rainger.

It was only the difference between one shade of grey and another, but it was there. He talked with great confidence to the people around him, he laughed a lot and made them laugh a lot, but he didn't seem to blend in quite as completely as his wife.

His dinner-jacket, like mine, seemed a little too new, of too modern a cut. My old dad wouldn't have cleaned the car in the ancient, almost verdigris-tinged clothes most of the men were wearing, but my old dad, like me, would have fretted about being considered too poor to buy a new one. The old Yorkshire money would have thought us not quite right in the head. Hadn't they taken a bit of a bath in the recession – they couldn't throw money about on new dinner-jackets when there was one in the wardrobe in perfectly good condition barely twenty-five years old.

Rainger's faintly suspect good looks also seemed to have been given rather too much arriviste attention. I studied them again, the longish dark-gold hair, the blue eyes, the slight tan, the compact frame. He looked to me to be exactly what his wife in her heart must know he was – a womaniser.

If his mistress was in this crowded room, which I very much doubted, I knew he was too astute to give any indication of it. In fact he received many admiring, if not almost hungry, glances, and a number of women were keen to tweak his sleeve as they drifted past his group. He had a warm smile and a ready word for them all, but was careful not to let himself be isolated by any one of them. He was like the skilled alcoholic, never drunk, always lucid, only ever taking the smallest sip from the glass that rarely left his hand.

It was at the end of this assessment, made a few seconds at a time, in between my contribution to the Finance Select Committee, that I seemed to detect another note of warning. It was faint but it was persistent, like a phone steadily ringing in another room.

Had he married for money? He seemed to live in some style for a man who worked in a location sales office. And was he spending his wife's money by the fistful on some other woman? And when I turned up the other woman would his wife give him hell for the rest of his life, knowing the life-style joined them at the hip? And would Rainger, pausing only to sharpen his knife to razor keenness, go for the messenger?

I'd had the suspicion before, but this surmise added a new and more sinister dimension. I didn't think there'd be any doubt about it, it seemed guaranteed that a man who looked as indulged and cosseted and fawned on as Rainger would have to go for someone's throat if life at home became unbearable.

It couldn't be hers, if the treasure chest was under her bed, so it would have to be mine.

But I was in it now. My presence here in a rented tuxedo meant I'd accepted the assignment. There'd have to be guarantees, guarantees that my name would be kept under wraps, perhaps even guarantees that she'd not tell him she'd used an investigator, but would say she'd gone do-it-yourself – I could tell her what to say. I sighed, recalling again how they'd eaten the builder for breakfast. These powerful men would all be on Rainger's team, men always closed ranks when it came to bits on the side. They'd wish him the best of British. If he fed them my name it would be like pointing a Rottweiler and shouting: 'Kill!'

'Oh, quite,' I said, dragging my attention back with an effort, 'they're certainly not to be sneezed at. The thirty-sixth issue was a snip. We'll not see eight and a half per cent nett guaranteed for a long time, perhaps not this side of the millennium. Probably better than a TESSA as it works out . . .'

My eyes strayed back to Rainger and, as I mulled over the unwelcome thoughts his appearance aroused, this happened. A coloured man came through the door at Rainger's end of the room, an Asian. He was dressed like the rest of us, but had added a red cummerbund. He was shortish and wore gold-rimmed glasses, and at a do like this he had to be some kind of professional – a consultant or a doctor or a minor diplomat.

As he passed Rainger's group, he touched his shoulder. Rainger turned round smiling, but the smile abruptly disappeared, to be replaced by a look of surprise that seemed to border on alarm. I had an impression that a glass was dropped or knocked over – a white-coat steamed discreetly up to put the matter to rights.

As he did so Rainger's face relaxed, and he began to smile again as he shook the coloured man's hand with every appearance of warmth.

No one else seemed to notice, not even his wife this time. The preprandials were taking hold and the only subtlety of behaviour that would really have stood out now against the hum of talk and laughter would have been someone dancing on a table.

But I was the trained observer and I'd noticed. And I wondered why the unexpected appearance of a coloured man should give him such a nasty turn.

Four

For one worrying moment I thought I'd lost him. After buying a second-class ticket, he'd slipped into the Gents. No need to follow him in there, there was only one door; I hung about near the paper-stand waiting for him to reappear.

But he didn't reappear. A man came out in a tweed suit and a cap, but no Rainger.

It was within minutes of the train's departure and it seemed as if I was going to miss it. I couldn't get it together. I went in the Gents myself. Deserted. I kicked every lavatory door with forty-five seconds to go – all empty. There was no other entrance and no window you could even squeeze a jockey through. I ran down the platform to the shuddering train and threw myself in through a door a guard was about to slam shut.

The man in the tweed suit and cap was sitting in one of those makeweight partition seats that are not overlooked across a table like the rest. He wore horn-rimmed glasses and had brown hair and a toothbrush moustache, and sat with a broadsheet paper close to his face.

I thought, nice one, Rainger.

The Rainger I'd followed into the station had been dressed in a dark-blue pin-stripe suit and was carrying an

47

old-fashioned rather bulky briefcase; it must have contained nothing but the change of clothes and the disguise. Even the briefcase had changed into a wooden-handled cloth bag; the briefcase would now repose inside the bag. He knew as much about changing appearance as I did myself. He'd left no detail overlooked.

I sat diagonally to the rear of him. For two and a half hours I could relax. It was the best kind of obbo there was – just sit tight and let InterCity take the strain. There was time actually to glance at the paper I'd held to my own face in the station forecourt, time to have a coffee, time to speculate on why Rainger was disguised like a private investigator and sitting in a second-class seat among ordinary people, when two nights ago I'd seen him looking so much at ease with Beckford's wealthiest and best that it seemed he'd never travelled anywhere second class in his entire life, and would scarcely know how to go about it.

Could it be, I asked myself, that he particularly didn't want to be recognised by the sort of men he normally travelled to London with, those men with the inch-wide document-cases and the aggressive cuffs, who ordered the Great British Breakfast in loud, confident voices on the way up and half-litres of chilled white wine on the way down?

The first-class carriages of the morning Executive were the first you came to on Beckford's Platform One. Rainger dressed as Rainger would have been seen and waved to by at least one man in four. Rainger in disguise had only been clocked by a private investigator – with great difficulty.

If he really was on his way to see some woman in

London, why disguise himself from his chums? His secret would be quite safe with them, that was guaranteed. They'd be having little affairs of their own, half of them, and the fact that they were all peeing in the same pot meant they'd be very careful not to splash each other's highly polished Grensons.

The train shot through the Midlands at its top speed, scenes of yellowing fields and hazy water and grazing cattle jump-cutting to the starker footage of industrial estates and neat rows of identical semis and car-parks filled with what seemed like coloured toys that glittered in the climbing sun.

Another thought spooled through my mind like a continuous tape. Was his girlfriend really a London woman? The more I thought about it the less likely it seemed. There might be women in London with whom he spent the occasional hour but, if he was having the kind of affair that his wife had latched on to, wouldn't the woman be local? In my experience they usually were. Forget the myth about not fouling your own doorstep – a man in the throes of a passionate affair wanted the mistress handy because time was at a premium. He wanted to be able to pop in on his way home from the office, drive her somewhere for lunch-time sex and sandwiches, see her at the weekend on his way to the garden centre.

If the affair was with a woman. Fernande had turned up a wild card on Wednesday night. As the train barrelled on, and Rainger continued safely reading his paper, I went back over our words in her flat after the party. Among other things.

'That was a lovely evening, John,' she'd said, putting the

brandies down on a small table and joining me on the couch, sitting close enough for our thighs to touch and her body heat to mix with mine.

'Glad you enjoyed it.'

After the cocktails at the house on The Hill we'd been taken to a dining-room for exquisite buffet food and wine like red velvet, and then we'd been gently ushered into another large room, which had tapestried walls of faded hunting scenes, where a man who gave lunch-time recitals at the Spinners' Hall had played some Liszt for us on a grand piano, and some Debussy. And then a lady who sometimes performed on Radio Two on Friday nights sang a Noël Coward song and a Cole Porter song and a selection from *Me and My Girl*.

It wasn't my scene, but there was an uneasy fascination in seeing how doggedly the Daisy Edgers clung to the same forms of entertainment their parents and probably their grandparents had enjoyed. It all somehow went with freezing out pushy builders and protecting their own from the dubious attentions of people like me.

Fernande had seemed suspiciously spellbound by it all, so much so that, despite the well-to-do background she'd hinted at, I wondered if she could really be accustomed to entertainment on this scale, relatively modest as it would seem to the Daisy Edgers, bravely battling their way through the recession. Nor did she appear actually to know any of the people there, which didn't seem to tally with a textile family upbringing, as a quarter of those around us would have made their original money in the same business.

I reminded myself that it didn't matter. We were simply using each other. I'd needed cover; she'd thought I was in with the big people. If I was careful I might be able to go on using her a little longer, before she found out I was a nobody. She'd got to have some kind of inside track to Rainger and his movements.

Meanwhile, it was nice to sit in her flat and sip her brandy and feel that encouraging thigh. I wondered if I'd be invited to stay the night. I wondered if I'd accept. The invitation would only be there because she thought I was well connected, and accepting on those terms seemed a bit naff, a bit of a con, the sort of thing that went with pencil moustaches and Old Spice. We wouldn't be using each other on equal terms.

'Do you go to many parties on The Drive?' she said hopefully.

'I'm afraid not,' I said, then added carefully. 'I only wish I did . . .'

She glanced at me quizzically. I was treading a narrow line. I spent a good deal of my time bending the truth, all investigators did, but I wasn't prepared to cheat my way into her bed. At the same time, I couldn't lay the full hand down until I knew more about Rainger.

'A one-off, I'm afraid,' I said, as casually as possible. 'To be honest, I'm not really in that league.'

'You could have fooled me,' she said brightly. 'They couldn't get enough of the money talk.'

It wasn't easy coping with an attack of decency with our bodies touching and her hand resting lightly on mine. There were few turn-ons quite like body heat mixing through thin clothing, as de Maupassant had once pointed out.

'Look, Fernande,' I pushed on doggedly, 'I was invited there tonight so that certain men could see if I was suitably house-trained. It was a great help to have you there.'

'I'm so *glad* . . .'

'If I'm hired,' I said, 'I go discreetly into some firm or other and examine the books. I look at credit-control and payables procedures, and see if there's some way of maximising cash flow. Sometimes, if someone thinks the cash might be flowing the wrong way, I'm hired to spot the employee who could have a hand in the till. So . . . in a way, I combine being an FA with being a sort of investigator.'

There, the dreaded word was out, but I didn't think I could go any further at this stage in the heavy-hint department.

'I *see*,' she said. 'And getting the Daisy Edge job is valuable because of the knock-on effect?'

'That's about it. I'm . . . just a man trying to make out . . .'

'Well, *I* think after tonight you're going to go a long way. Don't be so modest, John, they were lapping it up. I even saw one little man writing things in his diary.'

I wasn't making a conspicuous success of selling myself short. I sipped some of her expensive brandy and ploughed on. 'That woman I introduced you to . . . Mrs Rainger . . .'

I let her name dangle, like a baited line; she seemed almost to snap at it. 'Her husband's a Brit-Chem director,' she said. 'I saw him in the crush in the dining-room but he didn't see me. Miles. Do you know him?'

'Only by sight,' I said warily. 'I met his wife at some charity do. He's very much the type I'd like to cultivate. Top cat in the Beckford office, I imagine . . .'

'All but . . .'

'He must know everyone who is anyone.'

'Yes . . . he's done extremely well out of knowing the right people.'

'Seems to have the lot, doesn't he? Looks, charm, a house on The Hill, a top job. Shouldn't be at all surprised if he shared himself out with the ladies a bit too . . .'

She gave me a sour smile. I remembered the curt call she'd taken from him at the reception desk; the clipped, icy politeness in her tone.

'Yes,' she said flatly, 'being a Lothario *is* one of the impressions he tries to foster, among others.'

'He's not a favourite of yours, I take it.'

She sipped some of her brandy. 'I wouldn't mind it quite so much,' she said, 'the snobbishness and the conceit and the way he uses people, *if* he'd made the money himself. But he hasn't, it's nearly all hers, and it gives him a special kind of nastiness.'

I tried not to give any indication of my profound unease. She was only adding light and shade to the sketch I'd already blocked out. That spoilt, golden sod could easily cost me a dozen times more than the thousand his wife was paying me, if I wasn't ultra careful.

'As for being a stud,' she went on, 'the Brit-Chem women aren't too sure they buy it. He's well built and he dresses nicely and he has those rather glittery good looks, but we feel there's something a bit, you know, *other* about him.'

She lifted her hand and let it go limp at the wrist.

'You surprise me,' I said, and this time that was the exact truth. There were few secrets in any firm the tea-room maquis couldn't winkle out, and she seemed to be saying that if he wasn't exactly gay he wasn't exactly dong of the month either.

So where did that leave me? No better off on the face of it. *Good news and bad news, Mrs Rainger, there's no other woman involved, but have you by any chance met a colleague of his who wears a powder-blue jacket and two-tone shoes?*

Would she be able to cope with that? Some wives regarded a male lover as very much the lesser of two evils, something a blind eye could be turned to. It was other women who were the real threat, they didn't simply want sex or companionship, they wanted the package – the man, the money, the position and the prestige. Other women could wreck homes and fortunes. If golden-haired Miles were to hire the right kind of lawyer, Mrs Rainger could find herself in the position of having to hand out up to half the inherited dibs. Believe me, I'd known it happen.

'Ladies and gentlemen, we are now approaching King's Cross Station. Please make sure you have all your belongings with you when you leave the train . . .'

Rainger pulled his cap carefully over his brown wig, took hold of his cloth bag. His paper had been abandoned; for the last fifty miles he had seemed as lost in thought as I'd been. Could he really be bisexual? Seeing a man instead of a mistress? That still didn't explain the disguise. A man meeting another man in London didn't need to alter his appearance, even if he felt it necessary to do so for a woman; no one was going to look twice at two men drinking together or lunching together or walking together through St James's Park – not if they weren't hand in hand.

Rainger possibly a closet gay. Rainger in disguise. I wondered if these things added significance to his half-hour

54

wait in a beauty-spot car-park. Was it the sort of place where discreet middle-class gays hung out on the off-chance? The waste-basket had yielded nothing. I'd secreted the magazines back to the car, gone through them for loose papers. No luck. I wondered if the sort of rubbish placed in the basket was some kind of coded signal. Perhaps Rainger himself had deftly picked up something left earlier and hidden it beneath the suit jacket I'd noticed he'd left on, though earlier in the day I'd only seen him in shirt-sleeves.

This case, despite the worrying aspects of a come-back from a Rainger exposed, had looked to be boringly routine, a relaxing break before I went back to the normal daily round. This morning it had taken on a sudden new dimension, and I felt the first stirrings of instincts that seemed to have lain dormant for months.

Five

When Rainger walked at a leisurely pace along the King's Cross concourse and down the steps to the Underground, I breathed a sigh of relief. Had he kept on walking to the rank and taken a cab it would have meant me taking another cab and telling the second cabbie to follow the first. Films apart, the average cabbie isn't thrilled by this request. It's a tough option in London's dense traffic, and apart from that you might just, in these times, be armed, violent and looking for trouble.

Rainger took the Victoria Line to Green Park, and then the Piccadilly Line to Leicester Square. There's a lengthy walk at Green Park station between the connections, much favoured by buskers and beggars. A man played a guitar, a woman with a designer-grubby child asked for loose change, and there was even a trio playing the 'Meditation' piece from *Thaïs*.

Rainger paused to give them all money, tossing coins into the musicians' instrument cases, but handing the begging woman a note, which she gazed at slightly open-mouthed. It was a rather puzzling act of kindness.

He lingered for a full minute before the trio, and for an uneasy second or two I wondered if he had me clocked, if he would ensure I walked with the rest to the end of that lengthy connecting passage, before making back the way he had come.

But he seemed simply to be killing time. He drifted at length on to the Piccadilly Line platform and took the incoming train the two stages to Leicester Square.

After that it was straightforward. London was in full tourist swing beneath cloudless skies and hot sun. As Rainger wandered through the dense cosmopolitan crowds, so did I. And he wandered for some considerable time, down through the railed gardens in Leicester Square and along to Trafalgar Square, where he turned right towards the National Gallery, which he entered.

He glanced at many paintings in the busy interlocking halls, but he spent some time before two – Van Gogh's *Cornfield and Cypress Trees* and Velazquez's *The Toilet of Venus*.

I'd seen several prints of the Rokeby Venus, but I'd never seen the original. Even in prints I'd always considered it to be the sexiest painting in the world, with Courbet's *The Sleepers* second only by a millimetre. I looked at it now, from among the crowd, with the same appreciation that Rainger seemed to be giving it.

On the face of it it seemed rather to knock on the head the homosexual tendencies Fernande and Co. claimed to have identified. There were plenty of pictures of handsome men in various stages of undress to ponder over, but Rainger gave his closest attention to a female nude and a landscape of such power that the trees seemed to be growing out of the canvas.

After that, it was back into the heat and bustle of Trafalgar Square, with its fountains and its pigeons and its walls of grinding traffic, which seemed almost motionless in the shimmering glare. It rapidly became clear to me that Rainger was indeed a very attractive man. The wig and glasses appeared to do nothing to interfere with this attraction, the moustache and cap seemed positively to enhance it. It had to be admitted that he had an extremely athletic-looking body which he carried with an erect but relaxed grace. Giggly girls addressed him in different languages, often blowing him kisses and offering him popcorn or fried chips. Some, who were being photographed beneath a stone lion, invited him to join the group, expressing raucous good-natured disapproval when he shook his head with a friendly smile and walked on.

We then drifted along the Strand to a pub called the Coal Hole. It was the sort of place where office people gathered for lunch-time drinks and hot snacks, and was already busy. Rainger bought a half of lager and sat down at a table at the corner of the big L-shaped bar room. Nothing happened for about ten minutes, during which time I had a cheese sandwich and a pint of mild on expenses.

And then a man came in, bought a gin and tonic, and sat down at Rainger's table. He was middle-aged and coloured. He looked Asian and, though not the same, was not unlike the man who had given Rainger a shock at the Daisy Edge party. He was well dressed, in a dark business suit, and wore discreet items of gold jewellery – watch, links, ring. He had a broadsheet paper which he put down quarter-folded on the table, and began to do the crossword with a gold ball-point. He ignored Rainger, who'd not even looked up when he sat down. And it was somehow that scrupulous indifference to each other, that absence of casual politeness that went with someone taking a seat at an occupied table, that alerted me to the possibility that Rainger's London trip had reached its point.

After about fifteen minutes, a second gin for him, a second lager for Rainger, the man appeared to complete his crossword, and got up and left, the newspaper now abandoned. Exactly five minutes went slowly by as the young men in suits ate their sausage rolls and laughed and joked, before Rainger casually picked up the folded paper and whatever it concealed, because my trained eye had already told me it was bulkier than it should have been.

I had to hand it to Rainger, whatever he was up to had been handled in a thoroughly professional manner – the disguise, the deceptively aimless rambling through the West End, the exchange of the package. I'd realised, with hindsight, that when we'd walked along the Green Park corridors he had in fact been watching his back. It had taken every vestige of my own hard-won skills in surveillance to keep my cover intact. The jerkin I wore was reversible, and the nondescript ubiquitous camera bag slung over my shoulder contained my own battery of wigs and glasses and headgear. I had been three different people since leaving King's Cross, and he must have satisfied himself he was alone, or the exchange of the newspaper would never have taken place.

But, for the very first time today, his expertise wavered – there was relief in his good-looking face, relief that became pleasure. Through a gap in the jostling backs, I caught him smiling to himself, a smile that lasted for less than a second.

That transaction completed our London business for the day, and we returned to King's Cross to take the next train north. Following him now was easier because he was no longer quite so vigilant. He settled himself in his usual unobtrusive seat and I sat half-way down the carriage from him in shirt-sleeves and a final change of wig.

Just as the train was about to pull away, a man with ginger hair and a beard got on. He wore a crumpled sports jacket and a pork-pie hat. Our eyes met briefly as he came down the gangway.

It was the third time today I'd seen him.

He'd been on the train going up this morning. I'd noticed him because I noticed everything, it was second nature.

I'd also noticed him in the Underground – on the Victoria leg. That meant nothing, dozens of people took the Victoria Line from King's Cross. But the man was here again on a little-used train – little used, that is, by the sort of people who travelled up on the Executive. They'd not normally return on anything earlier than the sixteen-fifty; that gave them a clear five hours in the capital. Only people doing odd things, like Rainger and me, came back on the thirteen-fifty.

And a red-haired man with a beard.

It was almost certainly coincidence. In my business coincidence tends to be a dirty word, but there's a lot of it about, even so. I'd once taken an adventure holiday in Peru and half-way up the Andes I'd bumped into a man who lived across the road from me in Beckford. The bearded man was probably a messenger, delivering documents for a solicitor against a precise deadline. It happened all the time; I'd done it myself.

The thought edged me into depression. I spent half my life running errands. The rest of what I did didn't add up to much either – missing persons, legal traces, business theft, dodgy insurance claims, dick-sharing husbands. I was highly regarded in the business, but how often did a job come along even half as interesting as the Rainger case seemed to be turning out to be? Once, perhaps twice, a year.

It had been a day in summer, a day like this. I'd worn a new dark suit, a present from Dad, but I don't think it would have mattered what I wore.

Fred Goss's boy . . . you know . . .

How many times had I caught that phrase as I went along the corridors and into the sunny office in that modern complex opposite the Spinners' Hall?

Everyone was smiling. I was combed and polished, and Dad had told me the sort of things I'd be asked at the preliminary stage and what my answers should be, but looking back I knew we'd all simply been going through the motions.

I wanted in and they wanted me in. I was Fred Goss's boy and Fred's father had been police too. Certain families were police families, just as, in the old steam-train days, there'd been railway families. My best friend was Bruce Fenlon and *his* father was police, and they were seeing Bruce himself in this series of interviews, and everyone would be smiling again – two first-class types in the one day.

Because I'd have been very good. I'd have started where Dad left off. Fenlon was good, but not as good as me, I'd have used Bruce as a pacemaker. I'd have been the youngest inspector in the force.

If I'd managed to get into the force.

We finally cleared Greater London. Rainger had bought himself a *Yachting Monthly* and was immersed in that. I wondered if he was going to treat himself to a yacht, he seemed to have everything else. Why was he on the take, when his wife was so wealthy? She might be the sort of wealthy woman who provided a lavish life-style but could be difficult about actually forking out readies. Perhaps he needed mistress money – honey-coloured hair and freckled arms didn't usually come cheap. Assuming it *was* a mistress – I was uncertain about the economics of having a bloke on the side. If Rainger was on the take it would explain the disguise. It would have to be some sort of business scam, where it was essential he didn't bump into a colleague from the London office.

I had to remind myself it was nothing to do with me. My assignment was strictly *cherchez la femme/l'homme*. I gazed bleakly over the swirling landscape – the sheets of water and the lines of poplar and the yellow summer fields. I would find out what he was up to simply out of professional interest, but it would be completely academic. I'd have given my teeth to be wading into the drugs scene with Fenlon. While all Fenlon wanted was his holidays.

I got up abruptly and went to the restaurant car for coffee. We were equidistant between stations and there was nowhere for Rainger to go, unless he felt like jumping from a train doing ninety. I passed the man with the red beard. He was reading a battered kerbstone paperback that looked as if he'd bought it at Oxfam for fifty pence. He had to be a messenger. It was only messengers who threw that kind of money around on those kinds of books.

I sipped the scalding coffee and tried to fend off the depression by thinking of Wednesday night. In the end I'd stayed at the flat. After all, I'd *told* her, scrupulously spelt out that I was an ordinary Joe doing an ordinary job. In the end the body heat had been too much to cope with, that and the reflected light in her green eyes.

She'd gone through the second of the two doors that led from her living-room. I gave her five minutes, during which time I stripped down to the boxers, dumping the evening clothes on the couch. They were mine only for a day anyway. I tapped at her door. There was no reply so I went in.

She was sitting on a cushioned stool in front of the dressing-table glass. She'd been brushing her dark-brown hair and it hung loose to her shoulders. She was naked from the waist up and wore a pair of blue silk pyjama trousers. There was a single lamp on the table that gave her flesh a bronzy tint.

She smiled through the glass and put the brush down. I took her slender shoulders in both hands. Her breasts were firm and small-nippled but with areolae that must have been an inch and a half in diameter and of a colour more brown than pink.

She saw me looking at them and suddenly framed her left breast with the thumb and forefinger of each hand, the other fingers spread like delicate tracery over her bronzy skin. It reminded me of a painting I'd seen of a half-naked Scheherazade making almost exactly the same gesture, as if offering a rare and exotic fruit at its moment of ultimate ripeness. It was astoundingly erotic.

She put off the light then, and I heard the rustling of the blue pants as they fell to the floor in the total darkness. She took my hand and led me to the bed, where first she got in and then I, from the same side.

She was an almost unnervingly skilled lover. She

seemed to know every movement of that lithe body that would provide the utmost pleasure. Her hands, when not drawing my head to hers for moist, lengthy kisses, seemed to stroke my body with barely perceptible caresses from every direction. She had total control over the act itself, sensing the exact moment to still her body so that climax could be delayed. I'd never known sex to be as exciting or as gratifying as she could make it.

'Was that nice, John Goss?' she whispered finally.

'It was tremendous . . .' I put my hand again over the breast she'd framed with her long tapering fingers. 'How about . . .?'

But she slept then, slept as if anaesthetic had been injected into a vein, like some sleek, healthy animal that had been fed and watered and mated, slept perhaps before she needed to invent white lies about her own gratification. Because how could I begin to compare with some of the men she must have known, the men who'd helped her to perfect her skills to such a peak of artistry? They weren't the sort of skills you picked up from the occasional affair.

I slept myself then, until about five, when her hand resting on my thigh edged me to a state of drowsiness that was just less than being awake. We both seemed to be partly asleep when she eased one of her legs beneath mine and pulled gently at my shoulder.

We made love once more as the dawn sun through green curtains filled the room with a dim aqueous light. She lay beneath me, her hair spread fan-wise against the pillow, and this time it was a simple act, just our bodies pressed together, no arching or feathering or revolving, but only moving to a gentle almost languorous climax. It was difficult to decide which appealed most, the simplicity or the fireworks.

And then, still half in, half out of sleep, she suddenly murmured: 'Oh, Lymo, darling Lymo . . .' before plunging back into the total, enviable sleep of before. And as she slept, her breathing barely audible, I became fully awake, so awake that I knew I'd not sleep again.

I got up, showered and dressed, wearing only the white shirt and the black trousers of the evening clothes; I could leave the shirt neck open and carry the jacket when I went home. I moved into the kitchen, made a cup of instant and took it through to the living-room, where I drew the curtains back on roof-tops and hard blue shadows and the trees of Clifford Park.

I wondered about that skilled, attractive woman who slept like a child. ' "On a sofa upholstered in panther skin," ' I murmured with a wry smile, ' "Mona did researches in original sin." '

I shrugged. Whoever could afford her would be getting an object of the finest quality. He would probably never regret it, though he'd always have to keep glancing over his shoulder to see if anyone was creeping up behind him with more money, a better position, access to grander parties. It would keep him on his toes.

It had been a night I'd not forget. I supposed my mind would gradually block out the fact that I'd been standing in for Lymo. I supposed Lymo must be the one; if she was dreaming about him he had to be. Lucky old Lymo, to be so wealthy, so attractive, so far up the tree that he had access to women even more skilled at show-casing their breasts than Fernande. It rather looked as if Lymo was master class.

At least I'd be illusion free. I'd never really thought I was in her league. She'd seen me simply as a man who might be going somewhere and knew some nice people, nice that is if you equated nice with wealthy, a man, what was more, she was quite willing to give a good time in bed to, because then she could pretend it was the man she really cared about.

At least it ended any agonising about who was using whom.

A pretend-Lymo. I suppose I should have felt aggrieved. But I'd been pretend people before. I wasn't into long-term relationships in any case, and that meant you sometimes caught women on the rebound, women who simply wanted someone to go out with, party with, sleep with, while they got over the one who'd done a runner and looked round for the one who'd take his place.

I could live with it, especially if it provided the occasional night out with someone even half as desirable as Fernande.

The train was pulling in to Leeds. It wasn't a through train and we had to change here for Beckford. I followed Rainger down steps and along busy subways. It needed all my attention because I had to be ready for him to make a possible break in his journey here, to ensure I got through the barriers parallel to him, in case I lost him on the crowded concourse.

But he made for the Beckford platform and boarded the waiting diesel. It was only as the small train was pulling out that I realised that the man with the ginger beard wasn't on it. The detail nagged at my mind for the remaining leg of the journey. Why go walkabout in Leeds when he'd set out from Beckford? There could be a dozen reasons for it, but, as I may have hinted, investigation work was paranoia inducing, and being me I had to consider the possibility that he'd realised I'd clocked him on the way back. But that would mean he knew it was still me beneath the changed appearance. I wondered if it could be remotely possible I'd had to concentrate so hard on not being seen by Rainger there'd been no vigilance to spare, in those teeming London streets, for detecting that someone might be watching the watcher.

Six

'Saturday night,' Kev said. 'What a town! Dance-halls, theatres – three theatres – a pub on every corner. This is the only pub left of the old ones. I don't know – it was a different world.'

'Remember the Shalimar – Billy Bobbin used to play the mouth-organ.'

'He made more money playing the mouth-organ than he did as a bobbin-ligger.'

'Stan Sutton at the Eagle. Piano. Little tash. Get some vibes and drum-brushes behind him and you'd not have told him from Shearing.'

'They had a piano *and* a violin at the Stag's Head. Always a bit lah-di-dah there. The wool men used to go in their camel-hair coats. Shorts were threepence more than other pubs.'

'They could afford it. Remember 'Change days? All the chauffeured cars steaming up Spinnergate.'

'Where did it all go?' Kev asked sadly. 'Christ, we're only talking thirty years back . . .'

Fenlon gave me a weary grin. 'I suppose the dialogue *does* grow on you. What on God's earth was a bobbin-ligger?'

'I *think* it was someone who went round collecting full

bobbins from the spinning-frames and leaving empty bobbins. You'll have to ask Tom, he knows it all.'

'When I've got an hour to spare.'

'Is it next week you go away?'

'Was.' He sighed. 'They've asked me to rearrange it. Enid, as you can imagine, is not pleased.'

'Heroin?'

'It's really getting to Laurie. We put a DC on Dresden Place. Pony-tail, stubble, bomber-jacket, trainers. He kicked around for a few days, got himself known as a Social Security bandit and into bent motors. He starts buying H and he always has the folding – one day some guy in a Jag comes along and says he'll be our man's exclusive supplier, and that'll make sure he doesn't get ripped off. We're filming all this from an empty house, and we decide the guy's as high as we're going to get at street level. So we find out where he operates from and we go in. Only it's one of the terrace houses on Lead Street, and one corkscrew landlord owns a block of six. We have people back and front at the address, but the landlord's put a system of concealed trapdoors in that lead from one attic to another.'

'Very thoughtful of him.'

Fenlon shook his head bitterly. 'So chummy goes from one attic to another and comes out four houses up the street dressed in workman's overalls. Natch there's no one left in the house but a Dresden tom who rents the place. She knows nothing about nothing because she wants to keep her face in one piece. Only we search the place and we find four ounces of pure heroin – twenty grands' worth give or take – you know, before they've mucked it about for selling to the mugs.'

I nodded wistfully. It was a mark of our close, lifelong

friendship, and the trust he put in my discretion, that he felt able to tell me these things, things he wouldn't tell men he worked with unless they were directly involved.

'So we have it analysed and they say it's some of the best stuff they've seen, worth top money on the street, even cut to hell.

'But chummy's disappeared – he'll be in London or Manchester or Edinburgh now, they're always on the move, the bigger lads.' He shrugged. 'So we're no nearer knowing where it comes from or how it gets in.'

'Leave cancelled then . . .'

He took a cigarette out irritably, it was his third in half an hour. *I'd* have been indifferent to leave being cancelled, in fact I'd probably have been the one pushing for it. I'd not be affected by a wife and kids putting pressure on at home, not at this stage anyway, and as work would also be my hobby I'd never need to unwind.

'Trouble is,' Fenlon said, 'it's the knock-on effect. When there's a lot of a particular drug on the street, and users start to become pushers to fund their own habit, you can guarantee the increase in car theft, burglary, muggings, hold-ups. The money's got to come from somewhere and they can't *earn* the amount they need – you can see the graph rising for areas like Maltby and the districts next to it. And it makes them fidgety back at the nick. They get a lot of pressure upstairs from the do-gooders. What are we doing to stop all these kids wrecking their health on drugs? All right, I've got a kid of my own now, and it upsets me too, but I just wish the average family firm, JP, charity chairman, sodding do-gooder would spend a day on Dresden Place with the thin blue line now and then.' He jabbed out the cigarette and reached for another.

71

I ordered a gin and a half of bitter.

'Anyway,' he said, 'we've got a guy coming next week from something that calls itself the NDIU.'

'National Drugs Intelligence Unit?'

'Well done.' He gave me a brief admiring glance, then smiled faintly, sheepishly. 'They seemed to expect I'd *know* what the initials stood for and I didn't like to ask. This guy's a Customs man and he's going to tell us all the ways the stuff might be getting in, as if we didn't know. The advance word is that it originates in India or Pakistan – they've got people there who've become very skilled in refining it. And of course with our Asian population . . .'

He glanced at his watch and prepared to go.

'Well,' I said enviously, 'good luck.'

He gave me a glance that was faintly guilt-tinged because he wasn't getting as much of a charge out of giving twelve hours a day to the heroin problem as I'd have done.

The weekend proved uneventful on the Rainger front. In fact Mrs Rainger had left a message on the answering machine to say that surveillance was unnecessary on Saturday and Sunday, as she herself would be able to account for his movements, and that therefore there must be no charge for those days.

You always knew exactly where you stood with Mrs Rainger.

But the investigation had gone a little beyond where Rainger might or might not be running his ferret – as far as I was concerned at least – and I decided I wanted to keep an eye on him anyway.

Opposite the Rainger house on Daisy Edge Drive,

stood a house that was on the market. It had a note on the FOR SALE sign saying WITH VACANT POSSESSION. With the housing situation being what it was I felt reasonably confident there'd be no prospective buyers round at its asking price. The sign looked as if it had been there a long, long time, its crooked stance hinting at a battering by the sort of winds we'd not had since March. I'd parked my Sierra in its shady drive and stood watching the Rainger gates from behind dense shrubbery. I was wearing old jeans and a dark work-shirt; if anyone actually *had* come to the house I was going to say that I was just there to provide an estimate for tidying the garden for the agents. But no one came, not at a price that went with a market peak of three years ago. The Daisy Edgers had a kind of selective attitude to market forces.

The Raingers drove out in Rainger's Mercedes at eleven-thirty, and I followed them along Beckford Road, to join the new carriageway that provided rapid access to the Dales. We passed through Skipton and then up to Bolton Abbey, where they had a leisurely lunch at the Devonshire Arms, while I had cheese and biscuits and black coffee from my iron-ration kit.

From there we drove, on yet another day of blue and gold, into the heart of county-family country – North Yorkshire – with its space, its solid old houses, its stables, its fragrant fertile fields. Our destination was Claudia's at Ripon, where the Raingers spent an hour and a half buying clothes. I'd once worked on a case for Claudia; since then she'd extended into menswear, and it was now Claudia and Maurice. While Mrs Rainger was led off to a fitting-room by Claudia herself, a dark smooth-looking young man began to cover a counter for

Rainger with a range of sports jackets and shirts and ties and shoes, a large number of which Rainger nodded his head to, and which a respectful youth slid carefully into logo-emblazoned carrier-bags.

Eventually the Raingers emerged, to cross to the car in the middle of the square, followed by Claudia, Maurice, the youth, and a pretty dark-haired girl in a flowered smock, the youth now pushing the packages in a capacious trolley. I knew from the inside the sort of mark-up Claudia put on her designer labels – there could easily be five or six thousand pounds' worth of merchandise being lowered into Rainger's boot. In a single afternoon.

Who was paying, I wondered – Mrs Rainger from the family fortune? Or Miles Rainger from what had been wrapped in the pages of a newspaper at a pub on the Strand?

They drove back home then, to the house on The Drive, where, judging by the couples who began to saunter there from their own houses at around eight o'clock, they were to give a small intimate dinner for twelve. I remembered the fresh-ground coffee Mrs Rainger's housekeeper had prepared for us – I could see her now, chilling a really steely Chablis for the lobster, and airing a drop of the Eighty-five for the rack of lamb and the glazed new potatoes and the French beans the little old man would have pulled that morning from the kitchen garden.

I had to stop thinking about it – I felt almost faint with hunger after a long hard day on a bit of cheese and a few cream crackers. I got back in my car and looked at the phone, wondering if it was worth a throw. Surely she'd be out. She had a diary covered in engagements, she'd be *bound* to be out. I keyed the number.

'Hello . . .'

'It's . . . John Goss, Fernande. I wondered if you might be free this evening.'

'John, how *nice*! What *happened* the other morning?'

'Oh, I thought it best to leave you with a clear field. I helped myself to your coffee . . .'

'Are you wanting to invite me to another lovely party on Daisy Edge Drive?'

'If only I could. You are free, I take it . . .?'

'I was *supposed* to be partying, but it all fell through because people wanted to get away while the weather holds.'

'How about a party for two?' I said. 'I've got some Chinese in the freezer I could bring down . . .'

There was the briefest of pauses, but it was there – I felt it was the aural equivalent of the dismissive glance she'd given my car on Wednesday. I knew perfectly well she'd been expecting some restaurant like the Ash Tree to be on offer, at the very least. The problem was I'd had a heavy month for outgoings, my credit card was on its last legs and I hadn't got the couple of hundred readies I'd need for a decent night out, despite being healthy enough on paper. It was what we business folk called a temporary adverse liquidity situation.

'That sounds lovely,' she said, just that little too late. 'I'll put the cooker on. Let's hope it still works – I can't remember the last time I used it.'

She giggled, as if to indicate I mustn't take it too personally that she rarely, if ever, needed to eat in.

'About half an hour then, *chez toi*,' I said, smiling. 'I hope I'm in order to *tutoyer* you so soon . . .'

There was another fractional pause. 'I'll have to think

about it. See you soon, John Goss.'

I drove home, home being an average semi on Bentham Terrace, the family home until Dad had died and Mum had gone to live with Auntie Nora, selling me the house for about a third its real value, and only taking any payment at all because I insisted.

It was the reason I'd wanted to go to Fernande's and not vice versa. I'd carefully explained that I was working my way slowly up the ladder, but she'd have expected the ladder to have got me to a four-bedroom detached at the very least, with integral garage, two bathrooms, a downstairs loo and cable television.

I showered and changed into my best shirt, the only handmade one I'd got, and a lightweight grey suit. I took two Marks and Spencer's Chinese dinners for two from the elderly juddering freezer, and two bottles of Moët et Chandon from the fridge. I'd been saving them for a special occasion, which I decided had now arrived.

It would be over very soon, nothing was surer. And I needed to talk to her again about Rainger, try to get some kind of a fix on his movements next week, see if I could fill in any more detail on his position.

That was the official version. I put the food and wine into an old Adidas travel-bag, and reset the intruder alarm. But I couldn't stop thinking of the way she'd looked in the aqueous dawn light on Thursday morning, with her dark hair spread on the pillow and the thin coverlets pushed down to her waist because of the heat, to expose her relaxed and slightly flattened breasts with their large browny-pink areolae.

I knew Rainger was simply an excuse. Most of what I wanted to know about him I could winkle out for myself now, and would. The truth was that when I'd not been thinking about Rainger, during that long scorching day as I'd crouched behind bushes and hung about pavements, I'd been thinking about her and her feathering fingers and her darting tongue.

She was wearing a white cotton shirt and tight black pants, and her soft, wavy hair hung to her shoulders from a central parting.

'Come in, John Goss, with your goodie-bag . . .'

She closed the flat door and placed her full lips against mine. 'I've *missed* you!'

Or was it my promising future, more parties on The Hill, the terrace at Reid's, Saturday shopping sprees at Claudia's? Of course it was, but no one I'd ever known did it better.

'Bubbly,' I took the misted bottles out.

'John – my very favourite drink!'

Surprise, surprise. Even so I wished it could have been Krug. We put one in the almost empty fridge and filled a saucepan with ice for the other one, not being able to lay our hands on a silver bucket. The oven was on and clicking softly, and I opened the packages and put the meals inside on a baking-tray.

'What a lot of *food*,' she said. 'You must be a hungry boy.'

'Very hungry,' I said, glancing upwards, first at her body and then at her smiling eyes, as I knelt to ease the cork from the first bottle.

Champagne never hit an empty stomach more effectively than it did for me that evening. We sat on the couch in the declining sun, and the room was filled with the wistful throb of classical guitar music, music that seemed exactly right for my mood, with its evocations of heat and dust and primary colours, its promptings of indefinable desires.

She said: 'How long will the Chinese be?'

'About half an hour.'

'I wondered if I had time for a shower. I had one earlier, but I find in this very hot weather . . .'

'I couldn't agree more – one shower seems to go nowhere . . .'

She didn't bother with a shower-cap. She let the water drench her hair till it was plastered against her face. We could scarcely move in the narrow cubicle, her flesh seemed almost bonded to mine. She watched me, smiling in an artfully demure way as the spray cascaded over her flat, sodden hair, her delicate fingers giving me that familiar shudder because there was no indication where I'd feel their feathery touch next. She began to shudder too as I stroked the soft soapy flesh of her inner thighs upwards to the crotch, and I did it again and again, until she laid her head on my shoulder and rested her weight against me.

We drew the curtains of her bedroom then, and made love in light that matched that of the early morning two days ago. A faint odour of cooking drifted through from the kitchen, but one appetite had been replaced by another even more urgent, and I lost myself in her taste and smell, in the heat of her raised trembling legs and the skilled abandon of her thrusts and rotations, the touch of fingers that endlessly fluttered.

But I couldn't lose myself so completely that I could stop myself from wondering ruefully if the pleasure I gave her could even begin to compare with the intense pleasure she gave me, or with the pleasure she'd been given by the man she dreamed about.

★ ★ ★

When we came to open the second bottle of champagne and take out the overcooked food, the light of the long day had almost gone, and she lit candles in simple wooden holders for the table. My brain, already a trained instrument, seemed to be soaking in the fixing solution of memory the way she looked in the two garments she wore, the white shirt and the black pants. Her hair was still damp, but rapidly drying into the natural waves that so many other women put so much time and effort into achieving. She must have eaten almost as much as I ate myself, but with that unobtrusive delicacy I'd noticed before; the contrast between her grace away from bed and her abandon in it started a renewed flickering across my abdomen.

She brought out the good brandy.

'How long have you been here – in the flat?'

'Three months. It's on a short lease. I have an option to renew in September, but . . .' she shrugged, 'I'd like to be back in London by then.'

'London . . .?'

'I was modelling. My mother had a heart attack and I came back north. She's out of danger now.'

So *that* was it. A model. It explained a great deal – the presentational skills and the expensive clothes and the taste for good living. I had an instant picture of the life she'd be used to – fashionable restaurants, fashionable men and fashionable cars – the wonderful world of Lymo and Co. It was just as well I was being totally realistic about my own bit-part role in her life.

'I'm glad she's on the mend. You didn't stay at home . . .?'

She smiled sourly. 'When I was sixteen I resolved

never to live under the same roof as my father again – not even for a night. I've been going over evenings, weekends. They live in Harrogate now . . .'

'You . . . didn't hit it off . . .?'

'You *could* say that if you wanted to be extremely charitable.'

'That's very sad. When my father died it was the worst blow I'd ever had.'

'You were lucky, John. God, you were lucky.'

Her cat-like eyes, resting on mine in the flickering light but seeming not to see me, were unfocused and inward-looking. Suddenly, after a lengthy silence, she began to speak. 'We lived near Saddal in a house just off the moors. There was a small room upstairs that Mother used for storing bedding. We all hated it. The wind from the moors was worst in that room, and it creaked – it was really scary. He'd . . . he'd lock me in there for hours, half a day at a time. I used to think I was going mad . . .' She picked up her glass; her hand was trembling. 'He was master class at finding out what would upset you most of all, then making sure you got plenty of it. His other talent was for finding out what you wanted most and making sure you *didn't* get that. We'd be going on holiday and we'd be so excited and counting the days . . . and then he'd send me to stay with his sister, Aunt Helen, whom he knew I hated, she was as twisted as he was . . . just me, not the others . . . and they'd go to the coast without me . . .'

I couldn't have believed that that low gliding voice could have acquired such a harsh tone. 'I tried to be as cunning as he was. I knew even then it was the only way I'd survive. He taught me a lot about survival . . . One day a stray cat – Polly – sort of adopted us. I loved that cat . . . she sometimes seemed to be all I had that was mine . . . I had to pretend I couldn't stand her because I knew that was certain to make him force me to feed her and look after her . . . But he caught me one day . . . on my knees, petting her, playing with a ball of wool . . . it was obvious how much she meant to me . . . I never saw her again . . .'

She began to cry, suddenly, silently, unfussily, to cry as simply as she would fall into those deep impenetrable sleeps, large tears falling down the sides of her nose and round the edges of her mouth. Nothing had stirred me so deeply since my mother's uncontrollable weeping after the death of my father.

I went round the small table and put a hand on her shoulder.

'However naughty we'd been,' she said, in a strangled gasping tone, 'it was just me he picked on . . . always.'

'But your mother . . .'

'She was between us, you see. He had the money . . . he made the rules . . . She knew he was unfair . . . cruel . . .'

'You had brothers, sisters . . .?'

'They were sorry for me . . . but . . . but you accept the life the grown-ups make you live . . . you've nothing to compare it with . . .'

'But you've done a lot of comparing since . . .'

The glance she gave me was suddenly focused, glittering and hard. 'Oh, you're so right,' she said, in a voice now almost menacing. 'I've done a lot of comparing since then. I've never *stopped* comparing.'

We became silent, me standing over her, my arm still round her shoulders, my hand trembling slightly at my own anger at the damage inflicted on her. I'd heard

81

about that particular kind of middle-class viciousness before, that left the flesh untouched but shredded the mind. I did some comparing myself, her treatment against the care, guidance and affection my own father had always given me, and it made her treatment seem so much more appalling.

I asked no more questions. I was curious – it went with the job I did – but I knew it was best now to let her speak unprompted, if that was what she wanted to do. But she didn't speak again, and shortly afterwards she dried her eyes with an embroidered handkerchief, patted my hand where it lay on her shoulder and got up. I was to get to know that resilience extremely well.

'More coffee?' she said, in her normal voice, and went off to make some.

I crossed to the windows and looked out on glowing street lamps and squares of light in buildings across the road. They'd cut very deep, those dreadful childhood experiences. I wondered just how deep. I'd perhaps already seen the trauma's obvious legacy in the way she'd abruptly left home, achieved success in a demanding profession and developed a ruthless streak in dealing with people she considered of no use to her.

I wondered if that was the extent of it. I'd once been involved with a social worker in connection with a missing youngster. She'd told me that ill-treated children, especially the stronger characters, would keep the real pain inside what amounted to a sealed compartment of the mind, often for years. But they could be like Manchurian Candidates, sleepers, waiting for a certain signal that would unwittingly release the pain on to someone else, someone often as innocent as they'd been themselves.

I think it was Kierkegaard who said that life could only be understood backwards, and several months passed before I remembered standing at her flat window thinking these thoughts, and I realised then what a crucial element Fernande's disturbed childhood had been in the almost inevitable chain of events that was to follow.

She came back with a freshly loaded cafetière, smiling. 'Sorry about the waterworks. Blame it on the Moët. Alcohol and any mention of my father are always a seriously volatile mixture.'

'Look, if you want to talk about it . . . .'

She shook her head. 'I want another brandy and I want to put the clock back ten minutes to where that bastard hadn't taken centre stage.'

I pressed the plunger on the cafetière and poured.

'So you're a model . . .'

She sighed. 'Well, I *was*. It's not a career it's wise to take six months out from.'

I'd thought so too. If she was as tough as I'd considered her to be why had she abandoned a career so precarious to spend so much time with a mother who seemed to have been virtually useless when she was needed most?

'You took the Brit-Chem job to tick over?'

'I couldn't sit around doing nothing once she was past the worst. The job and I both became available at the same time.'

'When did you learn about computers?' I said, remembering those batches of complex-looking data on the reception-desk VDU she'd seemed completely familiar with, not a skill you readily associate with fashion models.

'Oh, I managed to pick up the basics here and there.

You never know when it's going to come in handy. What I really want to do is act. I paid for lessons out of the modelling money. But what happens when the modelling money dries up? I'd thought about trying to start my own agency if I could get the backing. I know the people and the business. The pieces are all in the air at the moment and time's running out.'

'But you'll be able to go on modelling for years yet. What are you – early twenties?'

'I'm old now, John,' she said with a wry smile. 'You've got about five good years from sixteen out. And the search for new faces never stops.'

It was a story I felt I could have punched a number of holes in, had she been one of those people I often talked to who stole stock or fiddled accounts or accepted slush money, but I had to remind myself yet again she wasn't one of my cases. She was simply someone I liked being with and had no illusions about. I'd already noted the acting skills up at the house on The Hill. I'd also reluctantly accepted that a good deal of acting went on when we were in bed. She'd only ever seen me as worth cultivating because I appeared to have contacts and might one day be fairly well off. The idea of starting her own business could quite easily be true – in which case the more men she could keep in with the better, even if one of them lived in the boondocks.

She was watching me now with a look that seemed faintly pointed and brooding. There were things I recognised about that too, it was a look I'd often detected when certain people had decided my casual chatty questions might be not quite as innocent as they seemed.

'And what about *you*, John Goss?' she said, almost brusquely. 'I let you into my flat, my bed, and I don't

84

know a thing about you. You could be a serial rapist for all I know.'

'They're protecting me,' I said, 'the big people on The Hill. They know about the serial raping but I know too much about the serial asset-stripping.'

We were sitting on the couch now; she put a hand on my arm. 'Come on, let it all out, the broken marriage, the relationships that didn't work. I bet you're searching for a Daisy Edge heiress right now, aren't you?'

She'd clearly decided that attack was the best form of defence. I smiled. 'Nothing like that. No marriage, a few relationships. I want to concentrate on my career until I hit the mid-thirties.'

Her eyes widened appreciatively. 'I like an ambitious man. They're often bastards, but so are wimps, so give me ambition every time. Where *do* you live?'

'Westbury,' I said vaguely, 'completely alone. It was the family house.'

She approved of that too. 'And you work for yourself?'

'You can't do enough for a good boss,' I said, giving Grandad's lone joke an airing.

'Nice shirt,' she said. 'Sea Island Cotton, isn't it, and handmade. Shirts off the rack never quite fit, do they – the sleeves are either too short or they have to be kept up with those absurd bracelet things.'

'By the way,' I said, keen to deflect a mind that seemed almost as skilled as my own from any further scrutiny of my background, 'it really would help me a lot to know more about your Mr Rainger, assuming I could get the chance to offer him investment advice. What exactly *is* he at Brit-Chem?'

'The biggest shit they've got,' she said pleasantly.

'You did say ambitious men could be bastards.'

'Ambitious men who do it their own way have a right to be bastards. But he's had it all done for him, hasn't he.'

'Is he *really* so unlikeable?' I said, recalling the ten-pound note he'd slipped the begging woman in the Underground, the instant appeal he'd had to foreign girls in Trafalgar Square.

'He's a snob, a bully and a hypocrite,' she said. 'He takes the credit for anything his people do well, passes the buck for anything that goes wrong. He treats the admin staff like dirt and they can't answer back or leave because of the recession.'

'What's his title?'

'Head of Sales.'

'Does that mean he's in charge?'

'There's one man above him, the Area Manager. It's a very big company as you probably know, international – Beckford's just one of the sales offices.'

'What kind of money do you think he makes?'

She shrugged. 'Forty . . . fifty, plus perks.'

I nodded. It was more or less the number I'd attached. 'Some of these questions might seem irrelevant but I'm just trying to build up some kind of profile of the man. Does he travel much?'

'Most of the time. It's quieter now because of the holidays. They use this period for meetings – forecasts, strategies, budgets . . .'

'Is he in London much?'

'At least once a fortnight. The Head Office is up there, of course, but he often sees customers from Europe, takes them out on the town. He's good at taking people on the town.' The wry smile became a sneer. 'He went to London once too often on Friday though. He'd gone without telling Ivor Fennell. Ivor was furious. He'd particularly wanted Miles in the office that day to help with the August projection. He asked Miles why he hadn't told him he was going to London and Miles said he wasn't a bloody office boy. I got it all from Ivor's PA. So Ivor said Miles *knew* the projection had to be faxed that afternoon and needed his input. And then he said he sometimes felt Miles's heart wasn't really in the business, and that he ought to consider stepping down and letting a more dedicated man take his place.'

I listened, so absorbed that the sensuous lips the words came from seemed to fade into the background, together with the damp hair, the smell of soap, the thigh that lay against mine, the drifting plangent music.

'Was that a definite threat, do you think?'

She shook her head, so decisively that her hair lapped against my cheek.

'Hot air. He's too valuable to Brit-Chem simply because of his background. But Jenny said he looked really worried for a while. She was delighted. We both were.'

The sneer had now been replaced with a smile of intense malicious pleasure.

Seven

Rainger was safely ensconced in a management meeting. He'd be there all day. It was another helpful detail that had come out in my discussion with Fernande on Saturday night. It gave me some free time.

On Sunday I'd returned to The Drive and kept watch once more on the Rainger place. Neither of the cars left the grounds all morning, and at noon people began to gather for what seemed to be a lunch party on the rear terrace, going by the distant laughter which carried in the hot, still air. It went on until the early evening. They seemed to like a drink.

I thought about it now, sitting in my car in the gloomy basement car-park at Hanover House drinking coffee. I could have stayed with Fernande. She'd let me stay Saturday night and I could have spent most of Sunday with her too. We could have had a gorgeous lie-in and driven out to Starbotton for a pub lunch.

Instead, I'd crept out early again and spent another day Rainger-watching, except that Rainger had done nothing worth watching.

It made no sense. She'd told me she'd be with him all weekend. And all I'd been engaged for was simply to find out where he was having it off. Whatever else he

89

might be up to had absolutely nothing to do with that specific brief. An entire day wasted that could have been spent with Fernande.

It was crazy. I screwed the cup back on the thermos. All I knew was that Rainger being angry about Fennell's veiled threats, Rainger *having* to go to London when he must have known the trouble it would cause, had aroused instincts in me that nothing seemed proof against – not Fernande, her bed, her skills, myself. Not even myself, with my hands filled with her soft, moist flesh.

At one o'clock I drove to Beckford Boys Grammar School and parked at the edge of the playing-fields. The entire school seemed to be out there – playing cricket or tennis, running, jumping, straining at a tug of war. It was the last week of term.

I went up the steps and through the open doors of the echoing main entrance hall. I told a doorman I had an appointment with Mrs Marsden and he took me along a parquet-floored corridor and into the ante-room of an office marked ADMINISTRATION, where he asked me to wait.

It was panelled in dark oak and had browning photographs on its walls of boys in football shorts staring fixedly at the camera. I sat down and rechecked my notes. I'd done some homework examining the background of a number of Beckford's prominent citizens to find out who'd been in the same year as Rainger at Beckford Boys'. Councillor Wendover had fitted the bill. Big in local politics and ambitious, he was aiming to make the Commons his next objective.

I'd then rung the Grammar School saying I was a member of Wendover's machine and I'd been given the job of writing a short biography of him for the divisional magazine. Could Mrs Marsden, the administrator, help with background and explain how the school trained its boys in leadership qualities? She'd loved that, fee-paying schools liked all the free discreet publicity they could get. She'd been more than willing.

The game-plan was to find out exactly which boys had been in Rainger's form. With luck I might be able to get her, or some senior master, to talk generally about them, where they were now, what they were doing. They'd certainly know about the ones who'd made the big time, like Wendover, schools always did; what I was really after was the names of the failures, if any, the ones who'd had an adverse effect on the school's reputation. Schools usually knew about those too. If I could get the name of a real wash-out and find out which boozer he drowned his sorrows in I might be able to get him to talk. About Rainger. Anything four-pound note about Rainger.

One of the first lessons I'd learnt about investigation from the man who'd taught me the business had been that if you wanted a true fix on someone's life-style you didn't talk to friends, you talked to enemies. You could usually rely on a failure to have the dirt on a success; if there was any, they had a perverted knack for getting it together.

It was tenuous, but it was all I had. Rainger lived a fine and private life in his Daisy Edge fortress, a life that seemed virtually impregnable. My only chance of dirt lay outside the charmed circle.

'Mr Goss . . .?'

'Mrs Marsden . . .?'

She took me into a small, comfortable office, all leather and velvet, and more dark oak and photographs.

The inevitable VDU stood on the tooled-leather desk-top, blending in with the décor as elegantly as a one-arm bandit in a funeral parlour.

'Do sit down,' she said. 'Now – how can I help you?'

She was a woman in early middle age, attractive in a plumpish way, with short, fair hair and reddish cheeks.

'Any information you could give me about Mr Wendover's last year would help. His sports background, achievements and so on. Any photos or school magazines would help tremendously.'

She said: 'Each year we take what's known as the Leavers' Photograph. I dug out the one of Tony Wendover's year for you.'

'Thanks awfully.'

She passed me the photo with its hundred-odd boys standing on a tiered structure outside the main entrance.

I recognised Wendover by his large nose and his ingratiating smile, attributes that even then seemed to be marking him out for political stardom. I also recognised Rainger by the immaculately combed locks, the perfectly knotted tie and a general air of being the jewel in Beckford Boys' crown.

'Tony did extremely well,' she told me. 'Straight 'A's in his A-levels, president of the Debating Society, Yorkshire breast-stroke champion and school captain.'

I nodded respectfully and wrote Hickory Dickory Dock in my notebook.

'Were you here yourself in those days?' I said.

'It was my second year. I remember the boys very well.' She smiled. 'It always amazes me how many boys I can remember when I've known so many. But it's the bright sparks that really stand out, of course . . .'

'Just by the way,' I said casually, pushing the photo

back over the desk and pointing at Rainger. 'I feel I know that face from somewhere . . .'

'Miles Rainger,' she said, without hesitation. 'Very much a bright spark. He's something rather grand in chemicals now. Married the Forbes-Walshaw girl – Fiona. Must have been for the connections because there was no money.'

I felt a sudden shiver run down my spine, as if my neck had been touched with cold steel. I'd not had that shiver since I'd finally worked out, after a sleepless night, how money and confidential documents could disappear from a safe to which only the owner himself had the combination.

'Really,' I said, almost indifferently. 'I thought the Forbes-Walshaws had so much they couldn't count it.'

'True once. They lost virtually the whole of their capital in some massive wool speculation, designed to corner the market. My father was in the wool trade and he got the inside story. The family never admitted it, but business people never do, do they? Anyway Thrush Hall was suddenly on the market and they buried themselves quietly in North Yorkshire in very reduced circumstances.'

'You surprise me,' I murmured politely.

She glanced pensively at the photograph once more. 'I must admit I was rather surprised when Miles did so well. He lives in great style these days. As you can see from the photograph, he thought a great deal of himself. In fact scholastically he was average. But he could talk and he had charm. *Such* charm. Wasn't it Barrie who said that if you have it you don't need anything else and if you don't have it it doesn't much matter what else you've got? Well, this young man had it by the sackful.

A little bit on the flash side, if you know what I mean; the sort who could go very right or very wrong. Perhaps even both. Too knowing for his own good, I often used to say.'

It was quite obvious that Rainger had had a profound effect on her all those years ago, and it was understandable if you considered that she was probably only a year or two older than him – she'd have been a golden girl then, much taken by a golden lad.

It was the sort of luck that made you forget the endless hours of waiting and watching, with often little to show for it. Like everyone else, it seemed, I'd assumed Mrs Rainger was loaded; I doubt it would have even occurred to me to delve into her background.

'Well, well,' I said, clamping calmness on to my manner, 'I was convinced Mr Rainger came from one of The Hill families and sort of doubled up everything by marrying into another.'

'Don't you believe it,' she said, with a malicious grin. 'He came of a perfectly average background. Father chief cashier at the Midland. But remembering that young man I believe he'd always try to foster that impression.'

'So he really is self-made?'

'I have to hand it to him, he seems to have got everything from life he always held dear,' she said, still in the tone of faint mockery of a woman who might once have been scorned, or, worse, not even noticed, by a Rainger spoilt for delicious choice.

We passed on to the bogus Wendover story; thirty minutes later I was driving back to the city.

Towards the end of the afternoon, my car back in the underground car-park, I disguised myself in longish black hair, rimless glasses and a droopy moustache, and hung about the entrance hall of Hanover House as if waiting for someone. I needed to know if Rainger would go down to the car-park or sneak out into the city on foot.

I wondered if he really was having an affair. I kept losing sight of what I'd been hired for. I'd even begun to hope not, a woman would now be an unwelcome complication. I'd not struck anything like the Rainger case before and I had difficulty sorting out the ethics. I had to keep reminding myself that anything he did beyond getting his rocks off should theoretically be ignored.

It now took a great deal of ignoring. London in disguise to get what was almost certainly a pay-off from a well-dressed Asian. A Daisy Edge life-style, a boot-load of expensive threads, a wife whose family had lost their shirt, so that Rainger must be funding the lot. *Out of fifty K a year?*

I wondered if it was that old favourite, the false invoices. There was a lot you could do with a dual set of invoices, especially in the Middle East – pay against the lower one, put the higher one through the books, keep the change.

If that was a runner what should I do about it? Advise Brit-Chem? I doubted they'd want to know. If he was meeting his sales targets they'd not want some nobody of a PI rocking the boat. They might even half-suspect and be seeing no ships – if you dealt with certain countries a kickback was the key to the door, and if Rainger got a kickback from a kickback good luck to him.

So why not simply concentrate on finding the pretty lady?

The offices were emptying and the entrance hall began filling with people. Fernande herself passed within a yard of me, in a pale-blue drop-waisted dress and white shoes, her hair in a pony-tail. I remembered I was in disguise, but the cool indifferent way she glanced at me seemed like a punishment for walking out on her on a glorious Sunday before she'd quite finished with me.

Then Rainger came into view, laughing and talking with a group of colleagues, in shirt-sleeves, the sleeves rolled back to reveal strong-looking brown arms, his jacket held over his shoulder, his dark-gold hair gleaming in a band of sunlight from an outside window. He went down to the car-park and drove directly home. I parked a hundred yards or so back from his house; after about ten minutes my car-phone rang.

'John Goss . . .'

'We'll be in all evening, Mr Goss,' she said in a low voice and put the phone down.

That was so I'd not charge overtime, even though we'd agreed a daily time-core that I'd assured her would almost certainly be adequate. It would have been nice to think she was sparing me a wasted evening, but I knew it was only the money.

I started my car and drove back along The Drive's green tunnel, past the large whispering motors of men on their way to showers and a change of clothes and preprandials on the terrace.

Why not just let the week go by, take the money and run? It made no sense to put all this additional work into a case that wouldn't yield an extra penny. But then, I don't suppose it made much sense that Schubert wrote all that music that no one wanted to buy. He did it because he had to.

I drove on auto-pilot, semicircling Clifford Park and then down to a block of flats that had once been a wool man's mansion. I drove, it seemed, from one obsession to another, from an investigation that seemed pointless to a relationship I should never have got into.

I pressed the button next to her card.

'Hello?'

'It's John, Fernande . . .'

'Oh, *hello*, Mr *Private Detective* . . .'

Eight

A lot happened on Tuesday.

First, I followed Rainger and his smoked-glass top-of-the-range Mercedes down to the office. I'd temporarily exchanged my Sierra for a Cavalier in order to make absolutely certain he didn't suspect a tail. I had an arrangement with a used-car dealer who lent me cars whenever I needed to ring the changes, in return for my leaning on people who owed him money. With Rainger settled in his office, I made a final fix on the kind of salary he pulled down at Brit-Chem. Yesterday, I'd rung the London office of Brit-Chem, pretending to be an official of the DOE, and had asked for the name of the personnel director, saying I had a confidential document to send him, to be opened by the addressee only. The name Hubert Black was readily provided and I rang off.

Then, altering my voice, I rang again and asked for him by name. This got me through to his PA.

'My name's Diplock,' I told her, 'and it's important I speak to Mr Hubert Black.'

'I believe Mr Black's just left for a meeting,' she said, with polite wariness. 'Perhaps you could give me some idea of the nature of your call so that he can ring you back.'

'I'm a reporter for Yorkshire Television,' I said. 'I'd very much like Mr Black's comments on the threatened day of action at the Dolphin Beach plant.'

'Day of action . . .?'

'By the shop-floor men over the proposed wage settlement.'

'Hold the line, please . . .'

He was on within seconds.

'Black here. What *is* all this?'

'We've had word that the entire Dolphin Beach plant will be brought to a standstill next week in a dispute over pay.'

'That's not possible. We've only just closed . . . Who told you this?'

'I can't divulge my source, I'm afraid. Let's just say that I trust it. *Can* you comment?'

'I fail to understand Yorkshire Television's interest, whether it's true or not. If there *is* a dispute, and I've heard nothing about it, then it's a routine matter for Brit-Chem to sort out. I simply can't see a news angle.'

'It's big news on the coast, Mr Black,' I said politely, 'seeing that Brit-Chem's the only real employer in the area. If there's trouble at the mill in times like these the people on the coast want to know about it.'

'I've heard nothing, absolutely nothing, so there's little point in my commenting.'

But I detected a faint note of grievance in his voice, an edge of suspicion – was some dickhead of a personnel manager up there trying to go it alone?

'In that case we'll probably run the story as it stands,' I said evenly, 'though we'd obviously like to give a balanced report . . .'

'Wait,' he said quickly. 'Let me speak to my people up

there. I'll ring you back. Let me have your number.'

I gave him the first number that came into my head. The point of the exercise had been to tape his voice on a cassette-recorder wired into the car-phone. Over the years, I'd worked hard at imitating voices, even going to an elocutionist to learn how breath and diaphragm control could alter tone and timbre. It was a valuable asset to a PI. There was absolutely no reason for Rory Bremner to get agitated, but I'd succeeded in producing some decent telephone sound-alikes when the occasion demanded.

I'd played the Hubert Black tape over and over in the car and I'd recorded my own imitation again and again on to a separate recorder until finally satisfied the average ear could be fooled.

And now, while Rainger was safe in his office, I was going to give the finished performance.

I keyed out Brit-Chem's Beckford number on the car-phone and when Fernande answered I spoke in mock-Black tones.

'Hubert Black here. I'd like to speak to Mr Mason.'

Bob Mason was the personnel man in Beckford. I'd found his name the same way I'd found Black's. Fernande's soft voice took on the added warmth her sensitivity to money or power invariably induced.

'One moment, Mr Black, it's ringing for you now . . .'

A respectful voice spoke. 'Hello, Mr Black, Mason speaking . . .'

'Ah, good morning!' I said in Black's booming tones. 'Look, Bob, I'm involved in a salary survey with the big twelve – Ford, Shell, ICI, et cetera – we run one every couple of years, as you know . . .'

'Oh, yes, sir . . .'

'Make sure we're not getting adrift in our own salary levels, do you see. Thing is, Bob, I need some details as a preliminary. Can you tell me how many of your professional staff you've got on salaries between fifteen and twenty K in Beckford. Approx . . .'

'I can tell you exactly, sir.' He rustled papers. 'Ten.'

'Right. And how many between twenty and twenty-five?'

'Fifteen.'

'Twenty-five and thirty?'

'Twelve.'

'Thirty and thirty-five?'

'Six.'

'Above thirty-five?'

'Just Head of Sales, sir, at forty-eight and the Area Manager at fifty-two.'

'Ah, yes, that's Miles Rainger and Ivor Fennell.'

'That's correct, sir.'

Fernande's instinct for salary levels had been spot on, but it had had to be checked out before I went any further.

'Good,' I boomed. 'That's all I need for now, Bob. I'll get back to you on a job breakdown later. Thanks a lot.'

'You're very welcome.'

'Oh, and by the way, Bob, I was impressed by that last report you sent up. Concise, well-researched and well-written. An excellent job of work.'

'Well . . . thank you, Mr Black. Thank you very much.'

I sensed his proud smile. Why not give the poor sod a high? Being a personnel manager in a sales office in Beckford meant, I was fairly sure, that he had as much chance of scaling the Brit-Chem heights as climbing on board Dolly Parton. Bring me sunshine . . .

I put the phone down. I now knew for certain that Rainger earned no more than forty-eight thousand a year which, combined with a company car and a lavish expense account and a probable profit-related bonus, came admittedly to a comfortable income for the north in the middle of a recession.

But it wasn't the kind of money that would pay for the parties and the domestic staff and the trolley-loads of new clothes and the second home – because all the Daisy Edgers *had* second homes, and we're not talking time-share here, or concrete flats on the Spanish coast; they had substantial villas by the North Sea or in the Dales or overlooking one of the quieter of the Cumbrian lakes.

And there was no inherited wealth – on either side. Plenty of style, a willingness to be readily satisfied with the very best, but no money in the original sock.

It looked to me as if Rainger was spending at least three times what he was legitimately earning. It strained my credulity to its limit to accept that he might be getting the shortfall from dodgy chemical deals. In a large, respectable, well-run company like Brit-Chem it seemed iffy, a lot too iffy.

For the rest of the morning, I waited. I'd discovered a small room off the entrance hall of Hanover House where cleaners kept their equipment and when the old commissionaire had been on one of his frequent absences from the desk I had slipped in there. By keeping the door slightly ajar, I could keep watch on the lifts and stairs. It was the ongoing problem of ensuring that Rainger didn't leave the office on foot.

Like most PIs, I liked to do the waiting in my car. Our cars were *our* second homes – they had books, magazines, tapes, elaborate radios. They provided distraction during the endless hours of surveillance. But of all the other types of waiting – in pubs, on city streets, behind hedges – the worst was being holed up as I was this morning, in darkness, unable to sit or stand comfortably or move about, with no diversion except the thoughts I really wanted diversion *from*.

'A private *detective*!'

I'd faced her again in that sunny attic flat, only this time there were no drinks on offer, and there was no classical guitar, no invitation to sit down even, as if I'd shortly be expected to leave.

'How did you find out?'

'Because you sneaked off again yesterday morning, and I wondered what I'd done wrong, and so I decided to ring you. And what hits me in the eye – John Goss, private bloody detective . . .!'

'Investigator,' I said. 'Detectives are in novels.'

'*Whatever!*' she said, with an exasperated shrug. 'And then John Goss listed again at some address on Bentham Terrace.'

It was difficult to decide which provoked the keener note of contempt – being a private investigator or living on Bentham Terrace. She wore an old faded T-shirt and jeans that had traces of oil down the front – it was probably a rig-out she used to clean the car in. She wore no make-up.

She'd not known I was coming, but I suspect she'd have kept the same clothes on even if she had. It didn't make her look any less attractive, it was simply that she was no longer bothered about flattering me with the extra patina of glamour that went with the good clothes and the subtly enhancing cosmetics. But the extra patina of glamour had been for a different John Goss, of course, one who still lived in the old family pile and advised the wealthy how to invest their hundreds of thousands, even though he'd once scrupulously pointed out that his work *did* include investigation.

'Why didn't you *tell* me? What were you *doing* at a place like Daisy Edge Drive?'

'I can't tell you. Someone retained me to keep an eye on someone, let's leave it at that.'

The feline eyes had a hardness in the setting sun that I remembered from the day I'd met her, when she'd regarded me as a nobody the first time round. And the low, gliding voice had developed the same edge.

'Why drag me into it then?'

'I was asked to come with a girlfriend as cover and I couldn't find anyone else in the time.'

'Well, thank you very *much* . . .'

'Oh, come on, I took you out to a bloody good do whichever way you slice it . . .'

'It was the *deception*. I wouldn't have gone if I'd known what you *were*. *I* don't want to get involved with a . . . with a . . .'

'Gumshoe . . .?'

I suspected the word she'd wanted to use had been much worse.

'It was such a *con*. All that financial talk . . . quizzing me about the Brit-Chem people so you could pretend to be going to sell them life insurance . . .'

She had not, thank God, appeared to tie up the questions I'd slipped in about Rainger, among many others, to the fact that Rainger might be the man I'd been retained to watch.

'It was all cover,' I admitted. 'I'm sorry, I expected

we'd simply go out for that one party and then . . .'

I broke off. I didn't know how to finish. I'd expected it to be as casual as the two or three other brief relationships I had each year. I'd expected to be able to walk away, perhaps with a regretful backward glance, but with no feelings I couldn't handle.

But that was before she'd delicately framed her breast with her graceful fingers in the bronzy light, before we'd showered together and her hair had been plastered against her head, before she'd lain beneath me, her hair now fan-wise on the pillow, and a single bead of moisture had gleamed in the groove above her top lip in the dim, aqueous light. Before I'd got so used to the spacing of her green eyes that I could no longer keep them out of my mind.

'Yes, it *would* have been better if we'd simply gone to the party and then home to our own beds, wouldn't it,' she said coldly, as if she sensed what I was thinking.

It hurt. Whatever I did for a living, I was young and fit and presentable, and I'd given her a good night out, a night she'd considered worth the granting of sexual favours. Could it really be down to nothing more than the position and promise I'd appeared to have?

Of course it was. She was a London model. When she was working she probably made more in a day than I made in a week. And she was used to men who earned even more money than she did herself, from acceptable occupations like the stock market and advertising and television. From where she sat, gumshoes probably came bracketed with men who cleaned windows and swept streets.

'I think you'd better go.'

'Can't we meet again?'

'I'm sorry, John, I can't go along with all that pretence. I just don't want to be mixed up with the sort of person who can't be honest.'

It was just the pretence. Nothing else. Nothing to do with not really being in with the big people and on the way to serious money, absolutely nothing – the only things to cause the damage had been the con-man patter and the economies with the truth.

My hands trembled slightly. I wanted to tell her to get lost. But I couldn't. I wanted to take her out again. She was the most materialistic bitch I'd ever known but I'd never imagined her to be anything else. And I'd dusted her body with talcum now and eaten Chinese in the candle-light and had that damned guitar music beaten into my brain, and she was in there too, like a virus in the bloodstream.

'Let me take you out to dinner,' I said, rapidly trawling my mind for the best restaurant in the West Riding. 'Let me take you to the Maison d'Or. I'm not really a man in an old raincoat poking round in people's marriages, you know. I've got a good reputation and I make a good living.'

It was too pathetic. If you had it you never needed to say so, the Porsche did it for you, and the Armani suits, the mews cottage in South Ken, the way waiters reacted at the Ivy.

She waited for some time in silence, the sluttish clothes suddenly seeming to enhance her attraction more than the fashionable ones, seeming to give her, with the absence of make-up, a ready availability. In a moment she would undo a single button, deftly remove two garments and take me by the hand towards the shower. I made as if to touch her arm, but she turned away abruptly.

'I don't know,' she said at last. 'It's been such a shock to me. I need to get it together. I have to think it through. I really don't know . . .'

Mid-morning. Men had delivered stationery, men had come to service the lifts, others to take away bin-bags of rubbish. They had all been querulously supervised by the old commissionaire, who now, almost certainly against orders, drank tea surreptitiously from a gigantic chipped mug, while reading the *Sun*, his lips moving slightly. No sign yet of Rainger.

It seemed I still had half a foot in the door with Fernande. Mention of the Maison d'Or had finally helped her to put her scruples on hold. If I could afford the Maison d'Or I couldn't be the type of investigator who got paid in used notes in a brown envelope. I sighed. Despite occasional cash-flow problems I really did make a good living. I could afford the Maison d'Or say twice a month. I'd certainly not be able to afford it, or places like it, twice a week.

I wished I'd never met her. It seemed to be the pattern of my life, not getting the only things I ever wanted. One depression appeared to merge seamlessly into another.

'Far-sighted as falcons,' Auden had written, 'they looked down another future.'

How often had I done just that, looked down another future where I'd not have met people like Fernande and Mrs Rainger, and would have been spared the problems they brought me?

'I don't know how to tell you this, John,' he'd said, 'but the medical people can't pass you. You've got some kind of irregularity in your heartbeat.' He'd smiled sadly. 'I don't suppose you even knew you had it, did you? Unfortunately, in such a physically demanding job we can't take the risk, however slight.' He shrugged. 'There are pension rights involved, that sort of thing . . . I'm very, very sorry.'

I'd paid to see a consultant privately and he'd made an independent examination. 'I could put it into technical language,' he said at last, 'but it wouldn't mean much to you. There *is* a slight irregularity, virtually impossible to diagnose precisely. You must believe me when I tell you that many completely healthy people have them. I can say quite categorically that it won't make a button of difference to your life or your longevity. If you'd been going into a bank, no doctor would think twice about passing you. But . . . the Police, the intensive physical demands, it does become border-line then . . .'

'If you'd been a police medic would you have failed me?'

He smiled wryly. 'I'm afraid so. When it comes to risking taxpayers' money we all become ultra-cautious. Apart from the politicians, of course . . .'

Where would I have been now, with my skills and energy, my single-mindedness and capacity for sustained work? On how many long nights had I measured my steady theoretical progress through the ranks, sensed my soul corroding at the promotion of my various police friends?

Too many. They'd helped to make me the man I'd become, those long, dark nights of the soul.

At one p.m. Rainger took his Mercedes out of the basement. I followed him to the centre of Beckford, where we drove up a ramp which led to an extensive open-air car-park built over a shopping mall.

He parked. I parked. It was very crowded and both of us had to manoeuvre. We were about twenty yards apart. I waited for five minutes, but he didn't get out. I waited another five; still no appearance. He was either waiting for someone or he was waiting for something to happen – shades of the Coal Hole.

I couldn't see his car properly from within my own; all I knew for certain was that he was still in it. Disguised in an auburn wig, fawn linen cap and sunglasses, and wearing T-shirt and slacks, I drifted casually towards the rear entrance of British Home Stores. The store's main floor lay at street level below the car-park, but the part of the building containing the offices, store-rooms and public restaurant rose above the end of it like the superstructure of a ship.

Inside, I ran quickly up to the restaurant floor, briefly checking from a landing that Rainger wasn't leaving his car. Then I slipped into the Gents and locked myself in a lavatory cubicle. It wasn't the first time I'd kept this area under obbo and I knew that the cubicles provided an excellent vantage point. The frosted-glass windows had a quarter-section at the base that could be pulled inwards on sliding arms for a few inches to provide fresh air. But these could in fact be pushed free of the section, which could then be opened fully. I released the section from its moorings and opened it until I could just see Rainger's car, then wedged it at that point with folded toilet-paper.

Then I took out a pair of field-glasses, small but powerful, and watched and waited.

It was a very difficult type of surveillance because of the continual coming and going of cars and the many people threading their way to the shops past stationary vehicles, and despite the years of experience I couldn't be certain that if anything significant *did* happen I'd be able to tell.

But it was experience that counted in the end. Amid the bustle, I became aware of a man standing outside one of the tiny single-storey shops that lined one end of the car-park. It was a florist's, its displays and bunches of seasonal flowers crowding the window and spilling out on to the pavement. The man seemed to be making a decision. There were perhaps a dozen people standing about along the pavement, but there was something faintly bird-like about this man's head movements, as if he were cautiously checking his back from his eye-corners. It took one to spot one.

He finally turned round. He carried a small travel-bag. He had wavy, rather coarse, fair hair and wore a medium-blue business suit. His features were regular in a curiously young-old face, which had an expression of resigned anxiety, like a probation officer who'd been assigned to look after the one who'd burnt down the school.

It was the man I'd seen in the lay-by overlooking the Aire Valley, who'd emptied rubbish from his car not long before Rainger had done the same.

He began to thread his way slowly along the narrow spaces between the banks of cars towards the front of the park. His path took him in the direction of the Mercedes. I smiled faintly.

The smile disappeared, because though he passed the car his strolling pace never altered. What was more, he was actually walking to a car parked nearby – a gold-coloured Audi. So what was the connection? Two men hanging about at the same time in one car-park, and then, a week later, hanging about at the same time in another, could not be a coincidence. The common factor at the beauty spot had been the waste-basket. I could see a waste-basket here, near the shops, but the anxious-looking man had gone nowhere near it. He'd simply stood about, obviously checking his back, and then, though he'd passed the Mercedes, had made no sign that I could detect, before halting at his own vehicle.

The man was now fiddling in his jacket pockets for his keys. I had a powerful sense that I was missing something, that some crucial detail was wrong. It was as if my eyes had registered some discrepancy and were transmitting signals that the brain couldn't yet decipher.

I edged the glasses back to the Mercedes but nothing seemed to be happening there. I moved them back to the fair-haired man, who had now got his keys and was opening his door. In a few seconds he'd be in his car and away, and though I'd automatically registered his number I'd not be able to confirm his involvement with Rainger if I couldn't pinpoint that small telling detail. It was so busy down there, the busiest part of the day, and the flash and glare of sunlight off the body-work of cars was making my eyes ache slightly.

I rapidly thought back to where I'd seen him, outside the florist's. The bird-like movements, the slow saunter along the narrow alley-ways between motors. Past the Mercedes, on to his Audi. Fiddling for his keys.

With both hands!

What had happened to the small travel-bag? He no longer had it. Somewhere between the florist's and the Audi it had vanished.

No prizes for guesswork. I let the slight smile return. Dropped discreetly at the side of the Mercedes, so that

112

Rainger only needed to open his door a few inches and hook it inside.

I ran downstairs. The Audi had gone when I hit car-park level and the Mercedes was just pulling out. I claimed my own car, threw card and coin into the barrier-booth and drove down the ramp. Fortunately, there was a queue along the narrow street at the foot of the ramp to filter into the dense traffic of the highway and I was able to keep Rainger in sight as he drove across town and on to Beckford Road. It was fast and busy at this time, and I could keep him in sight from several cars back.

Beckford Road ran roughly north-west out of the old wool town. We were soon clear of the great mills which no longer wove or spun, with a great deal of noise and smoke, but now stood cleaned and tamed and placid in the sun, metamorphosised into discount warehouses for carpets and fitted kitchens and Anything in Wood.

The road was the start of the pretty route, the one that led to Skipton and Gargrave and then a choice of destinations through little villages to either the Dales or the Lakes.

But at Keighley Rainger left the new fast road north and swung off a roundabout and on to one that led to Hawtrey, and beyond Hawtrey to Hebden Bridge. There was also, from that road, another that angled back to Beckford over high moorland. These were quiet B-roads, and I knew I could go no further and be certain of keeping my cover.

Which had to be why he'd chosen this route. And once more it was nothing to do with meeting a woman. I'd not yet followed a man on his way to meeting a woman who'd ever suspected a tail. Men on the way to leg-over

113

in a half-hour carefully garnered from a crowded day had wonderfully concentrated minds; you could follow them across the Syrian Desert on a camel and if they noticed you at all they'd assume you were heading for the next watering-hole for a fill-up for the camel and a sheep's-eye butty for yourself.

I parked in Keighley for one minute and then drove rapidly to Hawtrey. He might have kept on going to Hebden Bridge, but I suspected he'd be short on time by now. He was an executive, not subject to normal office routines, but he had a big department to control and a suspicious boss. Hawtrey looked favourite.

Hawtrey it was. I drove past the station and the industrial museum and up into the main street. It was busy with tourists and so again I had cover. The Mercedes was parked outside the post office, and as I drew to the kerb I was just in time to see Rainger go in. He was carrying a smallish package wrapped in brown paper. He was in there for about three minutes, then came out and drove off.

The same reason that had discouraged me from following him into Hawtrey too closely stopped me from following him out – quiet roads flanked by moorland. I had to take a chance he was returning to Beckford.

I went into the post office. A spare, elderly man stood behind the grille, looking as chirpy as a senior clerk who'd got his trial balance right first go. I smiled warmly, a smile developed over many years of trying to get people to tell me things.

'Sorry to trouble you,' I said. 'Could you tell me if a man's been in recently with a small parcel? Fair hair, blue-and-white-striped shirt . . .'

'Not two minutes ago, pal. You've just missed him.'

'It doesn't matter,' I said. 'Just so long as he's posted that parcel. Only we work together, you see, and he keeps forgetting to get it off. Had it in his car two days. Anyway, this customer of ours rang me today and said that if he didn't get that parcel tomorrow we could forget the deal. So I came after him because I knew he was going through to Hebden . . . anyway he's posted it, that's the main thing . . .'

'Definitely here, pal, stamped first class.'

'Good. Thanks a lot.' I set off towards the door, then hesitated. 'Oh . . . it was the *London* parcel he gave you, wasn't it, not the Birmingham one?'

He picked it up and peered at it through his bifocals. 'London it is,' he said. 'West One.'

'I can breathe again.'

I got back in my car. I could probably have got the name out of him too, but there was no point. It would almost certainly have been an accommodation address, and whoever picked it up would simply be a delivery man, skilled at shaking off tails, legal or illegal, as he tacked his way across London by cab, tube and bus.

With a parcel containing what?

What was small enough to be sent in a package through the post and yet valuable enough to help provide Rainger with all the gilt-edged goodies he'd ever desired?

Nine

She studied the menu carefully and then gave me precise instructions, and when the black-jacketed waiter came back I ordered for both of us. Behind him stood the wine waiter and I ordered a bottle of a St Julien reasonably high in the second division and a half-bottle of white Burgundy for the shellfish.

She sat opposite me at a small window table, wearing what was almost certainly another costly dress. It had dark sumptuous colours, pinks and purples and blues, relieved by subtle touches of white. Her hair and make-up were immaculate, the slightly eastern look of her wide-set eyes further enhanced by eye-liner that gave them the slightest upward slant.

None of it was for me, of course, it was all for the Maison d'Or and its clientele. Who knew, there might be a real wealthy man here she could smile at encouragingly instead of just a pretend one, who'd had his cover blown.

She'd ordered the most expensive items on the menu and chosen champagne as an aperitif. I was being made to pay for my deception, in spades. I looked at her over the candles and the carnations, obsession mixing uneasily with distaste. I was glad she'd soon be gone and I could begin to get back to the old life, the life I'd been able more or less to control.

What a difference a couple of days had made. Gone were the warm smiles, the suggestive glances, the friendly chatter. When I'd called for her this evening she'd opened the door with a look of faint amusement that had bordered almost imperceptibly on the patronising.

I was to be humoured. She was away from base, the friends she had in the area were on holiday, why not let the snoop take her to a restaurant that even Egon Ronay waxed guardedly lyrical about, with its window tables that overlooked the wide tree-lined river and a different waiter for each stage of the meal, apart from the main course, where you were allotted one each.

'Well,' she said brightly, 'have you had a busy day tracking down the missing heiress?'

I forced a smile. 'It was the second chauffeur – the Spanish one. She'd not been able to resist his flashing eyes and his curly hair. They've cut her out of the will, of course; I can't see Pedro lasting long once he finds she's penniless.'

I couldn't keep a bitterness from creeping into my tone, but she was getting such a deep almost erotic pleasure from the oysters she seemed not to notice.

'But what do you people *do*?' she said, in an amused tone. 'Really . . .'

I sighed inwardly and told her what we people did. The smile seemed to become a faint sneer. It sounded incredibly humdrum. It *was* incredibly humdrum. But it was the nearest I'd been able to find to the kind of work I'd set my heart on doing, and I was touchy about it, my own contempt for it being at times little different from her own.

Silver cloches were flicked simultaneously from gold-rimmed dinner-plates, to reveal artistically arranged main-course dishes, which lesser waiters in white waistcoats reverently surrounded with palettes of assorted vegetables. Then, after the Bordeaux had been tested and poured, they all backed off, bowing.

'How was *your* day?' I said.

'I'm counting the weeks now until I can get away from shits like Rainger.'

'He doesn't improve?' I said warily.

'Only a lobotomy could do that,' she said. 'Preferably one that went wrong and left him like a vegetable.'

Her voice was so much softer than most women's that the sudden harshness distorting it came as more of a shock.

'He's been in a bad mood . . .?'

'Quite the reverse.' She began to cut her duckling with sharp movements, though the delicate way she ate didn't alter. 'He went out for a long lunch and I thought thank God, with any luck he'll not be back at all, but it must have been a boozy do or he'd pulled some big stroke because he came back at his cockiest, which means his most repellant.

'I'm not a bloody tea-girl!' she said, her eyes glittering in the candle-light. 'I very nearly told him so. He had some people in during the afternoon and his PA was on holiday, so I had to take the coffee in. I was *not* pleased and I didn't pretend to be anything else, but he had the drinks cabinet open and they were all half-pissed. So then they came on with the macho stuff – I can't *stand* being treated like a bimbo!'

She stared angrily through the window, her hands trembling slightly, seeming not to see the beauty of the river's orange glow in the setting sun, only the demoralising scenes of the afternoon inside her head. She didn't like to be treated like a bimbo and yet she often behaved like one if she was down-wind of the heady scent of money. I was certain the soft-voiced charm wouldn't have slipped for a second, as Rainger's office had resounded with innuendo; it was me she let the aggro out on, as if I were the sort of timid husband some women used as a punch-bag.

I sipped about a pounds' worth of the wine. There were things about the outburst I couldn't get together. Why did he rub her up so badly? He was a professional charmer and I couldn't see why he let the mask slip behind the scenes. I had a workforce of one, but I'd learnt very early that if you didn't look after the staff they didn't look after you. It had to make good sense keeping on the right side of the receptionist, especially one as polished as Fernande.

Perhaps they were mutually antipathetic. She was a tough, knowing kid who'd been around, he was a self-regarding provincial with pretty looks that the in-putters thought were bisexual. From Fernande's ruthless standpoint all the strikes would be against him, and having little to lose she'd probably done nothing to stop the contempt hanging out. Didn't I know.

'Have some more wine,' I said soothingly, as concerned now to get her away from the subject of Rainger as previously I'd been keen for her to discuss him.

'I half-suspected his wife might be paying you to keep an eye on him,' she said, still slightly flushed.

'Good God, no!' I said, with a calmness not easy to sustain. 'I never take domestic cases if I can possibly avoid it. More trouble than they're worth.'

'I could see I was wrong when I thought about it. Why have you spy on him at Daisy Edge when she could spy on him herself?'

'Quite so,' I said, with relief.

'She just *seems* the kind of woman who'd hire some-one to watch him,' she said, emotion still giving her voice a rough edge, like a radio just off the station, 'because of all these women he's supposed to be screwing. If she's got the loot she's bound to want exclusive dick-rights.'

I smiled wryly at the new, coarser Fernande, a Fernande who saw little or no point in dissembling with the new John Goss. Even so, I had to admire a brain that could work out the angles so shrewdly. It was exactly the way I'd seen it myself until I'd found that Mrs Rainger's only money, including the money she'd be paying me to spy on her husband, came from Rainger himself.

'I think they're hovering for the dessert,' I said. 'Would you like anything else?'

Silly question. I'd been hoping she might settle for coffee at this stage, which would help to stop the bill looking like the price of a weekend in Paris, but she was inevitably drawn to the tiny paper-thin pancakes with a kiwi-fruit filling, which she said were the best she'd tasted outside London, and finally a little Brie.

'Would Madam care for a glass of Chianti with the Brie?' the wine waiter asked. 'It goes extremely well with a soft cheese . . .'

Another bloody silly question.

The restaurant had been gently air-conditioned; we walked out into air so hot it seemed as thick as the water that flowed darkly beyond the sycamores. We drove the fifteen miles to Beckford almost in silence. There seemed little to talk about – aspects of my life merely amused her and hers would be so richly full and varied that discussing it would only emphasise how far out of her league I was.

I was quite prepared for her to say goodbye at the door; in fact I wanted it that way because that would have ended it, probably at the right moment, when the keenest memories were of two people trying to give each other pleasure, even though I'd known it was really a game, two people with good acting skills, acting.

But she walked in as if expecting me to follow. 'Brandy?' she said casually.

'I'd better not. I'm over the limit as it is.'

'But you'll not be driving again . . .'

I watched her in the half-light.

'You . . . want me to stay?'

'Oh, come on, John Goss,' she said, with a smile that seemed to contain vestigial contempt. 'You can't go before the floor-show, not when you've paid Maison d'Or prices.'

It was my hands that trembled now. It was too much, besotted as I'd become. I should have left her at the door. I'd taken it all evening, everything she'd handed out, but this was an insult too far, that she didn't mind singing for her supper if I could go along with the wrong notes and the half-forgotten lyrics of a song she'd not bothered to rehearse.

'Don't you worry about any floor-show,' I said. 'You don't owe me a thing. I took you out because I wanted to go out with you. I know it must seem very naïve and provincial to a sophisticated bitch like you.'

She watched me, her face expressionless with shock. It was the first time she'd heard it, the tone I used for thieves and liars and cheats I'd finally cornered. It was over, of course. I turned away. But then she put a hand on my arm.

'Oh, *John*,' she said, in her low, gliding voice, 'don't be so *touchy*. I was only joking . . . I didn't mean to sound tarty . . . it was just a *joke* . . .'

It had been effortless, the instant return to the friendly warmth of the role-playing days. It threw me. I was certain I'd been right, that as I had no real money she'd put up with me as long as I spent freely what money I'd got and watched my manners.

'It didn't come across like a joke,' I said. 'It came across as if I was buying sex and should think myself lucky in view of what I did for a living.'

'Oh, John . . .' She put her arms on my shoulders and clasped her hands behind my neck. 'I'm over all that now. It *was* rather a shock, but I'm used to it. I've had a lovely evening . . . really, and I *want* you to stay with me. Now let's have a nice brandy and go to bed . . .'

She kissed me then, a kiss that seemed oddly chaste, a gentle pressing of her full mouth against mine. It didn't make too much sense and I couldn't help wondering what I could still have that might be of value to her. 'Please stay . . .'

I stayed. I think I'd have stayed even if I'd not lost my cool, even if she'd continued to be amused and patronising. I stayed because of the virus in the blood, the ineradicable images in the memory, which always began with a breast with a large dark areola framed by long graceful fingers in bronzy light.

It wasn't long before I found out what final use she was able to find for me. This night was to be nothing like the others. We simply took our clothes off in the

123

darkness and got into bed without any of the foreplay that in Fernande's skilled hands had seemed almost better than the act. She kissed me now with closed lips and a still tongue, and there were no fingers trailing across my skin and none of those whispered incitements: 'Is this nice?' 'Do you like this?'

She moved and thrust beneath me, but whatever she got from our love-making seemed to have an inward quality, as if she somehow wanted to receive and process her sensations in some part of her mind beyond my reach. As though the pleasure she got from my body, limited as it may have been, seemed not to come from me. I suddenly knew quite certainly that I was standing in for the man whose name she'd once drowsily given me in the dawn hours – Lymo.

When it was over she slept as she'd slept before, with that instant animal grace, leaving me to stare bitterly into the darkness. So that was it – I was to be the official stand-in for Lymo. Not someone she'd just called Lymo by mistake, coming out of a dream, but someone she could pretend *was* Lymo, as long as it was sex without the bells and whistles, where she'd have to relate to me and use my name, as long as it was sex in the darkness, in total silence.

She hadn't had to sing for her supper after all. I'd done that, as well as paying for it.

The man with the young-old face lived in a respectable white-collar district on the ring road, not far from the short section of motorway that connected Beckford to the M62 and M1. It was a neat and well-maintained semi, with carefully mown grass and trim beach hedges.

I'd got his name – Laurence Fielding – and his address

by supplying his car registration number to a contact in the traffic department who'd run it through the computer. Many doors in the force were open to a man who had so many policemen as friends. They knew about me, that I'd have been one of them but for the failed medical which had literally changed my life. You could say I was lucky to have such valuable contacts, except that real luck would have meant I was reaching my full potential in the CID, not having to make do with missing persons and husbands sharing their dicks.

This morning I followed the man Fielding along a wide, well-used road that skirted the River Wharfe as far as Ilkley. But in Ilkley he swung off at an acute reverse diagonal up a steep, straight road that led to the famous moor – he'd obviously compared notes with Rainger about using country roads if you wanted to make absolutely certain you were on your own.

I now had no idea what he was about to do next – meet a contact or drive on to an ultimate destination. I couldn't even make a calculated guess as I'd done when Rainger had gone to Hawtrey.

I pulled in and parked. The trail was cold. At the other end of the road that skirted the moor there were too many different roads the man could take. I might as well return to base, though I knew that Rainger would be tied up at the office in another meeting until noon. I sat gazing up the steep, quiet road, and beyond it to the rising moorland which, hazy in the summer light, reminded me, inconsequentially, of some distantly memorised poem about blue remembered hills. Where did Fielding get them, those packages that Rainger posted on to London? With such skilled operators would I ever know?

I *could* do it – with time. But I had a business to run, and soon I would have to report to Mrs Rainger and tell her her fears were groundless. About Rainger's cock not lying dormant, that was, away from home. And where did Mrs Rainger go from there? I think I knew where I went.

Just then a car came into sight, moving down the road from the moors. It wasn't Fielding's Audi. As it drew closer I saw that it was a Lada, an ancient rusting model with a noisy exhaust. It passed me. It was driven by a Pakistani, wearing the white skull-cap the males tended to affect at this time of the year to protect their heads from the merciless hammer blows of the West Riding July sun. He was the standard Beckford article driving the standard banger.

Except that this wasn't Beckford. It was Ilkley, and Ilkley was low on Pakistanis due to it being low on combing-sheds and taxis and double-decker buses.

And Rainger had recently made contact with an Asian. And maybe his ordinary-looking pal had made some kind of contact with the Pakistani in the rust-bucket, up there on some stretch of deserted road, where you could check your back for miles in every direction.

It was a hunch worth pursuing. Right now it was the only one I'd got.

I returned through Wharfedale to Beckford, keeping the Lada in my sights from four or five cars back. It led me to a road filled with shabby terrace houses no more than a mile from the centre of Beckford, called Drum Lane. The Pakistani carefully parked his motor against the kerb and went into one of the houses. I waited until lunch-time but he didn't reappear.

126

★ ★ ★

It was back, then, to Hanover House, to be in time for Rainger to lead me up to Daisy Edge. At first I thought he was going home, but he drove straight past The Drive and continued into what the locals called Old Daisy Edge. Here he parked in the car-park of a trendy restaurant called La Rasade. I circled round the village a couple of times, then returned to the restaurant in one of my many disguises.

Rainger was in the bar with a handful of men who had to be business friends. They were all talking in those loud, braying Tory voices that went with golf and Jaguars and vodka on the rocks, with Rainger himself the life and soul of the party.

I sat in a shadowy corner of the bar, nursing a Scotch and water. So this was Rainger being a high-voltage businessman. I could only admire his total mastery of the act. Several times recently, in moments when he'd thought himself unobserved, I'd seen him looking stressed and anxious, and I'd begun to be aware of the great strain his double life – if that was what it was – was putting on him. But here, with his business chums, none of it showed. He was the handsome chalk-striped executive, who only worked to keep his mind occupied, as there was plenty of money in the old sock, didn't you know, from both sides. Buy and sell the lot of us, the Raingers, I shouldn't wonder.

They all liked Miles. They all liked going to his spacious house and seeing his old-money friends and being invited to join those select groups that shot over dogs. Presumably, if your mind worked like Rainger's, the admiration of those true-blues at the bar made it all worthwhile, the trips to London in wigs and glasses, the meetings with coloured men, the waiting in car-parks, the errand-running.

I didn't stay for lunch. There was a simplicity about the restaurant – red-and-white-checked cloths, plain wineglasses, menu details scrawled on a blackboard – that was in an inverse ratio to the complexity of the dishes, the excellent service and the cost. Mrs Rainger wouldn't like me charging a La Rasade lunch up on expenses, not one little bit.

I returned to my car, parked unobtrusively beneath an overhanging tree, and waited. But not for long. I'd not even begun the crossword before Fielding came strolling casually into view, carrying a small travel-bag. He must have bought them by the job-lot. Glancing quickly round, he approached Rainger's Mercedes as if it were his own, opened the boot, put the bag inside, relocked it and passed on to the restaurant, where he would no doubt give Rainger an infinitesimal nod before sitting down to a well-earned snails and chips.

Two drops in two days. Whatever those bags contained the lads were certainly moving it along.

Ten

My car-phone rang at six that evening. It was Norma, my office staff. I had a recurrent nightmare that one day she might become ill, take a better-paid job, win a football pool or remarry. I'd inherited her from the man who'd sold me the agency and there were still things about the business where her knowledge was sounder than mine. She read me a summary of the day's calls and letters, and then, more slowly, the central details of certain enquiries she'd put in hand during the morning.

'Phil in London isn't going to charge – he says you'll owe him one. I managed to do the enquiries this end myself.'

'Jolly good – I'll have you doing leg-work yet,' I said, grinning.

'Not in a million years. The funny hours would do my head in.'

'Can you drop the report off at Bentham?'

'I'm not really paid to provide a delivery service, you know.'

'Oh, go on, you can't do enough for a good boss . . .'

'. . . as your self-employed grandfather used to say . . .'

The moment I put the phone down it rang again.

'My husband will be in all evening, Mr Goss. He'll be working in his study after dinner. We're hoping to spend time at our house on the coast during August and so he wants to get ahead with his paperwork.' She hesitated briefly and I heard a sharp intake of breath. 'Have you got anything to tell me – it's been a week and . . .'

'Nothing at this stage, Mrs Rainger . . .'

'He had a very long lunch break today . . .'

'With customers – at La Rasade . . .'

'And yesterday – he must have been away from the office more than two hours. He said he was with Ivor – that's Ivor Fennell, the area manager. He said they'd driven out to the Square and Compass to have a confidential discussion about staffing levels.'

I listened carefully. Was it those sorts of lies that had aroused her suspicions in the first place? I had to go along with the lie. I couldn't tell her about the games of Pass the Parcel, not right now, not until I'd thought it through, perhaps not ever.

'I can confirm that. He was with a rather thick-set man with brown hair starting to go grey . . .'

'That's Ivor,' she agreed, but a tremor of suspicion seemed to linger in her tone. 'And you've *nothing* to tell me? He went to London last Friday . . .'

I half-wished I could tell her there *was* another woman, I was beginning to think it might well be a more acceptable double life than the one I seemed to be uncovering.

'I'd like to continue the surveillance at least one more day, Mrs Rainger, and then I'll probably be in a position to give you a full detailed report . . .'

'Goodbye,' she said abruptly, putting the phone down. I assumed Rainger had entered the room she was phoning from. I clipped my phone back into its charging-stand, where it immediately rang again.

'You're as hard to get as the Prime Minister,' she said. 'Was it the heiress's father ringing to tell you Pedro had dumped on her?'

For once the jokiness about my job didn't grate. It had confused me that for the very first time she was the one making contact.

'Fernande . . .'

'Are you free, or do you have to drive through the night to bring her home?'

I'd left her flat this morning angry and bitter, knowing I'd never contact her again. The anger had seemed to fester in the continuing heat like a wound turning septic, had made me pick up the phone and put certain enquiries in hand, an action I'd quickly regretted.

I'd not taken into account that she might ring me. She never had done – let the gumshoe make the running had seemed to be the form.

'What . . . had you in mind?' I said warily. There'd certainly not be any fancy restaurants involved, that was for sure. It would be some time before my credit card had recovered from the Maison d'Or money-letting.

'Anything you like,' she said, with what seemed a note of hope. 'Or we can just sit here and watch the sun go down.'

'That sounds fine . . .'

'Great,' she said, with a brightness that may have concealed marginal disappointment. 'I've got wine but not much in the way of food.'

I smiled wryly. Perhaps she'd get round to shopping one day when she got too old to go on conning men like me into picking up all the tabs. 'I'll bring something then,' I said, trying to remember if there was *anything* in the freezer apart from a sliced loaf, two trays of ice and some cauliflower cheese. If not it would have to be pizzas – to go.

'Don't be long, darling,' she said.

I resited the phone for the third time and sat thinking for a few minutes. I still didn't know where I was – I'd been certain I'd not hear from her again and I'd been determined not to lift the phone myself, however strong the temptation.

I wasn't sure I wanted to go through with this. It was difficult to overlook her behaviour at the Maison d'Or, her deliberate, almost sadistic greed in ordering the most expensive items for every course from the à la carte menu, the way she'd used me as a stand-in for Lymo. I also had to take into account the new flaw that went with the hardness and the greed and the often barely concealed contempt – her deceit.

She'd done it all very well, the background she'd given herself, the easy manner with the formidable people on The Hill, the expensive tastes, but then, she was a bright kid with a lot of talent.

My hand hovered over the phone. Maybe I should ring back and tell her something had come up and I'd have to cancel. Apart from anything else, I had my reputation to consider. I was John Goss, an investigator with a clean ticket – it went a long way to bringing in the work. And image-maintenance tended to rule your life. It wasn't just you, it was the company you kept. If it was bad news people tended to include you in the same bulletin. I tried to remember if I'd ever stripped a false personality from anyone and found them still to be basically straight. One kind of dishonesty always seemed to go so easily with another. If she was going to get herself into some kind of trouble in Beckford . . .

I left the phone where it lay and drove on to my house. I showered, changed into the good lightweight and the handmade shirt. I was in luck with the freezer, there was some chicken pappardelle, oven chips and some garlic bread. There were also some salad materials in the fridge that Norma had brought in one day because she worried about my nutritional balance.

I wondered if she'd given herself a new background in order to obliterate the pain that went with the old one. Perhaps I'd have been tempted to do the same in her shoes. I was certain there had been pain, though not of course the middle-class cruelty she'd pretended it to be. That, I felt, had been a displacement for something infinitely worse.

I moved round the house, making sure I'd not left a window open, that the answerphone was in the correct mode. We both had flawed lives that we'd tried to make the best of in our own way. Maybe we could make another new start, accept each other exactly as we were at last, give each other some straightforward pleasure and friendship before we inevitably went our separate ways.

I went on hanging around, filled with an uneasiness I couldn't define. Perhaps it was some old mental programming; my mother, born in the Thirties, warning me about going around with 'naughty' girls and the trouble they could bring. It may have been partly that, but when I remembered it later, when it was too late, I believe the instinct to back off was almost a reaction to some future shock, to some catastrophe that was to act like a heavy stone thrown into a pond, sending powerful ripples backwards in time as well as forwards.

But in youth, as in manhood, 'naughty' girls always seemed to have been the most fun. Despite the trouble they could bring.

'Come in, John . . .'

She wore a simple pale-green button-through dress that seemed exactly right for a new beginning – low-key but stylish – and make-up so delicately applied it seemed more apparent than real.

'My favourite investigator,' she said, kissing me on the cheek, 'who must *never* be called a detective, complete with his Adidas bag crammed with the most *delicious* food.'

I couldn't help smiling. 'You'll be lucky,' I said. 'That was Saturday. I'm scraping the barrel now. Have you got a salad spinner?'

'Can you describe it?' she said, also smiling, but without that look of amused contempt I'd come to know and hate.

'It's like a very small spin-drier. It's normally plastic and it usually has a knob on top.'

'Doesn't ring a bell.' She opened the kitchen door. 'I suppose there *might* be one in one of those . . .' She waved vaguely towards some cupboards. 'Behind all those pan-things . . .'

It rather looked as if I'd have to prepare the food again as well as providing it, but there seemed something endearing now about her hopelessness around kitchens.

'Have you got a pair of wooden spoons then?' I said. 'No, don't tell me . . .'

'Sod the wooden spoons, Goss,' she said, 'why don't you throw me an easy one, like where's the booze?'

We both began to laugh then, and went into the

kitchen arm in arm. She took a bottle from the fridge which I opened and poured. It was an el cheapo but it was crisp and dry, and very welcome after a long day of driving and standing and sitting around in the unbroken heat. I began to feel a lot more cheerful.

I washed the salad ingredients as we sipped the first glass, dried them in a clean tea-towel, and then tossed them as well as possible with a pair of discoloured forks in the French dressing I'd also thought it prudent to bring.

'You're awfully domesticated, aren't you?' she said, but in a tone of what now seemed to be near-admiration.

'I had to learn the basics when Mother went to live on the coast.'

'I'd hardly know where to start. That's a terrible admission, isn't it.'

But perhaps it wasn't, for a working girl forever dashing about London, who'd earned enough money to pay for things to be done. I'd been too hard on her.

'I've been spoilt, I suppose,' she said. 'In London the cleaning-lady brought things in for me. Things I could bung in the micro. Not that I ate in much.'

'Whereabouts is your flat?'

'On the river. Just up from Westminster.'

'It must cost a *fortune*! Have you still got it?'

She nodded, shrugged. 'I needed a good address. It's a sort of marker in the business as to how well you're doing.'

'And you're doing very well.' It was more a statement than a question. These details at least, I supposed, were the truth. I'd known she couldn't have afforded this flat, the expensive dresses, the car, on a receptionist's salary. And I knew now there could be no money coming from the family. And so it must have been the modelling money, which, with the ongoing expense of a flat in central London, and no modelling work for several months, might be starting to run out.

'It hasn't been easy,' she said, holding her glass up to the light reflectively. 'People get such wrong ideas. Looks and figure are only a start. It's a slog. You have to be totally reliable – the set-ups are so dreadfully expensive. You have to arrive everywhere on time and you have to take great care of yourself. Plenty of sleep so there'll be no shadows or blood-shot eyes. Vitamin supplements to ward off colds. Working out to keep in condition – the standing *around*!' She smiled. 'You have to be very tough . . .'

It was odd to think how tough she'd had to be to achieve that delicate, almost fragile appearance. I glanced at her as she stood in the galley-kitchen, sipping from her glass, talking animatedly, her wide-set eyes gazing past me into that world she must be missing so badly, where the work was hard but the money and life-style more than made up for it. I reminded myself it was really no business of mine why she'd chosen to kick around in Beckford for two or three months, earning loose change.

The salad lay in a wooden bowl, glistening in its film of dressing. The pappardelle was in the oven, the chips and garlic bread ready to go in later. I tossed the tea-towel to one side and picked up my glass. 'Dinner in about half an hour,' I said, smiling. 'Just time for a shower . . .'

'What a lovely idea,' she said, putting a hand on my arm. 'Shall we finish this first?'

That seemed an even lovelier idea. Drink the whole bottle and bring desire to its keenest edge, till the sensations flickered in the abdomen at the thought of our bodies crushed together in the tiny shower cubicle and the soap sliding down her thighs like patches of melting snow. Afterwards, as we lay for five or ten minutes relaxed and satisfied, I could talk calmly to her about the fancy background she'd given herself, tactfully explain that I couldn't help a slight sense of grievance about the deception in view of her earlier attitude towards my own circumstances, tell her that when she'd achieved so much in her own right there had really been no need for embroidery.

We carried our drinks through to the living-room and sat on the couch.

'. . . But it's a good life,' she went on, as if the stylus had been lifted only briefly from the original track. 'Swimwear can mean Bermuda or North Africa, high fashion Paris, of course, style can mean *anywhere*. You know, if one year it's a Latin influence it could mean Rio de Janeiro, if it's eastern it could be Bangkok. Often they just photograph very English-looking clothes in exotic settings to emphasise the Englishness.'

She talked on and on, her gaze always unfocused and inward, about that world of black taxicabs and jet-planes and Annabel's, about dinners at restaurants co-owned by Michael Caine, about the celebrities she'd rubbed shoulders with, the glittering first nights she'd attended, the hampers at Glyndebourne, the champagne at Wimbledon, black velvet at Ascot, après-ski at Klosters.

'If only I could get *one* decent part on television. A sitcom, a soap, anything. I've done several commercials but I just need the break. Acting's the only thing I've ever really wanted to do – I know that now. You can forget yourself, you can be different people, you can forget *everything* . . .'

I didn't try to break in. I knew it was useless. The shower, love-making, that little chat about sorting ourselves out, it couldn't begin to compete with the shimmering towers that lay at the end of the yellow brick road. I wondered how I'd managed to convince myself that anything could be salvaged from this relationship. In the end I felt as if I had no real identity, but was simply like an upturned disc of a face that an actor glimpses beyond the footlights, and plays to intensely, but which is otherwise anonymous.

The food would be overcooked if left. I got up, went to the kitchen. She followed me, still talking. She talked through the meal and beyond, absently switching on the table-lamps as darkness filtered across the clear sky and the yellow squares began to appear in houses opposite.

At some point I stopped listening, but simply nodded and sat thinking my own thoughts. I didn't really exist for her at all, and it was this final acceptance that brought a special kind of pain, because I'd not known it before. Other women I'd taken out had often gone out with me to get over some other man; they'd rarely pretended otherwise. But for a few weeks I'd meant something in my own right, there'd been friendship, affection, fondness even. John Goss lived.

But I'd not lived for her, not as John Goss. I'd lived only as a series of two-dimensional figures – a business-man worth cultivating, an investigator worth exploiting, and finally a sort of fan-club of one, whom she could dazzle with the glamour of her life, while I drank it in in grateful appreciation.

You had to be very tough, she'd said. Tough, above all, to be a taker.

She finally glanced at her watch. 'Can it be so *late!*'

'It flies when you're enjoying life,' I said, but she was so wired that the flatness of my tone bypassed her. She put a hand on mine.

'We never had that shower, did we. Let's go straight to bed.'

I'd decided an hour ago I was going to go home. The moment she actually noticed I was there I was going to tell her I'd send a photograph of myself she could prop against the wine bottle and talk to. But I didn't. Her green eyes were gleaming with reflected light and I'd had a few drinks and I could remember the offered breast and the plastered hair and the murmured requests to define precise pleasures.

But nothing had changed. Her body was there, freely offered, but she herself continued living in the past, sighing, breathing rapidly, but never speaking. She was lending it to me but giving it to Lymo, and giving it with such intensity that it seemed Lymo was in the room with us, a shadowy presence that stood above us, gaining definition from the passion that seemed to surge round and past me like a flow tide. I might have thought how sad it was that the only time she'd ever really given she'd met with rejection, had I not been preoccupied with my own bitterness.

Afterwards, as usual, she instantly slept, it was a gift that must have been invaluable in preserving her eyes unshadowed for the cameras.

I slept for a few hours and awoke with that clarity of mind that I knew meant I'd not sleep again. It didn't much matter; I had to make an early start.

139

I ran my hand over her sleeping body for the last time, over the firm but relaxed breasts, the almost concave belly, the baby-skin softness of her inner thighs. Then I showered, dressed, drank instant coffee. I went back to the bedroom for one final glance at her in the familiar aqueous light. Unusually, she suddenly awoke, as if alerted by an inimical presence.

'John . . . darling . . . are you running off again . . .?'

I shouldn't have said what I said then. Enough was enough. I'd got neither a vicious nor an unkind nature, a fact she'd sensed very early on. The words seemed to slip past my guard, as if some subconscious self, wounded more deeply than I realised, wouldn't be stifled. 'Yes, I'm running off. For good this time – Fran . . .'

I'd pulled the thin covers over her body on getting up. There was a sudden flurry on the bed, a scrabbling and flailing of limbs, as if a non-swimmer had got into difficulties in a pool's deep end.

And then she was sitting bolt upright, her frightened eyes glittering in the strengthening light. 'What! What was that you called me?'

'Fran. That's your real name, isn't it, Fran Metcalfe . . .?'

I was in Drum Lane by six, parking a borrowed elderly Mini unobtrusively among the other old cars. The Pakistanis tended to have jobs calling for an early start and I wanted to be certain I got my man before he left home. The sort of thin, feathery cloud that went with continuous heat was still saffron-coloured before a rising sun, and the old terrace houses stood hard and black against the gathering light.

At the bottom of the road stood the wool-combing

140

works which probably employed a good many of the men in the area, one of the few surviving relics of a textile industry that had begun to succumb to its final death agonies in my early childhood.

I had often walked in this district with my father on Sunday mornings. It had been a beat he'd pounded as a uniform, and it had had a powerful nostalgic pull for him, forming as it did a sort of microcosm of the town's life and industry. There were mills that dealt with every process of the textile trade along these streets – sheds where the grease wool was scoured and combed into the sliver wool the industry called tops, mills where the sliver wool was drawn and spun into yarn, others where the yarn was woven into cloth, mills where it was dyed and finished.

Even then, in the Seventies, so many of the buildings had stood empty, their gates hung open on deserted mill yards, where grass was growing between the cobbles, their ground-floor windows plastered with garish posters for rock concerts, many of them poorly secured and flapping in the wind.

My father would shake his head sadly. 'When I was your age, John, entire families, whole streets, even *districts* worked in the textile industry. You know Fletcher's over on Hammond Street, the vertical-process mill where they did the lot under one roof – they employed *hundreds*.'

He looked in through the broken window of an abandoned dye-house. 'It was only in the Fifties, you know, when things were booming. Couldn't cope with the demand. We encouraged the Asians to come here then to help with machines that ran twenty-four hours a day. Did you know that, son?' He shrugged, and we

141

walked on. 'And now there's not much work for them and not much work for us, and it's going to be a long haul before we've attracted enough new industry to make up for it. And when people are idle and all they've got is dole money, that's when crime takes off. You watch. And it'll get more and more sophisticated because of modern communications and fast cars and the sort of money that's involved . . .'

I thought of those walks and those words as I sat there, and I wondered if I had stumbled on one of those sophisticated Nineties crimes he had sensed were in the pipeline.

The workers began to emerge from their houses between seven and half-past. They met in groups, talking volubly, then drifted off to their jobs, some in throaty old cars, some on foot. But the man I waited for didn't leave the house I watched – his car stood in the street exactly where it had been yesterday lunch-time.

Around eight, a white postman began delivering mail. There was a great deal of it, his hands were filled with letters and packets as he went from house to house. I was aware of his slow progress over long minutes as I kept my vigil.

When Drum Lane's mail had finally been completed he sat down on a low wall not far from my car, wiped his moist forehead with a grubby handkerchief and lit a half-smoked cigarette. He had the look of a man whose wife had really wanted to marry a used-car dealer. He saw me, flicked his head upwards.

'Bloody hate it,' he said, 'Drum Lane. There's more post for Drum Lane than what there is for ten other sods. It's all this crap they get from the old country – magazines and packets and God knows what else. But that's only half the aggro. The names is that similar, and a lot of them share houses – it's a work of art figuring out who gets what.' He gave a final drag on his dog-end, then added in a sympathetic tone: 'You collecting the television money then?'

'Something like that.'

I didn't encourage him. I didn't want attention drawn to my presence. I was parked on a long diagonal from the house I watched – I couldn't be seen from the house, but if my man emerged and spotted us he might get suspicious. That was assuming he was up to something – he might simply have been driving past Ilkley Moor to see the seventh wonder of the West Riding, the Cow and Calf Rock.

Fortunately, after another minute's whining, the postman shuffled wearily off. Fortunately, because a few seconds later my quarry emerged. He was dressed as before in an old brown suit and white skull-cap. A plastic Tesco carrier dangled from one hand.

He looked casually but carefully up and down the road, then crossed over and knocked on the door of one of the houses. The door was opened by a Pakistani woman, and something was handed to the man which he put in the carrier.

He then went to another house, and another, before crossing the road again further along and calling at two more. At each stop, something was handed to him which he put in the carrier. He then made his way back to the old Lada, where it only needed fifteen or twenty turns on the starter to have the engine singing as sweetly as a cement-mixer.

I moved warily on to his tail, and followed him along the bypass and into Beckford Road. I smiled briefly as he branched off several miles from town and on to the road that led to Ilkley. Once again, I drove along that wide, attractive route at the side of the Wharfe, low now and sluggish with the prolonged drought. He stopped short of Ilkley by about two miles and turned left on to one of the relatively deserted roads where I daren't follow him, and which, as I knew, went upwards to join the one that skirted the moor.

I parked my car on some broken yellow lines near a block of shops. It slotted together like Lego. When the Pakistani reached the moor road, he would drive *down* towards Ilkley and return to Beckford along the main road. But the young man with the old-looking face, Fielding, would drive almost into Ilkley and then *up* out of it on the moor road. In that way each of them could be absolutely certain he was not followed. Their cars would cross, and each would return to Beckford on the other's outward route.

And somewhere, high up there on that quiet road, where they could check their backs in every direction, something would pass from the Pakistani to the white man.

It was as tight as a champagne cork. It had been carefully thought through by professionals, who ensured that they themselves were insulated from the sharp end. As I read it, if the law managed to feel the Asian's collar, he would be regarded as expendable. Fielding too, though he was one step up the ladder. It would take a very persistent and expensive operation to get through to Rainger, and to get from him to any other link would almost certainly be impossible. Because if Rainger talked he'd never talk again, on account of the hardware lodged in his throat.

I waited among the Fiestas and Peugeots of middle-class housewives at the foot of the road the Asian had angled off along. If I was right, Fielding would presently be coming down it in his Audi, to return to Beckford.

I was and he did.

This time the drop was made at Beckford's railway station. Fielding parked in the short-stay section, entered the concourse, and put his travel-bag in a pay-locker of the type where you keep a key. He then went to a snack-bar. A few people, short on time, stood at the window that gave a view of the station VDUs, among them Rainger, a glass of milk before him. When Fielding passed the counter, accidentally jostling Rainger in the process, I had to admire the sleight of hand that got his key into Rainger's jacket pocket as the younger man apologised.

I went to the station bar and had a glass of lager and a pork pie. If all the pork pies I'd ever eaten in a hurry were laid end to end they'd stretch as far as the ulcer ward.

Another successful drop. Of what?

No prize bigger than a pound of Black Magic for guessing.

Eleven

I cornered into the drive of my semi at about eight-thirty that evening. Rainger and his boss had taken a small party of foreign businessmen in two cars to dinner at the Ash Tree.

When Fielding had slipped the locker key into Rainger's pocket, Rainger had lingered for a further five minutes and then retrieved the travel-bag, got into his car and made for Beckford Road. I'd not bothered to follow him – he'd only be going to some far-flung post office to send a parcel to London. No need to jump through that hoop again. I'd returned to Hanover House, seen him get back about three, witnessed the arrival of the businessmen and the lowering of sunblinds in the Conference Room, seen the businessmen leave at six, seen Rainger and Fennell pick them up from the hotel at seven, seen them all settled down for a nice long session of serious eating and drinking by eight.

The rest of the evening had been my own. I didn't even have to write up the official report on Rainger's movements for Mrs Rainger – there had been so many periods of inactivity involved that the report was completed to date in longhand – Norma would rattle it off in half an hour on the word-processor.

147

I'd have a gin and tonic, make some kind of a meal from fridge remnants and walk to the local for a couple of pints. It was a poor substitute for the times I'd had with Fernande, even the bad times, but I'd get used to it. I got used to most things. I wondered, as I tossed my jacket on to the living-room couch, if I'd ever mentally be able to call her anything but Fernande.

I glanced through the mail, isolating the envelope with my own firm's logo on, which Norma had dropped off. I held it for a moment, trying to decide whether to read it or simply tear it up. It was a report on Fernande/Fran's London activities I'd had put in hand in a fit of pique after the Maison d'Or dinner.

I'd already suspected the French background she'd given herself. On the single occasion we'd showered together, I'd said I considered *entrejambes* a word ten times sexier than its English equivalent, and she'd smiled a bright vague smile. Since then, Norma's local enquiries had told me the rest, about the pre-London days at least.

I looked again at the envelope. I didn't think I wanted to know about London itself. There'd be nothing in here that she hadn't covered in detail last night, between the first aperitif and the last brandy. None of that could be anything but the truth, she'd *lived* it as she told it, lived it so intensely that I could have been a cardboard cut-out.

In the end I opened it more from a sense of profession-alism than anything else. Phil had spent time and effort in getting it together, on a quid pro quo basis, and I should at least see what I owed him when the favour was called in, even if his work was to be consigned to the shredder.

When I'd finished it I wished I *had* destroyed it

unseen, because what I read gave me a profound sense of pity. And pity was the last thing I'd thought I'd ever feel, or ever want to feel, for the girl who called herself Fernande. I stared into space, my drink untouched on the occasional table. And then the doorbell rang.

It was Fernande. She was dressed still in what seemed to be office clothes, a white blouse and a grey calf-length skirt.

'. . . Fernande . . .'

'Can I come in,' she said brusquely, pushing past me into the hall.

'It looks as if you're in.'

She went into the living-room and stood on the hearthrug, watching me.

'This is a surprise,' I said uneasily, wondering if she'd waited in her car on Bentham Terrace for my arrival. 'Sit down, I'll get you a drink.'

'I thought you said you *weren't* one of those toe-rags that poked around in people's private lives,' she said, in an uneven, almost gasping voice.

She looked as she'd looked this morning when I'd called her Fran, the same trembling lips and glittering eyes, only now her whole body seemed to be quivering with rage. I'd seen her acting several parts in the short time I'd known her, acting with great skill, but she wasn't acting now. The real Fernande, it seemed, had at last stood up.

I said: 'Why don't you sit down and have a drink.'

'Because . . . because I wouldn't be able to stop myself throwing it in your face.'

My eyes fell from hers. I'd have given anything not to have flung her real name at her this morning. There'd been no excuse for it, no excuse for any of it, except anger and bitterness and, I suppose, little as I wanted to admit it, jealousy.

'I'm sorry,' I said at last. 'It was unforgivable.'

'You bastard! You *bastard*! I've known some scumbags in my time but you're the biggest scumbag of all. What else did you poke your shitty nose in that's none of your bloody business?'

'Oh,' I said, sighing, 'what does it matter . . .'

'What does it *matter*!' she cried, in the raw, gasping voice that was almost unrecognisable from the soft, gliding one I knew so well. 'I want to know who put you up to it and why. Of course it bloody matters, you stupid shit . . . this is my good name you're messing with, my reputation . . .'

I gave her a puzzled glance.

'Nobody put me up to it,' I said. 'I did it for myself.'

Her mouth fell open on white square teeth. She stood for seconds in silence and her shoulders gradually stopped heaving.

'For *yourself*?'

'For myself . . .'

'But *why*?'

'Because I got angry when we went to the Maison d'Or – I thought you were patronising me. I wanted to know if you were really what you seemed.'

'But we *settled* all that. I didn't mean to *seem* like that . . . and anyway it's only a *name*, for Christ's sake,' she cried. 'You can't go into modelling calling yourself Fran Metcalfe . . . we *all* change our names . . .'

'Do you all rewrite history too?' I said in a low voice. 'Pretend your Yorkshire wool-comber fathers are really businessmen of French stock.' I smiled wryly. 'You know, if you're going to give yourself French lineage you really ought to learn a few words of French.'

She looked away, the anger only showing now in her flushed cheeks. 'Yes, they do,' she said at last, 'change things. They invent all sorts of things for their CVs. We meet wealthy upper-class people, we *can't* call ourselves Fran and talk like factory girls.'

'But you don't, do you,' I said patiently, 'mix with the rich and famous? You have a bed-sit in Fulham and the stuff you model is completely routine – mail-order catalogues, chain-store photographs, face-cream. You've never modelled swimwear in Bermuda in your life.'

The flush deepened, as if she'd sat too long in the sun on the first decent spring day.

'You mean bastard,' she almost whispered. 'You mean, shitty bastard . . .'

I took her gently by the shoulders. They still trembled slightly. 'It goes no further than me. I shouldn't have done it and I apologise. It's your life . . . God knows you're entitled to your fantasies. We all are . . .'

She sat down suddenly, as if her legs had given way beneath her, in one of the armchairs of my mother's old three-piece suite.

'Why not have that drink?'

She didn't reply, simply sat staring ahead, her green eyes unfocused, those wide-set eyes that had been given a new significance by what Phil had written in his report.

I mixed her a gin and tonic, put it next to mine on the table and sat down.

'I can't believe it,' she said at last. 'I was so good to you. I let you make love to me whenever you wanted . . .'

'But I was pretty good to you too,' I said gently. 'I

gave you good nights out and when we stayed in not only did I donate the food but I cooked it as well.'

'God,' she whispered hoarsely, 'how many jumps do I still owe you?'

After a while I said: 'Why couldn't you simply have been yourself? You've got plenty going for you. You're very pretty and you're good fun. Just because you haven't made it to the Paris catwalks . . .'

'I'm not ordinary,' she said abruptly.

'You're not alone, you know,' I said with bitterness, 'in not getting the things you'd set your mind on.'

'But I will,' she said. 'I will get where I'm going. I know what I want and one day I'll get it. I may pretend I'm already there, but that's my way of encouraging myself. One day I'll get where I'm going and I won't need to pretend any more . . . and then you'll know just who it was you were lucky enough to get into bed with.'

She spoke in a calm, unemphatic way that seemed to lend the words more force than if she'd spat them out, as before. I'd thought there was nothing else she could say or do that could touch me on the raw, but she never seemed to run short of weaponry.

'But I didn't sleep with you, did I?' I said harshly. 'That's all part of it – it was Lymo who slept with you. I was just the dick who stood in for him – in more ways than one.'

I got up, as angry now as I'd ever been, and stood above the unlit gas-fire, with its dusty lumps of pretend-coal. I stood there for some time, trying to get my emotions under control, because I really hadn't wanted it to end like this.

Finally, I turned back. She was staring at me, her head shaking slightly, her face now bloodless, so pale with shock it was as if she'd undergone major surgery.

'How could you know about Lymo?' she said, the old gasping harshness back in her tone. 'How could you know about *Lymo*? How *could* you? How could you *possibly*? That's *my* name for him! *No one knows it but me and him*!'

'I know sod-all about Lymo,' I cried. 'I don't *want* to know. You called me Lymo that first night when you were half asleep. You've been letting me give you one and pretending it was Lymo ever since . . .'

Her eyes drifted from mine with the vague loss of focus that went with pain and shock; I'd once seen that look in the eyes of people badly bruised and shaken in a car accident. She put a hand out uncertainly, as if to make contact with some solid everyday object she could hold on to.

Then she began to cry, her lids brimming and over-flowing with tears slightly discoloured by the delicate eye make-up. They dripped off her chin and on to the wide collar of her blouse. She cried without sobbing, as she'd cried about her unhappy childhood, but with such volume it was as if the valve of a sluice had been opened. I had never known such a powerful blend of bitterness and pity, pity at such desperate unhappiness, and bitterness that it was because of some other man.

Suddenly she leapt to her feet and ran from the room. I walked slowly after her. The front door stood wide open and I saw the flash of her blouse in the darkness, heard the blare of a car-horn, the cry of an irate voice. Then she was in the white Fiesta and gunning the engine.

I let her go – surely it would be for good. I felt pity for her, genuine pity, but I didn't feel I could help to pick up the pieces. If I were to follow her with a bottle of wine, I might have to listen to the story of Lymo, just as I'd had to listen to the story of Fernande Goes to London. Only the story of Lymo would be true and I didn't think I could hack it.

I went back into the front room and finished my gin. I picked up Phil's report again, which had been on the sideboard face down as Fernande and I had snarled at each other. I had a shredder upstairs and I'd destroy it when I went to bed. I skimmed through it again, still scarcely able to believe that it could tell a story so different from the one she'd told in such fine detail, with such intensity, such nostalgia.

'. . . You were in luck, John, if I'd had to dig around in the usual way it would have cost you a fair few sovs, but as it turns out my PA's sister, Pamela, works for a fashion photographer as a gofer. She agreed to talk to me, so I took her to lunch. This is more or less what she said:

'Everybody in the business knows Fernande Dumont, and they have a certain wary respect for her. She's pushy, manipulative, charming when she wants to be. She tends to pursue people, mainly men, who have either money or contacts.

'She's obsessed about being an actress. The feeling is she's always acting. She's considered to have talents of a very high order, but so far has had no real breaks.

'Her biggest problem was her face. She's very pretty but apparently her eyes are set fractionally too far apart. Everyone's agreed this wouldn't have mattered had Vladimir not been involved – it was the type of flaw that can actually increase a model's appeal. You may have heard of Vladimir, the sort of David Bailey of the

Nineties (known to certain of the slightly more cultured of the model girls as Vlad the Impaler!).

'Very early in Fernande's career her agency was keen to give her the build-up, the full super-model track. They were on the point of placing her for a major promotion for a new scent, but it depended on how she looked in a set of trial photographs they commissioned Vladimir to do. (He would also be doing the photography for the promotion.) Well, as a perfectionist, Vladimir tends to make the rest look like Happy Snaps, but he did Fernande no favours. He said he couldn't get the eyes right whatever lighting he used, said they all printed out making her look slightly vacant. Pam's convinced had it been any other photographer she'd have been earning five grand a day by now, but she was just starting out and he queered her pitch. He's king of the heap and the feeling seemed to be that if *he* couldn't get it right the other names weren't even going to try, not with their time being such serious money. Ironically, she was said to be letting Vladimir give her one at the time, but he's not the type to let a small thing like that interfere with his artistic integrity.

'It put her in the second division – catalogues, house-journals, magazine small ads, etc. Also the dog-end of television commercials – soap-powder, sink-cleaners, what the business calls 2TK (two tarts in a kitchen!).

'Everyone was agreed it was a great pity because she really did have the drive and the talent. She's talked of starting her own agency, if she could raise the folding, as a back-stop to her acting ambitions, and it's thought she could make a go of it, knowing the business as she does.

'In about March she got involved with a politician. So what, you might ask, what girls aren't these days, but this particular MP, apart from being very able, was building his image on "family values" – fidelity, stability, kids, solid home life, etc. He was putting it about that it was the duty of people in public life to set a good example. He was touching a nerve with the punters and it was making him very hot politically, so much so that he was being tipped for office. So the Chairman of the 1922 Committee takes him on one side, apparently, and tells him that if he doesn't drop Fernande, like within the time it took to make a phone call, his career would be dead in the water.

'The feeling at Westminster was also that Fernande was being a total bitch. The guy was wealthy (that goes without saying) but there were plenty of wealthy men kicking about, and so why go for the one man she could damage most? The tabloids were on to it, of course, but besotted as he was he'd been too careful so far for them even to get the innuendo going. But it just needed time with a woman who regarded the only bad publicity to be no publicity. Draw your own conclusions.

'In about May, she suddenly left London, saying her mother was ill, but leaving no forwarding address. There were some who said she'd "retired hurt", but most were certain she'd be back and can't think what's keeping her.

'You don't say if it's a mis-per or a moonlight. If the latter, and there's much involved, you'll almost certainly have to whistle for it. She's always lived well beyond her means and managed to charm, or act, her way out of trouble. If you have any one-to-ones *do not be fooled*. Pam says the time she's at her most convincing is when she's acting most. Best regards, Phil . . .'

Norma had typed her own contribution at the end. It

wasn't long. It said, among other things, that Fernande had been born Frances Metcalfe in Beckford to a poor working-class family, had left a goodish comprehensive with indifferent O-levels at sixteen, worked in an insurance business as a clerk-typist, where she was still remembered for her looks, her excellent manner with clients, her ability to digest information and her unconcealed derision towards any of the male staff fancying their chances. She'd left within a year to pursue her modelling career.

I sat for a long time staring into space in the half-light. It filled in the remaining blanks. And it made me one of the three people who knew who Lymo was. It had to be the politician – whose name I had no difficulty in supplying – who was building his career on duty and devotion and dogs on hearthrugs and Sunday mass. Westminster had been right – it *was* sheer bloody-mindedness to pick on the one wealthy man whose career could be damaged, when London was knee deep in wealthy men whose careers would be positively enhanced by association with youth and beauty; if you could hack it in bed you could hack it in the boardroom.

But Fernande was a shrewd kid, definitely not a bimbo. She was not the type to go deliberately looking for trouble with an institution that had its own ways of dealing with troublemakers. And so it had to be love.

And she was in Beckford to let the heat off, using her mother's heart attack, which I was inclined to think was genuine, as an excuse to lie low, to let the tabloids focus silly-season attention on a more accessible scandal, a loose cannon at least defused if not yet securely clamped to the deck.

I supposed the money that had bought the dresses and

paid for the Beckford flat and the Fiesta had been the price of her isolation. It didn't really matter – as far as I was concerned nothing was more certain than that it was all over. I tried to tell myself that with a woman as unpredictable as Fernande it was the best thing that could happen. I supposed that that was what the MP was telling himself as he sat, in a snatched half-hour of quality time, playing Monopoly with his wife and kids.

I went upstairs and fed the report into the shredder. I wished there was some kind of mental shredder I could feed all the images of Fernande into.

Next day something happened that made no sense. None, at least, in the context of the theory I'd tentatively begun to outline about the Rainger affair.

I was diverting my attention now from Rainger to Fielding. I knew Rainger's role and it seemed unlikely to change much. He picked up something in a small parcel in a bag and posted it to London from an isolated moorland village. Now and then he went to London in person, apparently to pick up his wedge of some kind of pay-out. This double life meant he was uncontactable at certain times, and this had been the reason his wife thought he was having an affair (or another affair). But in almost nine days there'd been no trace of a mistress.

To some extent Rainger could be neglected, while the younger man might yield further information. Through his contacts, he might lead me to other parts of the city which Asians had made their own. I decided to take a chance on Rainger having a more or less normal morning at the office, and it was while I had Fielding under obbo that this happened:

I followed him at around nine from his neat home on

Runskill Avenue. He drove about a quarter of a mile along the ring road and then turned abruptly off back into the housing estate. I kept on to the next side road, where I also turned off, hoping I'd be able to get back on his tail, but not giving much for my chances.

Had he kept on going it would have been a lost cause. It was a large complex estate of crescents, ovals and culs-de-sac and, as I circled round cautiously, I felt I had as much chance of finding him again as touching up Sharon Stone, with or without her ice-pick.

But on my third revolution I suddenly saw the Audi from my eye-corners parked half-way along an avenue lined with maple trees. I drove on for about thirty yards, parked my borrowed van and took out a tool-box. I was dressed today in jeans and a dark-blue work shirt, and looked vaguely like a gasman. To encourage this illusion I'd fastened a badge to the shirt bearing the number seventy-three. I had a black wig that gave me a balding look and make-up that made me seem swarthy. To some extent I could understand the actor's sense of release when he was pretending to be someone else.

Everything in the estate seemed to have the word Runskill in it – this was Runskill Drive. I approached the Audi and passed it. Fielding was reading a paper and seemed to be waiting. They were great lads for waiting. They could have out-waited Estragon.

I was looking for a house that seemed temporarily unoccupied. This was young white-collar territory – most of the houses would be owned by couples with young children, or where both worked. The absence of children and cars was the obvious clue, a better one by far, as I knew from experience, was the lateral sunblind carefully adjusted so that it was difficult to see if anyone was in or not. Almost invariably they were not.

I walked up the drive of such a house and rang the back doorbell. Nothing happened and so I took some keys from my tool-box. The doors of most houses in newish estates had standard locks that could be opened with standard keys – I had the full set. At the ninth attempt the key turned. There was no intruder alarm to go off, I'd already checked on that, they mustn't have had their first burglary yet, lucky things. As I was about to enter, the back door of the adjoining semi opened and a woman came out. She looked thirtyish, had a puffy face that bore traces of old make-up, wore a shell-suit that was too small for breasts and buttocks of roughly equal dimensions, and had the sort of hair on which, had she been modelling for Medusa, serpents would have made a nice improvement.

'Gas, love,' I told her. 'There's been a leak reported.'

'She generally tells me,' she said aggrievedly. 'We've had men round here before now *pretending* to be gasmen.'

'Well, you can come in if you like, love, but it could be a long job. Anyway, I'll have to check your house as well, so you'll be able to tell if I'm genuine.'

'You'll have a job on,' she said, 'we're all-electric.'

'There could be secondary seepage, don't you see,' I explained obscurely, 'through the underdrawing. It'll all have to be checked out with the hygrometer.' I tapped the wooden tool-box significantly.

'Oh . . .'

'And I've got my card here,' I added, holding up the section of my wallet that displayed my all-purpose card, with a photograph that matched the disguise.

She gave a sudden wide smile. 'Oh, I knew you were

genuine really. You look too honest to be anything else. It's just that you can't be too careful these days, know what I mean . . .'

'If more people were as careful as you, gel,' I said, 'those beggars that go round pretending to be gasmen would all be locked up.'

The smile became hideously friendly. 'Would you like a cup of coffee', she said in a warm voice, ghastly in its implications, 'when you come round to see to mine?'

The houses had curving bay windows, and from behind the upstairs curtains I had a perfect view of Fielding's vehicle. The waiting period went on for another fifteen minutes – time enough for me to wonder what in hell I thought I was playing at. I had entered a private house without permission. The *police* couldn't do that, not without just cause, not without a warrant. I'd worked ten years to get where I was, and if I was caught it would go for nothing. My hands trembled slightly with the chance I was taking.

But it wasn't enough to get me out of this nice bedroom with its nice flowered duvet covers and matching pillowcases and satin-weave curtains. I'd had two obsessions this past week, and one of them had gone, leaving more energy for what had always in any case been the more powerful of the two. I had to know what these people were up to. I didn't know what I'd do with what I found out, if anything, and there was never going to be anything in it for me you could put in the bank, but I couldn't leave it, not until I'd added detail and perspective to the first rough sketch I'd pencilled in.

A woman came into my field of vision, walking a dog. She turned in at the drive opposite Fielding's car. Two minutes after she'd entered the house, Fielding strolled down her drive and rang her doorbell. The woman opened the door. It was clear she knew him. Almost before he could speak she began to smile and nod. She turned back into the house, then returned almost at once. She was holding a brown-paper package about the size of a thick book, which bore postage stamps.

She handed it to him. He glanced at it, nodded, and put it in yet another of his travel-bags. He seemed to be thanking her effusively, and as he put the package away he took out what looked like a box of chocolates and gave it to her. I could hear their faint laughter. He turned from her, still smiling, and walked back to his car, in his nice dark suit and striped tie. With a final wave from the car he got in and drove off.

I left the house, carefully locking the door.

'I'm all ready for you!' the plump woman cried. Her make-up had been renewed in vibrant primary colours, and an ill-advised attempt had been made to back-comb her hair into a piled-up style that leaned ominously to one side. The shell-suit pursued its hopeless battle against cellulite. 'How do you like your coffee, chuck?'

'With and with, darling,' I said. 'Just need a bit more tackle from the van. Shan't be a tick . . .'

I drove down to Beckford, parked beneath Hanover House, waited. It made no sense. An Asian collecting from other Asians I felt I could begin to get together, but an ordinary cheerful-looking housewife – where did she figure in all this? Whatever theory had begun to emerge had now been blown apart.

The transfer this time took place in a reading-room at Beckford Central library. The long school holidays had begun and the room was almost empty. Apart from Rainger and Fielding, lurking behind separate fixtures,

162

there were half a dozen students poring over textbooks, and a librarian inputting a VDU and surreptitiously eating a cream bun. It was a fifth-floor room and the roar of the city's traffic was like the distant whisper of a turning sea.

Fielding eventually emerged from behind his fixture, minus travel-bag, and five browsing minutes later Rainger appeared from behind the same fixture, plus travel-bag.

I needn't have come along – I'd seen it all before, three times. I think it was professional interest in the endless changes that kept me going. Such extreme precautions weren't necessary, they could have used the same method every day – the railway-station locker would have been the least troublesome. But I knew, if I were to trail them for a month, that they'd never use the same venue twice. Because these men were part of an organisation that watched its back so meticulously that it was virtually impenetrable, except by chance, except by someone like me, looking for one thing and stumbling on another.

I didn't bother following either of them from the library. Rainger would be on postal duty, Fielding would be returning to his respectable city office. I stood by the window on the library landing, looking down at the city, with its pretend-Gothic cathedral, its pretend-Venetian palace and its pretend-French château. There had been other Victorian buildings which I dimly remembered from my childhood, graceful wool warehouses with flat Palladian parapets and clearing banks with majestic eastern cupolas, but they were long gone.

There was no fancy dress in the modern buildings. The office blocks, tall, white and curtain-walled, could contain nothing but offices, the stunted malls nothing but identical shops, the hotels nothing but temporary machines for living in. It was as if the old wool city had lost its sense of fun when it had lost its sense of purpose.

How could a placid-looking woman on Runskill Drive be involved in a grimy business where packages in travel-bags went from hand to hand and large sums of money were made? And if she wasn't involved why was she receiving packages? And where were *her* packages coming from? Surely not Pakistan . . .

Twelve

Kev said: 'I was once in Market Street and I counted eight lorry-loads. Eight! And that was normal.'

'We brought it in from everywhere,' Tom told him. 'Uruguay, Argentina, South Africa, Australia, New Zealand. We dealt in what they call speciality fibres too – mohair from Texas and Turkey, alpaca from Peru, even a bit of vicuna . . .'

He looked sadly into his Scotch. 'Wool used to be the bread-and-butter commodity and now they regard wool itself as a speciality fibre at the side of all the other crap they make cloth and carpets from.'

Bob said: 'Ellerman's shipped so much wool in they'd throw a dinner-dance on the flagship every June as a thank you. Every wool man and his wife. Do you remember, Tom, the captain presenting each lady with a corsage?'

'Never known food and wine like it . . .'

'The servants were Lascars, you know, one Lascar for every four people. Bring anything you asked for in half a minute . . .'

'A full orchestra . . .'

'A cabaret . . .'

'Remember that blonde dancing-girl with the green glittery knickers . . .?'

'Those knickers have lived in my mind for a quarter of a century.'

The laughter died down and then Tom said: 'Wages and salaries weren't high in those days, you know, but everyone had a job. Which is best, lowish pay and full employment or this new carry-on where those in work are highly paid and those out of work get a few quid from the dole? Is that what society's been working towards, three million sat around penniless with nothing to do? We were better off when we *all* had less . . .'

'And if they're sat around penniless they start to go out and grab it,' Kev advised us. 'Look at burglary – is there anyone here who hasn't had his house done over or knows someone who has? And drugs – don't get me going about drugs. I won't have any of that kind of carry-on in here. I can *smell* trouble . . .'

Fenlon turned to me. 'Vox pop,' he muttered. 'And not so far from the truth – the view from the station is that society's going nowhere. It *was* better when we had less, my old man says exactly the same as Tom. What benefits have money and technology brought? In Taiwan they probably pay themselves a fifth of what we do but they're all in work and out of trouble.'

'Which Roman emperor was it said that when a slave wasn't working he should be sleeping?'

'Did he have it right.' It was a statement not a question. The other smiled for the first time. 'Sorry, old son, I've been on a bit of a downer. It must be nearly a week since you were in . . .'

'Single case. The lady had the folding and the lady wanted round the clock.'

'Leg-over and chips?'

'Well, she'd ruled out secret devil-worshipping.'

'Let me guess. He's a chartered accountant and he needs to stay back nights because they're up-dating the computer. And he has this *really* brilliant assistant who needs the overtime to pay for the double glazing, and *she* can't help it if she looks like Kim Basinger . . .'

I grinned. 'The last one I kept tabs on actually left his wife in the end. Last time I saw him he looked just as pissed off with the mistress as he had with the wife. But this time it's a rather superior kind of sales-exec. Big house on The Drive, lah-de-dah wife.'

'These business lads get the lot, don't they? Big salaries, expense accounts, fancy wheels, women on the side. If you can run a mistress as well as a wife you've got to be loaded. Where did we go wrong, chum?'

The trouble was he half meant it. He was a born copper and he'd never really be able to imagine being anything else. But he'd never begun to have my kind of single-mindedness, and I'd never forgotten the way they'd looked when they'd had to let me go, *Fred Goss's boy*. Being able to hire Bruce hadn't begun to make up for that and I knew it. He was my closest friend and he'd been a great help to my agency, but he'd got a job that I'd never stopped brooding about, and he'd never be able to grasp the extent of my bitterness at not even being eligible to enter the race, a race that by now would have seen me two-thirds of the way to the first prize.

He was a hard-working capable policeman, but the dedication was missing, he might or might not reach DI but he'd get no further. He'd be reliable, dependable, a good boy scout, but already he was succumbing to the siren-calls of family life, a wife wanting him home nights, tapping his foot to the television jingles, a kid wanting to be played with, a dog wanting to be walked.

He could be on the verge of one of the biggest cases to hit the city, but he regarded it all as a wearying nuisance, calling for overtime, paperwork, a break with the familiar routines. Had it been me I'd not have been able to get it off my mind. And I'd never have felt tired, the adrenalin rush would have seen to that. I'd have been as excited as I'd been since the morning I saw Rainger get on a train in disguise. I knew me.

'The last time I saw you you said a chap was supposed to be coming from the NDIU,' I said casually. 'About the increase in heroin.'

'He got here Tuesday. Seconded from Customs and Excise. He said there was a new dodge of getting the stuff into the country. They *posted* it – from places like India and Pakistan.'

The ice rattled in my glass and I had to put it down and turn away, to cover the sudden flush, the sudden jubilation, with a spasm of pretend coughing. I *knew* it, I'd known it since Wednesday. What it had taken the NDIU with all its people and resources to work out, I'd worked out with a man and a dog. It *was* heroin I was on to and they *posted* it!

'You all right?' Fenlon said, tapping me on the back.

'Gin down the wrong alley. Carry on, Bruce . . .'

'Well . . . this guy makes out it comes in in rolled-up magazines and newspapers, even in letters.' He smiled sourly. 'He says they thought of Beckford right away – the NDIU, that is – along with Birmingham and Leicester. He says he's just putting us in the picture at this stage until they've got a genuine lead.'

And I *had* a genuine lead. Elation slipped directly into bitterness. I had a lead and soon I'd pass it to Bruce, who'd never really wanted to know, and he was the one who'd reap the rewards of my vigilance.

He lit a cigarette, the battle against nicotine now decisively lost. 'He came across very positive but me and the lads don't think he has a price. You can imagine how much Pakistan mail hits this town; you might nail one receiver but what about the others? Sending it in penny numbers spreads the risk like insurance.'

'I thought the Pakistanis were law-abiding on the whole,' I said, genuinely puzzled.

'They are. Most of them haven't a clue what's going on, they're sure of that. Innocent people are involved apparently, who get a packet of the stuff and are just asked to hold it till it's collected, as a favour to a countryman. Do a raid on one of *them* and they simply don't know they've got gear worth twenty-odd grand in that rolled-up newspaper – and they certainly don't know where it's come from.'

I wondered how much the Pakistani in the old Lada had collected the morning I'd kept watch on Drum Lane – a hundred thousand pounds' worth at the least probably. In a single *day*.

Fenlon said: 'The feeling is there are just one or two genuine dead-eyes running the import side, and finding them would be like finding a virgin on Dresden Place. And we have to go steady – we don't need any hassle from the Race Relations Board, it doesn't take them more than half an hour to start talking harassment. It's all very well these experts flying in for half a day with all their theories, but we have to live in the real world.'

'Oh, come on,' I said, 'political correctness can't possibly extend as far as protecting genuine villains dealing in drugs that wreck lives.'

'You're not in it, John, you don't understand how

carefully we have to tread with the ethnics.'

I wondered if he and some of his colleagues were tending to play the race card as an excuse for a lack of commitment to a course of action that without inside knowledge would admittedly be time-consuming and costly. They'd follow orders in the end, of course, but the negative responses going up the line wouldn't be without their effect on men who controlled budgets and resources.

I said: 'So you've taken no action so far on the postal aspect?'

He shrugged: 'They're kicking around the idea of a task force – mail interception, long-term surveillance in parts of the inner city – but we're so stretched at the moment it's finding the bodies. We feel we need a genuine tip-off and that's not easy from such a closely knit group. The customs guy said why didn't we borrow a plain-clothes Asian from a Midlands force and plant him.' He finished his beer. 'We had to explain that putting a plant among the Beckford Asians would be like putting a Chinaman on Shetland.'

He prepared to leave. 'We'll get a break in time, we usually do. Let's just say we're ninety per cent certain there *is* a Beckford connection, but right now it's on the back burner while we concentrate on people we can actually see.'

'The pushers . . .'

'That's all we can really do at the moment, put out fires.'

We walked towards our cars. I was tempted, very tempted, to tell him what I knew on the spot, to make his day even as it dismantled mine. I owed him. It would give me a buzz to tell him what he needed to know.

But I didn't. From a mixture of motives. Until I'd worked out where the woman in Runskill Drive fitted in the job was only half done. How much more of an achievement to clean up the story-line. I was also genuinely uneasy about the ethics involved in passing on, at Mrs Rainger's expense – both emotional and financial – what I'd uncovered by chance. I needed more time to think it through.

I tried to tell myself those were the only reasons, but I knew they weren't. I didn't want to let this case go, that was the true bottom line. Because of enjoying every moment of it, because I'd used skills I'd thought had almost atrophied, because life this week had had a vibrancy and colour that owed nothing to the endless sunlight.

I gingerly took hold of the metal handle of my car-door, which seemed as hot as a cooker ring. 'So,' I said. 'To sum up, the NDIU man thinks the H comes in from India-stroke-Pakistan in cardboard newspaper tubes, small packets, et cetera, to, by and large, innocent Pakistanis, who simply pass them on to a gang member.'

'That's about it,' he said. 'But it can get more complicated. From time to time that track overheats. So the people at the refining end start posting to drops on the Continent, and those drops repost it over here, to a hotel say or a block of flats or an accommodation address, where someone with a phoney name waits to receive it . . .'

I became very still. I'd been half in the car, opening windows to release the nauseating heat, but I felt the perspiration seeming to chill on my body. 'Not . . . not *private* addresses?' I said, striving to keep the excitement out of my voice.

He shrugged, as impassive as I was elated. 'It's been
known. The form seems to be that they send it from the
Continent to an innocent householder. Once it's on its
way they send a con-artist to the address and he asks the
householder if he or she would mind looking out for a
parcel. He tells them it's really for him, but he's just
found out the sender's got the address slightly wrong and
it corresponds with the householder's. He'll be well
dressed and plausible. They nearly always believe him.

'Then, when it *is* delivered he just goes back and
claims it, once he's certain the coast's clear.'

'So,' I said, struggling for a tone as casual as his, 'if the
law manages to intercept it, all it's going to do is lead
them to someone who's outside the frame.'

'Right on,' he said wearily. 'That's the trouble with the
whole sodding carry-on.'

'Yes?'

'I'm from the Post Office, madam,' I told her,
opening my wallet on my card. 'We've had a report of
a misdirected package.'

She frowned slightly. 'Well . . . yes . . . but it's
been sorted. The person it was really for picked it up
yesterday.'

She was blonde, faded and matronly. She had two
teenage children, an Old English sheepdog and a husband who was doing quite nicely at the Woolwich. She
didn't look remotely bent and she wasn't – I'd checked.

'I see . . . was it a mix-up in numbers or something . . .?'

'Well, the number was right but the street name was
wrong – it's with all the names being Runskill round
here; I don't know why they do it. The gentleman it was

really for lives at Runskill Avenue and this is Runskill Drive. He . . . well, he just asked me to look out for a package. You see, he knew it had the wrong street on because he'd been on the phone to his business friend abroad, and it came out in the conversation. He was very cross about it. It's easily done, I suppose. He just asked me if I'd mind accepting it because he needed it very urgently. He said if I returned it to the postie there'd be such a delay till they sorted it out.'

She began to look anxious. 'I hope I didn't do wrong. He showed me his driving licence as proof – well, you can't be too careful, can you, not that he didn't seem a trustworthy business person. You can always tell, can't you? *Did* I do the wrong thing?'

I smiled reassuringly. 'Well, the correct procedure *would* have been to return it to the postman, that's the rule, but as long as it's sorted out there's no need for me to take further action. What was his name, just for the record?'

'Caine,' she said, then seemed to search her memory, 'Mr C. O. Caine.'

The outfit wasn't without its jokey side. She hadn't asked me how I could have picked up on a private arrangement between her and Mr C. O. Caine, and women were usually very good at spotting those little telling details. Except nice, vague, middle-aged, middle-income women like Mrs Webster, who kept her husband's shirts immaculate and would be rather worried for a few days, not entirely convinced the Post Office had overlooked her irresponsibility.

I sat in my car for five minutes, savouring the satisfaction. The Beckford force had had seminars about it; I'd done it. It was now more or less complete. Letting it go would be like having teeth drawn.

★ ★ ★

My doorbell rang. It made twice in less than a week. It normally rang twice a year. Fernande stood on the step. I watched her warily.

'Can I come in?'

'I don't think there's anything more to say.'

'Please let me come in.'

I stood aside to let her pass. She was in jeans with a white crocheted top worn over the waistband. Her hair was in a pony-tail and she carried a sort of patchwork bag that clinked slightly.

She handed me the bag. 'Will you have a drink with me? They're nice and cold.'

There were two bottles of Sancerre in the bag and two cartons of food.

'Jambalaya,' she said. 'I thought you might have a meal with me as well. There are some crusty rolls underneath and a ready-made salad. It only needs tossing if you'll show me how much dressing to use.'

There was a touching hopelessness about her total lack of domesticity that I wasn't sure I wanted to be affected by. I smiled faintly. 'I'll cope with the dressing.'

She smelt of the same scent, delicate and elusive, that she'd worn the first night we'd gone out. I could detect a white half-cup bra through the top's open-work and glimpse minute areas of the flesh of her upper breasts.

I took her into the living-room, then went to the kitchen and turned on the ancient cooker, put one of the bottles in the fridge, opened the other.

She was looking round the room when I went back, at the chocolate-box paintings of North Yorkshire coastal resorts, and the glass-fronted cabinet full of Reader's Digest condensed novels, china ornaments and sherry

174

glasses, and the sideboard, with its silver-framed photographs of my parents' wedding, of me as a two-year-old, as
a schoolboy, as a man of twenty-one.

I glanced at her defensively for any return of those
familiar looks of amused contempt. There was none, but
I still found myself saying: 'My parents' taste. The house
is mine now but I left everything as it was until . . .'

Until when? Perhaps for ever. The house's banal
timelessness comforted me during the brief hours I spent
in it.

'I like it,' she said simply. 'I wish I'd been brought up
in a house like this where people . . .'

She too let the sentence hang. Where people loved
each other, was that what she'd been going to say? I'd
certainly had plenty of love and care – my youth and
childhood couldn't be faulted for happiness and hope.
Fate seemed to have decided so too, because it had then
corrected the balance.

'I'm sorry, John . . .' she sat down. 'I did use you. I
did pretend to be something I wasn't. I'm very sorry.'

I handed her a glass of wine. I wondered if she was
really sorry or if she was acting being sorry. I wished I'd
never read Phil's report – it would always be difficult
now to forget his warning about one-to-ones. But for
that bloody report I'd be able to believe her as much as I
wanted to believe her.

'And I'm sorry too,' I said at last. 'Your life's your
own. It wasn't for me to pry . . .'

She held her glass near mine. 'Will you accept my
peace offering? It doesn't go near making up for the
lovely meals you've given me.'

I looked at the green eyes that had helped to lose her
super-model status because they wouldn't satisfy

Vladimir's artistic integrity while the rest of her body was satisfying his lust. I looked at the very dark brown hair and the full mouth and the body with its deceptive air of fragility.

'And what you've given me can't be measured in anything it ever cost me,' I said in a low voice. 'I mean that . . .' I broke off. 'I was going to call you Fernande. Is that what you want to be called?'

'Call me Fern. That's what I've always been in London. *Anything* but Fran. I see Fran as a large, jolly girl with coarse black hair and big knockers who crews boats and goes pony-trekking and has a boyfriend called Trev.'

We began to giggle. The cold, lively wine went down like nectar and I began to feel very good. I didn't know where we went from here and I didn't care a toss. They said she never stopped acting and I didn't give a damn about that either. She was back, and if she was a different woman every day I was going to get several dozen for the price of one, all equally exciting.

She patted the couch. 'Come and sit with me.'

I refilled the glasses and joined her. She slipped her arm through mine. 'Can I tell you something? It won't be a fairy story about my blinding career in the fashion business and it won't last until dinner and out the other side.'

'Of course, but only if you want to. Your life's your own and what you do with it is none of my damned business.'

We looked at each other with faint, wry smiles.

'There *was* a man called Lymo. You were right in everything you said – you're a very perceptive man, John Goss. I couldn't get him out of my mind, even when . . . Well, there's not much to tell. I knew a lot of men in London and there's not much point in pretending I didn't try to use them. You know, the Lombards . . .'

'Lombards . . .?'

She grinned. 'Loads of money but a right dick-head . . .'

'I like it. I've known a few. They deserve to be used.'

'Well, the sort of men who pursue models and actresses know exactly what everything's about. They want to be seen with attractive women and the women want to be seen in the right places. It's supposed to give you a profile, not so much with the punters as with the people who really count, the insiders.

'Lymo . . . didn't seem like that. He didn't want to use me as a sort of . . . you know . . . trophy, it tended to be low-profile stuff at quiet restaurants. He had a lot going for him, and he was very wealthy and very very attractive. Married, of course, but then most of them were.

'I . . . fell for him. It's not the sort of thing I did, to be honest. My career had always come first. But . . . it just got out of my control. I *thought* he'd fallen for me. There was talk of a future and I believed it. But in the end it all seemed to get too heavy for him, and he dropped me, so he hadn't really been much different from the others. That's it – the end.' She smiled now with sad cynicism. 'Thank you very much . . .'

A darker blue was filtering slowly across the clear sky and lawns were taking on the liquid, almost pool-like appearance a summer dusk gives them. We sat in silence for a time. As she said, I'd been right in every particular.

I nearly always was. It was why people I'd worked for told their friends: 'Send for John Goss.' I got up, switched on wall-lights and poured the rest of the first bottle of wine.

'You didn't mind me telling you?'

'Not if it helps.'

'You're the only person I've told. I'm not really into letting my hair down with the girls. When I got home . . . the other night, I thought about it a lot. I was in love with him . . . probably still am . . . but he's gone. And you're here, and you'd make ten of Lymo . . . and . . . and I couldn't stop using you as if you were one of *them*, the ones who expect you to be using them because they're using you.' She drank some of the wine. 'I don't suppose I'm making too much sense. Can we . . . try again? Nothing . . . you know, heavy. Friends. I don't know where I am or where I'm going just now, I've got a lot to get together. But if I had you by me for a month or two – till I go back . . . someone I trust . . . and respect . . .'

We sat down to the jambalaya and the crusty bread and the glistening salad very late. Before then we'd showered and then made love in the room I'd had since childhood, with its battered desk and its woolly elephant, its bookshelves and its model aeroplane, its midi system, watercolours and answerphone – artefacts, it seemed, from every stage of my life.

We'd rewound the tape, and it had been back to the wet hair and the patches of soap sliding over her soft flesh. Back to me towelling her dry and dusting her body with masculine talc, at which she'd giggled and said she hoped it wouldn't grow hair on her chest, back to the murmured requests I'd thought I'd never hear again – 'This way . . .?' 'Do you like that . . .?' 'Shall we . . . go for it . . .?'

As if sensing what I'd longed for more than anything else, as I'd withdrawn the towel from her large, dark areolae she'd even arranged her graceful fingers over her left breast in the offering gesture that dogged my memory.

After dinner, we sat in the lamplight and sipped Drambuie, and she expanded on the new relationship she'd have with a John Goss who'd not bullshit her, who'd provide uncomplicated friendship and sex without strings. She'd been in Town too long and become case-hardened by men who simply wanted to display her like a new car. She could never remember any of them saying what I'd said to her, and that she'd not forget – that she was fun to be with. How could a bimbo be fun? They were too thick to be fun, and that's all she ever was to them – a bimbo.

I warned myself it was all Fern Rediscovers the Decent Guys Back Home, and yet there seemed such simple honesty in the fragmented sentences and the faint sighs, the eyes that rested on mine with a rueful smile, even though I'd never needed Phil's report to know how many-sided she was, and how easy it was to be dazzled by the facet the light was currently picking out.

'Look after me, John,' she said later, just before falling into instant, enviable sleep, 'until I've sorted myself out. Maybe I've been out with so many flaky types I don't know where I'm at any more.'

If she really was acting that night it was some of the best I'd ever seen. And I couldn't have cared less. What did it matter if she *was* acting if the entire audience consisted of me?

Thirteen

During the night the heavy cloud had drifted over from the west which had been forecast for two days; when we got up it was sluicing with rain. It beat against the window and clattered in an overflow from a blocked roof gutter, and it flowed down the drive, past Fern's Fiesta, in thin bubbling streams. Only the parched lawns could cope, soaking it up like blotting paper. The long dry spell was over.

'I like rain,' she said, looking out through the kitchen window. 'When the roofs and pavements have that whiteish shine and everything's sort of clean and sharp-edged, as if you're seeing it after a couple of drinks, and . . . sort of cosy. I don't want to go to the office today, I want to sit in a corner of your living-room and read *The Wind in the Willows*. *Your* copy's got coloured pictures . . .'

I put a hand over hers. 'You can read it next Sunday while I make brunch. After a long lie-in.'

'You won't go off investigating again, will you, in the middle of the night?' she said with mock petulance. 'It's awful waking up and having no one to play with.'

I smiled. 'My Sundays are my own for the foreseeable future, thank God.'

181

I tried to inject a note of genuine feeling into it. After all, instead of crouching behind bushes in heat and discomfort watching the Rainger house I'd have Fern's considerable sexual artistry in compensation. And yet, had the case not been more or less over, I knew perfectly well that Fern would again have taken second place behind the greater thrill of piecing together Rainger's other life, of seeing the picture slowly take on definition, like a print beneath an enlarger. Even though when I *had* been crouching behind bushes all I'd been able to think of was Fern's expertly writhing body in the half-light.

We sipped black coffee for a while in silence in the welcome coolness.

She said: 'A friend of mine once wanted to hire an investigator to keep an eye on her husband. I said if it were me I'd not bother. I'd definitely know if he was losing interest, and if he hadn't stopped losing interest within a month I'd go and see the best divorce lawyer in town.'

She spoke in the calm, unemphatic tone I'd heard before, which had a peculiarly convincing ring of truth.

'You're going to get drenched', I said, glancing at my watch, 'just going to your car. Would you like to borrow a raincoat of Mother's? She's about your height if not *quite* your shape. You'll have to pretend you're modelling for Oxfam.'

I brought the coat and rain-hat down, and helped her into them. 'My favourite bag-lady. Let me just smear a handful of mud on your face to get the full effect.'

She loved them, pirouetting in front of the hall glass, loved the waif-like appearance they gave her, the sweet urchin in hand-me-downs. I could see her at nine, putting on her mother's lipstick, bidding for the attention that, from what I could make out, had only ever been given reluctantly – attention, that was, that bore thinking about.

I kissed her.

'You'll come and see me tonight, won't you? Early. You won't be doing boring old surveillance . . .'

She spoke lightly, but it was the second time she'd referred to my work taking precedence over her, and I realised it must have been a situation as unusual as it was resented.

'I'll be there. Sixish. I'll provide the sweet and sour if you'll provide the imagination.'

I held the door open. 'Can you go out kind of ostentatiously. There's an old lady across the road who'll write it all down and send it to Mum. It keeps Mum in touch, she says she gets a lot more news from Mrs Firth than she does from me. She'll *love* you wearing her raincoat – that's definitely daughter-in-law stuff.'

'But what about me staying the night in the family home? *Unchaperoned*!'

'Next time she rings she's bound to ask if I made sure there were clean sheets on the guest-room bed.'

I drove along The Drive, rain cascading on to the roof of the car in filtered rivulets from the broad-leaf overhanging trees, the tyres sizzling over the road's flooded surface and throwing up spray like the prow of a speedboat. The single minute change in the appearance of The Drive itself was the emptiness of the gardens, where before, in the days of sunlight, you could occasionally glimpse, through the arched gateways, ladies in white hats, sitting at white tables, sipping iced drinks. Today, they'd all be sitting in one another's conservatories, reminding each other grimly that the weather in England could never be trusted for very long, and making plans for holidays in countries where it could.

'It's Goss,' I said, 'to see Mrs Rainger.'

'Are you expected, Mr Goss?' the thin-faced woman in the green smock asked guardedly.

'No – but I think she'll see me.'

I was left in the hall this time until it was ascertained if my confidence was justified. The old place looked as elegant as ever; because of the day's almost November gloom small silk-shaded lamps were lit here and there, giving a glowing richness to the highly polished surfaces of tables and cabinets constructed by hand when the queen who'd given her name to their legs was still getting about on her own.

'Perhaps you'd like to come through, Mr Goss . . .'

I was shown into the drawing-room with the marble fireplace and the Chinese rugs and the silver tray loaded with hand-cut glass.

'Mrs Rainger will be along shortly. Would you care for some coffee?'

She must already have been brewing up because a single fragrant cup was brought to me on a small tray. I drank it slowly with the reverence it deserved. I looked at the pictures – fine oil-paintings of moorland, lowering skies, grouse, dogs. I looked at the intricate patterns on the rugs, the vibrant muted yarns they'd been woven from. I looked at the decanters, the jewels of light reflected from their faceted stoppers, that would be filled with the finest brandy, whisky and gin that money could provide. And I looked through the leaded windows at the carefully shaped trees, the Porsche coupé on its turning circle, the sweeping lawns, flawless and emerald, despite a hose-pipe ban that had left most ordinary folk tending yellow stubble.

I wondered what it must be like. They said it was the little things in life that really got to you. You could cope with illness and death and the house on fire, the nervous breakdown stuff was a leaking roof and a faulty car and a negative equity mortgage. But the wealthy even had people to take care of the little things. They never got shoe-polish over a new shirt-cuff because the shoes came to hand ready shone. The lives of the rich were all their own.

I sat down on one of the couches that angled from the fireplace. I suddenly realised I was envying a mirage. The Raingers were wealthy but their lives were certainly not their own. Their lives, this luxury, depended on certain powerful and dangerous men in London. Who needed Rainger, but not one tenth as much as Rainger needed them.

I could understand now why they'd chosen Rainger, and I could guess how they'd done it – the charming stranger, the apparently casual encounter over drinks at the Inn on the Park, the skilfully oblique dialogue, the hints of a need for a northern contact, the delicate suggestions of very rich pickings.

I could only admire the research. Rainger was a man of respect, married to a woman with class but no money. He had a good job and a fair salary in his own right, and he had no form of any kind – I'd checked. He had highly developed administrative skills.

He was also a bit of a Flash-Harry. He liked the good things, and he had a taste for danger and intrigue that didn't have to be dug for too deeply.

Above all, he was blackmailable. Normal underworld

figures tended to move around with others of their ilk – they had their own inverse aristocracy of necessity because the world of straight money and Norman blood wouldn't give them houseroom.

Rainger was unique in bridging both worlds. He made a great deal of funny money and he lived among the old wealth. And because the life-style meant so much to him, any threat to remove it, to expose him, would make him one very obedient servant.

'You wished to see me . . .'

She came in wearing a grey silky house-dress that looked both simple and costly. She also wore gold-rimmed half-spectacles which for some reason gave her an appearance of intense sexiness. She took them off as she came across the room – no doubt she'd been casting a careful eye over the household accounts. I remembered the powerful emotions that ran beneath the iron composure, the unhappiness that had briefly distorted her features as I'd turned to her in the hallway on that first morning, the hungry adoration in her face on the night of the party as she'd gazed at her spoilt golden man through the shifting crowd.

We sat down, she on the opposite couch.

'Well,' she said flatly, 'is it good or bad?'

'Let's just say there's no other woman.'

If this gave her an overwhelming sense of relief there was nothing you could notice.

'Are you . . . sure?'

'Positive. I've followed him everywhere for a week and a half.'

'The agreement was supposed to be for a week.'

'If it's going to leave you strapped I'll throw in the extra days.'

She rose effortlessly above this display of lower-class churlishness.

'If there's no other . . . woman why does he lead such an irregular life?'

'He's a sales executive – he can't work nine-to-five hours.'

'I'm aware of that, but at one time I always knew where he'd be. There weren't unexplained blanks about which he was evasive.'

'I assure you he's not having an affair.'

'How can you be quite so positive in such a short time?'

'I've done a good deal of this kind of work. Up to now, almost all the men I've kept under surveillance *were* having affairs, and married men who play around are like schoolboys who've just realised girls are a different shape. Not to put too fine a point on it, they can't let it alone, not for half a day.'

'Then what does my husband *do*?'

I shrugged. 'He works hard, irregular hours.'

'He went to London a week last Friday – what did he do there?'

'He met a business contact and they had lunch together in the West End.'

'But why didn't he go to Head Office and work from there? He always used to.'

'He seemed to be there specifically to see the one customer . . . it was a long lunch and he came back mid-afternoon and returned to Hanover House . . .'

'These lengthy lunches,' she went on, with clipped doggedness, 'in the Beckford area . . .'

'As I told you on the phone, he went one day with Mr Fennell, another day with business friends to La Rasade . . .'

'When he wasn't taking people to lunch, Mr Goss, he'd always come home for lunch. In summer we'd sit on the terrace and have rolls and cheese and a glass of wine . . .' She broke off abruptly, aware that the last sentence had been irrelevant, but not before I'd detected the note of almost desperate longing that had given her voice a slight unevenness, almost a throb. It moved me more than I could have believed possible, coming as it did from a woman I'd decided I didn't much care for.

'. . . What . . . did he do, at lunch-time, on those days when he wasn't with Ivor Fennell or at La Rasade?'

'Management meetings that ran through lunch. A sandwich at his desk . . .'

'Now *you're* being evasive,' she said, accurately. Silence fell slowly over the room, a silence broken only by the endless patter of rain against the windows and the soft, ponderous tick of a wooden-cased wall-clock.

'I thought you'd be *pleased* to know he's not sleeping around,' I said defensively. This abrasive cross-examination had been the last thing I'd expected. I'd been certain she'd be so relieved that an independent professional could find no evidence of dick-sharing that she might even have awarded me my very first smile. I wondered if she'd known more than she'd admitted at our first interview, had positive proof of that elusive other woman. In that case, the only assumption that could possibly be drawn, following my days of obsessive scrutiny, was that Rainger was between affairs, or had had a single affair whose completion had coincided with my secondment.

'Has someone made it worth your while to tell me there's no other woman?' she said abruptly. 'Has Miles or some . . . person . . .?'

It was the first time such an accusation had ever been levelled and it threw me off balance. I flushed, began to feel my hands trembling slightly.

'Mrs Rainger,' I said, in the coldest voice I could muster, 'I don't honestly care how little you trust your husband, but I care very much how little you trust me . . .'

'It wouldn't be the first time someone in your . . . profession worked for the other side . . .'

'I wouldn't make any more remarks like that if I were you.'

Our glances met and held. The clock whittled away slow seconds, but I neither spoke nor let my eyes leave hers. Eventually, it was she who looked away. She got up and went to the drinks table, picked up a decanter.

'Can I . . . get you something?'

'No thank you.'

She returned to the couch with gin in a heavy tumbler.

'I forgot', she said, 'that you tend not to drink during the day.'

She was suddenly trying to be affable. It didn't go as far as smiling, but the sharpness had left her voice and there was a sort of regal warmth in it that it probably had when she was congratulating the gardener for knocking the moss problem on the head.

'Mr Goss – I'd like you to continue your surveillance. It's important to me to be absolutely certain that this . . . that there is no other woman.'

I wondered if that had been a Freudian slip, if it meant she'd been about to say that *this time* there is no other woman. The knuckles of the hand clutching the glass were glistening whitely.

'Mrs Rainger . . .'

'Another week at the same rate. Any reasonable expenses . . . plus a bonus . . .'

'I'm sorry, but no.'

After a lengthy hesitation, she said: 'I spoke hastily . . .'

The words had taken a great deal of effort. She was of the class that didn't explain and didn't apologise – especially to the hired help.

'It's not that,' I said. 'My back's broad enough, even for aspersions on my integrity.'

'A week . . . ten days,' she said in a low voice. 'It may not be long enough. He may be playing for time. I know . . . *please* continue . . .'

The breeding could no longer entirely conceal the wretchedness – it showed like a bone through broken flesh. I felt genuine pity then that the breeding hadn't helped in her choice of husband. She'd know a genuine antique from repro at fifty paces – why hadn't she been able to tell an upstart from a gentleman? Or had the difference been the attraction, the looks and the Flash-Harry ways the real turn-on for a woman whose girlhood had perhaps had everything but glamour and charm. Perhaps she too had once looked down a different future, and then decided on one that gave every indication of being a lot more fun, even if the times of desperate unhappiness could already be sensed, because of Miles's sinisterly easy way around women and the hungry glances in his direction she must already have been intercepting.

'I . . . can't, Mrs Rainger. I'm sorry . . .'

'*Please* . . .' The voice fell almost to a whisper.

I sighed. It seemed the only way I could relieve one kind of unhappiness was to replace it with another. But in any case perhaps ethically she had to know. I'd struggled with the problem half the night while Fern slept that deep animal sleep, her arm laid across my chest, her cheek against mine. I'd not had a satisfactory answer and even standing on Mrs Rainger's doorstep this morning I'd still been uncertain what I should tell her, had decided in the end to think on my feet when the time came.

'Look . . .' I said at last, 'your husband isn't involved with a woman but he is involved . . . in something else . . .'

Our eyes met again. Her glass stood neglected, the gin barely touched. Finally she said: 'Go . . . on . . .'

'I need to say this. Have you ever given careful thought to how your very lavish life-style is funded?'

She frowned. If she was puzzled she was also very put out. The unhappiness was suddenly sidelined, not proof in the short term against the instinct to repel boarders. She watched me with the previous imperious hauteur. 'I'm afraid I can't see that our finances are any concern of yours. I can't see what they have to do with anything.'

Had I been seeking an excuse to go no further, here it was. I couldn't begin to tell her even a little of the truth because she'd been born a Forbes-Walshaw, who'd no sooner talk about her finances with an outsider than she'd talk about her sex-life, assuming at this point she had one to talk about.

I said flatly: 'Your husband makes about fifty thousand a year and that dress you're wearing must have cost him a week's salary. You have a very expensive motor, a Daisy Edge house, a substantial second house, antique furniture. You entertain lavishly, you have expensive hobbies, staff, foreign holidays. It all adds up to a lot more than fifty thousand – in fact I'd say the Rainger

191

life-style was out of synch with the Rainger income by about four to one . . .'

'That will do, Mr Goss,' she said brusquely. 'Our income is no concern . . .'

'*Your* income?' I cut her off. '*Your* income? You do mean *his* income, don't you? I feel certain I don't need to remind you that your own family ran short of folding money in the Sixties. They had a lot of respect, and still do, but respect doesn't pay for Daisy Edge houses and Porsche motors and little old men to cut the grass.'

This time she didn't even reply. She simply stared. It bore no relation to the earlier stare. We'd played the eyeball game then because of a clash of minds about integrity. This one was about money and it left integrity out of sight. Some two hundred years of Forbes-Walshaw gentility went into that stare, and it worked. No servant caught unlocking the tantalus could have felt more like touching his forelock and shuffling his feet. My hands seemed to be twisting a non-existent cap. Without moving her eyes from mine, she opened a drawer in the sofa-table that stood between us and took out a cheque-book in a leather cover, and a gold-topped pen.

'I believe a thousand pounds was the figure we agreed for your services,' she said evenly, 'and two extra days would make it fourteen hundred, if we work on the basis of a five-day week. Plus expenses. Should we say fifteen hundred in total . . .'

As she was already writing, I assumed the question was rhetorical. I had to admire her unswerving control of the cash flow, even though she seethed with contained anger. A hundred pounds fell well short of the real expenses of the case.

She flicked the cheque across the table with a finger-nail. It slid over the Mansion polish and on to the rug. It would be nice to say I left it where it had fallen, got coldly to my feet and exited without a word, like those investigators in novels, but with an office and Norma to run I couldn't afford lofty gestures. I picked it up, and pausing only to ensure it was signed and dated and that the figures agreed with the words, put it carefully in my wallet. I was now free to go. I'd tried to warn her, I'd tried to point out the discrepancy between income and expenditure, but I was no match for the guarded crenel-lations and the lowered portcullis of Mrs Rainger's upbringing.

She smiled in icy contempt. The irony of it being the first smile she'd ever given me wasn't lost. 'I'm sure you won't mind which part of my income that particular cheque comes from.'

'It comes from the legal part as far as I'm concerned. It comes from the part he earned selling chemicals.'

I should have left well alone. I'd had the derision and I'd had the money, and I should simply have gone. The smile slowly faded and she sipped a little of the gin. Then she sighed and shook her head in exasperation.

'Mr Goss,' she said at last, 'this is all so *irrelevant*. I engaged you to find out if my husband was having an *affair*. Nothing else. I may have seemed rather annoyed, but I certainly didn't want you trying to find out how much money he makes.'

I couldn't argue with that. It was something I'd told myself – a hundred times.

I shrugged. 'You're right, of course, it's absolutely nothing to do with me. I can give you my word he's not having an affair and the full report is in this envelope.' I

193

tapped it where it lay on the couch at my side. 'Perhaps we should simply leave it at that . . .'

I made to get up, but she raised a hand in delay. 'Mr Goss,' she said, in a more reasonable tone, 'you're an investigator, a very skilled one, I'm sure. But my husband's a very skilled businessman. He's very successful. The economy depends on people like him.' She hesitated, then said, choosing her words with delicacy: 'If . . . he and his colleagues sometimes bend the rules a little and find ways of paying themselves more than their basic salaries, don't you think a society that benefits so much from their efforts ought to be prepared to turn a blind eye?'

I began to feel the weariness slowly descending over me that I only ever felt when I had a problem that seemed to defy solution, however lateral the thinking. That would be the accepted wisdom, that he was making a bit on the side. That attitude would be in her genes too, from that fine old business family she'd been born into – the payments in kind, the wife listed as secretary, the foreign holidays in the guise of selling trips, that the wealthy so often tended to believe was none of the Inland Revenue's damned business.

I said wryly: 'I wish I *were* only talking about the office slush-fund.'

'Oh, Mr Goss! Miles is a respectable businessman. He's never been in any kind of trouble in his life, not real trouble.'

'Neither had Robert Maxwell,' I said flatly, 'but he *would* have been, wouldn't he, if he'd lived?'

'Oh, *really* . . .'

I got up. The problem had found its own solution, as the real toughies often did. It would have stretched her credulity to breaking point to accept that Rainger could ever land himself in any kind of mess that he and a creative accountant couldn't somehow sort out. The way he was making his money would always pale into insignificance against the possibility of his making some typist. I can't imagine why I even bothered with one more throw, unless it was conscience.

'Well,' I said, 'don't forget that you heard it here first. I think I must warn you that you could be facing a lot of changes in your life, all of them for the worst.'

Her brown eyes flicked distractedly from mine, but not before I'd caught a glimpse of inner turmoil. Had I got through to her at last, touched some nerve that hadn't been entirely atrophied by the deadening comfort of the life she'd lived? Did I detect the faint echo of some inner cry of pain: *Oh God, what has the bloody fool done this time!*

I looked down at her, with her costly dress and her dark, sleek hair, sitting among her exquisite possessions. Studying people had been my life and I knew she simply could not be compared with the type of women who knew they were married to professional crooks. She'd been bred to a life of quality – there had always been someone to provide it. She was like an exotic fish in a tank that had been given every semblance of a corner of the Pacific – it might be sheltered and artificial but it was all she knew. The men did things in city offices and the life-style just rolled effortlessly along. She might be scrupulously careful with the loose change, because the Yorkshire rich had that bred in the bone too, but she'd never have tried to put an actual figure on Rainger's income because she didn't need to. Whatever she wanted she was given.

195

She looked up at me again. 'Mr Goss . . .' I could barely hear the words.

'I'm very sorry,' I said gently. 'To be frank, the sort of trouble he could be in, I wish I *could* have told you he was only screwing his secretary . . .'

'Mr Goss . . . I'm sorry for anything I've said that may have upset you. I've been under a great emotional strain. I *must* know that Miles is being completely faithful to me, my . . . well-being depends on it. Please say you'll continue your surveillance for me for one week more, *please* . . .'

I seemed to feel myself trembling on the verge of hysterical laughter. It was like being in some group in a bar-parlour where everyone talks and no one listens. I'd searched my soul half the night for what, if anything, I should tell her, and *if* I told her how I should break the news, only to find that Miles could only be tried on a single issue, all else being inadmissible evidence. I realised then that she could have turned a blind eye to him robbing a bank as long as his mistress wasn't driving the getaway car.

No woman had made an impact on me as Fern had, and this last week I'd thought I'd begun to understand something of the nature of that kind of obsession. Compared with what Mrs Rainger felt towards Miles, what I had seemed more like a mild and unremarkable infatuation. I suddenly felt an inexplicable tremor of fear, and I had an overwhelming urge to get away from this house, this wretched woman's blinkered misery. I'd had enough.

'I'll have to go now, Mrs Rainger,' I said. 'Thanks for the cheque. I'll send you a receipt. I really don't feel I can help you further. If I followed him for a month I don't think I'd find another woman . . . if that's any consolation. I'll see myself out.'

I crossed to the door. Half-opening it, I glanced back. She looked so small and vulnerable in that great room. She seemed scarcely aware of my departure – she sat motionless, eyes unfocused, as if trying to cope, ironical as it seemed, with the fact that Rainger *wasn't* being unfaithful.

Because I was beginning to sense that she'd have preferred me to bring news of a definite affair. I'd left her defenceless when she wanted ammunition she could use in some battle that might win an eventual war.

I wondered if that was how it had been in the past – some frightful scene followed by days, perhaps weeks, of tears and reproaches, followed by weary promises from him that it wouldn't happen again. And probably it *wouldn't* happen again, for six months or a year, because of the effect on his nervous system and the smooth running of his home life. Perhaps, for a little while, he'd be entirely hers and she could live in hope once more that he'd be hers for good.

My catching him between affairs must have been the last thing she'd wanted. By not finding Miss Scarlett I'd failed, because I'd not been able to provide her with even a temporary respite from the relentless corrosion of her neurotic jealousy. I'd brought her peace and she'd wanted a sword.

The thin-faced housekeeper stood in the entrance to the kitchen. Behind her I caught a glimpse of a large, airy room, with anything resembling an artefact taste-fully concealed behind panels of light oak. An equally invisible music-system was playing very softly Liszt's third 'Liebestraum'.

'I'll open the door for you, Mr Goss, it's got a rather complicated security lock.'

'What difficult times we live in,' I said abstractedly.

She suddenly shivered, a moment later I felt cold air seeming almost to cling to my body, as when you opened a front-loading freezer.

I glanced round. 'The air-conditioning must have been a godsend last week . . .'

'Air-conditioning . . .?'

'I thought you must have a portable unit in the kitchen.'

She shook her head. 'There must be a window open . . .'

But she looked uneasy. The rain still sheeted and it was cooler today, but the atmosphere was very humid. The cold air that seemed to surround us felt as if it had travelled across a frozen lake.

I was reminded then of the coldness of the hall the first time I'd come here, which had seemed to issue from the kitchen. Yet, as today, it had not been there when I'd arrived, only as I left.

We exchanged glances; I sensed that mine was as uneasy as hers.

'Goodbye, Mr Goss,' she said, manipulating the many-levered lock and opening the door wide, as if welcoming the mild, moist air that was drawn inside. 'Would you like an umbrella to get to your car? You can leave it just inside the gateway . . .'

'Please don't bother,' I said. 'I'll run.'

I didn't even want to stay for as long as it took her to find an umbrella.

Fourteen

It was hard trying to adjust, very hard. I'd been immersed in the Rainger affair for a week and a half, and it had seemed like a time out of life, especially with Fern adding to the dream-like quality. Whenever I remembered Fern in the future, and it would be often, I would also remember the Raingers, the heat and the light, the waiting, the tailing, the shadowing of Rainger through the cosmopolitan crowds in Trafalgar Square.

'Come on, my lad,' Norma said, at half-past eight on Tuesday morning, 'you've got a lot of catching up to do.'

I sipped the scalding black coffee she always had infusing in the cafetière first thing, and looked with a sigh at the bulging wallet-file she had in front of her.

We worked on the invoices first, for my percentage of the proceeds of work I'd farmed out to take on the Rainger case, and then went on to the routine legal work, and after that the individual cases – two mis-pers, a life-style check, a persistent stock loss at an electrical goods warehouse.

'. . . Finally, a woman called Garner wants an eye keeping on her husband. She's found an hotel receipt . . .'

'No chance,' I said. 'I can't face another leg-over, not

199

after Mrs Rainger . . . in fact I may pack it in for good . . .'

'It pays well,' she said, glancing at Mrs Rainger's cheque where it lay on top of the paying-in book. 'I think I could overcome my scruples for that kind of money.'

'You go and bloody do it then, while I sit here with my feet up . . .'

'I *knew* I was going to have a bad week with you. You're always the same when you've been off enjoying yourself on a single case.'

How right she was. I buried myself in paper, trying to lay the boredom by the sheer volume of work I forced myself to accept.

'Here are your snaps, by the way. He's not a patch on that *gorgeous* Mr Rainger.'

I flicked through them. During one of the many times I'd turned on to Shilling Street, where the Brit-Chem offices were situated, I'd seen once again the man with the red beard I'd noticed on the outward and return journeys of Rainger's London trip. He was walking in my direction on the opposite side of the street away from Hanover House, and I'd managed to pull into a twenty-minute-stay section and photograph him surreptitiously several times with the long-focus lens fully extended, through the car windows. He'd worn the same battered sports jacket and pork-pie hat I remembered from the train, and had carried a document-wallet under his arm.

I'd been tempted to shadow him, but I couldn't leave the car, nor neglect Rainger for too long, on the off-chance the beard was doing anything but delivering house-title deeds.

I said: 'Who is he?' as I handed them back to her.

'How do you mean?'

'Well, you know all the PIs and messengers . . .'

'He's not a PI. Not unless he's a new boy. But I don't think he can be. You can't be a man of a thousand faces when you're wall to wall red fungus.'

'Quite so. He couldn't be more conspicuous if he wore a stocking mask.'

Which was probably why he went on kicking about in my mind. If I were to be scrupulously honest with myself I'd be forced to admit that he'd probably not have made the same impression on me had his appearance been completely nondescript.

'He *could* be a messenger,' she said. 'They turn over so rapidly you can't always keep track. Why did you take his picture?'

'He just *seemed* to be in places where Rainger was, once or twice. I've absolutely no proof of it, but for a time I thought Rainger might be a closet gay . . .'

'Rubbish! Not a lovely man like that . . .'

'Just because they're good-looking doesn't mean a thing. Look at that old film star who died – Rock Hudson.'

'He wasn't *gay*! They just say things like that to sell newspapers.'

'Norma, he had pool-parties where there wasn't a woman in *sight*.'

'That's because his wife didn't want him tempted by a load of starlets. He *was* once married, you know,' she said triumphantly, 'to a *woman*.'

You tampered with Norma's icons at your peril – her information on them was all-embracing, if selective.

'All right,' I said, 'can we just *pretend* that Rainger might be bisexual and didn't want it known in the circles he moves in. The mixture of a bisexual Rainger, a bearded man who seemed to be lurking about, and blackmail, just crossed my mind. For one reason and another I've gone off the idea, but I'd still like to know who the guy is so I can take him out of the picture.'

Norma only knew that I'd shadowed Rainger because of a possible mistress, there was nothing in the official report about the handing over and posting of parcels. Normally I told her everything because her advice was always worth having. But I'd hesitated to tell her about his criminal tendencies because I knew what her reaction would be. Straight to the Bill. But it wasn't quite as simple as that. I could have walked through the case and concentrated solely on the brief – was he or wasn't he having it off. Many investigators would, and I couldn't honestly find it in my heart to blame them. But that wasn't my way, and now I was sitting on information I'd not quite thought through how to handle. It *would* be presented to Fenlon, that went without saying, but a delicate question of timing was involved.

'There *are* a few lawyers on Shilling Street,' she said. 'He could be working for one of those. In fact I believe there's a firm actually in Hanover House. Hang on . . .'

She slipped a disc into the side of the word-processor, called up a file. She had all Beckford's solicitors listed in various ways – alphabetically, by city street, by speciality. 'Pike, Rathbone,' she said, a few seconds later. 'Newish practice. They've had the mail-shots but they've not been in touch so far. Concentrate on conveyancing and commercial . . .'

'That's got to be the answer,' I said. 'He's a paper-boy.'

'*Blackmail*,' she muttered derisively. 'A hunk like Mr Rainger. They're trying to make out James Dean was gay now. *James Dean*! You know, *Rebel Without a Cause*. Ronnie and I saw that when it first came out.'

'Wasn't that the night Ronnie had his collar felt? Doing forty-two on the ring road in his Robin Reliant . . .'

The following Saturday, I drove Fern north to the Dales. We walked from a tiny village called Kettlewell over the steep moorland of Cam Head and down to a tiny hamlet called Starbotton, where we sat in the bar-parlour of the Fox and Hounds and had beer and sandwiches.

It was a day of walking in what Yorkshire people modestly called God's country, with good clear views across the valley. The rain had gone now but it was a lot cooler than it had been, with a strong wind and drifting galleon clouds. Fern loved it, loved the effect of the wind through her hair and being able to display herself in a thin white parka and tight pants and a turtle-neck sweater. She revelled in the impression she made on the sweating back-packers as we crossed over the bridge in Kettlewell; no one could have played it better, the pink-cheeked county gel who lived for the moors and the fells and the big skies.

She reached the table of flat land at the top of the incline ahead of me. She turned round and stood against cloud and sky, her hair blowing sideways across her forehead, her green eyes catching the light. She smiled and blew me a kiss.

I felt I understood now something of the motivation that drove her to conceal the real Fern behind the many roles she immersed herself in. A Fern being someone else could relieve herself of the traumas of a girlhood the real Fern could only begin to contemplate at all by pretending the traumas were mental and middle class. In

203

the end I'd begun to overlook her faults – the false charm and the main-chancing and the way she used people – because they were all aspects of a toughness I could only admire for the way it had helped her to force her way out of her background, as you admire the perfectly formed wild flower that forces itself through a barely perceptible crack in a concrete path.

After lunch, we walked back to Kettlewell, hand in hand, along the winding valley road.

I said: 'When do you go back to London?'

'When my notice expires. I handed it in yesterday. Trying to get rid of me?'

'I was hoping it wouldn't be too soon.'

She put her free hand on my arm. 'I've got to get back in the swing, John. Before they forget my face altogether. They make people with Alzheimer's seem like memory-men.'

'What's the game-plan?'

'You tell me. I'll be able to tick over on modelling work. As for acting jobs . . .' She shrugged. 'I'll go and queue up for the walk-on parts with all the others.'

We went on for some time in silence.

'It could have been so different,' she said, with a faint sidelong smile. 'You'll probably think I'm bullshitting again, but because one man couldn't get my eyes to photograph exactly as he'd decided he wanted them I missed out on the real loot.'

'Your eyes are your best feature.'

'I was advised they made me look vacant. Charming. The irony is that most of the girls *are* vacant. They had the flawless looks, I had the ambition.'

I sensed she didn't want to say any more about something I knew to be the exact truth. It had to have been one of the most upsetting events in her life, but her tone was detached and calm, giving an impression of still water that conceals a powerful undertow. If she could have talked about her home life as it had really been I suspected she'd have used exactly that tone.

'I know the country well,' I said.

She glanced at me.

'You wanted to be a super-model; I wanted to be a super-cop.'

I told her the story of John Goss. She was the first person I'd ever told, and I did it to comfort her, because she'd mapped her life out as meticulously as I'd mapped out my own, and had the gods shrieking with the same laughter.

'I can't see you as a bobby, John. It's all so structured and disciplined. You seem a lot more laid back . . .'

'You can't see me as one because I never got to be one. The metal's the same, but if I'd gone in the force it would have been beaten into a different shape.'

'Poor John . . .'

'Poor Fern . . .'

We walked for some time in silence, through long grass, which the ebb and flow of the wind flattened in sudden narrow paths that seemed to run along the ground like the passage of a stalking dog.

She said: 'I once saw a nature programme about small birds emigrating hundreds of miles to the south. They're guided by the sun, they have a kind of mechanism in the brain that locks on to it, and it guides them where they have to go. I think people like you and me are like that, guided by *something* that's going to get us to what we should do with our lives, even if it's not what we thought it was going to be . . .'

205

★   ★   ★

She stayed the whole weekend at the house where I'd been born, and we slept together in the room where my mother had read to me about Paddington, where I'd had the measles and done my homework and played pop records and worked out the details of buying the agency and brooded over the complicated cases. Like Rainger.

We'd had large gins on Saturday night and then a simple Goss meal of fillet steak, baked potatoes, salad and a bottle of Beaune. We'd been so drowsy with the walking and fresh air that even as we reached for each other in bed at midnight we'd fallen asleep; me, like her, slipping for once into instant oblivion.

And I'd never known a keener pleasure than to wake up eight hours later, completely refreshed, with her body in my arms. It was a day of broken weather, cloudy and showery, with flashes of sun, and her eyes glinted in the gloom as we stroked each other to arousal. We lay in a drifting state until almost noon, drowsing, stroking, making love. And then, driven from our cocoon by a different hunger, we'd gone downstairs, where I'd begun to assemble the ingredients of the only breakfast I ever had.

'There's the *Sunday Times* if you want something to read,' I said.

She smiled. 'I was promised *The Wind in the Willows* . . .'

It was a perfect day for escape – dark, wet, cold enough to set a low gas flame licking through the pretend-coal. Her act today was one of her most appealing, that of a woman fleeing from the disappointments and complexities of adult life into a cosy, affectionate and protected girlhood. She sat for most of the afternoon curled up in one of the armchairs, barefooted, twisting a lock of hair round her finger, and reading, with a faint smile, the adventures of Mole and Ratty and Mr Toad.

I picked up the *News Review*, but my mind wasn't on it. I *had* to make some decision about Rainger.

I knew what I *should* do. Go to Fenlon first thing in the morning and tell him all I knew. I could pretend to myself it wasn't ethical to divulge information I'd come by inadvertently, but I knew perfectly well the question of ethics wasn't involved with a man like Rainger. He was a common criminal and it was my duty to unleash the dogs.

But I couldn't get that poor woman's face out of my mind. She deserved a breathing space. I knew she simply didn't care that Rainger might be a criminal, but her life was going to change out of all recognition and she ought to be given time to prepare for the crash.

One more week. I'd do nothing for another week. At the end of that week I'd hand Fenlon the secret dossier on Rainger, the police would mount their own investigation, and by the end of August that would be the beginning of the end for Yorkie One.

I had to consider, of course, that the operation could be endangered by waiting another week. Mrs Rainger might warn her husband, and he might revert overnight to being a respectable citizen. But I didn't think she would. If she warned him, she'd have to say she'd found out from someone who'd been following him around to see where he was getting the extra-marital. I felt certain she'd not be able to tell spoilt Miles she'd hired a pro. I didn't think it had ever worked that way. I felt she'd be too afraid she'd push him too far, so far that he walked out on her. The story would always be that she'd done her own snooping.

I also had to consider that I was making noble excuses for myself, that a certain amount of casuistry was going on here. Because if I gave that poor woman a week to come to terms with the roof falling in, I should also conveniently be giving myself a week to see if Rainger went again to London, and whether I'd be able to follow his *London* contact to the people who might run the show.

I could then give Fenlon the sort of break that would make him a star. Because the people in the Smoke would do the lot – heroin would merely be a division. They'd be bringing cocaine in too, they'd control Ecstasy, LSD, pot, anything that would help turn a regular million.

If I could follow Rainger to London again I could do it. I'd sorted the Beckford end out on my own and I was certain I could go the distance. There'd be nothing in it for me you could put in the bank or attach to your epaulette, the glory would be all Fenlon's, but *I'd* have done it.

I thought of Fern's words, as we walked in the sun and the scouring wind, about us being guided by *something* that would get us where we had to go, and perhaps I'd been guided to Rainger to face the biggest challenge of my life, the chance to break what was almost certainly a national drugs ring.

'You're not reading, are you? You've been staring at the same page for *ages*.'

She was sitting beside me on the couch. I'd not noticed her make the switch from the armchair. There was a slight edge to her voice; she hated not being noticed. 'Man,' she said, 'when you get something on your mind you really kick it around . . .'

'I'm sorry, Fern. I thought you were still lost in the

Wild Wood with the night coming on.'

She began to smile. 'I'm a quick reader. It all ends happily.'

'What would you like to do now?'

'I suddenly remembered, we both fell asleep last night before . . . Do you think we ought to sort of . . . catch up . . .?'

'Is that why you didn't bother putting any knickers on?'

'I didn't think you'd noticed. I was hoping it might come as a nice surprise . . .'

Daisy Edge Drive gave on to a road called Elm Lane that ran down a steep hillside to join one of the main Beckford roads. I waited in Elm Lane early each morning, in a different car, in a different disguise, and would follow Rainger's Mercedes to the city. If he went to Hanover House I would go on to my office, there was nothing else I needed to know about his Beckford activities. I was interested only in the next London trip.

It was Hanover House both Monday and Tuesday.

On Tuesday evening I finished in the office about eight-thirty and went home. I wasn't seeing Fern as she was going to a leaving party for one of her Brit-Chem friends. I sat and unwound for ten minutes with a gin, and just after nine walked half a mile to a Chinese takeaway for a carton of sweet and sour, and on my way home I bought a couple of tins of lager. It wasn't what you would call one of my bigger nights.

I wondered if he'd go to London on Friday as he'd done before – it was going on three weeks now since they'd passed him his last wedge and life on The Hill wouldn't be getting any cheaper. Perhaps they had other ways of getting money to him and going to London had been a one-off. What if he *didn't* go on Friday? Should I extend the week's grace to a fortnight? Convince myself that the poor woman would need more than a week to prepare for the biggest culture-shock since Oscar Wilde had gone inside?

The car seemed to come from nowhere in the darkness. It may have been an illusion, but it was almost as if it had been coasting with the lights off. I was half-way across Carron Avenue when suddenly there were flaring headlamps and a roaring engine where before there'd been a clear road.

I could have been seriously injured, even killed, depending on how I hit the ground. Perhaps what saved me was the job I did. Investigation work developed quick wits, and the long hours on your feet kept you fit.

As it was, the car's off-side wing gave me a heavy glancing blow to the left buttock. Had I not already been running, I'd have been under the wheels. The impact flung me to the opposite roadside, where I sprawled heavily on the tarmac. The car didn't stop.

I lay in the road, groaning. In the gathering silence, I could hear my tins of lager rolling in the gutter, beyond that the small indifferent sounds of suburbia; a dog barking, a householder whistling, a window being closed.

'You all right?'

An old man in a flat cap stood above me in the light of a distant street lamp, trembling with shock.

My arms and hands seemed to be all right, and before attempting to move I felt both legs and ankles carefully. The left ankle was tender and painful, but nothing more. I ached everywhere and I could feel wetness on the buttock that had taken the impact.

'You all right, son?' he quavered again. 'Bugger were driving like a bat out of hell . . .'

Wincing and grunting, I got slowly to my feet.

'I don't suppose you saw his number, Dad?'

'It's me eyes. I don't see too well these days, not even with me specs.'

'Any idea what make of car?'

'They all look the same to me mate. Never had one of me own.'

'Not to worry . . .'

'Bleeding disgrace. He *must* have known he'd hit you. Driving like a maniac. Too many fools on the road these days. This your bit of supper . . .?'

The tins of lager had stopped rolling when they'd reached the mound of pork, rice and vegetables.

'You're right,' I said. 'He knew he'd hit me. Joy-riders. They knock a car off and they can't control it. It wouldn't have made much difference if you *had* seen the number.'

'They want locking up. Whatever age they are. If you can't walk the streets, what's the world coming to? Come home with me, son. Wife'll make you a cup of tea. Drop of whisky in it. We're just round the corner . . .'

'You're very kind, but I'm afraid I'm bleeding rather badly. I'd better get along to the Infirmary. I'll need stitches and penicillin . . .'

'You could've been killed . . .'

I limped home, put a pad on the buttock and drove to the hospital, wincing every time I put my foot to the clutch. They cleaned me up and put ten stitches in the wound. There was little or no damage to the ankle, despite the pain; it would be stiff for a day or so, nothing more. Everything else was superficial bruising. I was told I'd been lucky.

They asked me if I'd contacted the police; I lied that I had. They'd catch the sod sooner or later without my help, and then the magistrates would take his youth and disadvantaged childhood into account and sentence him to cutting lawns for old ladies for six weekends, and he'd leave the court grinning.

I knew it was some kid – joy-riding was getting to be a chart-topper, in this area as everywhere else – not only was it jolly good fun but the training came in handy for when they started on the ram-raids.

It had piss-artist written all over it: the headlamps suddenly coming on, the engine given too much gun in low gear, the lousy steering. Added to which, I hadn't been dressed too conspicuously, but had been wearing the dark casual clothes I generally used for night surveillance.

I thought no more about it.

Until the parcel arrived.

Fifteen

He didn't go to London on Wednesday either, and I had a relatively routine day in which only the thought of seeing Fern in the George at six helped to hold at bay a boredom that shaded inevitably into depression when I contrasted the work I'd have to do for the rest of my life with the sort of work I could have done. I half-wished I'd never known about Rainger, because of what he'd shown me I was missing.

She was waiting in the bar-parlour, completely at ease with the ageing wool men, themselves invariably at ease with attractive women.

'They've been telling me about when beer was a shilling a pint,' she said. 'That's five pence, isn't it? You could get a hundred pints for a five-pound note, except that according to Kev the five-pound notes were white and crinkly and as big as a lady's handkerchief.'

'And I suppose if you got two of those a week you were doing extremely well.'

'What *happened* to the wool business?'

I shrugged. 'All kinds of things. Men stopped wearing suits and overcoats because of central heating and heated cars. They began making carpets of synthetics. The emerging countries started to develop their own textile industries. All sorts of reasons and all at the same time. I'd love to have known it in the old days.'

It was accepted now that we met every night. She appeared to have few female friends. She seemed popular enough, but I suspected she'd save her warmest regard for the sort of women who could be helpful to her, and women rapidly sensed that. There were obviously no other men. Just me. And I was there to help her get over Lymo. He must have been quite a man to have affected so profoundly Fern's total control over Fern.

I remembered the pocket-book she'd taken from her bag on the day we'd first met, a diary black with the entries that denoted a hectic social life. All part of the meticulous detail of the daily charade, I supposed. Fern as a girl men stood in line for. Or perhaps she was just comforting herself for the London days, when life really had been a whirl.

'Are you all right, John? When you came in you seemed to be limping slightly.'

'It's nothing. I pulled a muscle somehow, moving things around in the office.'

I had spoken in an instinctively guarded way. I was always guarded about anything that happened to me in the course of my work, but being knocked down by a car had nothing to do with my work.

It had simply been a joy-rider, so why hadn't I told her about it? I wonder if even then I was reacting to some tremor of suspicion almost beyond evaluation, like the soft throbbing note of a double bass that you sensed rather than heard below the cataract of a symphony orchestra's trumpets and violins.

She slipped her arm through mine as we sat at the bar

214

and gave me a lingering smile, as if I really was the only man in her life. 'Why don't you come to London with me? You could make a lot more money, a clever boy like you. You could do your thing and I could do mine, and we could share the expenses of a decent flat. There's so much to *do*. We could see all the plays and shows . . . you'd enjoy it . . .'

'Are you serious?' I said, with a sceptical smile.

'I'd not say it if I weren't.'

'You mean . . . a relationship?'

She wrinkled her nose slightly. 'We-ell . . . we're not really into relationships, are we? But we could try it for size, see how it went . . . we get along . . .'

I signalled Kev for fresh drinks. 'This needs serious consideration.'

We began to talk, but I knew that that was all it was, talk. She'd hit a low and she regarded me with genuine affection. I was useful. I could cook and cheer her up, and I wasn't too bad in bed, if not in the Lymo class. Why not import me to London, where I could go on with the good work as well as paying a share of the flat which, if I knew Fern, would rapidly escalate from fifty per cent to a hundred?

Yet it was tempting. I could do my sort of work anywhere, and breaking into the London competition might provide the kind of challenge that would ease the endless boredom that tormented my soul.

But how could it last long, with Fern? Once she was back in the old stamping ground among the Lombards, who'd be able to take her to the Ivy every night. And what if Lymo reignited? He might have dumped on her, but he'd have had time to reflect on what he was missing, and what he was missing about Fern must be resting very

215

gentle on his mind very often, if my own experience was anything to go by.

But it made for a lovely evening. Drinks in the George, then round the corner for a curry. It proved to be her classiest act yet – two young folk, brought together in sadness and misunderstanding, and now growing to care deeply for each other, deciding to walk away from the wreckage and make a bright new start in the big city together. I could almost see the panning shot of the Thames and hear Eric Coates at his most elegiac. We talked about it endlessly, as excited as children, right up to bedtime in the bronzy light of her room, and beyond.

When I got to my own house on Thursday evening there was a Post Office note with the mail, on which was printed in pencil: PARCEL IN OUT-HOUSE. It happened often. I got a number of packets, mainly textbooks, and I always left the out-house unlocked. It would be the hard-cover tax guide I'd recently sent for. The out-house, so-called, was in fact the small store-room set into the side of the house in the cavity beneath the bedroom steps, which had once held coal and now held gardening equipment. When I opened the door the parcel was laid on top of an upturned plastic bucket.

I still wake up sweating, my heart thumping like a donkey-engine, when I think what might have been.

My mind occupied with meal arrangements for when Fern arrived, I put the parcel on the hall table. I took a shower and changed. I reached for the gin and glanced at the television news, then brought the parcel into the living-room.

Many people have a recurrent bad dream. A past

girlfriend woke up shaking one night – in childhood a large red spider had scuttled over her bare foot; she still dreamt, at least once a month, of red spiders by the dozen, all over her body. In Bruce Fenlon's dream, he was always opening the front door to find himself staring into the barrel of a shotgun, levelled by some villain he'd once helped put inside who was now ready for vengeance. Mine was flying. Always, I was holding a large gin, the cabin was flooded with sunlight, people were talking and laughing – and the great plane was flying steadily into a mountain.

From the day of the parcel I never dreamed about planes again. Just parcels.

My hands moisten now at the memory. I'd almost begun to unfasten the knots. I'd have cut the string with my pocket-knife except that I'd left it upstairs when I'd changed.

STRING!

I laid it down as if it were antique china. *String*. How many parcels in this day and age were fastened with *string*? It was all jiffy-bags now, stapled at the flaps or swathed in heavy-duty adhesive tape. I couldn't even *remember* the last time I'd seen a parcel fastened with string.

I could feel sweat beading on my forehead, trickling down my back and down the side of my leg.

I touched the parcel gingerly with the tip of an index finger. It seemed very hard. A book with stiff covers felt hard, but this seemed more of a metallic hardness, unless it was my imagination now working at full stretch. I picked it up gently. It seemed no *heavier* than a thick tax guide. I put it carefully back on the table and sat down. Then I got up and put it back in the out-house, came back to the living-room and thought. And thought. I broke my concentration only once – to ring Fern.

'I'm sorry, Fern, I'll have to cancel tonight. Something's come up.'

'Oh, *John*, I was so looking forward to coming over.' The familiar petulance was there, that anything, anything at all, could be allowed to come before her.

'There was an urgent message on my answerphone. I'll have to deal . . .'

'Is there something wrong? You sound odd . . .'

'No . . . I'm just pissed off about breaking the date.'

'*John*, I'm seeing Mother tomorrow night. I shan't see you till *Sunday* . . .'

'I'll be at the flat at twelve on Sunday.'

'You'll have to take me somewhere really, really nice for lunch to make up. Somewhere pubby with delicious casseroles in little earthen pots . . .'

'I know just the place . . . beyond Gargrave . . .'

'And then we'll come back to my place and try and think of something else to pass the time . . .'

Her throaty laughter would have lingered in my mind for an hour on a normal day; tonight she was simply a minor distraction from a total preoccupation.

At midnight, I stopped thinking and began acting. I'd once had a motor cycle and upstairs I still had the gear – the stout leather jacket, the leggings, the gauntlets, the goggles, the crash helmet. Now and then I used them as a disguise.

I put the outfit in a plastic refuse-sack, then threw the sack into the car boot. I also transferred the parcel to the boot and packed four bags of lawn-sand round it. Finally, after a search, I located an old tree-pruner of my late father's. It was like a pair of secateurs but mounted

218

on a nine-foot pole. By pulling a trigger, a thin metal cable running the length of the pole activated the blades. It enabled you to prune garden trees without climbing ladders.

I oiled the action of the pruner, tested it and laid it diagonally from the passenger seat to the rear of the car. Part of it poked out through the back window but it was barely noticeable in the darkness.

I drove along minor roads until I came to the main Beckford–Keighley highway. I stayed on it for about six miles, then branched right up steep zigzag gradients to the high deserted moors. I pulled the car off the road into the denser darkness beneath a stand of chestnut trees and set off on to the moor on foot with the pruner and the refuse-sack, into which I'd now put the parcel.

I walked cautiously on uneven ground beneath a clear, starry sky for perhaps a quarter of a mile until I found what I was looking for, a smallish bowl-shaped piece of ground, rather like a crater. Here, I dressed myself in the leathers. Then I laid the parcel down in the hollow and gently eased one of the blades of the secateurs beneath the string that crossed the parcel widthways. The way I'd thought it out, nothing could happen when I cut the widthways string, but it had to be cut before I cut the lengthways string, otherwise it might possibly foul up the action of the object inside. And I didn't want that to happen. I had to be sure.

Fenlon had told me that he had once seen a parcel-bomb that worked on the mousetrap principle. A spring-loaded metal tongue, hinged to the centre of the base, flew upwards in an arc when released. It didn't need to travel far, a circuit was completed almost instantly, which triggered an explosion that at best only blew your hands off and blinded you, and at worst killed you.

The only safety-catch, once the bomb was wrapped up, was the string. The second the lengthways string was cut the bomb was a going concern.

This explained the anachronistic string itself. The device was too volatile for a jiffy-bag or a cardboard folder, the metal tag had to be securely held against the base until it was in the right hands, those it was intended to blow off.

I returned to the other end of the pruner, which protruded over the top of the hollow. I lay full length outside the hollow and at right angles to it, wincing from my recent bruises. Then, adjusting the goggles and the helmet, and with the gauntlets protecting my hands, I gently squeezed the pruner's trigger and felt the string give.

Silence – apart from the wind that whined softly through springy moorland grass. I went warily down into the hollow again.

Suddenly, there was a noise that sounded exactly like the rustle of brown paper. I felt my heart lurch. I flung myself to the ground and waited, first for an immediate explosion and then, during elongated seconds, for a delayed one because the mechanism had temporarily jammed.

Nothing. I got shakily to my feet, almost ready to abandon the thing and run. But I *had* to know. If the parcel contained a tax guide, then the car knocking me down had been joy-riders. If it contained a bomb, the driver had been a hired killer.

In the end, I decided that the rustling must have been the flight of some animal and went back to the parcel. The widthways string had been cleanly cut, the lengthways string remained intact. Very, very slowly I inserted a blade of the secateurs beneath the remaining strands and withdrew to the top of the hollow. Lying flat, head down, with only my gauntleted hands protruding over the top of the hollow, I squeezed the trigger slowly and firmly.

The force of the explosion wrenched the rod from my hands. It lit up the immediate area like a flash-gun, and as briefly. A few small pieces of hardware and soil pattered over my leathers. And that was it. The noise hadn't been too loud, just the sort of noise a large firework might make, but it had definitely been a killer, not merely a maimer.

I lay there for five minutes, drenched in sweat and trembling with shock, unable to get my mind off those near-fatal moments when, relaxed and euphoric with gin and the thought of Fern's naked body, I'd almost begun to undo those knots.

Legs still shaking, I went down into the hollow. The smell of the explosives mingled with that of burnt grass. The ground was littered with fragments of metal, brown paper and string.

Slowly I returned to the car. It was police work now – I'd had enough. It had to be Rainger. She'd have told him what I'd told her, and he'd have told her not to bother her pretty little head about a thing. Then sent for the heavies.

But *had* he? I put my tackle in the car and sat in the driving seat, waiting for my hands to stop trembling and my head to come together. What if she *hadn't* told him, hadn't really taken me seriously in the first place, being totally preoccupied with the far more heinous crime of Rainger having it off elsewhere? With a woman as neurotic as Mrs Rainger it was a possibility I had to take seriously.

But if I worked on the assumption that she hadn't told him, that ruled out both Rainger and Fielding, because I was certain neither of them had known at any stage they were under surveillance – had they had the remotest suspicion, they'd have phased out their particular method of operation within minutes.

But there had been a third man in the team – the Pakistani. Could there have been the slightest possibility I'd been clocked that morning in Drum Lane, before I'd followed him to Ilkley? I remembered only too well my unease when the chatty postman had chosen to sit on a wall about a yard from my car and smoke a dog-end. Had he set going some kind of bush telegraph? But if that was so, and the Pakistani had somehow got wind of me, why hadn't he alerted his immediate boss – Fielding? Perhaps he'd realised that if he did it would blow the postage scam out of the water and he'd become redundant. But if he took me out himself, a nice quickie with a stolen car or an exploding parcel, then everything might carry on as what passed for normal. It seemed a short-term view but perhaps at his level any other kind was an impossible luxury.

I also had to think again about the man with the ginger beard. Reluctantly, because I'd virtually eliminated him from the case, and because I didn't like to think that *anyone* could follow me without my being aware of it. And yet I had to accept that I'd had to concentrate so hard on the various marks I'd tailed that I'd not had much attention to spare for my own back. I ran my mind over those different pursuits – Rainger, Fielding, the Asian. I knew I'd have been aware of any car behind me that stayed the same, but what if the cars had been interchanged by people as professional as I was?

I sat, staring into space. It could have been five minutes, or half an hour. I was still too shocked to follow any coherent train of thought for very long. I began to drive home along silent roads. There could be yet another problem if I involved the police at this stage. Two attempts had been made on my life; both had failed. The moment these people realised they'd missed again their minds would be wonderfully concentrated. They'd tried to kill me with great skill and unnerving anonymity. The motor could have been joy-riders, the parcel-bomb the work of one of the cranks that most investigators pick up along the way.

Theoretically I *had* to tell the police my life was at risk. But if I made one step towards a police station they might assume I was going to tell them a lot more, about packets collected in Drum Lane, reparcelled and sent to London. One whiff of the Bill – and they'd have noses like gun-dogs – and it could be open season on John Goss. I could buy it anywhere at any time.

But if I didn't go to the cops they might eventually decide to leave me alone, might reckon that if I *did* know anything the car and the bomb had put the frighteners on, that I'd had such a shock that the only singing I'd do now would be in the bath. They were clearly pros and, unless they had a nutter on the books, wouldn't really want to try a full-frontal on a well-connected PI and stir up the kind of investigation they'd be only too anxious to avoid. Would they?

I didn't know. I wasn't making too much sense. I was tired and badly shaken. I'd been within a granny knot of death or appalling injury and I couldn't hack it any longer. I needed sleep, or at least the pretence of it, and a clear mind to think it through logically.

I put the car in the garage instead of leaving it in the drive, and I tested the door and window locks. I also reset the intruder alarm, something I only normally did when leaving the house unoccupied. I had a large Scotch and soda and I went to bed. Oddly enough, I slept quite well, it must have been something to do with total exhaustion.

I was dragged out of sleep at seven by a loud knocking on the front door. There *was* a bell, a gentle two-tone affair that would have aroused me without the threat of cardiac arrest, but some people, invariably men, were knockers by nature.

My heart was having quite a work-out just lately; when I opened the door it was to look into the pale-blue eyes of the man with the ginger beard.

Sixteen

'I'm police,' he said. 'Plain-clothes. It'll be better if we talk inside.'

'And I'm Danny La Rue,' I said, 'so I think we'll stay right here on Mother Kelly's doorstep.'

'Look, chum,' he said, in what sounded like an East London accent, 'if I say we talk inside we talk inside.'

He moved towards me.

'Take one more step, chum,' I said, 'if you want a crutchful of running-shoe.'

'You're doing yourself a lot of no good . . .'

But he came no further. He looked tough but then so did I – if he gave it I could give it back. He'd fight, I thought, to the death in a tight corner, but he wasn't going to waste energy for the sake of a point he couldn't be certain of making. Which meant he was definitely not a piss-artist.

'If you're Bill,' I said, 'I want proof.'

'If you don't want serious trouble you'll take my word for it.'

'I wouldn't take your word for the way to the gate.'

He had gingery hair everywhere – it licked off his head like frozen flame. It covered his chin and cheeks, it met dense eyebrows, it grew up to his eyes like reeds at the

225

edge of water. His eyes watched me steadily – pale, unemotional, unblinking – like eyes sewn on to a woolly toy. Finally he said: 'You've been keeping tabs on a guy called Rainger . . .'

'So . . .'

'Me too. That's how I came to know what you're up to.'

He waited. I waited. Smudge, the next-door cat, sat on a wall and waited.

'We've been watching Rainger for a long time,' he said, 'and we want to know if you've found out anything we've missed.'

'Not a thing.'

'My colleagues will be very upset if you don't give me all the help you can,' he said softly. 'Very upset indeed . . .'

'Which colleagues are these – the Black Hand Gang?'

'My colleagues in the Force. They don't like private dicks to begin with, but private dicks who withhold valuable information can get them very twitchy. They can put the word out up and down that John Goss is a bit four-pound note, and then the lawyers start dropping you, and before long the only work you've got is tracing lost dogs.'

'I hear what you're saying . . .'

'Then you're using your head . . .'

'And I think it's crap . . .'

He watched me. While we waited, the cat jumped down and sat on the step near my feet. It was the friendliest cat I'd ever known, but in passing the bearded man it had almost flattened itself against the wall. I had a faint memory of reading a Huxley essay called *Sermon in Cats*.

'If it's all the same to you I'd like to get back inside and get ready for work,' I said, 'now that I'm up.'

'Close that door on me and your name's a dead letter in this town.'

'Look,' I said patiently, 'anybody who is anybody in the Beckford Bill knows John Goss. What's more, they like John Goss. We help each other out. It's a symbiotic relationship – you want to look the word up if you can find out how to spell it. Believe me, if I *had* seen anything dodgy when I was tailing Rainger I'd have passed it on the same day.'

'You might have seen something that wouldn't mean anything to you but might mean something to us,' he said, 'so I'd like you to run through your activities when you had him under surveillance.'

'I will, if you come back here with one of the coppers I know and trust.'

A peculiar grimace distorted his thin lips, as if he were about to lash out at me – I stepped back instinctively, my body tensing. But then he spoke, and I realised he was trying to smile, using facial muscles that appeared to have had little exercise in the past twelve months, if ever.

'Look, John,' he said, the friendly tone seeming to contain more menace than the normal one, 'this is the pitch. I've been drafted in from the Met, and I'm playing it as close to the chest as I can. Two reasons. The local lads get temperamental about guys from NSY operating on their patch, and there's just a possibility one of the home-grown Bill has got hisself in up to the neck in what I'm investigating. I've got nothing on me to identify myself because I'm supposed to be a bloke involved in fertiliser sales to farmers. We thought that looked right because if there's one thing you're not short of in Yorkshire it's farmers.'

I didn't think I bought it. We went into another of our watching and waiting sessions, the cat's head resting companionably against my foot. Finally I said: 'My only involvement with Rainger was to see if he was having it off on the side. His wife was certain of it. I followed him around for more than a week but I could find no evidence of it.'

I hesitated, then picking my words carefully, added: 'He did one or two odd things, agreed. He went to London in disguise one day, sat in a pub on the Strand, came home again. He spent a lot of time sitting around in car-parks and station buffets. He once drove to Hawtrey and then back to Beckford – I couldn't get that together. And that was it. If he *was* up to something bent it passed me by. If I'd found out what it was I'd have told the police, but I haven't got the time to get involved myself. My brief was to find out if he was getting the knickers off the parish spinsters – that was the job she was paying me for and that was the job I did.'

The sewn-on eyes rested on mine for a good ten seconds. The grimace that stood in for a smile must have made his face ache too much and he'd abandoned it. Nothing in that hair-covered mug gave me any clue which way he was thinking – another mark of the pro.

'And that's it?'

'That', I said firmly, 'is it. His wife's still convinced he's free-lancing somewhere but I could find nothing so she paid me off. I've not seen the guy since.'

His eyes still unblinkingly on mine, he finally nodded. 'All right,' he said. 'What you've told me might help. If it doesn't I'll be back to go over it again in detail.'

He turned and went slowly along the path. Half-way down he turned round. He wore shapeless brown pants, a hairy dark-green jacket with leather buttons hanging off it that looked like small footballs. 'If you're bullshitting me you're in trouble. Don't ever underestimate what we can do to people who piss us around. And . . . their friends . . .'

He climbed into a battered-looking Range Rover. It ground throatily into life. His shallow blue eyes gave me a final lengthy glance as he moved off.

I dressed rapidly and had a single cup of strong black instant. I drove to Elm Lane, knowing that if Rainger had taken the early train to London I had now missed him. But he hadn't; he drove to the office at the usual time, as he'd done each day this week. It was a heavy, humid day, the sort of English day I most disliked, when low white cloud made the eyes ache slightly and the lightest clothes hung moistly to the body. It seemed to deepen my sense of foreboding.

There was plenty to do, but it was all routine. On normal days I would work through paper with Norma for an hour, then begin the series of personal calls she'd set up for me, with solicitors, with people desperately seeking other people, with the employers of certain high-rolling employees. It was auto-pilot stuff, and again and again my mind went back to the bearded man, who knew my name but hadn't offered his.

My gut reaction was that he couldn't be police, but I had to concede that the sort of policemen who needed to mix regularly with hardened criminals often became coarsened themselves. A London drugbuster would have to be very tough. He had certainly sounded like a

229

Londoner. His cover too had an authentic ring – there *were* a lot of farms in the Ridings, and the fact that he had found smiling almost beyond him made his fertiliser salesman seem like inspired casting. There could be few Yorkshire farmers who'd not be intensely suspicious of a man who approached them smiling, let alone bearing gifts in the shape of free herbicide samples.

I didn't know. All I knew for certain was that I'd almost been killed, twice, and whether the bearded man was bad lot or Bill, in the end I'd wanted him to be quite sure I'd seen nothing, heard nothing and said nothing. That way I might get to go on breathing – a habit, I'd recently realised, I was seriously into.

There were other possibilities – too many. He might genuinely be police or he might be one of Rainger's paymasters, suspicious that Rainger was playing both ends against the middle.

In any case, it was time to hand over to Fenlon. The week's grace I'd allowed Mrs Rainger and me was almost up, and though Rainger hadn't gone to London again I didn't think I wanted to keep an eye on him until he did. I'd told the bearded man I was off the case now, and whether he was straight or bent I was pretty sure I'd not like what he'd do if he found out I'd been lying.

I'd had the most absorbing time of my career, but nothing was worth losing my life for. It was policework now. It had been that from about day three but I'd not accepted it.

These unsatisfactory and inconclusive thoughts passed through my mind all that heavy and enervating day. Overlaying them was an uneasiness I couldn't pin down, a sort of fear that evaded analysis, like the kind you wake up with from a bad dream that has left nothing behind it but the fear itself. I stumped along city streets in a mizzle of fine rain, striving to give the miasma shape and focus.

It always came back to the bearded man. It wasn't so much the words – or so I thought then – as the stress he'd given to certain phrases. It seemed almost as if there'd been some specific message encoded in the things he'd said. Or maybe the bomb and the flying car had made even the most normal dialogue seem portentous.

It was Friday and that didn't help. The days of the week usually meant little more than markers. I would often work Saturdays and Sundays as if they were no different from the rest. But I was seeing the weekends now in terms of Fern – Fern standing against sky and cloud, or sitting in a bar room with her arm through mine, or reading my childhood books with no knickers on. And this weekend she was going away, up to Newcastle to see her mother, whose illness was one of the few sound threads in that original web of deceit. I wondered if she'd arranged it at a time when it was possible to see little or nothing of her father.

In any case I'd be alone when I particularly needed the sort of distraction she was so skilled at providing.

'There were four,' Kev told us, 'if you count the Empire and the Spinners' Hall. The Viscount was a proper rep – acting one, rehearsing one and learning the lines for the week after next. Then there was the Little Theatre, amateur, but that's where all the new talent came from. The Empire was mainly variety, but they did a lot of plays in the spring and summer. And then the heavy brigade at the Spinners' – Shakespeare, *The Importance of Being Edgar*, that class of carry-on . . .'

A woman called Dee Dee said: 'I believe it was *The*

Importance of Being Earnest, Kev, and Oscar Wilde
wrote it.'

'Didn't he do time for being bottled beer?'

'They had acting groups at some of the bigger mills,
you know,' Tom said. 'It wasn't *all* brass bands and
ferrets. I saw a lot of plays in works canteens. Some of
the acting was quite incredibly good.'

'Bertram Feather began at Dyson's, you know. Him
who plays Sydney in *Paradise Court*. Dyson's, the Little,
then the Viscount, there were so many places for them to
learn the business in those days. They didn't earn much
but you couldn't put a price on the experience. And we
got to see live actors.'

'They say there are twice as many actors now as there
were in the Sixties and half as many parts . . .'

I sipped my gin. And Fern was part of the fall-out. I
felt she'd have loved the repertory days – she need never
have been herself from one year to the next. Perhaps if
she'd had that kind of experience she'd have been
spotted by now, that was how it had worked.

The talk went on, of bygone Beckford, a city which,
when compared with the Beckford I knew, of drugs and
discos and unemployment and endless theft, seemed to
have all the innocent folksy charm of the old MGM
musicals my mother loved to watch on television, where
everyone lived in white houses with balconies, and had
pretty daughters, where people sang to each other in
tram-cars, where youngsters staged incredibly talented
shows in old barns, and where the sun invariably shone,
except for the isolated occasion when a small dark man
in sodden clothing had danced dementedly along a
flooded street in what seemed to be a tropical monsoon.

I sighed. I was indulging myself, listening to it all with

total absorption, to give my mind a break from the endless, fruitless speculation.

I was certain something was wrong. It was nothing but intuition, but intuition was my stock-in-trade. And it was buried somewhere in something the bearded man had said. I reran his words for the hundredth time.

I discounted any personal threat that might have been contained in them. They'd had two goes at my life, assuming he wasn't police, and I was fully geared up to guarding against any third attempt.

Was it the Raingers? Had I somehow increased the danger they already seemed to be in? I couldn't believe that any threat to them would make me so uneasy. If Rainger was in trouble, he'd gone out and bought it, but I couldn't see them harming his wife – they were pros, they'd only nail the man himself.

Fenlon said: 'I wasn't sure if I'd find you in here. You've been a bit elusive.'

'There's a girl I've been knocking about with . . .'

'Kev told me. A cracker, according to him. And really friendly with it. Not a bit of edge . . .'

Fern practising being warm and ordinary with the little people for when she was signing autographs after the Aspel show. Fenlon gave me a wry smile, suddenly envious of a kind of freedom he'd not have known how to cope with if he could have had it.

I glanced warily round the bar-parlour. I went nowhere now without checking my back. It could be very bad for my health to be seen talking to Fenlon, if the bearded man and his people weren't police – and I was becoming increasingly certain they weren't.

'Anything new on the heroin front?'

He shook his head. He seemed indifferent, but it

could have been fatigue. He'd never had my kind of nervous energy.

'We cracked down on Dresden. Some of the toms are users, and if they don't push themselves they know a man who does. So we took a lot of snaps and felt a lot of collars of men who mix with them but not for leg-over. So it's all gone very quiet for the moment, but all we've really done is move it to some other city.'

'No leads on the letters?'

'None. They're still working on a co-ordinated approach, tying in with the Post Office, tracking a piece of mail from its source, but even that will only get the tiddlers. The big people sit well back. We need a reliable informant to get us up the line and it won't be easy.'

We sat for a minute or two in silence, Bruce as hooked as I had been by Kev's reminiscences of Beckford in its MGM days, when you could leave your doors unlocked and pretty girls in gingham cheerfully sang as they loaded bobbins on the spinning-frames. When the only punch-ups you ever heard of were at the Dublin Boy and even those proved to have had an endearing, almost ritualistic quality, and no one ever, Kev asserted, never *ever*, threw a bar-stool, let alone a pint pot or a pick-axe handle, whenever Patrick O'Shaughnessy stood on his bucket to sing 'Rose of Tralee', God rest his soul.

Bruce was bored. He wanted his holidays, to take his wife and child to some cottage where he could sit in the sun and read a Dick Francis.

When I and Bruce had been kids of ten or eleven, we'd play at being detectives. One day we picked a man at random on a city street and resolved to find out everything we could about him.

We'd followed him to an office, waited till he came out

again at five and then to where he parked a Cortina on a
strip of waste ground. The following day we were at the
waste ground at five with our bicycles, and we trailed
him in rush-hour traffic to the third set of lights in York
Road. We lost him then on the stretch of dual carriageway that led to the ring road. The following afternoons,
by waiting at different points along the dual carriageway,
we eventually saw his car turn off into Mulberry Lane.
The next day I went to Mulberry Lane alone because
Bruce had grown bored with it all and gone swimming
with Curly Tyzack.

Within two weeks I knew where Keith Moorhouse
lived, what his job was, the names of his wife, his
children and his dog. I found out about the mistress too,
though it was several more years before I understood she
was a mistress; then, she was simply a woman he drove
from the office some lunch-times to a quiet corner of the
city, where they would eat a sandwich and smile at each
other. He also visited her two evenings a week when he
was supposed to be playing chess with a friend. It was
only when I'd grown to manhood that the full eerie
sadness struck me of a kid of eleven knowing so much
more about Keith Moorhouse than the woman who'd
lived with him for fifteen years.

I suppose the differences had been emerging between
me and Bruce even then, despite being best friends. He
couldn't understand my dogged pursuit of Keith Moorhouse when it was summer and there were so many other
things to do. But I'd said I'd do it and I had to finish it,
that first attempt at surveillance, and in any case it had
taken such a grip on me that in the end I couldn't let it go
until I knew everything there was to be known. I
couldn't fathom the compulsion any better than Bruce

could. Perhaps it was the example of my father, getting home late and grey-faced but quietly triumphant, having got it together on some villain who didn't inhabit Kev's sun-drenched corner of Memory Lane. Bruce had thought me very odd.

But my kind of oddness was exactly what they needed in these complex times, and what they'd got was Bruce, a good lad who worked steadily and did what he was told without making any obvious waves, and who wore himself out in the daily juggling act of sharing himself between a demanding job and an equally demanding home.

'You don't suppose there's anyone working under cover on this thing?' I said finally. 'Anyone from the Met or the NDIU or the RCS.'

He glanced at me. 'In this area?'

'I mean, would you *know* if someone were moving around up here, following, say, leads that had brought him from London?'

'*Someone* would have to know or we'd be getting crossed lines. We might think the undercover guy was one of them and vice versa. It would have to be co-ordinated and it would depend on the Chief how far down the line it went. The uniforms would be out of it, of course, but you could safely assume the jacks would know, to my level at least.'

'What if', I said slowly, 'you had a bent copper on earners from the drugs people and this guy was sent to suss him out?'

He shrugged. 'It's a possibility, I suppose, but believe me, if we had a bent copper on the patch we'd *know*, the lads, that is, and unless we were all on the take we'd have the bugger nailed for our own sakes. We all know what everyone earns, and anyone not living more or less the same way the rest of us do would stand out like a nun in a pub.'

He finished his beer, ordered another round. 'What brought all this on?'

I sipped my second gin. I was torn. Despite the many warnings I'd given myself I still hankered to follow Rainger to London once more, and do the business on the Coal Hole Asian I'd done on Rainger, even if it meant staying in London at my own expense; even though the bearded man was almost certainly not police, and to continue alone would be a bit like playing the advanced version of Russian Roulette – five live and one blank.

'The thing is,' I dragged the words out at last, 'I've been following a guy around recently, the well-heeled one I was telling you about whose wife thought he was lobbing it out. Well . . . he did certain things and went to certain places that had nothing to do with ferret but had a lot to do with being bent.' I smiled ruefully. 'I thought of my old friend Fenlon right away.'

'That's what friends are for,' he said. 'Tell me more . . .'

Friends!

'I've got to go, Bruce. I'll give you a bell at home,' I said, turning distractedly from the bar.

'For Christ's sake, John, you've not finished your drink.'

By then I was half-way across the bar-parlour. He came after me and in the entrance hall caught my arm.

'*John* . . .!'

'Sorry, Bruce,' I pawed his hand away. 'It's . . . it's a document for a solicitor – I was supposed to hand it to

him personally this afternoon. I'll have to go to his
house . . . he must have it . . .'

He watched me sceptically. He knew I didn't forget
things, knew my obsession with detail. 'It's something to
do with what you were going to tell me, isn't it?' he said
quietly.

'No . . . no, absolutely not . . . I'll ring you . . .'

'This guy you were tailing,' he said doggedly, 'why
didn't you tell me what he was up to last time we met?
You'd been following him a week.'

He may not have had my edge, but it didn't mean he
wasn't sharp.

'I've *got* to go. I'll *ring* you . . .'

'You're a dozy bastard, John, this isn't your first
attempt at do-it-yourself . . .'

But I was already through the outer door and running
along Spinnergate to the back street where I'd parked.

It all seemed as obvious now as the town-hall clock.

I thrust the key in the ignition, drove off as rapidly as I
dared. A bead of sweat trickled down my back and my
mouth had a metallic taste. Every light on Beckford
Road seemed to change to red as I approached.

I couldn't believe I'd been so obtuse. '*And . . . their
friends . . .*' had been his final words, and those had
been the ones I'd given the least significance to. Friends
– I had no friends except policemen and they could look
after themselves. I was otherwise a loner.

I had a trained memory and I'd gone over every word
he'd said again and again, except those three final words
that had seemed almost a throwaway – a sort of bet-
hedger, implying that if I *was* involved with anyone else
on the Rainger case we could both expect aggravation.

But I wasn't working with anyone else, and my mind

had switched off there and gone back over the rest in an endless loop. It had never once struck me that the phrase could include Fern. She was a civilian, she'd had no part in the Rainger business. She *was* a friend, very much a friend now, but surely not in the sense the bearded man had meant. Surely to God not.

It was the last set of lights – the ones near the main gates at Clifford Park. Yellow was a fraction of a second off red as I approached, and I almost kept my foot on the throttle and took the chance, but fear kept me cautious – all I needed now was a collision.

Fern, like Rainger, worked at Brit-Chem. Perhaps that, and the fact that she was going about with me, seemed too much of a coincidence to the beard. Perhaps, in his thorough way, he'd decided that if I knew too much she also knew too much. I didn't know. I just knew I had to get to her.

The car was rolling again. I realised, within a few hundred yards of the flat, that I should have used the car-phone. Had there been no reply, I needn't have gone there. I could have taken off straight after her, foot on the boards, up the A1, hoping somehow I could catch her up.

And if I did catch her up, what then? I didn't know that either; right now I was acting as instinctively as an animal and would know what to do when the time came. If it came. I just wished to God my instincts had made me pick up the phone first.

I swung on to the drive where she had her flat. Even here there were frustrations. One of the yuppies was having a party and cars lined the short street bumper to bumper. I had to leave mine off the drive altogether, on the road that ran up to the main highway.

239

It took only seconds but I needed every second I could lay my hands on. I ran along the quiet tree-lined pavements in the gathering darkness and through the entrance. The car-park that had once been a front garden was crammed with expensive cars. There was one cheap one – her white Fiesta.

Relief was like physical pain, like warmth returning to fingers deadened by frost. I sagged against a wall, dragging air into my lungs. Legs shaking, I went to the front door and rang her bell. The speaker clicked instantly and she said: 'Hello!' in a tone of irritation.

'It's me . . . John . . .'

'Oh . . .' The irritation changed to surprise; she tripped the lock.

She was waiting with the door open, looking flushed. Her bag stood just inside it and she was dressed in jeans and a thin sweater.

'John . . .?'

'I don't know why you haven't set off,' I gasped, 'but thank God . . .'

'That *prat* in Flat Three,' she burst out. 'Did you *see* how he was parked? I'm *blocked* in. He's gone to a meeting somewhere in someone else's car. I played bloody hell to his wife, but she doesn't know where to contact him, and she's no spare set. *Ugh*! He won't be back till nine and I wanted to be away at six. Christ knows what time I'll end up in *Newcastle* . . .!'

She spoke with such pent-up anger I couldn't get a word in. Suddenly she stopped and looked at me in a less preoccupied way. 'But . . . why are you here . . .? Not that it isn't lovely to see you . . .'

'Something's wrong, Fern.'

'Wrong?'

'Can you put off going to Newcastle?'

She stared at me uneasily. 'Not go . . .'

'Look, does anyone else know you're going?'

We watched each other. A faint pallor had taken the place of the flush of exasperation.

She shrugged. 'The office people. The garage – John what do you *mean*, something's wrong?'

'The garage. What happened at the garage?'

'It . . . went in for service yesterday and they found something amiss with the cylinder-head something or other . . . all right round town but no good for a journey. I told them to do it. Look . . . John . . .'

'They kept it overnight?'

'They had to take the engine out. I picked it up this afternoon . . .'

'Main dealer?'

'No, someone called Ken Underwood. John, for Christ's *sake*!'

'Smallish place on Beech Hill. Fenced compound, second-hand cars . . .?'

'Yes . . .'

'And standing on its own,' I said, almost to myself. 'Locks on the gates you could breathe on and they'd fall off . . .'

'John, John, *John*,' she almost cried, '*please*!'

'In a minute, Fern,' I said, putting my hands on her arms. 'Look, does *anyone* apart from the office and the garage know you were setting off this weekend? Anyone at all.'

'No . . . no . . . absolutely not . . .' She broke off abruptly and focused slowly on my eyes, looked away. 'There *was* something, yesterday lunch-time. I was out to lunch and a man rang, saying he was from Head

Office and doing a survey on phone traffic to see if it would pay the company to use Mercury. Karen told him I was out, and he said he'd be out for the rest of the week, but he'd ring me at home either Thursday or Friday evening. And . . . and Karen told him it would have to be Thursday because I was setting off for the weekend after work Friday. But . . . he didn't ring last night.'

'She didn't give him your number?'

'He didn't ask for it . . .'

'He wouldn't need to . . .'

Her lower lip trembled. 'John, this is getting really, really scary. What's all this about my car? Is it one of those funny men . . . it once happened in London. Breathing down the phone . . . *John, please tell me what's wrong*!'

'I just don't know. But something *is* wrong and I'm trying to work through the possibilities.'

It wasn't necessary to work through any more. The explosion was like a gas-main going off.

Seventeen

It briefly lit up the gloom, like a powerful rocket bursting, making the windows of Fern's attic room rattle and blowing in the ones further down, before settling to a roaring blaze.

It was what was left of Fern's Fiesta.

She stood completely still, open-mouthed, white-faced as someone with a disease of the blood. I left her standing while I turned off the lights. I opened the door one inch. There was no one about at this stage; shock resting over the big house gave it an air of Sunday afternoon tranquillity. Within seconds people would begin rushing downstairs and out to the car-park. At that point we would have to go.

I had rarely felt more alert, more in control. It was as if the explosion had provided total release from the preoccupations of that long, sultry day. Something dreadful had happened, but it *had* happened, and it left me with reflexes that seemed to work at the speed of electronics.

'Fern,' I took her by the arm, 'is there a back way out?'

She gazed at me absently and I had to force myself to be very patient, because I could remember how I'd felt when death had been waiting for me on an upturned bucket in the out-house.

'Fern,' I said, slowly and distinctly, 'this is very important. Is there a back way?'

She went on gazing for a second or two more, then shook her head as if trying to focus her brain. The rushing of feet had already begun lower down in the house, and I could hear faint horrified exclamations. There was also a gathering hubbub from the street as people came running from other houses.

'. . . Fire escape,' she whispered. 'There's . . . a door . . . every back landing . . .'

'We've got to go down it . . . now . . .'

'John . . . oh, my *God* . . .'

I put my arm round her. 'Trust me,' I said, '*please* . . .'

I made her put on her parka and we crept to the deserted landing of the floor below. I'd picked up her travel-bag; she might need it. I had additional clothes of my own permanently available in the Sierra's boot.

We went down the fire-steps and along the back garden, keeping close to the wall, and out through a small gate on to a narrow cobbled track that led along the rear of the houses to the road that went up to the main highway. She ran mechanically, her hand in mine, the whites of her eyes prominent in the gathering dusk, still half in shock. After a long, dark day the darkness of night was closing in early and helped conceal our progress from back windows, not that we needed much concealment when probably every occupant of every flat was watching the blazing car. I was very glad now I'd been unable to park in the drive at the front of the flats. Any attempt to drive rapidly away from a bombed car in front of horrified onlookers could only be open to one interpretation.

I pushed her into the car, clipped her seat-belt, and drove away on half-lights. As we came to the main road we heard, coincidentally, the distant shriek of a police siren.

'Why don't we go to *them*?' she suddenly cried. 'The *police*. You've got a phone here. I could have been killed . . . I could have been *killed* . . .!'

'We will go to them,' I said grimly, 'but I have a call to make first. Because if I don't make it they'll never give up. We've got time to spare because they'll assume your car went up on the A1. It was meant to seem like the sort of accident where a tyre blows and a fuel line gets severed and the car's demolished. The experts would sort it out but it would take time. So they'll think they can relax now – you gone, me scared shitless. But it didn't work, and it puts us marginally ahead. But going to the police now would be too dangerous unless he goes too, they could only give us limited protection . . .'

'I don't know what you're talking about,' she said, her voice uneven because of the trembling of her lips. 'I don't know what you're *talking* about. Who are *they*? Why did they blow up my *car*? Who are you going to *see*?'

I'd been trying to clarify my own confusion by thinking aloud; I realised what gibberish it must seem to her.

'Fern,' I said, slowly and gently, 'I'm going to see Miles Rainger. He's a criminal, heavily involved in the drugs trade. The people he works with are the ones who blew up your car.'

We were on The Hill now and I cornered on to Daisy Edge Drive. 'That can't be true,' she almost whispered.

'Are you *crazy*? *Miles Rainger*? You must be out of your *tree*!'

I was even more preoccupied now, trying to decide where to park. Not too near the Rainger place, not too far away. Should I park in the grounds of the place that was up for sale?

'Give me a minute, Fern, I'll try to explain . . .'

The great silent houses rose up behind the dense trees and the high walls, with occasional squares of yellow light cut out in the dark fabric of their façades. The wealthy would now be settling down to their food and wine in the candle-light, chatting about the golf and the fishing, and the MGM Beckford of 'Change and wool sales and restaurants where palm court trios had once played 'Bells Across the Meadow'.

The Beckford that lay two or three miles away, where people pushed drugs and pimped harlots and arranged to kill people, would seem as remote to them as the things they saw on *News at Ten* about Bosnia and Mogadishu.

Yet it had all started on this drive. My youth seemed scarcely more distant than the night I'd sipped Chivas Regal with Fern, in the green dress, on my arm. So much had happened, the hours elongated by excitement and tension and fear, and I'd allowed myself to be swept along in the thrill of the chase. I realised now how massive the self-indulgence had been and how appalling the price. Not just my own life at risk, but hers, a woman who was innocent, a civilian, totally uninvolved.

I made my decision on parking, did a U-turn, and halted about a hundred yards from Rainger's house, so that the car faced in the right direction for a speedy getaway; The Drive being in fact a cul-de-sac, blocked off at the far end by woodland.

I took her hand, so overwhelmed by guilt that I couldn't speak for a moment. Fenlon had been right, I should have told him ten days ago. He'd been right about the do-it-yourself too, it hadn't been my first attempt, only this time it had almost led to two deaths, had reduced Fern to a state of terror and shock she was still struggling to come to terms with.

'It *is* Rainger, Fern,' I said. 'Take these houses for a start, and the cost of upkeep. How can a man live like he does on what he makes at Brit-Chem?'

She shook her head, again and again. 'He doesn't *need* to. His wife has money. She pays for at least half of it, everyone knows that . . .'

'Except me. *I* know that his wife's family lost their shirt on a business deal that went wrong in the Sixties. I've checked it out three different ways. The only thing she inherited was expensive tastes.'

'How do you know all this?' she said, her lips still trembling.

'Because Mrs Rainger hired me to watch him – she thought he was having an affair. Yes? Well, he wasn't having an affair, he was running drugs . . .'

'I can't *believe* it . . .'

'I swear it's the truth . . .'

She was silent, shivering all over, like a child who'd bathed in the sea on a cold day. Then she suddenly cried: 'But what's it got to do with *me*? Why blow up *my* car? John . . .'

'I'll tell you everything,' I said, 'but not now. There's too much to do. All I can say now is how sorry I am.'

Her face was a pale disc in the darkness, the whites of her eyes still showing. Suddenly she put her arms round my neck. 'Take care of me, John, *please* take care of me.

247

I'm so *frightened*. If you hadn't come when you did, if you hadn't *come*. I was just going to put my bag in the car, I was even thinking of cleaning it to pass the time till he got back . . .'

I think I saw the real Fern at last, the one she carefully concealed behind the daily remakes. Fear had robbed her of her usual mastery and technique, she reacted to it as messily as everyone else did in real life, as I'd done myself the night before. She trembled uncontrollably, her palms were damp, her hair tousled, she seemed to have shrunk into herself like a small, threatened animal. It was as if I could see across the years the vulnerable child who'd been forced in the end to take refuge in any other persona than her own.

I slowly released myself. 'I've got to go to the Raingers' place . . .'

'You can't *leave* me, John. Let *me* come . . .'

'It's best if I go alone. I don't know how he's going to take this. I can't involve you any deeper . . .' I fitted a small key in a mechanism beneath the dashboard. 'Look, I'll leave the keys in the ignition, and this other key will activate the alarm if you turn it to the right. I'm certain you're safe here, but keep the doors locked, and if you see anything suspicious either sound the alarm or drive to the central Police Station and ask to be put in touch with Bruce Fenlon. Have you got that? Bruce Fenlon . . .'

Finally, and unhappily, she nodded.

'I don't know how long I'll be. I have to talk him into coming with me to the police before anyone tries anything else.' I clenched my fists. I was going to get Rainger and the police together in the same room tonight if it meant a do-it-yourself operation on changing his face.

248

I circled Rainger's house three times to satisfy myself no one was watching it, then crept past the immaculate lawn. The house seemed ominously dark. The only light came from the faint glow of a hall lamp. I pressed the bell, heard the discreet chimes in the distance. Nothing happened for a good ten seconds; cursing, I was about to give it one more try. Then I saw a faint movement behind one of the stained-glass panels that lay to each side of the door.

A voice spoke carefully from behind it: 'Who is it?'

The housekeeper.

'John Goss. I did some work recently for Mrs Rainger.'

The door opened a few inches on a chain. An outside lamp flared. We looked at each other. She wore outdoor clothing, a white raincoat, a grey beret drawn to one side.

'I'm sorry, Mr Goss, but I'm alone in the house. I had to be sure to whom I was speaking.'

'Please don't apologise. I respect your caution.'

'Did you . . . *want* Mrs Rainger?'

'No. Mr Rainger. It's very important.'

'They've gone to the coast, I'm afraid. They went early, about six. They have a house near Esk Head. They'll not be back until Monday morning. I'm just on my way home.'

'I'll have to go out there then. Can you give me their address?'

'Could you not phone? They should be there now.'

'I'm afraid not. It's absolutely essential that I see him. Believe me, the last thing I want to do is go to the coast at this time of night.'

She watched me, the professional servant, trying to

decide whether she could release the information. She suddenly decided in my favour. One of the reasons I got so much business was an ability to look at people steadily without blinking, something I'd trained myself to do after hearing Michael Caine say what it had done for him. I wrote the address in my pocket-book.

'Thank you. Does anyone else know they've gone away . . . apart from their friends along The Drive?'

'I think the only people who know, Mr Goss, are you and me. It was a spur-of-the-moment decision. Mrs Rainger's been under rather a strain recently.'

I could believe it.

'If anyone *does* contact you, anyone at all, would you please *not* tell them where the Raingers have gone. Say they're touring and you have no address.'

A faint look of alarm crossed her thin features. 'I . . . shan't be here anyway, as I said. Any messages will be recorded on the answerphone. But this all seems very odd . . .'

'There's been a crisis. I'm afraid that's all I can tell you. I must go now. Thanks for your help.'

'I do hope whatever you have to tell them won't spoil Mrs Rainger's weekend,' she said, with controlled agitation. 'She does so need a change, she's not been herself for some time. She suffers rather badly with her nerves.'

'What happened?'

I started the car. 'They're not there. They've gone to the weekend place.'

'Esk Head?'

I glanced at her as I released the handbrake. 'You know about it?'

250

'I've . . . heard it mentioned in the office. Where are you going now?'

'The weekend place. I've got to.'

I heard her indrawn breath over the sound of the idling engine. I put my hand on hers.

'I've got to see him. And right now *anywhere* will be safer than Beckford. If we stayed here till he got back too much could happen.'

'I'm so *scared* . . .'

I let in the clutch and began to drive the seventy-plus miles to the north Yorkshire coast. We went via Ripon and Thirsk and Sutton Bank, along deserted unlit roads running past prime farmland, full beams scything through the darkness and giving trees and hedges and white-washed cottages the harsh transitory brilliance of night scenes in old black-and-white feature films. I was doing a Rainger, driving through country where it was impossible to be tailed without being aware of it, especially at this time of night.

On the way, I told her everything that had happened, from that bright, sunny morning when I'd first driven up The Hill to see Mrs Rainger, to this moment when we sped through the night. At first I heard the sound several times of her suddenly indrawn breath, then she listened in total silence until I'd finished.

'But why me?' she said at last, her voice almost calm. 'Why *my* car? I've nothing to do with any of it.'

'I don't know. I can't really get it together. All I can come up with is that you work at Brit-Chem too, and you know me. Perhaps they thought you had some kind of an inside track on Rainger and told me about it, a professional investigator, and they decided we might both know too much.'

'But who are *they*?'

'Again, I don't know. Possibly just heavies trying to keep the heat off a valuable asset. Possibly men from a rival operation. Drugs are big money, big risks and big danger.'

We drove on then in silence. When we were a few miles from Pickering, I pulled off on to a wide grassy verge and parked.

'I need a drink. I've got some brandy . . .'

She got out of the car and walked slowly to a dry-stone wall that bordered farmland. A field of stubble stretched away, in which stood large cylindrical bales of wheat in a regular formation, awaiting collection. Better weather must have been pushing in from the east because we had exchanged the cloud and humidity of the West Riding now for air that was clear and dry. There was a waxing moon, and stars that seemed to flicker with an almost sub-tropical vibrancy. I followed her to the wall.

'You are a shit,' she said.

I could see her features clearly in the pale light, her head held slightly back, her eyes narrowed, her lips set in a thin line.

'I've known some shits in my time, but you lead . . . Christ, you're out there up front . . .'

'Fern . . .?'

'You *knew*,' she said harshly. 'You knew what the swine was up to a week ago. *A week ago*. That's when you should have told your tame bloody policeman, not wait for them to start blowing my car to pieces.'

I stood for a while in silence, as insects creaked softly in the grass. I put my hand on her shoulder. 'I know that,' I said in a low voice. 'I had the same bollocking from Fenlon. You can't begin to understand how badly I feel about the danger I put you in.'

'You don't give a monkey's!' She knocked my hand away. 'You're *enjoying* all this. You don't think I *believed* all that crap about giving her a week to sort herself out. You were giving *yourself* a week and you bloody know it.'

I'd tried, very hard, to keep emotion out of my voice, to present the surveillance of Rainger as a dry catalogue of events that I'd reacted to with impersonal conjecture, but I knew that some of the triumph, the sense of achievement, had crept imperceptibly into my tone as I hurled the car along dark, silent roads. 'I'm very sorry . . .'

'*Sorry!*' The echo of her scream of rage seemed to rebound over the peaceful fields. 'I could have been *killed*! I could have been killed, you stupid prat, I could have been *killed*.'

'I was almost killed myself, don't forget,' I said. 'Twice . . .'

'What do you think *I* care? What do you think I care about some bloody ten-pound detective? *I'm* the one with the future, *I'm* the one who's going somewhere. I haven't struggled half my life to get blown apart because of some provincial gumshoe.'

I felt myself flushing. The words had pierced the stout insulation of delicate nerves, torn back the first sliver of flesh from a wound that had never completely healed.

'Look . . . Fern . . .' I strove to keep my voice under control. 'It *never* crossed my mind you'd be in danger. If it had I'd have seen the police the same day. I still can't understand why they thought you were involved. You must accept that I'd never knowingly put you at risk.'

'You'd put your *mother* at risk. That's what you're all

about. Anything to be one up on the local Plod. You're not fit enough to be *in* the Plod so you want to go along there and say: "Hey, guys, guess what I've been up to while you've been taking car numbers – I've cornered the Beckford connection." That's what you're about, John Goss, and as long as you're getting your kicks what does it matter who gets hurt?'

I turned away, shaking with an anger I could no longer contain. This wasn't just a tender nerve she'd touched, this time she'd ripped my soul open. No one in the world could have guessed at the convuluted motives that had driven me in the Rainger affair, no one except a wannabe actress, filled with the bitter, uncanny perception that resulted from similar unrealised dreams.

'And what about *your* kicks, bitch!' I shouted. 'And the people *you* use. They have to warn public figures off you because you're such bad news. Anything . . . *any-thing* to be noticed, so they'll always think of you when they want some tart to come on strong with a box of soap-powder – the empress of 2TK herself . . .'

It seemed incredible that someone so slender, so fragile-looking, could punch so hard. The blow caught my cheekbone and almost knocked me over, with a scattering of coloured lights.

'You bastard!' she screamed. 'You bastard, you bastard, you bastard!'

I straightened up, shook my head, looked into eyes that gleamed wetly in the pale light and smiled ruefully. 'I'm having a drink,' I said. 'That's what I stopped for.'

I went to the boot. In what I called my ever-ready bag, apart from the change of clothes, there was brandy and wine and a kind of iron-ration pack of processed cheese, biscuits, nuts and plain chocolate. I poured some of the brandy into the flask's cap. It was an unremarkable brand, but just then, after all that had happened since I'd fled from the George, it tasted like the finest liquor ever distilled.

She came slowly up behind me. 'Can I have some?'

'Of course . . .' I refilled the cap and handed it to her.

'I've got some beef sandwiches in my travel-bag,' she said. 'I was going to pull in at a service area on my way north. I knew there'd be nothing waiting at home. There never is.'

We got back in the car, and ate like fighting dogs that hadn't been fed for two days, all the food there was, with the wine. She also had coffee in a thermos, good strong coffee, made from grounds in a cafetière, her single culinary skill.

We didn't apologise for the things we'd screamed at each other, either then or later. I think in some strange way we almost respected the cruel matching perception that had enabled us to inflict such wounds. It seemed to bring a new closeness.

It was as if the pain was like an acid running over the treated surface of my memory, burning in the details of that night so that they remained as sharp and timeless as an engraving – the fresh clean smell from the fields, the clear light, the faint sound of wind soughing along telephone wires, the hunger and the enhanced taste of simple food and cheap wine, the outline of her face as she gazed through the window.

And I knew we shared it, the feeling that every sense was transmitting each nuance of those minutes, as if along fibre optics, simultaneously and in exact detail. I could tell by the quality of her silence as she looked across the silvery fields. We were on a complex high, and an incredibly rare one; despite the danger, we were seeing life with all the colour and definition of people who'd narrowly avoided losing it.

We set off again, reluctantly, up over rising moorland, covered with heather so dense that it seemed to sweep like a purple tide to the edges of the narrow road. Then we began the long descent to the coast, with its distant view of the moon's glittering track laid across the North Sea, and the ruins of the priory standing against it on the cliff top, sharp and black as a woodcut.

We avoided Esk Head itself by taking a skirting road to the north shore. Rainger's weekend place, according to the housekeeper, lay between the fishing village and Beacon Point, somewhere beyond the nine-hole golf course that ran along the cliff top.

I slowed as we reached the end of the golf course, believing an isolated house would be seen easily against the plateau of fields beyond the links. But it wasn't. I dropped another gear, slowed to a crawl. About a mile or so along the road I could make out the lights of a hamlet called Cliffs End – between us and it there seemed no other habitation.

Suddenly she said: 'Perhaps this is it . . . to the right . . .'

I gave her a puzzled glance, but braked. A cinder track ran off towards the cliffs, with hedges on either side. Approaching it, I'd thought I was looking at a single hedge, dividing farmland. I wasn't certain, in this light, I'd even have seen the track when we were abreast of it, not first time round at least. But she seemed to know it was there almost before we were upon it.

I said: 'I thought my eyes were pretty good.'

'It's not that,' she said. 'I just had a really odd feeling

it was there. Sort of *déjà vu*. I used to come here as a girl, perhaps I walked past it. It might not lead to the house anyway.'

But it did. The track dropped down to a wooded hollow, not visible from the road. We followed it on foot. Beyond the wood stood a trim two-storey house with white walls, shutters and the pantile roof of the region. A pergola, smothered in white blossom, ran from the left of the house to an open-ended summer-house. To the right, the Mercedes stood beneath an ivy-covered carport. Perfect lawns sloped gently from the wood to the house.

'That's it all right,' I said in a low voice. 'Just one more reason why Rainger's Brit-Chem salary can only be a fraction of his real income.'

'What . . . are you going to do?'

'What I was going to do in Beckford – some hard talking. He's got two choices – either he comes back to Beckford and gives himself up or I ring Fenlon and they come and collect him.'

'What if he's armed?'

'He's certain to be armed. He shoots and fishes. He's licensed to carry hunting-guns. That mob he's involved with, I doubt if he goes anywhere *unarmed*.'

'What I mean is . . . if he's armed, he might be dangerous to you . . . us . . .'

'No chance. He's a Daisy Edger, a respectable citizen. He'd not even think of harming people like us.'

'If you threatened him he might,' she persisted. 'You're giving him a choice of two different ways to go to prison. I can't see him being keen on either.'

We stood above the house, behind a sycamore tree. We could hear the soft, steady roar of sea over shingle. I didn't reply for some time; she had a valid point. There was a lot of difference between facing Rainger in Beckford and Rainger in Esk Head – seventy miles of it. I'd been so anxious to confront him I'd not thought it through. There was an element of danger in either place, but I couldn't see him doing anything dramatic with a gun in the heart of Daisy Edge, with people on every side. Here, in the total isolation of the weekend house, the temptation might be too overwhelming – two shots, two bodies, two weighted bags. Kepwick Nab, a spit of land from which the churning tide never receded, would do the rest.

'You think we ought to get him away from the house? Neutral ground . . .'

'Why don't we go somewhere and get some sleep, and decide what to do in the morning?'

I shook my head in bewilderment. 'For Christ's *sake*, Fern, this isn't something we can think about, like where we'll go for a holiday. They've already made three attempts on our lives, we've no *time*.'

'But nobody knows we're here. And according to you, nobody knows the Raingers are here either. We've got *some* time. If you go in there angry you might put his back up. His temper can get very short too, when he's had a bad week, and that seems to be most weeks these days. And what if he denies it all? You might be in there for hours and not get him to agree to anything, and then by tomorrow you'll be worn out and not thinking straight.'

I stood silent again. She was right about the mood I was in, that was true. Her near-death was down to that bastard, however tenuous the connection between cause and effect. It wasn't the kind of mood that went with cool words and logical thinking.

I was reluctant to accept it, but we did need a proper break, a period of calm after the turbulence, a time to retreat behind the lines and lay careful plans for the best form of attack.

'If we come back early tomorrow,' she said. 'In daylight, with people about . . .'

It made more and more sense, impatient though I was for instant action. She was a sharp kid. We could make an ostentatious return, rested and ready to talk Rainger into what he had to do, even if it took all day.

'You're right,' I finally admitted. 'We need time. They're in there, that's the main thing.'

We stood a little longer. As we watched the house, our eyes fully attuned to the sort of darkness that went with moonlight, we detected a movement at one of the unlit bedroom windows. A curtain was slowly drawn, a figure stood there.

I took out field-glasses. The figure was in a white shirt, I caught a glimpse of gold-coloured hair. He kept his vigil for some time, two or three minutes at least, just looking out over the silvery lawn. It could have been a man admiring the view.

Or a man waiting.

Eighteen

We drove south the three miles to Esk Head. It was late and the streets were almost deserted. The bigger hotels fronted on to the sea on North Cliff; before them the lamp standards were hung with bunting and unlit fairy lights. Trailers stood at the roadside, of the fairground type, and what seemed to be carnival floats, on which were mounted the insubstantial wooden structures that backed milk-queens and jazz-bands.

'Regatta?' I mused.

'It must be. That's probably why the Raingers came. He's supposed to be into yachting.'

'That means we'll almost certainly have to sleep in the car.'

But we were in luck. The Cliff Lodge had had a last-minute cancellation and there was a double room they were delighted to find guests for. The night porter showed us to an airy sea-facing room with twin beds.

She threw her bag on to the nearest. 'A shower,' she said. 'Jesus, do I need a shower.'

I craved hot water too, going in as she came out, soaping myself again and again, standing for minutes beneath the jets, in urgent need of the familiar illusion – that hot water would wash away the stress and frustration

261

of that endless day along with the gallon of sweat.

When I re-entered the bedroom, she was lying on the bed naked, in the light of a single lamp, the covers thrown back so that her body was exposed as far as the mid-thigh.

Neither of us spoke; I simply got in the narrow bed with her. It bore no relation to anything we'd known before. We neither of us had time for the nuances of love-making, those drawn-out sybaritic phases of touching and stroking, of breast-nuzzling, of fluttering fingers, of moist, lengthy kisses, of even slowing down sex itself by periods of immobility, as some people ate water-ices between courses, to prolong the sensual pleasures of taste.

We made love like wild animals, gasping and lurching on the tousled bed, as if both united in a desperate search for total release from the anxieties of that flight from the city. We never spoke from beginning to end, endearments would have seemed misplaced. I don't think either of us could have explained an act that seemed almost like a frenzy, but we sensed in it the shock of near-death, the fear, the endless tension, the pain and hate we'd aroused in each other, and that new undefined closeness.

I grasped her body with such force I could feel her bones bending, her arms round me felt like metal clamps; it was as if we were trying to force our bodies into one. It appeared endless, the seconds seemed to fall away like drops from a slow-leaking tap. The room had total coastal silence, but for our rasping breath, the rustling of sheets, the gasps and groans of near-pain.

Orgasm seemed almost unattainable, as if our bodies couldn't comprehend our relentless quest for it, after the danger we'd come through. We were now in a state of safety, so why did we need sex when we could have had peace and calm?

It was sex as we'd never known it, just as food and wine, during the time in the car, had stimulated taste-buds we'd never known we had.

When our bodies were finally pitched into a shud-dering climax, the orgasm itself felt endless, as if we were high on the sort of drug that is said to give that effect.

She slept the moment she was still, her arms slacken-ing round my shoulders, her legs still arched. How I craved that ability to plunge into a sleep that I knew only too well would be deep and unbroken. It was as if her mind left her body totally, only to return at the precise moment of completed repair. I'd heard it said that a soldier who could sleep like that on the eve of battle would be one who would survive, or at least die only one death. It was a valuable gift for an actress who had so many roles to create.

I eased myself away from her, straightened her limbs, and drew the covers to just below the large brown areolae of her relaxed breasts. Then I got into my own bed and also slept, but not on the same profound level as she did. I awoke as the rising sun brightened the curtains, my mind immediately turning over the best tactics for handling Rainger.

I drew the curtains at six, having ordered a room-service continental breakfast for half-past. I wanted to be at the Raingers' between seven and eight. The sun had risen blood-tinged out of a sea that lay flat, reddish and dull. I stood watching for part of a minute.

'Would you say it had a wine-dark look?' she said from behind me.

'Is that the only word of Homer you can remember too?'

' "He saw the cities of many peoples and learnt their ways. He suffered many hardships on the high seas in his struggles to preserve his life and bring his comrades home . . ." '

Her gliding voice, controlled and vibrant, seemed to fill the room. She stood naked at my side, her body gilded slightly by sunlight. She shrugged, smiled.

'I could go on for hours. I learnt great chunks of it for my acting classes. I learnt great chunks of everything and ended up saying: "They're as white as the day I *bought them*!" '

I stroked her face and put my arm round her, and we stood for a few minutes in silence. Then we each took another shower and dressed in pants and T-shirts. It was going to be hot, the sweaters and coats could go in the boot.

The fresh croissants, rolls and coffee arrived precisely, and we sat at a small table the waiter erected in front of the window.

'Is this the first time I've eaten anything at this time of day in my entire existence?' she said, but went on to tuck in with a good appetite.

'When shall we eat again is the point,' I said. 'I can't see Mrs Rainger getting the larks' tongues and Chablis out, come lunch-time.'

'You think it's going to take so long?'

'You know the guy. He's a sales-exec, born talking. He'll talk all day, I shouldn't wonder.'

'He won't give himself up, John,' she said, softly but

decisively. 'Not Miles Rainger.'

'I think he will,' I said, 'if I get the script right. I've been working on it since dawn.'

Her eyes slid from mine and caught the light as she looked over the flat sea. An old man in a cap and cardigan slowly passed the parked cars on the front with an old, stiff dog.

'I once stayed in this hotel,' she said, 'with Auntie Irene and Uncle Ronnie. They took pity on me. I wonder if I had a premonition I'd come here again in strange circumstances. I can't remember it.'

'I came with my parents as a kid,' I said wistfully. 'We could have had a lot of fun at the Regatta. We could have gone to the fair and watched the folk-dancing and had a few drinks at the Cod and Lobster . . .'

We fell silent as we reluctantly adjusted to the realities of the heroin business, remorseless killers and the problem of Miles Rainger.

We left the hotel at seven. It was cloudless and already hotter than it had been in Beckford during the dry spell. Men, stripped to the waist and deeply tanned, were erecting stalls on the cliff-top lawns for the sale of hamburgers and seafood, and a Mr Whippy ice-cream van was already manoeuvring into position to take full advantage of the season's most lucrative day. Finishing touches were being put to the float vehicles, and young girls dressed as fairies and milkmaids and queens were beginning to drift along from the village, giggling excitedly. The quayside fairground was hidden by the cliff's overhang, but even at this hour we could faintly hear canned hurdy-gurdy music and the throb of generators.

'Let's forget it happened,' she said. 'Let's get a double Ninety-nine and walk along the prom . . .'

I drove back to the house in the hollow against a steady stream of traffic. The Regatta was a powerful attraction and locating a parking spot within half a mile of the village after nine would be virtually impossible.

I pulled off the road at the entrance to the cinder track and we got out slowly, carefully drawing attention to our arrival by talking and gesticulating for some time at the side of the car, actions to which Fern brought her usual flair. If mine was a face you didn't much remember, hers was a face you wouldn't forget.

Then we walked, her hand trembling very slightly in mine, down the track and through the copse to the top of the long, sloping lawn. If the house had looked good in moonlight it looked incredibly attractive in the morning sun, with its green tiles, white walls and blossom-smothered pergola, dreaming against blue water and blue sky. A little old man was hoeing flower-beds. He could have been a clone of the one at the Beckford house, it was as if Rainger travelled with one in the boot.

'Daisy Edge by the sea,' I said. 'It must cost almost as much to run as the other.'

'The car's gone!'

'I know. They'll have taken it round the back to load the hamper and the ice-box. They *can't* have set off yet, he'll have privileged parking at the Yacht Club . . .'

But I was uneasy as we crossed to the door and rang the bell. I wasn't remotely surprised to find it being answered by a woman in a green smock. She had grey hair and glasses, and the sort of reddish complexion that went with stiff sea breezes.

'Could I see Mr Rainger please?'

'I'm afraid not. They left half an hour ago.'

'For Esk Head?'

266

'It is Regatta Day, you know . . .'

'But surely the racing doesn't start till mid-morning.'

'He likes to be there in good time. He helps them tinker with the boats . . .'

'Is he racing himself?'

'Not this year. Next year, when his own boat's built. He *could* have hired, but he said to me: "Mrs Shann," he said, "you can only race properly in a boat you know like your own car, and so I'll just have to be patient till my own's ready." It should really have been ready *this* year, by rights, but Bobby up the yard, his best man had that bother with his heart. Coronation thrombosis,' she added importantly. 'So *he* won't be back to the boats before the autumn.'

'Mrs Shann,' I said, forcing myself to smiling patience, 'have you any idea what time they'll be back?'

'Six. He was very certain about that. They've been invited to a cocktail party for the yachting folk at seven, and then they're going on to dinner with some of the members. They're very popular. Who should I say called? I only work mornings, bear in mind, but I can leave a note near the gin bottle.'

'Please don't bother,' I said, trying to keep the grimness out of my smile. 'I'd really prefer it to be a big surprise. We're the last people he'll expect to see.'

We went back to the car, the gardener saluting us politely in the approved manner.

She said: 'What now?'

'The Yacht Club. It's just about as unsatisfactory as it could be, but we've no choice. I couldn't have believed they'd have set off so early. Detaching him from his pals will *not* be easy.'

'But safe . . . with all those people about . . .'

'But what protects us protects him. If he doesn't like
the sound of what I start telling him he can get in his car
and drive off. He couldn't have done that here because
my car blocks his drive.'

'Why not just come back at six? We've been clocked
by Mrs Thing and the old man. He can't try anything . . .'

'No. I was against leaving it overnight, we can't leave
it another ten hours. Those people in Beckford, they'll
know now your car didn't blow on the A1. They'll know
I'm not at home. They might also have worked out that
Rainger's over here and we've followed him. They've
got degrees in second-guessing.'

'The Yacht Club then. You're the boss.'

I glanced at her. Sleep seemed to have made her over
again, even in these circumstances. If she was afraid it
was a fear, beneath sunlight and clear skies, she could
handle. There was a slight flush to her unmade-up face,
but it seemed more from excitement, an excitement I felt
I sensed because I'd woken with it too and hoped it
hadn't shown.

The Yacht Club overlooked a wide natural basin in the
river, about a quarter of a mile inland from the harbour.
My spirits sank when we reached it. In my childhood
days the general public had had unrestricted access to
the pathway that skirted the sheds and landing-stages.
Since then the area had become a fully fledged marina,
and was now enclosed by sturdy chain-link fencing and a
long, barred metal gate that was closed and immovable
even today, and accessible only to key-holders.

'Shit!'

We stood by the gate in the intensifying heat, but
anyone going to the club seemed to be already there, like

the Raingers – we could see expensive motors double-
and treble-parked on hard standing at the rear of the
clubhouse.

There was nothing else to do but get back in the car,
roll down the windows, and wait. It was a long, frustra-
ting wait, during which Fern flicked from station to
station on the radio, singing fragments of pop songs,
while I beat out an endless tattoo on the steering-wheel.

After about fifteen minutes, a Jaguar whispered down
to the gate and an elderly man took out a plastic card.
He needed only to display it at a certain point on a metal
pillar and the long gate rumbled slowly open. He drove
out, then braked as we approached him. He wore a
blazer and a crested tie, and had grey hair brushed
smoothly back from a widow's peak and a rounded
rather shiny pink face. Like Rainger's gardener, he gave
an impression of ubiquity – I seemed to be looking at the
same face the television cameras invariably homed in on
at Lords and Cowes and the Trooping of the Colour.

He glanced at our clothes with what seemed a
repressed shudder, then coldly spoke those immortal
words of the privileged the western world over, warily
guarding their privileged strips of land from the sub-class
– 'Can I help you?'

'We're looking for Mr Rainger, sir,' I said humbly.
'His housekeeper gave us to believe he might be at the
Club.'

His face softened slightly, at what seemed to be clear
evidence that I knew my place and was prepared to stay
in it.

'Can I give him a message?' he said cautiously. 'I'll be
seeing him later.'

The protective instinct of wealthy people for other

wealthy people seemed bred in the bone. He'd automatically assumed I'd be the last person Rainger would want to see on Regatta Day, even though I was washed and shaved, and seemed to know my manners. You daren't give much rope, if any, to the type of person who wore T-shirts and drove Ford cars.

'I'm from Brit-Chem, sir, Mr Rainger's firm. I'm here on holiday, and there's a message I need to pass to a colleague urgently; I can't get through on the phone. Mr Rainger's going back on Monday and I wanted to ask him to do it for me.'

'I see,' he said, his voice another degree warmer. I could have been the bar-steward, putting his drinks together for him. 'Well, look here, I'm afraid Mr Rainger's left now . . .'

'Left . . .' I wondered if the waxwork was instinctively lying.

'He and his wife decided to go down to the harbour to get a good spot for the start of the races. But I'll be seeing him later if you'd care to give me a number where he can get in touch . . .'

'Thanks all the same, sir, but we'll try to catch him in Esk Head. Have you any idea where he'll be?'

He shook his head. 'He could be on any of the piers. They'll have to take their chance with everyone else, I'm afraid.'

His tone implied nostalgia for a time when men like him and Rainger needed only to walk on to a pier for the sub-class to fall respectfully back, for a forehead-touching man to spring from a prime spot saying: 'Just keeping it free for you, sir, and God bless you.'

We went back to the car, Fern giggling surreptitiously, her shoulders shaking. 'You grovel *superbly*. You were like something in *The Forsyte Saga*.'

I let in the clutch, turned again towards Esk Head.

'Learning to dissemble is lesson one in private investigation. Anyway, you weren't even born when they were running *The Forsyte Saga*. I was only a kid myself and it must have been a rerun then.'

I assumed she'd not read the books. I'd never known anyone who had.

'Someone . . . bought me the full set of videos. About twenty-four glorious hours of it. I'd have *killed* to play Fleur . . .'

I glanced at her. I think she'd have stopped short at murder, but not far short.

I said: 'Have you ever seen an old film called *Rosemary's Baby*?'

'Why do you ask?'

'The husband sells Rosemary's womb to the Devil to get a major acting part. You'd be in his corner, wouldn't you?'

'You've got to admit', she said, grinning, 'it was a neat career move.'

By having to waste time at the Yacht Club we'd lost the remotest chance of parking in the village itself. I inched in a circular route with all the other grinding traffic, but it was hopeless and we were wasting more time; in the end I parked out on the road that led to the moors, the one we'd come in on last night.

'Needle in a haystack time,' I said, as we returned to Esk Head on foot. We passed the big hotels on North Cliff and went down to the harbour by way of a flight of stone steps let into the side of the cliff itself. It brought us out near the fish-quays, which, for this single day, housed the paraphernalia of the fairground – the throbbing generators, the arcades, the merry-go-rounds and the blaring speakers. Beyond the fairground, an overnight city of stalls had sprung up, selling toys and ornaments and cheap clothing. We came through this to a clear stretch of road that led along the harbour wall to an iron swing-bridge which gave access across the estuary to South Cliff, the older part of the village.

'We'll do it methodically,' I said, as we stepped on to the bridge, choked with traffic. 'Most of the small craft are parked on the south side, and that's where Rainger will probably be. We'll go to the end of South Cliff Pier, and then work our way back. He may not be too difficult to spot – if I know anything he'll probably be dressed like something out of Somerset Maugham anyway.'

She gave me a wide smile, difficult to interpret – it was odd, now that she knew of his criminal activities she no longer talked scornfully about him, as she once had, almost as if she were impressed by his other life. It made me vaguely uneasy in the moments I could spare from scanning faces in the crowd. It might be exciting, but it was a serious business. I never lost sight of what it was all about, but she was a night's profound sleep away from yesterday's shocks and the slate seemed wiped clean. It could be very dangerous if she began treating it as a sort of game, lulled by colour and music and kiss-me-quick hats.

We crossed the bridge and turned off on to a narrow curving street called Spice Lane. A man with an accordion and two others with fiddles were playing folk music to which young boys and girls, dressed in white, gravely stepped an intricate reel. Fern was instantly engrossed, the performer instinctively drawn to a performance, and she looked on almost wistfully, her lips slightly apart, as the boys bowed, the girls curtsied, and the couple at the top of the lines spun down to the bottom. The narrow pavements were jammed with people, and it took us several minutes to pick our way to the other end, and though we kept moving, her hand in mine, her eyes went back again and again to the dancing children.

'Nothing's changed,' I said. 'There were kids dancing on Spice Lane when I came with Mum and Dad in the Seventies. And Mum said it was just the same in the Forties.'

'I wish I'd been a dancing kid . . .'

I'd not heard that particular note of yearning before. Her eyes met mine, slid away for one final glance behind her. 'How could you have fitted it all in,' I said, smiling faintly, 'dancing in Spice Lane *and* being Regatta Queen?'

She squeezed my hand as we pushed on, from Spice Lane into South Cliff Street, threading our way through the crowds, past the odours volleying from tiny shops, of wet fish and newly baked bread and ripening fruit, past narrow passages, known as ghauts, which ran between close-packed cottages to give sudden blinding glimpses of white sails against glittering water.

Scrutinising faces as we went, we came to the end of the street and passed on to the main pier, which angled diagonally towards its sister pier across the harbour's mouth. We walked, more rapidly now, towards the small lighthouse at its end, over planking laid lengthways with inch-wide gaps through which we could see the sea surging heavily over the barrage thirty feet below. No Rainger.

We came to the lighthouse, so freshly white and

shining in the clear sun that it slightly hurt the eyes. I took out field-glasses. Between this pier and the bridge, two smaller piers right-angled from the harbour side at a lower level. The racing had been going for some time now, and at intervals of about ten minutes we heard the crack of a starting pistol as a group of yachts positioned in the middle of the harbour set out for the open sea, their spinnakers bellying sluggishly against a down-breeze from the river, the foam from their bows creaming over water that had now turned cobalt in the climbing light. The smaller piers were crowded with sightseers; I edged the powerful lenses along the rows of faces again and again.

Perhaps I'd never have spotted him had my guess about his clothing not proved right. Rainger was a dressy man who'd almost bought a yacht, and he chose to give a subtle hint of this special status by the blazer, white trousers and white cap that suddenly identified him as he moved out from behind a group of lesser mortals in T-shirts, some even printed with humorous slogans, at the edge of the second pier.

'Success!' I said jubilantly. 'The Captain of the Pinafore himself.'

As I watched, Mrs Rainger appeared at his side in a white dress, dark glasses and a wide sun-hat.

I pointed them out to Fern. Now that we had a fix they could easily be distinguished with the naked eye in those sorts of clothes.

'They seem to be going,' she said.

'Mrs Rainger pointed towards North Cliff. They may have decided to walk over there, you get a better view of yachts in the open sea. Let's go – by the time they get off the pier we should have reached them.' I took her hand.

'This is the drill – we stay on his tail till we find a place to talk. Sooner or later they'll go somewhere for a drink, some up-market spot like the Lounge Bar at the Cliff Lodge.'

We ran, or tried to, back to South Cliff Street, but our pier was filling up too, and we were badly hindered by the drifting trippers, at one stage being almost carried back half the pier's length by a crowd of boisterous men and women running to cheer some yacht on its way out of the harbour. As we forced our way through this human tide we were just in time to see the Raingers emerging from their own pier and turning in the direction of the bridge.

We were within fifty yards of them when they turned into Spice Lane. We got there ourselves as its curve was taking them out of sight. At that point the pavements were clear; there had been a break in the dancing during which time admiring onlookers had gathered round the youngsters. But as we ran into the lane the music suddenly struck up, the spectators flooded back to the pavements and we were engulfed again. By the time we'd pushed through to the half-way point of the lane, the Raingers were once more out of sight. Cursing with frustration, I craned about to see if they'd stayed to watch the dancing; that slowed us down even more. It must have taken five minutes for us to get from one end to the other. When we finally came out into the main road, it was to see the Raingers walking off the far end of the bridge.

I snatched Fern's hand and we began to run again. The bridge seemed oddly empty now, both of cars and pedestrians, with knots of people standing at each end. But I was so intent on keeping Rainger in sight that I didn't grasp the significance.

'*Stop!*' someone shouted. 'You can't go now! Are you *blind!*'

I stopped, glanced round. A man with sun-bleached hair, tattooed and stripped to the waist, stood at the door of the bridge-house, pointing upwards. A barrier of the level-crossing type was floating down towards us.'

'*Christ!*'

'What is it?' she cried. 'What's happening?'

'They're only opening the bloody thing, that's what's happening.'

Three tall-masted yachts were gliding down the estuary towards the bridge. As they did so, it split itself in two and began to swing its halves apart on massive turn-tables. It was a sight that was always worth watching, except for those million to one occasions when the man who was just disappearing from view on the other side of the harbour was the one man in the world you urgently needed to be on the other side with.

'Not to worry,' I said bitterly, 'they'll have it all back together again by the time the Raingers are part of that cast of thousands over there.'

I turned away, seething with frustration . . . to look into the flat unblinking eyes, further along the barrier, of the man with the red hair and beard who'd stood on my doorstep yesterday morning, pretending to be a policeman.

Next to him stood the man with the young-old face called Fielding.

Nineteen

The second of the yachts was moving past. In another minute the third would be through to the harbour and the bridge begin to close.

The bearded man was talking rapidly to Fielding, but before the younger man could look in our direction I pulled Fern with me so that a bunch of burly youths stood between us and them. Fielding might already know us by sight from secret observations or he might not. If not, I didn't want to make it easy for him.

'We've got company,' I told her in a low voice. 'Just along the barrier – the pretend policeman I told you about, and the one called Fielding, Rainger's leg-man.'

She watched me, her face paling, the excitement of a chase she'd been rather enjoying now gone. 'How could they *know*?'

'I'm afraid there was always that possibility. They're cunning. Look, the bridge is closing – as soon as the barrier's up we move across with the crowd. There's nothing they can do with all these people around. That's . . . if they wanted to do anything, and we've got to assume it's a strong possibility.'

She shivered in the blazing sun.

'Let's go back', she said, 'to where the kids are

277

dancing. If we're waiting for the bridge they'll assume we're going over it. But instead of that we go back. They'd never find us in the crush.'

The two sections were now grinding slowly together.

'They'd outguess us, Fern,' I said, covering my agitation with a calm tone. '*Never* underestimate them. The beard will have thought of that. What they'll do the second the barrier's up is run across and stand at the far end. That way they'll be able to check whether we've crossed or not. If we don't cross now they'll wait there till we do – as long as it takes.'

'Let's go to the next one . . .'

'It's about five miles up-river and my car's on the other side. And it's imperative we get to the Raingers before they do . . .'

The bridge finally locked itself together with the explosive crump of a ceremonial cannon. Fielding and the bearded man scuttled across it the moment the barrier cleared their heads.

'Excuse me . . .' Fern said in her most seductive tone to one of the young men standing next to us. 'There's someone we particularly don't want to see at the other side of the bridge. Could you and your friends sort of cluster round us till we're across?'

Born street-wise, his reaction was nano-second. 'Right you are, darlin', as long as I can stand next to you. Hey guys, bunch up . . .'

It was the story of their lives, getting twelve bodies into various enclosures with eight tickets, and they worked with almost military precision, cheerfully swinging haversacks clanking with tins of beer on to their shoulders, and arranging themselves skilfully round our hunched bodies so that we were lost to sight behind a thicket of muscular brown legs.

'You having trouble, darlin'?' The first man's voice came to us from above as we were half-way across. 'Mean to say, if there's someone needs seeing to, know what I mean, me and the lads can sort it, no bother . . .'

We glanced at each other, hunched and shuffling inside our human palisade. How tempting to let our new friends loose on the two who waited, to let them have some of what they were so good at dishing out. But I shook my head; for all their toughness these boys would be lambs to the slaughter – those two would have silenced guns in their hands before the first punch was thrown, weapons they'd have no hesitation in using.

'No thanks,' Fern said sweetly. 'It's not that kind of trouble. Awfully kind of you to offer.'

'Yeah, well, we're getting kind of bored with boat-racing and fiddle-dancing and that. Not much action in the pubs yet, either, know what I mean . . .'

We crossed then from the bridge to the harbour-side, and I caught a single glimpse of the bearded man, his flat-looking eyes darting everywhere in the heaving crowd the barriers had released. We went along with the young men for another fifty yards and then, judging it to be safe to break cover, we thanked them and separated; they to go off in search of a nice pub to demolish, we to continue our search for Rainger.

'Where now?' she said.

'North Cliff. I'm certain they'll be going that way.'

We walked as quickly as we could through the drifting crowds, past the reek and bustle of the seafood stands and the hamburger hotplates, then back through the tented village of market-stalls to the fairground.

I glanced back. They were both following us, casually

but steadily, incongruous in city clothes, the jackets of which they couldn't remove because of the armouries they'd be concealing.

'It's no good,' I said. 'They're on our tail.'

The bearded man would have thought it through exactly as I'd done myself. That we had to be on this side and time was running out. Fern's quick thinking with the yobbos would only have fooled him briefly. We had to be *somewhere* in that river of bodies, and there'd be little he didn't know about bunching from his own misspent youth.

'If they're supposed to be after the Raingers,' she said shakily, 'why are they following *us*?'

'I think they got a fix on the Raingers on the south side and hit the same problem as we did when the bridge opened.'

'But why follow *us*!' she said again, her voice rising against the jolly music and laughter of carnival day.

'I can only think the beard's realised we're as anxious as he is to get to the Raingers and thinks we might have the best hunch for finding them . . .'

'I think they're just after us,' she said in a voice I could barely hear. 'They tried to kill us in Beckford, and now . . .'

I was suddenly quite certain she was right. I'd tried to reason it out, as I'd always trained myself to do; she'd simply reacted to her instincts.

'Why are they searching Esk Head anyway?' she cried. 'If they're after Rainger they'll know where the house is . . . all they have to do is go and wait . . .'

'Maybe they *don't* know where it is . . .'

'They know every other bloody thing!'

'Maybe he never told them about the seaside place.

That wouldn't stop them finding out, but perhaps they don't know the exact address. The Daisy Edge woman wouldn't give it to anyone she didn't know, and the phone will almost certainly be ex-D . . .'

I spoke in a preoccupied way as we plunged into the fairground crowds – I was trying to reassure her but I was also trying to think out both a short-term and a medium-term strategy. There was, too, some niggling detail scratching around in my mind, some small incongruity about the men behind us that went beyond the unsuitability of their clothing, and might or might not be significant.

The bearded man carried an attaché-case. Why?

I had three premises to work on. That they were pursuing Rainger. That they were pursuing us. That they were pursuing Rainger *and* us. Whoever they were after they'd almost certainly be carrying weapons – guns or knives. But not in an attaché-case. No weapon could be produced speedily from an attaché-case.

Money? Was it stacked with banknotes? If so, why, when Rainger seemed to look after his own pay arrangements. Was it for *collecting* money waiting to be laundered? But if they were going to collect money from Rainger, surely he'd already have it packed up and waiting in a case of his own.

There was one other possibility about that case that I thrust to the back of my mind.

'We've got to shake them off and get back to the car,' I told her. 'Forget Rainger for the time being. Give me your hand . . .'

Hunching down again, we moved into the thick of the crowd, darting this way and that, past children playing hoop-la and blue-rinsed old women playing electronic bingo, past barkers with hand microphones, past banks of space games whose simulated explosions vied with the ringing staccato of stray pellets on a miniature rifle-range. Above it all, the speakers were blaring an old pop song called 'The Day We Went to Bangor', a song that was shortly to seem like the most terrifying music I'd ever heard.

I had a sudden premonition of danger, a realisation that crowds weren't the answer. There was supposed to be safety in numbers, but these were intensely preoccupied numbers. They had their heads full of flashing lights and deafening music, they were so engrossed in Kelly's Eye and metal ducks they'd scarcely have noticed if we'd been leading a tame bear. It suddenly seemed safer for the bearded man than for us. They had cover, cover to use weapons, weapons no one would hear or see, cover to slip away into the teeming streets.

I thrust that thought to the back of my mind as well and went on with Fern at a half-run. I was over-reacting; it was the strain of the past few days. The bearded man seemed to be a total pro, surely it would offend every instinct to do anything violent in the open.

In any case, we were almost through the fairground, and the two men were nowhere to be seen. I gave her hand a reassuring squeeze. We seemed to have made it – the circuitous route and the back-tracking had paid off, and they must still be prowling among the slot machines.

'They could spend ten minutes in there thinking we're still around,' I shouted. 'That's all the time we need to get to the other end of the village. This way.'

I drew her down a sort of alley between a caravan and a truck pulsating with generating equipment. They were sited at the perimeter of the fairground, and beyond them was a relatively deserted section of fish-quay with its open-sided packing-sheds.

The bearded man was standing in one of the sheds as we emerged from between the vehicles. He was holding the attaché-case at almost waist level and was pointing the end in our direction.

The shock brought it all together – the brilliant spot of light only moved on my T-shirt for a fraction of a second before I'd dragged her away at an angle.

'Zigzag!' I cried. 'For Christ's sake, *zigzag*!'

I scarcely heard the muffled burst, but I definitely heard the splintering of wood as the bullets ripped into the stout panelling of the old caravan.

Fear had honed her reflexes to razor sharpness, and she followed my every move as tightly as a shadow as I pulled her along the fish-quay, feinting rapidly left and right, until seconds later we came to a different crowd about thirty yards beyond the fair.

We plunged into it, gasping with relief, and paused to drag air into our lungs.

'You were right,' I said grimly. 'It was us they were after.'

'Just . . . us?'

'I don't know. Don't worry about it now. We need to concentrate on getting back to the car.'

We could hear music again, similar to that we'd heard in Spice Lane. We pushed our way steadily to the front line, where we could see adult folk-dancers, semi-professional men and women in green and yellow clothes, dancing to the usual fiddles and accordions. There were also mummers, dressed as clowns and knights and horses, morris dancers with sticks and bells, and a trio of sword-dancers, all waiting their turn to entertain the crowd.

They made their way into the dancing area through a corridor in the dense mass of trippers, which those not performing kept intact by making a sort of human fence, like policemen on crowd control. Beyond this corridor was open road, relatively clear, as far as the steps that went up the cliff side, and the beginning of the route that would take us back to the car.

As I studied this, the dancing ended. One of the women began to speak, her voice carrying thinly to us above the murmur of the onlookers and the cries of seagulls. 'Now, ladies and gentlemen, this is *your* turn to join the dance. We want ten ladies and ten gentlemen to come forward. It's an easy step and we'll guide you. Don't be shy . . .'

I said: 'Let's go . . .'

She gave me an incredulous glance.

'Where will they be looking?' I said. '*Not* at the dancers. They'll be combing the crowd. Out there we're safe for a short time. They'll get deeper and deeper into the crowd, and after a few minutes we can make a run for it through that opening across there.'

She suddenly grinned. 'We once did a play like that – the waiter poisoned the drink because no one looks at waiters.'

It was both endearing and impressive that in the worst danger she'd ever known, an incident from her acting life was the first thing that came to mind.

We moved out into the group of folk-dancers, who led us to the centre of the area. There, two circles were formed, the women on the inner, the men on the outer, and when the music started we began walking, the two

284

circles travelling in opposite directions. When the music stopped on a chord, we were each claimed by the nearest folk-dancer of the opposite sex, and when it recommenced, expertly guided in a simple waltz step.

'We're having a singsong tonight,' my partner said, as she drew me round to the jolly tunes. 'At the Crown and Anchor after the fireworks. Would you and your lady like to come?'

'We'd love to,' I said fervently. Crime belonged to cities and mean streets, and even now, with Fielding and the bearded man trawling doggedly through the crowd, I found it hard to accept that these things could be happening in the magical sunny land of my childhood summers.

I saw him then, the bearded man. As I'd surmised, he had no time for the dancers. He seemed to have cunning but not much imagination. He was in the middle of the mob, peering carefully at faces and almost at the furthest point from the human corridor when the music stopped again, a signal to the dancers to re-form the circles.

I dashed up to Fern, grasped her hand and made for the opening. We ran through it and within seconds were climbing the cliff steps. We were two-thirds up before I looked back at the dancing.

The two men were half-way between the crowd and the cliff steps, and walking rapidly.

'Sod it!' I gasped. 'He must have had Fielding posted somewhere outside the crowd. On the harbour wall maybe . . .'

'We'll *never* get to the car . . .'

'You're right.' The men had started up the steps. It was just as well that I took the bearded man so little for granted that I had some kind of alternative in place.

We reached the top of the steps and passed on to the cliff-top flower-beds and walkways.

'Run,' I said, 'but not too fast. I want to make sure they stay with us at this stage . . .'

We began to jog along a sloping road that led down from the cliff and into the shopping streets that lay behind the harbour. I glanced back. They were on to the cliff top themselves now and also jogging. We came to the first of the shops and then, darting right and left past the inevitable bunches of trippers, to a pub called the Esk Head Clipper.

'In here,' I said.

'But we'll not get *out*!'

'There's another way . . .'

'But they'll guess that *too*!'

'I *want* them to. I know how they work now.'

She let me take her in. The pubs had been open almost since breakfast time, and this one was heaving. This meant that whichever of them followed us in would have to spend time checking each room.

The Esk Head Clipper also had a side door, off a cobbled passage from the street, which led directly into a tap-room, a relic of days when fishermen weren't encouraged to use the same entrance as men who wore a collar and tie.

I was praying that the pair stuck to form and split up as they had on the quays, one to follow us in, one to guard the doors. Because Fern and I were going out through the beer-garden. It was reached by a small door near the bar, a door which almost seemed to blend with the dark panelling, and which gave a strong impression of being the entrance to the landlord's private quarters. In fact that was what I'd always thought until my father, who'd given considerable patronage to Esk Head pubs over the years, had taken me through it on another Regatta Day. It led to a small garden with a few tables and benches that tended to be used almost exclusively by a handful of old regulars who sat for an hour or so over a pint of mild. A narrow gateway at the rear led between high walls to a maze of back streets.

I took hold of the door-handle.

'You'll find nothing down there!'

I felt as if cold steel had touched the nape of my neck. A heavy grey-haired man in shirt-sleeves spoke from behind the bar as he pulled beer from a hand pump. It was a good few years since I'd been twenty. Pubs changed hands, they were renovated, beer-gardens became kitchen extensions. We were trapped.

'The toilets is over back of the Snug. If that was the toilets it would say toilets on it, wouldn't it . . .'

'We were looking for the beer-garden. It used to be through here . . .'

'*Beer-garden!*' he said incredulously. '*On Regatta Day!* I need every man-jack I've got up here . . .'

'But we can go in it?' I said, a bead of perspiration breaking from my hair-line and trickling down my forehead. 'We can go in the beer-garden?'

'Nothing to stop you going *in* it. Just don't expect these girls to come running down there with ploughman's lunches. And if you take glasses down there you bring them *back* – understand?'

Across the bar-parlour and in the crowded hallway, I caught my first glimpse of the bearded man looking carefully into corners. I almost bundled Fern through the door.

'You'll have to take drinks with you!' the landlord

cried irritably before the door swung shut, silencing the sounds of revelry as if a radio had been abruptly switched off.

We ran down stone steps, through an open doorway and out once more into the glare of the sun.

A graveyard could scarcely have been more peaceful. Half a dozen ancient men, sitting over their drinks like waxworks, showed minimal interest as we flashed past them and out through the narrow gateway.

To freedom.

Twenty

'Why did he point that case at us?'

I said: 'Inside that case was a Heckler and Koch sub-machine-gun, guided by a laser sight. The laser produces an aiming-spot. That spot of light is synchronised with the gun itself – when the spot's on the target the gun can't miss. It might sound James Bond, but it's hard fact. They're used by the SAS and the Metropolitan Police for protecting VIPs. They're expensive, not easy to get hold of. It's another example of the kind of money and expertise these people can lay their hands on.'

We sat in the clearing of a small wood not far from a village called Egton on Goathland Moors. It was a beauty spot, but deserted today because of the Regatta. The car stood in shade beneath trees.

On leaving the Esk Head Clipper, we'd run through back streets, rejoining the road through the shopping centre a quarter of a mile further on. I'd drawn her to a halt then.

'We've got to walk now, Fern. If we walk we blend, if we run we stand out.'

It was agonising, but we both knew I was right. We walked steadily but not quickly along the teeming pavements. Every few seconds I glanced casually back, but couldn't see them. With those two, as I'd learned the hard way, it meant nothing. We might have fooled them this time, but the bearded man would once more be working logically through options. At the same time, he'd almost certainly have decided that if he guessed right about which way we'd jump next he could take no more chances; if he saw us he would kill us, no matter where we were or who we were with, even if others got hurt. I had seen his eyes as he lined up the case on me and the jolly music about going to Bangor had swirled round us, and I knew that if I looked into them once more it would be for the last time.

We finally came to the road that ran through the outskirts of the village before climbing steeply up to the moors. It was lined with cars, and we had to pass at least fifty to get to mine. They were still not behind us, or seemed not to be, but they could be playing our game, walking steadily through the crowds so as not to stand out. On reaching the parked cars, they could hunch down and creep along the off-sides and take us the moment I put the key in the lock of my own.

But we reached the car safely and got into it. I checked the door-mirrors carefully but could see no one creeping up either side of the line of vehicles.

She flopped at my side. 'God – the *heat!*'

The temperature build-up was so intense it would have killed a dog in minutes; I felt as if I were sitting on hot bricks. Other people could throw their doors open, allowing the car to cool down before they drove off; we had no time for such luxuries. I drove at sixty in a great semicircle towards Egton over open moorland, checking following cars obsessively, pulling twice into lay-bys until the handful behind us had passed by, not setting off again until the road behind us was quite clear. At the second halt, I handed her a blonde wig and dark glasses, and put on a dark brown wig and glasses myself.

'A *woman's* wig!' she cried, giggling. 'You've even got a *woman's* wig! What's your *other* favourite old movie – *Some Like It Hot?*'

I smiled as I carefully applied a thin moustache to my upper lip. 'Only trouble is, I can never get a dress that fits really well across the shoulders. Not even at Claudia's.'

She gave an involuntary smile of pleasure as she tucked her own dark hair into the wig, it must have been the same smile she'd had when making up for a photography session or a poetry reading or a 2TK. She spent long, careful minutes arranging it, so that the finished appearance corresponded exactly to some inner perception, and during these minutes it seemed as if nothing else mattered, even pursuit by armed men.

'How does it look?' she said finally, in a preoccupied tone.

'Let's ask the man with the beard,' I said wryly, 'next time we bump into him.'

She barely listened, her hands still patting and primping as she turned her head from side to side in the sun-visor glass. She applied make-up then, for the first time, from a narrow case she kept in the back pocket of her jeans, toning her eyebrows to match her hair, with some mixture of powder and cream, and touching her lips with bright, tarty lipstick. She was still recognisably Fern, but an even sexier-looking Fern than normal, if that were possible; a Fern with that sort of vulnerable availability of women in a certain genre of Fifties movie the critics called *film noir*.

Before we set off again, I screwed false number plates over the car's original ones through tiny holes I always had specially drilled in my cars.

'I'm impressed,' she said.

'We're up against impressive enemies. They'll almost certainly have clocked my number back in Beckford. If we meet them again it won't be any good us looking different if the car doesn't.'

We drove on then to the beauty spot, and I walked alone to the village pub on the principle that if the bearded man did somehow home in and ask around, no one could say they'd seen a man and a woman together.

I brought back great sandwiches of salami and salad in long crusty rolls. We were both ravenous again, as if our bodies were crying out for replacement of all the mental and physical energy we'd expended since leaving the hotel.

I opened a bottle of cream soda. 'No alcohol, I'm afraid,' I said. 'Not until this lot's over.'

'I could *slaughter* a large gin. Clinking with ice and a slice of really fresh lemon floating on top. I can just see that bluish tinge . . .'

'Don't be sadistic . . .'

The only sounds were the trickling of a stream, bird-song, the distant chugging of a tractor. We ate in silence, perhaps both reminded of that other meal we'd had in the open, last night near Pickering, though neither, I felt, experiencing the same onslaught on our senses.

Perhaps the first hit was always the one that counted, in life as in drugs, perhaps we were never going to reach that pitch of emotion again, that powerful rush of shock and anger and fear. Nothing seemed to have changed – we were still running, people were still trying to kill us, we could see no clear way out of danger, and yet our reactions were altering, however imperceptibly. I'd had three attempts on my life, she two – it was as if it were becoming familiar, incredible as it seemed, as if we were almost getting used to it, and this was the way life was now.

There were noticeable changes in Fern. She'd had that deep metamorphosing sleep, had reinvented herself yet again to the point, it seemed, of heroine on the run. As though sensing it was the role of a lifetime, she seemed to be playing it for all she was worth. There'd been signs of it all morning – the eagerness in her face as we'd tracked down the Raingers, the alluring voice she'd produced to get the youths to bunch round us on the bridge, the intense almost sensual pleasure it had given her to draw the blonde wig over her hair. She'd gradually become the sparky gamine who'd run along station platforms with Robert Donat, had scrambled over a monument of a president's face with Cary Grant and escaped across the state line with Steve McQueen and a case stuffed with dollar bills.

I looked on with an uneasy mixture of admiration and alarm – she had so much energy and spirit, such an ability to bounce back, lived in that deceptively fragile-looking body with such confidence. She'd been almost blown up in a car, shot with an attaché-case gun, yet her life force still swept her on to what it now appeared to seem certain to her would be eventual safety.

I wished I could share that overwhelming optimism. I'd had a lot of excitement, lived life more intensely than ever before, I had to admit that, but I knew a lot more than she did about what Arendt had called the banality of evil. These men were out to kill us and it was simply a job of work. The fact that Fern was pretty and young and pretending to be Eva Marie Saint, and simply did not deserve to die, wouldn't register in their minds; they'd kill her as indifferently as they'd take a shower or eat a meal.

'I'm sorry,' I said. She glanced at me, about to thrust a large piece of roll into her mouth; her delicate way of eating had been abandoned since our rush to the coast. She raised her strangely pale eyebrows but did not speak. 'For getting you into this terrible business.'

She shrugged, smiled, went on eating for a few seconds more. 'It's not your fault. You didn't mean to involve me, I know that now.'

We sat side by side on my old car-blanket. She put an arm on my shoulder. 'And no one could possibly know more tricks for keeping us in one piece. My . . . sort of feel for things, and your brains, make us a hell of a team, kid.'

I had already sensed that the sheer fun she was beginning to get out of it all was partly based on her growing conviction that I could somehow get us out of any trouble, however great the odds. It was an over-whelming responsibility to add to all the other strains I was working under.

She said: 'What do we do now?'

'Take it easy for an hour, then go back to the Raingers' place and wait. That's what we should have done in the first place – laid low somewhere and gone back later. You were right. You were right about the beard too – it *was* us he was after, not Rainger.'

'But how could he know we were in Esk Head?'

I'd never stopped thinking about it in some part of my mind. 'Let's try this on the dog,' I said slowly. 'Let's say the beard and Fielding were coming to Esk Head anyway, that there's been some problem or crisis at the London end and they must contact Rainger. Only Rainger's not at home. So they come to find him.'

'But how did they know to come to Esk Head?'

'Because Rainger made no secret about having a place here. You people in the office knew about it, the Daisy Edgers would know about it, and so ten to one the mob would have known about it.'

'Why was the beard wandering about then? Why not go straight to the house?'

'Perhaps he didn't know the exact address. Maybe he thought Esk Head was so small they'd have no trouble finding it.'

'Do you think they'd *seen* the Raingers – before the bridge opened?'

'Impossible to be certain. The Raingers were leaving the bridge when the barriers came down. They were in a dense crowd and we could only see them because we knew what we were looking for. I really don't know. But clocking us took their minds off the Raingers, that's for sure. You're supposed to be dead and I'm supposed to be scared shitless. The way I read it the beard made an instant decision to put Rainger on ice till they'd seen to us.'

She no longer paled or trembled at the idea of sudden death. The renowned John Goss, with all the cool skill, clever thinking and iron fists of detectives in novels, would get her safely past every Moriarty going. She finished the last of her sandwich with obvious pleasure. 'What will they be doing now, those dreadful men?'

'They'll have looked for us for perhaps half an hour or so, and then the beard will have realised we're completely out of the picture. I think they'll have concentrated on the Raingers again, not so much searching the crowds as finding the house. If they'd known it they'd have gone straight to it, as you pointed out. Finding it won't be easy. I had *directions* and it wasn't easy. It's not even in Esk Head itself. The phone will be unlisted, Mrs Thing will do all the shopping and the only people who'll really know are the people at the Yacht Club, and they're not going to tell *anyone* where he lives, especially if they look as inviting as the beard. And with all the trippers about and the public offices shut . . . they couldn't have chosen a worse day.'

'Lucky for us . . .'

We sat in the clearing until a distant clock chiming across placid meadows told us our hour was up, an army of two that had retreated, refreshed itself and re-formed.

'It means an awful lot to you, doesn't it, nailing Rainger?' she said, as I folded the blanket and put the bags and empty bottles in a wire basket fastened to a tree.

I glanced at her warily, remembering her furious anger last night at the danger I'd placed her in; her inspired accuracy in guessing why I'd not gone to the police earlier.

She smiled. 'Don't look so defensive, I'm not cross any more. I know the country. It won't make any difference financially, and all you'll get from the police is a free ticket to the ball. I know about that too. There's a kind of . . . of purity of motive. We're very similar. I've spent a lot more on learning to act than I've ever got from acting jobs. Perhaps I'll *never* get anything out of

acting. But I'll never give in, even if the break doesn't come till I'm fifty and only good for character parts.' She took my hand in both of hers. 'John . . . we can't go our own way after all we've been through together. Come to London with me when this is all over and you've done what you have to do . . . we'd have such a lot of fun . . .'

The tenderness in her voice vied with the brash sexiness of the lipstick and wig, recalling again those potent-looking blondes in the old black-and-whites, who'd made so many promises to those tough men, street-sharp but insecure, who'd been so desperate to believe them.

But I wasn't insecure. Scratch the surface cynicism and there was another layer of cynicism, like the many coats of paint baked into a modern car. I knew she acted most of the time and I'd been advised that the best acting seemed to come at the point where she seemed most sincere.

But I was ready to go with her. I put my hand on her cheek. Even though I knew it all, knew she'd be sucked into her cliquy world, would use me for settling bills and sleep around as readily as she shook hands or kissed a cheek if she thought it might get her anywhere. But a lot of it would still be fun for two people who nursed the same hang-ups and weren't into relationships.

'Let's get through today,' I said, 'and then we'll talk about it. Yes?'

As I reached for the ignition, she said: 'Do you think blonde hair suits me, John? Perhaps I should give it a try. Not this bottled harlot stuff, of course, perhaps if I started with streaks . . .'

I drove cautiously along North Cliff, despite the

disguises, which had even extended as far as different-coloured T-shirts. We saw no sign of them, or of the Raingers.

The red-tiled houses across the harbour had had an almost Canaletto-like definition this morning; now, in the shimmering mid-afternoon heat, they had the hazy softness of an Impressionist print. The open sea had merged with the sky almost imperceptibly, two slightly different shades of what seemed to be the same faded blue vapour.

' "August for the people . . ." ' she said, in her soft, gliding voice. ' "Daily the steamers sidle up to meet the effusive welcome of the pier." ' She broke off, giggling. 'I once recited that at a reading in that illustrious seat of culture, Milton Keynes, would you believe.'

'Lucky old Milton Keynes . . .'

She put a hand on my thigh. What a day we could have had, drifting with the crowds, lunch-time drinks, walking hand in hand along the shore-line, showering together and making love in that quiet period between getting back to the hotel and going down to dinner.

Though even the day we'd had wasn't one we'd forget.

I nosed on to the coast road. It had become almost deserted, as few people were now going to the Regatta, and it was too early for many to be returning. When we came to the shady cinder track that led to the Rainger house, I kept on driving.

'There's a caravan site about half a mile on,' I said. 'I noticed it this morning. I'm going to leave the car there. I don't want Rainger to see it when he comes back, or anyone else for that matter.'

The site had a stretch of hard standing, and I left it positioned for a fast, easy getaway. I also gave Fern a set of keys in case of any eventuality I couldn't at this stage foresee. We then returned to the house as unobtrusively as possible by walking through fields behind the dry-stone wall that fronted to the road.

The house seemed deserted, but I made a careful check, glancing in through downstairs windows. It had been built into a slope of the land, and the rear door was a good way above ground and reached by a flight of stone steps from a tiled patio area. That and the front door were the only ways in or out.

I finally returned to Fern, where she waited behind a tree in the dense copse that stood above the garden and screened the house from the road. I wondered if the bearded man could possibly find it without help, assuming that he was in fact looking for Rainger.

We waited then, sitting with our backs to the tree. We were very early. The housekeeper had said they'd not return before six, but they might have had enough before then, and I wanted to be on the safe side. We were both, because of our occupations, accustomed to waiting around, had developed an ability to relax our bodies and retain energy, and were very still as shadows lengthened across close-cut turf, birds whistled in the echoing silence and a distant tide endlessly turned. The peace was broken only once, by the Red Arrows display team skimming along the coastline or spiralling into the cloudless sky and releasing their plumes of multi-coloured vapour. That would be the Regatta's high point.

We barely spoke for the best part of an hour. The things I needed to say to Rainger spooled through my mind like a continuous tape.

But Fern had a reflective look I'd not seen before, her

face unusually impassive. I had an impression that now we were almost at the point of seeing Rainger she faced it with mixed feelings. There was an oddness in coming up against a man she worked for in such strange circumstances, of course, but there was also the fact that she'd always intensely disliked him, and I'd thought it might have given her a certain satisfaction to see his shock and embarrassment at the news I'd be delivering.

But her reaction to the fact of his criminal life had always been difficult to interpret. She had scarcely commented on it, and by not doing so had given an impression of indifference, despite it being at the bottom of everything that had happened to us; indifference, that is, to the criminality itself. There had also been that faint, disturbing admiration I felt I'd detected for a man who'd made a great deal of crooked money, and, up to now, got away with it.

These thoughts were abruptly broken off by the arrival of a car; the barely perceptible throb of costly engineering and the crunch of tyres over cinder.

Twenty-One

The Mercedes prowled past us, where we crouched behind rhododendron bushes, and purred down the tarmacadam drive at the side of the long sloping lawn and into the carport. We watched them get out – he in cap and blazer, she in the white designer dress – and enter the house.

We gave them five minutes. We'd removed our wigs just before leaving the caravan site. We walked quickly and quietly down the drive, and I pressed the doorbell. After a pause, a lengthy one, there were finally footsteps on the tiling of the porch and we saw a diminutive blur of white through frosted glass. Mrs Rainger opened the door.

Her eyes widened fractionally. After a second's hesitation, she said: 'Mr Goss . . . and Miss Dumont, I believe.' She had the socialite's trained memory. She must have been astonished to see us, but the breeding ensured she kept it to herself.

'I must see your husband,' I said. '*Now.*'

She watched me impassively. The last time I'd met her it was to tell her her husband was a criminal. It rather looked, from the leisurely day they'd spent, that she'd neither really believed it nor done anything about it. I'd always suspected, on the rare occasions I was being honest with myself, that that would be the case.

She had, it seemed, ignored it, as if by doing so it would eventually clear up, like a heavy cold. And behind that calm exterior, I sensed she was in a quandary. My trailing them to the holiday home had to be bad news, something which could only threaten serious disruption to that life of well-ordered luxury and comfort.

'Mr Goss . . .'

'I've *got* to see him. I know he's in there. You're in danger. We all are. And every second counts, believe me . . .'

Again she was silent. But this time I seemed to catch an almost subliminal glimpse of the desperate unhappiness I'd seen in her eyes on that day of ceaseless clattering rain when she'd pleaded with me to go on with the case.

'You'd better come in,' she said, with extreme reluctance.

She led us across the porch and into the hall. Rainger was standing there, in shirt-sleeves, he'd obviously been there since the chiming of the doorbell. He looked wary and alert, but if he was uneasy, or even scared, he didn't show it.

He watched me in silence as his wife brought us to the middle of the hall. I'd seen him many times, but always at a distance; close to I realised for the first time that he was not simply good-looking, with his dark-gold hair, regular features and compact muscular figure, he had genuine presence, gave off an almost palpable air of something I can only call domination. It came as a shock after two weeks of assuring myself he was both spoilt and easily led, a Flash-Harry. His eyes never left mine, did

302

not waver, or blink; he looked like a man trawling his memory to see if he could find my face. I felt that memory would be as comprehensive as a data-bank.

He then took his eyes from mine, to glance for the first time at Fern, who'd fallen behind me as we entered the hall.

And that look released more powerful forces than I'd ever known in a group of people. The effect was almost tangible, like displaced air. It was a moment of knowledge and shock of the sort that meant that nothing from then on, in our varying relationships, would ever be the same. It was a bizarre irrelevance to the danger we were in and had all the banal absurdity of life itself, like a condemned man spending his last night distracted by a raging toothache.

'*Fernande* . . .'

He spoke just that one word, but it was a word that said everything, that and the uneasy tone he said it in – and the involuntary glance he gave his wife.

I could only admire the way he caught himself in mid-air. 'What a *surprise*!' he said, in the hearty tone I remembered from La Rasade. 'Fernande! Fiona, this young lady is our receptionist at Brit-Chem. Whatever brings you here, my dear, and your friend . . .?'

He papered over the cracks like a cabinet minister on the *Today* programme, but the fissures ran deep and wide. His wife and I looked at each other; in my look there was rueful commiseration, in hers a blankness that almost certainly concealed great pain.

It all came together. It was like one of those dialogue games that seem to make no real sense unless you're in possession of a key word or phrase. And now I had it, the single link that connected many chains. Mrs

Rainger's utter certainty there was another woman, Fern's total contempt, in the early days, whenever Rainger's name was mentioned, her knowledge, in darkness, of the cinder track that led to his holiday home. It explained too that most puzzling of all incidents – the bombing of Fern's car. They'd not bombed it simply because she worked at Brit-Chem and was seeing me, but because they suspected, possibly with good reason, that she *had* to know too much.

They'd bombed it because she and Rainger had been lovers.

I wondered how long she'd known about the heroin. My eyes went reluctantly back to her. She was looking steadily at Rainger with a smile so hard, so filled with distilled hatred, that I understood now about the pensiveness out in the copse – it had been gloating anticipation of the sheer bitchy pleasure she was going to get when ex-mistress met neurotic wife in front of hapless husband.

'We need to talk, Rainger,' I said, with a curtness I'd not intended. 'For a long time.'

'Well, well,' he said, 'I don't know what it's all about, but it had better not be *too* long – we have a dinner engagement – come through and have a drink.'

His eyes never lost their watchfulness behind the breezy charm. He led us to the drawing-room. It was almost as large and airy as the one in Daisy Edge, and though the furniture wasn't in quite the same exquisite class it was still very good – a bureau bookcase, a drum-table, solid wing chairs, oil-paintings of sailing ships, a broad-based ship's decanter and crystal glasses on a silver tray.

'Gin all right?' he said. 'Do sit down.'

We all moved to separate chairs. There was a sofa, but at that stage none of us wanted to sit with anyone else.

'Don't sit on that one, old chap,' he said. 'It's dicky. When one leans back it tends to fly over too far. I'd have it seen to, but we never use it. It was my father's, rest his soul, its value is purely sentimental.'

I sat elsewhere. I found it out of character but oddly. endearing that he should keep a valueless and unattractive rocking-chair in memory of his father. I'd kept my father's favourite chair too, and it was unlikely a dealer would have given me fifty pence for it.

He brought the gin. I remembered how Fern and I had longed for just such a drink at lunch-time; now they were before us we were indifferent.

'Well . . . tell me what your problem is, Mr . . .?'

'Goss. John Goss.'

'Go ahead . . .'

'I'm a private investigator. Your wife hired me to see if you were involved with another woman . . .' He glanced sharply at his wife, but she stayed in her own world, staring straight ahead. 'I could find no evidence of another woman, but I did find out about the heroin. *Everything* about the heroin.'

Silence gathered in the old room, filled with the slanting rays of the late-afternoon sun, the only sounds the ticking of a long-case clock and the snapping of ice in our tumblers.

'You'd . . . better go on,' he said at last.

I talked for ten minutes, summarising and telescoping the events of the days following my first visit to the house on The Hill. He listened with great concentration, occasionally resting his blue eyes unwaveringly on mine, sometimes looking slowly, and with an obvious effort, towards his wife.

She sat, small and dainty, looking now sidelong at Fern, with an almost wondering expression on her smooth olive-tinted face. Her gin, like ours, stood untouched. Fern herself went on watching Rainger with the same smile of what seemed almost malevolent glee at the separate loads of trouble we'd contrived to dump on him.

'That's about it,' I said. 'I don't think there's much point in denying it, do you?'

He watched me for some time in silence. 'What's your angle,' he said at last, 'blackmail?'

'I just want to go on living,' I said. 'It's as simple as that.' He didn't speak so I went on. 'Do you know a man with red hair and a beard? Stocky, about five-nine, drives an old brown Range Rover.'

He thought carefully, then shook his head. I had to assume he was being truthful – if he wasn't it threw another set of pieces in the air. I thought rapidly back over the surmises I'd talked through with Fern. The bearded man and Fielding couldn't possibly have known that Fern and I had made for Esk Head, therefore they must have come specially to search out Rainger. But Rainger denied knowledge of the man who was clearly in charge.

'He knows you,' I said. 'He knows you very well. He's roaming round Esk Head with your side-kick, Fielding.' I hesitated. 'You . . . wouldn't by any chance have been skimming, would you?'

He shrugged, seemed about to shake his head, then gave a faint sheepish smile. It provided the rest of the answers.

'They're after you then,' I said bluntly. 'They're heavily armed, and if they find you they'll kill you because they can't let a skimmer go free, otherwise they'd all be at it. And frankly I couldn't give a toss except that the beard now thinks Fern and I know too much about you, and they've tried killing us to be on the safe side. Parcel-bombs, exploding cars, machine-guns – you name it, they've thrown it at us.'

More silence. Rainger picked up his gin and sat looking at it. He could have poured glasses of tap-water for all anyone wanted to drink. Mrs Rainger continued looking at Fern with brooding eyes.

She took some beating for inappropriate emotions. Had she not engaged me to spy on her husband, Fern and I wouldn't have been exposed to all this danger. It wasn't her fault, but our involvement with them had cost us dear, and a little concern for what we'd had to go through wouldn't have come amiss. But she ran completely true to form. All she could think of now, as always, was where Rainger had been flying his zeppelin.

And I knew then what I'd suspected for some time. That apart from being spoilt, self-centred, humourless and neurotic, she was also unbalanced.

Rainger suddenly said: 'Fiona . . .' and then dragging the rest of the words out with an effort, went on '. . . I'm sorry about all this. It's . . . it's true. I've been a fool. I've always liked the goodies too much, and they cost an awful lot of money. More than I could ever earn at Brit-Chem . . .'

She turned slowly away from Fern at last, like a woman sedated on tranquillisers, and looked over at her husband. 'I thought you were a man of honour, Miles,' she said in a low voice.

The phrase had that fine, absurd, *fin-de-siècle* ring to it that could only have sounded right coming from her lips. But as usual, in her inverted scale of values, it was clear she considered the rogering to have dishonoured him, not the lives he'd helped to wreck in heroin dealing. You got used to it.

My eyes met his. There seemed in his some shadow of the exasperation I felt. With the sort of trouble he was in now, such as the possibilities of torture or death, or losing his job and his place in local society at the very least, leg-over came at the end of a sizeable queue.

'If you're not blackmailing me,' he said, 'what *are* you aiming to do?'

'Talk some sense into you.' He watched and waited. 'First, you've *got* to understand we're all in the gravest danger, and time's running short. We can't afford to stay here much longer. The beard knows you have a place here, but he obviously doesn't know where. But they'll be asking around at the best hotel bars, and sooner or later someone will connect you with this house. They'll be keen to do the business here because if you get back to Beckford it's going to be a lot more difficult with your high profile.'

He gave a slight nod, as if he accepted my summary of the situation.

I went on: 'I . . . have a personal friend in the Beckford police. I can talk to him. I'm positive they'd deal . . .'

I let the words hang in the air to try and estimate his reaction. He gave nothing away. Eyes steadily on mine, he said: 'Are we talking plea-bargaining here?'

'You must be in a position to name some fancy names.'

'They'd let me go?'

I shook my head. 'That's a popular myth. You'd have to do your time. But it wouldn't be a lot of time, and if it were a really valuable list and your life would be endangered, they'd give you and Mrs Rainger a new ID.'

He abruptly shook his head. 'I can't do that, John. I can't go inside. I've been a fool and I accept it. More than a fool – God knows I never realised what a filthy business I'd got into. It hasn't been too easy to live with myself a lot of the time. But I can't do bird.'

I watched him. I'd been contemptuous of him all along, because of the dressiness, the Flash-Harry ways, what I'd considered to be his monumental conceit. But I couldn't suppress a sneaking regard for him. His realism was impressive. No bluster, no lying, no self-justification – simply a trained business mind rapidly accepting the inevitable and trying to decide the next step.

'What choice have you *got* . . . Miles?' I said. 'You've had your hand in the till and they'll kill you. You might keep ahead for a few weeks, but they'll get you in the end.'

'We could give ourselves new IDs.'

'Not like the police. They can spirit you away and change everything except your fingerprints. Go it alone and you'll have to mix with some very dodgy characters to get new documents and plastic surgery, and they'll take your money and then sell you out. And whichever way you slice it your old life is finished – Daisy Edge, this place, yachts, staff . . .'

Silence fell yet again. Mrs Rainger brooded, Fern smiled her ghastly smile. It sickened me, the intense pleasure she was getting from his downfall, even if he deserved it. He must have hurt her very badly. And yet she knew the world of high-voltage men, must have been aware of how easily they moved from one affair to the next and understood the ground rules. Hadn't she played exactly the same game herself, contriving to be seen around London with men just like Rainger, though well-known, so that she might become well-known too to the sort of people who produced plays and films?

But those men – the London men – would be scrupulously careful to make no promises, to offer nothing they might later not wish to deliver. What you saw would be what you got – lavish hospitality at the best night-spots, on the clear understanding that imaginative sexual favours would be granted in return.

Had Rainger not followed that careful code, one that he, of all men, must have had a feel for? Had he taken the favours and reneged on his side of the deal, whatever that had been considered to be? It seemed a strong possibility in a man who could become a criminal and then short-change the criminals.

Rainger was looking around him as if he always wanted to remember this charming old room at its sunlit best.

'I can't face prison,' he said decisively. 'I'd rather take my chances . . .'

'There aren't any to take. *And* you owe us – Fern and me. The heat won't go off us till you're with the police. Once they know you've blown the whistle they'll not bother trying to kill us. No point.'

'Look . . . John . . .'

'You'll get a fairly nominal sentence . . .'

'How nominal is fairly nominal?'

I shrugged. 'I can't say, to be honest. Maybe five – half that with good behaviour. You'd be safe and they'd take care of your wife. You'll lose a great deal, but you're a good businessman, and you'll make a new start. You'll not live like this again, but it'll be a lot better than being dead.'

He thought for some time, time we couldn't spare, behind a face impossible to read. It would be the sort of face he'd have when trying to decide what fancy package of credit terms would help him swing a tough deal. My skin seemed to crawl with frustration. We couldn't leave the house till I'd talked him into going to the police, and I'd given myself a bare hour to wrap it up. There were ten minutes left of that hour. I could not rid my mind of an image of the bearded man doggedly walking the streets of the fishing village, with that dreadful absurdity of an attaché-case hanging from his hand, ready to kill us all as a convenient job-lot. It only needed some barman somewhere, with a knowledge of the area, to connect dressy Rainger with the poshest holiday home on the coast. The bearded man would have sent Fielding to do the asking, because he looked so respectable.

'No deal, John. I'm sorry. We'll take our chances.'

'And condemn us to death?'

'It won't come to that. Now this is what we do,' he said briskly. 'We'll go now. Your car's not in the drive so I assume you've got it hidden somewhere. We'll take you in our car to where yours is, and I'll make sure you get to Esk Head safely.' He smiled grimly. 'They're not the only ones with guns. If we see any sign of them I'll draw their attention while you make for the moor road. When you reach Beckford see your police friend and tell him everything. By then Fiona and I will be a hundred miles off. I . . . have a contingency fund for something like this. You'll be safe. My people – the heroin lot – will know inside twenty-four hours that I've done a runner and they'll not bother about you any more. Believe me. Their greatest worry, as you correctly surmised, was that you and Fern might get me to a police station. This way, all the police will get is Fielding and a couple of Pakistani dead-eyes, and *they* don't know enough to shop the organisation's pet cat. You *will* be safe, John, you must know they'll not waste any more time and money trying to eliminate you two when I've disappeared and, by inference, have no intention of grassing.'

I could see him in a conference-room, incisively cutting through waffle, telling colleagues exactly how next year's business-plan would be achieved. I wondered if any of them had felt as agitated as I did at failing to talk him into anything he'd set his mind against.

I got up and walked distractedly about the room. Acid seemed to be burning holes in the lining of my stomach. Everything had gone wrong. How *could* the bastard expose us to such danger, danger I was certain would never end while he was on the loose, two people who, for all our separate brands of foolishness, had been drawn into this mess by pure chance? How could I go to Fenlon with such a half-baked story, that I knew who the Beckford connection was, but unfortunately he'd done a runner because I hadn't told the police soon enough?

I halted in front of a stone-mullioned window that looked out over the peaceful sloping lawn, my cheeks suddenly flushing with guilt. The danger had nothing to do with my frustration, and I knew it. It was because I'd set my heart, if not my soul, on delivering Rainger to the Beckford police, ready to tell them everything he knew. It was a goal I'd never lost sight of from the moment I'd realised what was in those packages. Only I'd never bargained on dealing with a Rainger who had such confidence, such presence. He'd been typecast in my mind as a middle-aged spoilt brat, a man I'd be able to browbeat into doing things my way, and it was like trying to kick a steel door open with slippers on.

'You'll *never* be free,' I said agitatedly, so angry with him I simply wanted to rub his nose in the mess his future life would become. 'They'll not let you go because it would look too easy to anyone else who had the same idea. The beard will follow you to Mongolia, I *know* that swine now. The only freedom you could *ever* know is by going inside, because when you came out it wouldn't be you any more. I bet you've forgotten what that kind of freedom's like, Miles, haven't you, since they bought your soul?'

I turned on him, hot, furious, glaring. I had expected nothing but indifference, polite contempt, perhaps even a faint smile at my outburst. He'd made up his mind and that was that, decisive men didn't vacillate. But I saw none of those things. Somehow I seemed to have said something that had pierced the almost impenetrable armour of his total self-confidence. It had been like fiddling about with a combination-lock and suddenly, by a fluke, getting the numbers in the right order. His face changed even as I stared at him, the watchfulness seeming to leave it, giving it an appearance of boyish, almost urchin friendliness. I could see then why he got on so well with men and seemed so fatally attractive to women. He wasn't so much an evil man as a rogue. The main emotion in his face was profound relief, and I knew that the key word had been 'freedom'. I knew, too, with equal certainty, as he glanced at his wife, the double interpretation he was putting on it. She'd brought valuable assets of her own to his life in terms of social contacts, in the unerring taste she'd shown in turning him into the sort of man who fished and shot and knew the best wine to serve with game that had reached the correct level of decomposition. But the price had been high.

It wasn't simply freedom from the heavy gang, it was freedom from her. After all, if the life-style had to go there was no point in spending the rest of his life with a neurotic bitch.

Her eyes never left his face. He was the only human being in the world she really cared about, and it seemed as if she must be as sensitive to his reactions as he was himself. I could understand any man wanting to free himself of possessiveness on that scale. But then, I would.

'You know, John,' Rainger said at length, 'you really hit a nerve then. I *hadn't* stopped to think how controlled I'd become. And you're quite right – they never will stop searching. I'll never be free of them. You know, I think I might, I think I just might, consider playing it your way.'

There was a small crash. In her sudden agitation, Mrs Rainger had knocked over her glass. The gin flowed across the polished walnut of the sofa-table and would bloom the surface if not quickly mopped up. But that no longer mattered.

'You can't,' she said in a strangled voice. 'You can't, Miles, you can't, you *can't*!'

He looked at her with what seemed to be genuine contrition, though I wasn't entirely convinced.

'Fi . . . I can't tell you how sorry I am about this. There's not even time to talk about it now. We've got to get back to Beckford. There'll be time to talk it through later. We'll make a new life somewhere. I'll work hard, you'll see . . .'

A voice said: 'I wouldn't count on it, Miles, not now.'

We swung round. Fielding stood just inside the door, which had been ajar. He held a gun.

Twenty-Two

We all sat very still. The anger I felt seemed mirrored in Rainger's face. The front door had been left unlocked. Rainger's lips moved as if he were whispering curses. How could two men so cautious have overlooked something so vital?

Fielding edged into the room. He seemed alone. All he'd had to do was turn the knob and walk in. It went back to those moments of shock and truth when the four of us had come together in the hall. Mrs Rainger had been the last into the drawing-room, perhaps Rainger in his confusion had assumed she'd secure the lock, perhaps she in hers had left it to the housekeeper, forgetting that here the woman worked only mornings.

Fielding said quietly: 'Put your hands on your heads.'

'Laurence!' Rainger began, in a tone of bright enquiry. 'What on *earth* . . .?'

'Shove it, Miles. You know why I'm here. You're the best talker in Beckford, but no one's listening any more.'

'Laurence, whatever can you be on about? Do put that ridiculous weapon away. I thought we were friends as well as . . . colleagues.'

'Yes, well, they don't like your top-slicing habits. They're very funny about top-slicing in the Smoke.'

'Me, Laurence, *me* – get a hand in the till? You can't be serious. I know them better than you do, *know* what the penalty would be.'

I could only admire the remarkable acting talent. It was almost in the Fern class; perhaps it was one of the things that had attracted her to him. He must have been as scared as the rest of us – fear seemed to hang in the air like body odour – but the expression of puzzled innocence was flawless. It was what Hemingway had defined as grace under pressure.

'They did a test package,' the other said. 'They gave me it, and they watched me and it every inch of the way till it was in your Merc. So stop pratting about.'

Rainger duly stopped. 'What'll buy me off the hook?' he said, switching from one track to the next as effortlessly as an InterCity crossing points. 'If I were to give them a refund? If I were to work free for six months? Surely they'll deal. You could be my broker.' He acted a suave chuckle. 'I was going to say honest broker, but perhaps in this context that wouldn't be the most felicitous word.'

'You couldn't buy out if you were God,' the other said simply. 'I don't need to tell *you* that.'

'You wouldn't let me down, Laurence,' Rainger said, in a warm vibrant voice. 'You and I, we're a team, we're *friends* . . .'

'There's no friend in the world I'd risk getting topped for.'

'Laurence, *surely* we can . . .'

'There's a guy out there called Red Harris,' the other cut him off. 'He's something else, believe it. He works for all the firms, and he has one job – seeing to people like you. Bent – he could change you an eight-pound

318

note for two fours. You've no way out. He's rung the Smoke, because he was pretty sure the gumshoe would have got to you, and the Smoke's sending some local talent in from Leeds just to be on the safe side. So he's out there and I'm in here till they clock on. I've locked the mortices on the back door and thrown the keys through the window. I suppose you could try jumping from a back window if you wanted to break your leg, with that slope the land's got. So even if you jumped *me* there's only one way out and that's through the front of the house. And if Red sees anyone coming out of anywhere at the front, anyone who doesn't look exactly like me, he'll start blasting. He asked me to explain that to you very carefully.'

We sat with our hands on our heads, the faces of the women clenched and white with fear, their lips trembling. My own fear was still in place too, but like Rainger I was forcing myself to keep calm enough to work through possibilities. There didn't seem to be any. Rainger had done a first-class job, but the strain was beginning to show. I could see knuckles gleaming on the hands clasped over his dark-gold hair.

He faced certain death, and it wouldn't be quick or clean; we both knew this wasn't a simple matter of a pusher trading on the wrong end of the street, who could be quietly eliminated; this was the criminal world's equivalent of corporate fraud. They'd take him south and they'd gather a few of the men together who were Rainger's equivalent in other areas, and they'd make them look on while Rainger was ferociously beaten and then killed, to make quite certain they passed on to their contacts that death was finally the best thing that could happen to a skimmer.

As for me and the women, there were no possibilities here, only the one stark certainty. It would be the attaché-case machine-gun and the house doused in petrol and torched, and no forensic department in the country would ever come up with anything that would lead to the real truth.

I tried to force my mind on to more constructive thinking, while trying to look as insouciant as Rainger. It was a small thing, but two men looking confident and relaxed when they should have looked tense and nervous could only unsettle a man like Fielding, who'd almost certainly been forced to play a part he'd not wanted or expected. He stood, covering us with the pistol, trying without success to conceal his own uneasiness, that almost permanent expression of worry on his face deepening the lines to corrugations. He was a clean-cut looking man, probably in his early thirties, of middle height and with a slender, wiry build, and long, rather coarse fair hair. In the four or five times I'd kept tabs on him, I'd never seen anything in his face except the near-anxiety that seemed to be rapidly lending it an appearance of premature middle age. I gave him a warm, friendly smile.

He began slowly sidling across the room, behind our chairs. As he drew near the rocking-chair, Rainger said casually: 'I'd not sit there, old son, it has a habit of folding up on you. You'll find it safer on the sofa.'

'Do me a favour, Miles,' he said, almost petulantly. 'If you're recommending the couch it's because you want me there. So I'll have you and the gumshoe on each side of me. You must think I fell off a Christmas tree.'

He hovered near the rocker which, from its corner position, provided the best over-all cover. I could sense

Rainger, like me, willing him to sit on it. It was of the type suspended on two sleepers and didn't look at all unsafe.

I had renewed admiration for Rainger's chess-match brain. He'd advised Fielding against the chair as solicitously as he'd advised me against it, and even at a time like this, with an executioner at the gate, the words had seemed natural and unforced, appearing to display the instinctive concern of the perennial host. I could sense Fielding's increasing agitation at the seriously inappropriate signals he seemed to be receiving. Why weren't we sitting pale and strained, and speaking in voices not fully under control; why were we so friendly and relaxed; what secret messages were we passing to each other? The man's nervous disposition was proving to be one of Rainger's most valuable assets.

The subtlest aspect of the ploy had been the way he'd delicately implanted in Fielding's mind the idea that if it was to be a long wait it would be nice to take the weight off his feet. In two brilliant double-bluffing sentences, Rainger had tempted him to relax, and ensured that if he did, it would be in the worst possible place.

Time passed. I don't suppose it was much, perhaps only as long as it took an electric kettle to boil, but a little seems a lot when you have a mental picture of violent men speeding across North Yorkshire to give a killer a helping hand with his killing.

Rainger crossed one leg gracefully over the other and sank back luxuriously into his wing-chair. Fielding looked on with what seemed like weary envy. He'd almost certainly spent most of the day on his feet, in heat that had been almost sub-tropical.

More time passed. Shadows inched across the Chinese

hearthrug. The clock ponderously ticked, the swing of its pendulum seeming to grow like the blows of a hammer in the deep silence. All at once, I saw Fielding's foot begin to push one of the sleepers so that the rocker faced our group more squarely on. It wasn't easy trying to control the sound of my exhaling breath at the partial release of tension. Fielding lowered himself with a faint contemptuous smile at Rainger – no one was going to tell *him* where to sit.

Nothing happened. But then I remembered that nothing would so long as he didn't lean back. I looked on, trying to control my dismay behind the cheery smile. It rather looked as if actually sitting down was the only indulgence he was prepared to allow himself. He perched carefully at the end of the seat, gun-hand on arm-rest.

'Laurence . . .'

'Save it, Miles . . .'

'A drink, old son. You can't deny us a noggin at a time like this. Just put the gin on the table and one at a time . . .'

'From the state of your glasses it looks as if you've all got plenty to drink, assuming I'd let you take your hands off your heads. And the lady doesn't even seem to want hers because she's thrown it all over this nice antique table.'

Fielding was guardedly amusing himself for the first time, probably to relieve the strain. His voice had taken on what I assumed he imagined to be the silky yet menacing tone of the super-villain in some opulent underground suite, who was allowing himself a few minutes' pleasure toying with a captive James Bond.

'I was just about to refill the lady's glass when you

joined us so unexpectedly. It was an accident. And the others need sweetening, fresh ice . . .'

'Dear me, we shouldn't expect a lady to sit with an empty glass, should we. And yet, much as I trust you, Miles, I can't get rid of the sneaking suspicion that while you were seeing to her drink, and I was watching you, the gumshoe might *just* feel tempted to think he was in with a chance.'

'A cigarette, then. There are some in that box on the table a little to the rear of you on the left-hand side.'

'Yes . . . put the box on the centre table, would you. You can't expect us simply to *sit* here, man, without a decent drink or a cigarette.'

It was Fern. She spoke in a perfect upper-middle-class accent, the words seeming almost separately chiselled in their rapid, precise delivery. It was the formidable voice of assured breeding and wealth, the voice that got scurrying attention in dining-rooms and reception areas. It had the edge even on Mrs Rainger's.

It threw Fielding. He was so startled for a moment that he seemed to half-reach for the onyx box on a reflex. Then he stopped himself, suddenly brandishing the pistol.

'Shut up!' he shouted. 'Shut up, all of you. I'm not your bloody servant!'

His Charles Gray impression was quite gone now, beneath the onslaught of signals that had almost undermined him. He was badly rattled. I gave Fern an admiring glance. It must have been obvious to a born actor within seconds that Rainger and I were hamming up an appearance of being completely at ease. So she'd joined in, because that's what actors did. She'd been very frightened, but actors knew how to control that too, the fear of facing a live audience.

And Rainger's inventiveness seemed boundless. Neither Fern nor I smoked. I'd never seen Mrs Rainger smoke, and if he himself had been a smoker he'd certainly have smoked this evening. Which meant that only Fielding liked a drag, and Rainger was pointing him to where the cigarettes were, skilfully abetted by Fern, who might not have guessed what Rainger was up to, but had sensed that her own haughty two-penn'orth could only add to Fielding's disorientation.

Fielding's hand trembled ever so slightly on the pistol. If he was a smoker the effect we were having on his nerves must mean he was now craving for tobacco. Rainger had probably deduced that his own cigarettes would most likely be in his right-hand jacket pocket, not easy to get at without transferring the gun to his left hand and taking the risk of being overpowered.

He glanced peripherally at the occasional table behind him, with its gleaming onyx box, a sight that must have been as tempting as a box of continental centres to a chocoholic. Then he looked stolidly back at us. A minute passed – it felt like five. And then, in a tide of relief from Rainger and me that seemed almost tangible, he began to feel out with his free hand towards the table, his body moving almost imperceptibly backwards on the rocker.

The chair suddenly snapped back like a mousetrap being sprung. In the same instant that the gun fired wildly, smashing an overhead globe, Rainger, with a single bound, was standing above Fielding and chopping down at his wrist with a hand that looked as stiff and hard as the edge of a spade. Fielding shrieked with pain and a second later was doubled over, holding his wrist to his chest, and the gun was in Rainger's hand.

'Well, Laurence,' he said mildly, 'I did warn you about that chair, old son, but you seemed to think you knew best.'

I wanted to laugh hysterically at the delicious irony of his words, and the overwhelming relief I felt that Rainger was now in command, but the wretched figure Fielding cut stopped me. His eyes were filled with tears of pain and he began to whimper. Sending a man like Fielding into a room with Rainger had been like matching a spaniel with a pit-bull terrier.

Rainger said: 'Right, John, action-stations.'

I looked at him with an admiration I didn't attempt to conceal. 'I've never seen anything like it.'

He gave me his urchin grin. 'They say as you go through life you only use a fraction of your brain-cells. Well, that's only true if you're not involved with this lot. Do you know about these?'

He handed me the pistol. I looked it over, snapping the magazine out and back. It was fully loaded apart from the single round that had shattered the light-fitting. I said: 'I'm beginning to wonder how Heckler and Koch got along without them.'

He laughed briefly. 'Keep Laurence covered. I'll not be long.'

I glanced at Fern and Mrs Rainger. The older woman looked drained by the reaction to tension and fear, but Fern was flushed and triumphant as she gazed with shining eyes at the whimpering Fielding, as if the curtain had just gone down on a production in which the cameo role she'd played had been, none the less, crucial to its complete success. Her hatred of Rainger apparently sidelined, she seemed back in her old favourite role of

Girl on the Run, to whom nothing really serious was ever going to happen despite a few fun-fair shocks along the way.

Rainger returned, almost jauntily, carrying a shotgun. He'd changed into pants and a jerkin and a thin crew-neck sweater – travelling clothes. The blazer, shirt and white trousers hung over his arm.

'Laurence,' he said, 'I'd like you to strip down to your underclothes, old son.'

Fielding looked up slowly from nursing his swollen wrist, his cheeks still wet with tears. He wore an old brown-checked sports jacket, grey flannels and a cream shirt open at the collar, and he glanced from these clothes to those on Rainger's arm. He couldn't make the connection. I thought I did, but was too appalled at the idea to believe that Rainger could have come up with something so monstrous.

'What's going on, Miles?' I said uneasily.

'Exactly what you think. The ginger bastard starts shooting the moment anyone appears at the front of the house who doesn't look like Laurence. So we send Laurence out through the door looking like me. He's about my height, and with the white cap and blazer in the fading light . . .'

'You can't do that! That's murder. That's cold-blooded murder!'

Rainger shook his head wonderingly. 'John, what do you think they'd do to *us*? For God's sake, man, you and I *know* what we're dealing with. Do you seriously believe Laurence would be alive now if I hadn't got a date with the Bill? *I* can't afford to see to him – there'll be enough on my charge-sheet without homicide. So it'll have to be done by proxy.'

'I can't believe I'm hearing this . . .'

'It gives him a chance,' Rainger said in a reasonable tone. 'Don't you see? When he goes through that door he's got about two seconds to get it across to his pal that he's not really me. That's good odds, the sort of mess he's in.'

'If he goes through that door and lives that makes it *worse*. That means he's back with them making it harder for us.'

'That doesn't worry me. They're out there and we're in here. We need only shoot in self-defence, and this shotgun's fully licensed, so the law will take a lenient view. Meanwhile we phone the Esk Head fuzz . . .'

'You can't imagine the phone-line's still intact . . .'

He hesitated for a fraction of a second. 'Dear me,' he said, with a faint smile, 'where are my brains. It'll have to be distress rockets, I've got a boxful in the cellar. They'll be round here in minutes . . .'

'On Regatta night? With the fireworks due to start on South Cliff after dark?'

He smiled again, wryly this time. 'Ah . . . the fireworks. What a mind for detail you've got, John. No wonder you managed to find out so much about Laurence and me.'

'Fielding goes with us, Miles. We'll all go out the back way. We'll prise the door open somehow. I suppose there's some kind of a track down to the beach, yes . . .?' Finally, reluctantly, he nodded. 'From the beach we get back to the road by one of the paths further along. My car's at the caravan site. We'll all go back to Beckford in that.'

Rainger said: 'If you insist, but let me assure you Laurence will be a big risk. He's not without a certain low cunning for all the unlikely figure he cuts. He could give us the slip, expose our position, slow us down . . . you can imagine how ecstatic he'll be about helping the police with their enquiries.'

I glanced at Fielding, who'd finally managed to extract a cigarette from the box that had caused all the trouble, yelping slightly whenever he had to use his swollen hand. I picked up a table lighter and held it to his cigarette. The end glowed almost incandescent as he sucked in smoke by the great, urgent mouthful.

I said: 'We'll just have to take a chance, Miles.'

'Right you are,' he said briskly. 'Let's get moving then . . .' There was something intensely refreshing about his decisiveness, even in accepting lost arguments.

Fielding suddenly began to speak, through clouds of exhaled smoke. 'I . . . want to go out the front door,' he said. 'Give me your gear, Miles.'

We all stared at him.

'You can't be serious,' I said. 'That maniac missed me by an inch this morning.'

He said: 'If I go with you you'll have to carry me out. I mean that.'

I glanced at Rainger. He smiled faintly, shrugged. I looked back at the hunched Fielding. Going back with us would mean he'd be tarred with the Rainger brush. But, unlike him, because he was small change, he'd be in no position for fancy dealing. And the police, still brooding about having to trade leniency for names with Rainger, would throw the book at Fielding to make up. They were like that. I respected them, I got on with them, I'd wanted to be one of them, but I had no illusions.

Fielding sensed all this. And he was a young man. He saw some of the best years of his life go in being banged up, with the sort of woman he'd almost certainly have married gone in the first month, a record, and the heroin men scarcely able to remember his face.

And he preferred to take a chance.

He'd smoked the cigarette down to the butt. He stubbed it out. I gave him a new one and a light.

'Come with us, Laurence,' I said in a low voice. 'I have a friend in the police. I'll do everything I can to get him to give you an easy ride.'

He looked up at me with an almost pleading expression in eyes that were still moist, as if he desperately wanted to believe me, but had been tricked so astutely it was almost beyond him. This would simply be another trick, like pretending to be unconcerned when he had us covered, like demanding the cigarette box in that haughty voice.

'John . . .' Rainger said urgently. 'Time's running out. You yourself wanted us to be away half an hour ago at least . . .'

'Look, Laurence,' I said quickly, 'I won't pretend it's going to be easy, but if you admit your guilt and express contrition and keep your head down, you'll not be in too long. I feel certain you were of good character until you got caught up in this business. That'll count for a lot . . .'

He affirmed the clean record by silence, stroking his chin with a shaking hand, shooting quick glances at me, as if he detected the note of genuine concern in my voice. He looked down again, seeming to consider my words.

I could have written his biography; I'd known several Laurences. He'd be married to a cuddly blonde who'd trade super-sex against an insatiable urge for clothes and holidays and Fiesta Ghias. He'd have got into difficulties, been turned down for a loan by respectable lenders, gone to the sharks. He'd not have been able to repay them the principal, let alone the grotesque APR. The sharks would have given him two choices – broken legs or payment in kind. The ripples would have circled out from one shady bunch to another, and Fielding would have found himself running errands for people who did things with drugs. He'd have cleared his debt, but the sort of money he could make, almost enough to satisfy his wife, would have kept him in the game. He'd have been exactly what they wanted – an office worker with a nice job in the city, who had a clean record and looked too honest to put a private letter through the office franker. It must have seemed as if they'd got the dream team when they'd paired him with Rainger.

And here he was, forced into actions he couldn't have envisaged, even while accepting he was earning bent money, on loan to mad Red Harris because he knew Rainger so well, given a big frightening gun to carry, promoted well beyond his abilities, because the Peter Principle applied in crime too, just as it did in the straight world.

'*John*!' A note of irritation was marring the almost total control Rainger had over his voice.

'What do you say, Laurence?'

He stubbed out the cigarette with an unfamiliar decisiveness.

'Give me the clothes, Miles . . .'

'*Laurence*!'

'Oh, for Christ's sake, John, it's his decision. Look we've got to *go*!'

'Laurence, you can't want to *do* this . . .'

He got up, wincing as he put his swollen hand on the chair-arm, and began to shrug off his jacket.

'Leave it, Laurence!' I said. 'If you go through that door you go in your own clothes. It won't make much difference to us . . .'

'Now hang on,' Rainger grasped my arm with a hand that felt like a pair of pliers. 'Are you saying we just return the enemy with a pat on the back? Knowing our plans. And us – by your own admission – unable to use a phone or attract attention with the rockets. Let me repeat, if I weren't going to the police Laurence would now be dead. And he can either go with us or he can go out dressed as me, when he gets one chance, not much of a chance admittedly, but it's his choice. I'm not prepared to argue about this, John . . .'

I turned to the women, who stood near the fireplace, looking on. 'Why can't you two say something?' I said angrily. 'We're talking about a man's life here. Why can't you help me to persuade him to come with us?'

Mrs Rainger still had the trance-like look, as if her mind could no longer cope with the things she'd seen and heard since I'd rung the doorbell of her holiday home – heroin, bombs, violence, a man outside with a machine-gun; it was an awful lot to take on board for a woman of gentle birth.

'Why should *we* help him?' Fern said harshly. 'He blew up my car, sent you a parcel-bomb. If he wants to go, let him. I couldn't care less.'

'It wouldn't have been *him* who did those things,' I said irritably. 'He wouldn't know how to – Christ, look at the man!'

'I think they're all as bad as each other.'

She still had that flushed, triumphant look of helping

to fool Laurence, was still a little to the left of centre stage. Good had triumphed over evil, after many scary twists of plot, and to tidy everything up the bad guy had to take the rap. It was as if Fern's emotional depths were contained in a graded swimming-pool, and the things that had happened to her whenever she'd ventured near the point where her feet couldn't touch bottom had conditioned her into straying only rarely from the shallow end.

I turned back to Laurence with a sigh. 'Keep your own clothes on,' I said. 'I'm not letting you go out in his clothes if we have to stay all night.'

'I *want* to put them on!' he suddenly cried. 'It doesn't matter! Don't you see – it doesn't bloody *matter*.'

I did see then, saw what must have been obvious from the start, had I not been so agitated. To Fielding, it must have seemed his only chance of any kind of freedom was to risk his luck with the blazer rig-out, to prove to Red, if he could stay alive long enough, that he'd been forced out in Rainger's clothes under duress, so that Red would be fooled into killing his own man. Going out there in his own clothes wasn't going to save him. It would delay his end, perhaps until the others arrived, but that was all. In Red's simple, cunning mind Laurence should either be guarding us or, if overpowered, should now be dead. If he wasn't guarding us and he wasn't dead, but was walking freely from the house, he was obviously involved in a double-cross, had treated with the enemy and could not be allowed to bring to fruition any scheme engineered by me or Rainger. In this business, as Rainger had pointed out, you didn't turn the enemy free from compassion – that would be a concept well beyond the reach of the brain of Red Harris. I glanced round at the others. It seemed to be a concept beyond everyone's mind but mine. I gave it one final shot: 'Come with us, Laurence . . .'

But he was already stripping down to his vest and shorts, still groaning with the pain of his wrist. Rainger helped him into the handmade monogrammed shirt and adjusted the waistband of the white flannels with the same friendly charm he'd have helped a business colleague who'd pulled a muscle on the squash court.

'There you go, old son,' he said, directing Fielding's ballooning hand into the armhole of the blazer. 'Not a bad fit at all. Just the cap now . . .'

Fielding stood ready. The perfect summer light was purpling into dusk, and in the gloom and in those clothes, he bore more than a passing resemblance to Rainger.

But the stylish clothes seemed only to emphasise his nondescript qualities, the colourlessness that should have guaranteed him a secure anonymity with a decent, simple woman, and an undemanding career in motor claims. I had once read that in the early days of photography exposures had needed to be so lengthy that, in the photograph of a street, people could walk in and out of the camera's range without being recorded on the final print. It seemed as if Fielding's progress through life had left as little impression; he didn't deserve the spotlight of this sudden powerful drama, for which he was as unfitted as he was unprepared.

'Right,' he said, 'I'm going now.' He suddenly held out his hand to Rainger, his left undamaged one, and added ludicrously: 'Been really nice knowing you, Miles; we *were* friends, weren't we, like you said.' He then offered me the same hand and held mine in a soft, moist grip, his mouth suddenly twisted and trembling.

The three of us walked slowly across the hall. Rainger opened the door a crack. Across the tiled porch, the outer door stood open. Beyond it was a darkening lawn and the trees and bushes of the copse.

'It's all yours, Laurence,' Rainger said. 'Good luck, old son.'

The man's forehead was beaded with sweat, and I looked him steadily in the eyes, willing him to change his mind, to go back with us and face the music, and for a couple of seconds he seemed to hesitate.

Then suddenly he was gone, through the door and across the porch. As he went through the porch door he shrieked: 'Red, don't *shoot!*'

But Red was already shooting. As the evening silence was shattered by the muffled roar of the sub-machine-gun, Fielding's body ran one more step.

But Fielding himself was quite dead.

Twenty-Three

Rainger flattened himself against the porch wall, moved rapidly sidelong, kicked the outer door shut and secured the lock. He moved back down the porch and through the inner door, which I slammed and locked behind him.

But we'd seen the crumpled body in the half-light, all three of us, because at some point when we were ushering Fielding off to his certain execution Fern had come quietly into the hall behind us. She stood now, visibly shaking.

'You should have helped me,' I said bitterly. 'He wasn't a criminal, he was just a weak fool. He didn't deserve that. If you'd helped me we could have talked him into going back. No one can be as persuasive as you when you set your mind to it. He was almost ready to see sense, I'm certain . . .'

'Oh, come on, John,' Rainger said, 'you gave him every chance. He didn't *have* to do that. All your assumptions are correct – he wasn't your classic bad-hat, he was simply too easily led and not much upstairs. He had no future worth a five-pound note whatever he did – he'd worked that out for himself. Considering the life he had before him it had to be the best career-move he could have made.'

335

For Rainger, the matter was closed. I could see him in his sales office, running a tight ship, taking the one with the slipping sales graph to lunch, giving him his severance cheque with the coffee, and dismissing him from his mind.

'He was too young to die,' I said in a low voice. 'He could have made a fresh start. We could have helped him.'

Rainger smiled, something in the smile still of his surprise at the fuss he considered me to be making about a matter that to him seemed perfectly straightforward – Fielding's hide or ours.

'John,' he said, 'don't ever be tempted to operate on the wrong side of the law. You haven't got the stomach for it.'

I glanced at Fern. She'd scarcely moved, her unfocused eyes still gazing towards the door. It had given her a shock almost as great as seeing her car blown up, another glimpse of the squalid and mundane savagery of serious crime. She'd appeared as ruthless as Rainger when I'd appealed to her for help with Fielding, but I felt she'd not been able to picture him crumpled and bleeding on the peaceful lawn, completely dead. It was as if, when he'd made his dash into the gathering dusk and the gun had begun its muffled drumming, a director would cry 'Cut!' and Laurence would pick himself up, walk back to the house, change his shirt and strap fresh sachets of Kensington Gore across his chest, to have yet another attempt at giving his death run the graceful verisimilitude discerning television audiences had come to expect.

Rainger glanced at a pale-gold watch. 'For God's sake,' he said, 'we've got to *go*. Those lads from Leeds can't be too far away.'

'The back door?'

He nodded. 'Your plan.'

'What if Red goes round there?'

'He won't move a muscle till the heavies arrive, if I'm any judge. We've fooled him into reducing his head-count by fifty per cent, and it'll have thrown a scare into him. He'll know now we're armed with at least one weapon. My guess is that he'll be guarding my car as our only effective means of escape. He may or may not be certain you're here, but not finding your car on the road he'll probably assume you came on foot, or even found me in Esk Head and came back with us. As it took him so long to find the house, he's obviously not familiar with it and won't know there's a footpath down to the beach. Few people do – it was virtually impenetrable until I had my man cut back the undergrowth. I think we assume Red stays put.'

I was practised in deduction myself, but couldn't begin to match his effortless speed.

'Well, ladies,' he said almost cheerfully, as we went back to the drawing-room, 'time to move on. Sensible shoes, Fiona, and change into something warm and dark, would you. You'll have to manage in the dark, of course . . .'

She went off without a word, as obedient and unquestioning as a Stepford wife. The rest of us went into the kitchen. It was almost dark now, and Rainger let down sunblinds over the window and drew curtains. He then considered it safe to turn on a single strip-light over the breakfast-bar. He went down to a cellar and reappeared with a crow-bar and some sacking. I muffled the instrument while he displayed considerable strength in forcing the stout oak door. It gave a single splintering crack,

337

which sounded loud in the enclosed space but wouldn't travel far outside.

He went off again on some final errand, and I glanced at Fern in the illusory cosiness of the breakfast-bar light. I wondered if there was anything left for me. As her eyes met mine her look seemed almost as impersonal as the day I'd walked into Brit-Chem's reception area.

She'd had a very different look for Rainger. When he'd forced the crow-bar into the gap between door and jamb, and the fine hairs had glinted on his bare arms and the veins had stood out like cords, I'd caught a different expression on her face from the savage earlier smile of revenge. Perhaps the fact of Laurence remaining quite dead, deciding on a wrap instead of going for a retake, had helped to throw her into a state of vulnerability. Because this was a look of hunger and longing, it could have belonged on the face of Mrs Rainger herself, and at one point, as I swaddled the crow-bar with the sacking, I saw her lift her hand and almost make to touch his shoulder, before directing the gesture into the smoothing of her tousled hair. Perhaps I'd have been jealous of this man, who still meant so much to her, if there'd been any time.

Mrs Rainger reappeared in a cashmere turtle-neck sweater, black woollen trousers and kid-leather moccasins – even her running-away-from-murderer clothes were of the finest quality. She seemed still in some intense inner world. The two women stood almost side by side, facing me, as if awaiting instructions, but ignoring both me and each other. It gave me a feeling of extreme uneasiness that seemed grotesquely inappropriate when there was a man in the copse waiting to kill us all. It was the old absurd irrelevance, but it couldn't be ignored. They were both obsessed with the same man; with one it passed for love, with the other for hate – from where I stood it looked much the same thing. It injected a powerful distracting charge into the atmosphere at a time when the only thing on our collective minds should have been survival.

When Rainger came back he was wearing a navy cap that almost concealed his dark-gold hair. 'Thought it might be an idea to hide my light under a bushel,' he said, still cheerful, still apparently unaware, or choosing to ignore, the atmosphere created by his two women, which to me seemed as tangible as static electricity.

'You and me first?' I asked Rainger. 'We're armed. If we can get across the garden safely we can cover your wife and Fern.'

He smiled, shook his head.

'No chance. I go alone. When I'm across the rest of you follow . . .'

'Two of us, two chances . . .'

'No,' he said firmly. 'I owe you one for all the trouble I've given you. The only one he wants is me, and if I buy it you'll know to make yourselves as secure as possible and send the rockets up when they've finished with the fireworks.'

I watched him, with his good looks and his engaging boyish smile. He was a bad-hat, a despicable character, but now I actually knew him I knew that nothing he could ever do would stop me from admiring him for his qualities of courage and resourcefulness, his way with a decision.

'All right then, Miles. The best of luck.'

'We all meet at the back gate – it's in a straight line from the back steps.'

'Miles!'

Mrs Rainger had woken from her trance. She laid a hand on his arm, 'Miles, you *mustn't* go alone. Mr Goss is right – let him go with you, there's more chance . . .'

Of Miles getting across the garden while Mr Goss got his head blown off. Sod Mr Goss. You learnt to live with the relentless consistency. I might not have felt quite so totally expendable had Fern not been nodding urgently in agreement.

'Now Fi,' he said gently, taking her hand from his arm and patting it, 'I got us all into this so the risk must be mine.'

Before she could speak again he'd doused the strip-light, opened the door, and slipped out into the night.

'You *should* have gone with him, Mr Goss,' Mrs Rainger said in a low voice, in a tone I remembered so well from the interviews at the Daisy Edge house. 'He mustn't be allowed to take these appalling risks on his own.'

'I *offered* to go with him. You heard me, for God's sake . . .'

'You should have *persuaded* him. He's headstrong . . .'

'Like you helped me to persuade a foolish young man to stay alive?'

I knew the words were wasted as I spoke them. She'd almost certainly have decided that it was Fielding himself who'd led her husband astray, and therefore deserved what he'd got. I was becoming expert in guessing how her mind worked; every brain-cell in it was engaged in the protection of Miles – from other women, from criminals, from his own utter foolishness in not taking

340

me with him so there was an even chance I'd get shot in his place.

She subsided. I stood listening to my heartbeats, half waiting for the ghastly muffled drumming of the attaché-case gun.

Silence. I felt a bead of sweat trickle down my back. I let a minute go by and then I whispered: 'Right, let's go. Keep close behind me.'

I eased the door open and we went slowly down the long flight of stone steps to the back garden. Beyond the patio area, with its tables and chairs, there was the usual immaculate lawn, with dense hedges to each side, and a low wall at the rear for the sea view. We walked steadily and quickly across the lawn until we came to where he stood by a wrought-iron gate.

I could see no path; an apparently impenetrable tangle of trees and bushes seemed to lap to within yards of the gate. But Rainger drew back the foliage on one side, indicating that I should do the same on the other, and the narrow footpath then emerged. It appeared he'd deliberately arranged for that screen, as if sensing that one day he might need it. Beyond the screen, the brush and branches had been cleanly cut back and we were able to walk rapidly in single file down a steep track that brought us to the beach. The day's second flow-tide was running and it turned heavily about fifty yards from us, the breakers throwing up a fine spray that was almost like a mist in the clear moonlight. To the north, we could see the lights of the cottages that clung to the side of Cliffs End, to the south, the rocket-bursts of the Esk Head fireworks display – the traditional Regatta Day finale – lighting up the ancient bones of the Priory. We all stood for a moment at the foot of the track, as if reflecting what a lovely night it must have been for ordinary people.

Then Rainger led us along the beach for almost a quarter of a mile, keeping close to the overhanging cliff. At the next break in the cliff wall there was a narrow gorge which took us by well-used footpaths back up to the coast road. The entrance to the caravan site was not far away, and as most of the occupants were still in Esk Head it was practically deserted.

'Shall I drive?' Rainger said. 'We come here so often I know one or two short cuts.'

'Be my guest . . .'

The engine firing was the sound of the year; we gave a simultaneous sigh of relief. He drove as quietly as possible out to the road, then, turning south to pick up the moor road to Pickering, stood firmly on the throttle.

We flashed past the hooded entrance to his summer place – it was deserted.

'He'll be parked in the wood,' Rainger said, 'so that I'd not be able to get to my car past his. Or Brit-Chem's car, should I say. What a lot of loose ends will need tying, John . . . Two houses to dispose of, and all the bits and pieces. Some kind of house or apartment for Fiona . . . the list is endless . . .'

I nodded. 'I'll help. The police may want to keep it all under wraps, but they trust me and may be glad to off-load a lot of the detail. I'm in constant touch with my friend – he'll make sure you know what's going on.'

He glanced at me. 'That's very decent of you, John. If there were someone I could trust to look after my affairs it would make a deal of difference.'

As usual, there'd be nothing in it for me, but that wasn't the point. I felt I'd have done anything for him within reason. He was coming back to Beckford, he was ready to name names and he was going to give me the only genuine achievement I might ever have, even though no one would ever know it, apart from a handful of police, who were welcome to the glory.

I liked him. I couldn't help myself. He'd been engaged in a filthy business, had seen poor Fielding slaughtered without a backward glance, but he had such incredible style and charm. I remembered the administrator at his old school quoting Barrie – if you had charm you needed little else and if you hadn't it didn't much matter what you did have.

The good fairies had stood in line at Rainger's cradle, to give him brains, looks and ability as well as charm – and it made him into a man impossible to dislike or even be indifferent to. Even when your girlfriend seemed to be falling in love with him all over again.

Minutes later, we were on the outskirts of Esk Head. Our route bypassed the harbour, but we could see the fireworks exploding around floodlit ruins, dropping their delicate globes of green and yellow and red out of the darkness, and we caught occasional glimpses of the harbour lights, reflecting themselves in the glassy water beneath, where the yachts and the cobles, their races run, lay dark and still.

The day-trippers from inland had departed by now, and the road that snaked over Goathland Moors was almost deserted. Rainger drove as expertly as he did everything else, hurtling onward along the bright tunnel punched through the darkness by the Sierra's full beams.

Within a couple of hours we'd be back in Beckford; so much had happened since last night it seemed like a week. Rapidly as he drove, I urged him mentally to greater speed. I couldn't wait now to see him off-loaded – and talking. My personal gratification was very much involved, but a massive burden would also be lifted when Fern and I were finally out of danger, which would only be when Rainger was talking, and what we knew was no longer worth killing us for.

We were at least out of immediate danger. We were armed, and the men going to help Red were travelling in the wrong direction and would not find Rainger's house easy to locate, however precise the instructions. By the time they'd cautiously ascertained that the house was deserted we'd be half-way home.

I'd never stop reliving this past twenty-four hours – the exploding car, the flight to the coast, the way her naked body had looked this morning gilded by sunlight, the cat-and-mouse chase through the crowded, jolly village, that almost idyllic time at Egton when we'd virtually agreed to throw in our lot together.

My spirits suddenly sank. So much had happened, from the moment I'd pressed the doorbell of Rainger's holiday home, that it was as if my mind hadn't had time to spare to attach the emotion to the stark fact that Fern was as much in love with Rainger as his wife was. If she couldn't have him she might or might not be prepared to make do with me, but after what we'd been through, and what she'd come to mean to me after this long frightening day, I didn't think I could now accept being consolation prize.

I could sense the monumental depression awaiting me tomorrow, when it was all over. After tomorrow, I might never see them again, these people who'd brought such danger into my life. And colour. And excitement. I sighed. Perhaps they themselves would see little of each other. Rainger was humming softly to himself, a sound that could just be heard above the sound of the engine. He was on the freedom kick, couldn't wait to be born again and away from it all – the heroin men, his wife, his ex-mistress. And what of them, the two women who loved him to distraction? There'd never be another man for either of them, I knew it with total certainty, no man who could stand comparison with the golden boy. I could almost pity them their future lives, never again to be lit up by the aura of his personality. If I hadn't been pitying me.

We crested the top of a steep, curving gradient that was the last stage of the long climb from the coast to the moorland plateau. And there, at the limit of the light cast by the full beams, in the middle of the road, their car half on the grass verge, stood two policemen, their right hands held up as an indication that we must halt the car.

Twenty-Four

Rainger drove slowly towards them in third.

'When I get abreast of them,' he said, 'I'm going to pretend to slow down, and when they come towards us I'm going to put my foot down.'

I said: 'Over my dead body. They'd put my number out and we'd have half the county on our tail.'

'John . . .'

'I *need* them. My life has to go on after all this, and half my work comes from police referrals. I'm having no trouble with the law, not for anyone or anything . . .'

'You can't imagine they're genuine law!' His voice was high with surprise. 'Oh, come *on*!'

'They get sheep-rustling on this moor. It'll simply be a routine check.'

'Those men are *not* police . . .'

He was driving as slowly as he could, but we were almost on to them by now.

'John,' he said grimly, 'They're *funded*. You *know* that. They can produce anything – uniforms, police-cars, attaché-case guns . . .'

I grasped the handbrake. 'Either stop or I pull this on.'

He sighed and began to brake, finally stopping a yard in front of the men. They came to his window. He wound

347

it further down. I was anxiously aware of the shotgun laid alongside Rainger's right leg, of Fielding's pistol in the glove compartment in front of me.

'Yes, officer,' he said in his usual breezy manner, 'what seems to be the trouble?'

They looked from one to the other of us, then at the women in the back.

'Is one of you gentlemen called Rainger, sir?' one of them said.

'Yes,' I said quickly. 'I am.' I touched Rainger unobtrusively on the knee and thanked God the cap covered most of his hair.

'Do you own a house near Esk Head, sir? Just past the golf-course.'

'Well, yes . . .'

'A man's been found dead in the garden.'

'I'm . . . afraid I don't understand . . .'

'We need to talk to you, sir. I'll have to ask you to come with us.'

Rainger, inevitably, had been right. I knew a lot of policemen; any similarities between them and these two men were minimal. They didn't look or sound right, and they were reading the wrong script.

'There must be some mistake, officer,' Rainger said easily. 'Everything was in good order when we left Mr Rainger's house. If there's been some nonsense with Regatta Night rowdies at the property I hardly see . . .'

Like me, he was playing for time.

'I'm sorry, sir, but because of the circumstances I'll have to ask Mr Rainger to come along for questioning.'

Real police, investigating such a serious matter, wouldn't have thrown their ace away by talking about a dead man in a garden. They'd have been a great deal more circumspect, they'd have begun by asking me if everything had seemed as usual at the house before we'd left it, they'd have said they were looking into an 'incident' or an 'injury', and they'd have been politer in their approach, asking me a good many questions on the spot before inviting me to visit a police station. Nothing was more valuable in police detection than the reactions of a suspect to a crime not fully specified.

'We'd better all come along then,' Rainger said. 'We've got to get the poor chap home somehow. I'll follow on behind.'

'No, sir, that won't be necessary, we'll make sure he gets home. The rest of you are free to go.'

That clinched it. If there was a dead man in a garden, and we'd all been together at the Rainger house, then we were all equally involved.

I got slowly out of the Sierra. The two big men fell in one each side of me, and we began to walk towards the pseudo, or stolen, police car. It was as bad a moment as any that day. With that brain of his, Rainger would probably have worked out why I was pretending to be him, but what if he decided not to play along? He was a charmer, but he was also a criminal and a realist; at the end of the day the only survival he was interested in was his own. What if he decided that the best way to ensure it now was to drive on and leave me to it in the corner I'd painted myself into? I couldn't see his two women protesting too much, if at all.

I almost thought he'd made that decision. My palms were wet and iced water seemed to be trickling across my stomach. I cursed my foolishness – had I set myself up for his execution?

We were within a yard of the white car. A handful of

tourist cars, bunched together behind a slow, careful driver, went by, the drivers clocking us as they passed between my car and the police car, but keeping their eyes carefully to the front, not wanting to be involved in any kind of questioning that might incidentally lead to the production of breathalysing equipment. It was exactly what my own reaction would have been, but their indifference to my plight seemed almost callous as the sounds of their passage faded into silence.

'Officer!' Rainger suddenly cried. 'That man is *not* Rainger. I'm Rainger. He's had a gun on me all the way from Esk Head.'

It made no sense if you had time to think about it, but surprise was the essence. The men stopped dead, began to turn. As they did so, I let the man on my right have it very hard in the groin with my bunched fist. He doubled over with a groan of pain and I followed through with the same fist on the back of the neck. As he hit the ground, I kicked him once in the belly very, very hard. He lay hunched up, moaning softly.

The other man was standing very still because Rainger was pointing the shotgun at him, its barrel gleaming bluely in the moonlight.

'Move a muscle,' he said, 'and I'll blow you into the valley. Hands on your head. Check him for hardware, John.'

I checked him gingerly from behind, locating the gun in a waistband holster beneath the police tunic.

'Right,' Rainger said to him, 'take the gun out very slowly and throw it to the side . . .'

The man did so, but was getting too much of our attention, and it was almost our undoing. The men were basically heavies who'd not got much going for them upstairs, which was why Rainger's ploy had worked so well. But what a lifetime of rough trade had developed in them to an incredible degree was an instinct for survival.

We'd assumed the other man to be temporarily out of the equation. I was a handy lad and I knew where and how to strike. What I'd not allowed for was that despite the pain he wasn't so disabled that he couldn't work his own gun from under his tunic as he writhed about.

I saw it appear in his hand barely in the nick of time, and even as I kicked that hand the gun went off – into the rear off-side tyre of the Sierra. It deflated with a sound like a horse snorting.

'Right,' Rainger said softly, 'does anyone want to try anything else?'

It seemed nobody did.

'You on the ground,' he said, 'get up.'

Cursing and grunting with pain, the man did so.

'John,' he said, 'position that car of theirs so it's as near to the edge of the valley as possible, would you, broadside to the road. The keys are bound to be in the ignition.'

They were. Before getting in, I glanced briefly at the car's exterior. It was a white Ford Prefect, and what seemed to be an authentic beacon was in fact a good model, attached to the roof with suction pads. The insignia, the body-lines and the word POLICE on the sides were cut-outs of glossy adhesive paper, which could be attached or peeled in seconds.

Rainger had known. He knew everything about these people. I'd never imagined them to be amateurs, but my credence had stopped well short of false police cars. It filled me with sudden awe, mixed with foreboding. What had I taken hold of? I'd known for some time how important he must be to the organisation, but what kind of star status merited what now seemed to be a full-blown man-hunt?

Shivering slightly, I started the car, backed it on to the road, then drove across the verge at right angles, edging it as near to the point where the land fell sharply away to the deep valley as I could safely manoeuvre.

'Leave it in neutral with the handbrake off, John.'

I did so, then returned to the Sierra.

'Right,' Rainger said to the men, 'start pushing.' They watched him with uncomprehending frowns. 'Push the car over the side,' he said, as if to children. 'That's if you don't want a hand blown off.'

They moved then, quickly, the injured one wincing and gasping with pain. It took them only a few seconds to get the car rolling. Almost soundlessly, it vanished over the edge, and then we could hear it crashing down the slope towards the valley floor.

'You as well,' Rainger said, getting out of the car. 'Last one down gets the ale in.'

'Aw, *shit*!' one of them muttered, and then, with final baleful glances at us, they moved to the edge and began to pick their way gingerly down over the scree-like ground, frequently slithering, the sound one cursing volubly, the damaged one giving regular yelps of agony.

As we watched, the car, almost at the bottom, suddenly burst into flames.

'What a pretty sight,' Rainger said.

We stood for several minutes – minutes we couldn't spare but which had to be sacrificed to ensure the men were so far down that climbing back up would give us time to be off the moor.

'Why did you say you were me?'

'Oh,' I shrugged, 'you had the gun near you and you have the quickest mind in a tight corner. I knew you'd conjure up some kind of *deus ex machina* if I could get them away from the car.'

I could make out his cynical smile in the moonlight. 'Not to mention that if there *was* any shooting involved it had better be me that did it, so you could stay the good Boy Scout.'

There was little point in denying it.

He said: 'Well, I don't blame you. In your shoes I'd probably have done the same. You're a bit of an arm-chancer though, aren't you?'

'Takes one to know one.'

He chuckled, as the noise of the scrabbling men grew fainter. Then he said: 'Do you know why I came into this game?'

'The way you live, it's got to be the loot.'

'Boredom. I could have made all the money I needed legitimately.'

'At Brit-Chem?'

'I'd have been European Director by now if I'd been willing to go to Brussels. You can't *believe* the pressure put on me to relocate. The eventual package, virtually guaranteed, would have given me everything I've got now, plus a block of shares, plus private use of a small company jet.

'I can sell, you see. I'm not particularly well qualified, but you don't need to know too much about chemicals to be able to sell them. I could sell bottled tap-water. I can talk, I can amuse, I can flatter – that's all you need. Best of all, of course, I can motivate.'

That last quality must have been the one that had made him seem such a prize to the big people in the

Place Madou. I could see men and women sacrificing their leisure in their eagerness to meet targets set by Rainger, longing for that hand on the arm, that wide urchin smile, those jewelled words, 'Well done!', that would reward success, just as they went in trembling fear of the cold blue gaze, the brutal honesty and the rapid demotion that would be the penalty for failure. Whether it was carrot or stick, they would always respect, admire and even revere him, because he would never ask them to do anything he couldn't do himself, because he was such a charismatic man, because, though his charm would always conceal it from them, his ruthless self-interest would pull out of them qualities they'd never known they possessed. None of them would have seen the ludicrous side of Fielding shaking him warmly by the hand on his way to the firing-squad.

'I was less than enthusiastic', Rainger went on, 'about Brussels. They did not like it. It confused and annoyed them that I could turn down such an offer. They never really forgave me. They wouldn't even put me in charge of the Beckford office then, they put a man over me whom they knew I disliked and regarded as second-rate.'

He shrugged. 'I couldn't hack it, couldn't face the Brit-Chem system for the rest of my life, finding it all so easy, meeting men day after day who were as brash and boring as I just pretended to be. With nothing in it but a comfortable life and the executive toys . . .'

He glanced at me. 'They caught me at just the right psychological moment, the heroin people. Oh, the big money came in handy, I don't deny it, but the charge, the *real* charge, was the challenge of setting it all up in Beckford. And the danger. The danger was the hook, not the money – they can never get their minds round that. I suppose men like me, during the cold war, got involved in spying on the Russians. The money couldn't have been the draw, that's for sure, because as far as I can make out the government paid you out of the petty cash and when you got in trouble pretended they didn't know you from a bent tycoon.

'I suppose that's why I began top-slicing too – I'd got the set-up running so well it was getting to be as boring as Brit-Chem.'

I said: 'It's a hefty price to pay for getting bored easily – Red Harris or going inside.'

'Where's the thrill without the gamble? Playing around with women – that was another part of it. I'm not really a womaniser at heart, it was just the fun of playing around and seeing if I could get it past Fiona, who could make really serious trouble if I didn't, believe it. She once went for me with a kitchen-knife – it took some very fancy footwork on my part. There's still a mark on the pantry door where I'd been standing. Moral: never confront a woman in a well-appointed kitchen!'

He chuckled again. I wondered if that was why he'd not left her before now, because of that incendiary atmosphere of jealousy and guilt that made some married people so unhappy but which at a different level they seemed almost to crave. Or had he stayed because of the finishing-school gloss she'd brought to his development, the contacts with the sort of people who could afford Daisy Edge? Whatever it was, he was hell-bent on leaving her now – he knew it, I knew it and she knew it.

'I can't imagine Mrs Rainger getting so angry she lost control. She always seemed so self-possessed.'

'Few people can. The trouble is there are times when I'd try the patience of a saint. Anyway, after that, whenever we argued I always made sure we weren't standing near anything heavy, sharp or corrosive she could lay her hands on.'

We could no longer hear the two men scrabbling down the valley wall. I said: 'I think we can go now . . .'

He was silent for a few seconds more, peering down into the darkness. 'The trouble with men like me, John, is we have natures that tend to shape our destinies. I have dark and dreadful days when I feel that however often I switch roads they all eventually end up in Samarra.'

I have never forgotten those words.

'Right,' he said briskly, 'let's go. But one more thing . . .' Turning towards the car, we faced each other. 'I wish it weren't hello and goodbye. I'd like to have got to know you. I've known a great many men in my time, but I can't think of one I'd sooner have with me when my back was against the wall.'

'The feeling's mutual . . . Miles.'

We returned to the car, his arm lightly over my shoulder. The women stood in the road now, after the blowing of the tyre. They were weary, their faces almost expressionless in the moonlight. There had been so many shocks, what difference did one more make in a nightmare that seemed to have no end.

Rainger said: 'A man as organised as you, I needn't ask if the spare's in good shape . . .'

'*And* holding the correct pressure.'

He laughed shortly, and between us we had the car jacked, the wheel off, and the spare on in three or four minutes. Rainger said: 'Red outflanked us. When Laurence bought it, he must have taken no chances, must have assumed we'd somehow do a runner. He'd have got his Leeds contact on a mobile phone. They would have contacted the heavies and told them to set up the police trap. That's how it was all ready and waiting. Is that how you see it?'

I nodded. 'Why take just me though? Or me supposed to be you?'

'Too dangerous out here to try anything on with the lot of us, not with trippers still driving past. They *had* to have me, but they could catch up with the rest of us later. That must have been the thinking.'

I nodded, glancing up and down the deserted road. 'We could be in a box. Uncle Red behind us and more of them ahead.'

'Agreed,' he said, looking at me pointedly. 'Except that this time we don't stop for anyone, not even if it's an ambulance and half a dozen bodies lying in the road, not even if we have to drive over the bodies. Do I make myself clear, young Goss?'

I nodded, with a sheepish grin. He opened the back door. 'Come on, girls,' he said gently, 'we just have to get off this damned moor and we should be all right. I'm very sorry for all the trouble I've brought you.'

He may have meant it or it may just have been a PR job, but, like everything he said, it had an authentic ring. When they were inside, we ran quickly across to the valley's rim, to ensure the men weren't making too rapid a come-back.

We could hear nothing beyond the normal creaking sounds of insects on a summer night, but in the distance, on the road skirting the valley, the same road that would eventually climb steeply to the point where we now stood, a lone car moved rapidly, its full beams looking like twin glow-worms in the darkness.

Twenty-Five

We got off the moor without further mishap, driving on to the Pickering roundabout ten minutes later. It gave us a choice of three roads.

'Which one, John?'

'Helmsley and Ripon. It's the long slow route. They'll be expecting us to take the short quick one.'

'By now it's probably academic which one we take.'

Even allowing for his fatalism about roads, I had to agree. We weren't more than ten miles along the northern route before we knew for certain. Rainger had been driving slowly on half-lights, even dousing them completely when cornering on to fresh sections of the road and driving by moonlight, sensing that if anything was going to happen it would happen within the first ten or fifteen miles.

We had just crept cautiously round another bend when he suddenly braked and drew into the side beneath trees. Remarkable eyesight was yet another of the advantages life had showered on him – I could only just make out the shape of a bulky estate car in the distance, with behind it a trailer almost as long, car and trailer parked broadside across a narrow part of the road.

Rainger sighed. 'If they'd wanted to increase serious-money crime, if they'd wanted to speed it up and make it more efficient, they couldn't have done better than encourage everyone to buy a car-phone.'

'We . . . could get round it,' I said hesitantly.

'Agreed, but it would mean driving partly on the verge. Ten to one they've found a spot where there's a ditch. At best we could end up with a disabled car, at worst, if we went at speed, we could injure ourselves. Either way they'd have us.'

'Back to Pickering?'

'Too late, I think. They'll have done the same thing behind us.'

'Take off?'

'No alternative. This is farmland and there'll be trees and hedges. We could probably camouflage ourselves until the morning when the roads get busy again. They'll come after us but we'll have the advantage of surprise. We'll have to play a lot of it by ear, but it'll be much safer than sitting here in the car.'

'Agreed . . .'

'Well, Fiona, Fernande,' he turned to them, 'we seem to be on the run again.'

The women began to prepare themselves without a word. Rainger was the natural leader and his nerve and brains hadn't let us down yet. I glanced at them briefly. There seemed a new determination in their shadowy faces. Speeding across the moor, it must have seemed to them we'd made a clean escape, that whatever problems of adjustment lay ahead we were at least out of physical danger. I'd thought that way myself, and I could imagine the special kind of shock it must have given them to realise that even men who looked so reassuringly like policemen were to be feared and mistrusted. The weariness, the near-apathy of their reactions to that new setback seemed to have gone now, as if they were getting used to danger again as a fact of life, were calling up new reserves. In Mrs Rainger it was the breeding that seemed to show, a childhood of being told that gels of her background didn't cry or complain, even when they fell off their ponies, but held their heads up, gritted their teeth, and set an example to those of less sound upbringing. And then, there had always been the example of Miles; whatever other faults he may have had, no one she could ever have known could have reacted better in a crisis.

I saw also in Fern a glint in the eyes that evoked memories of her earlier role, the one she'd loved so much and clearly hated to relinquish – the action-girl, the one who could face with spirit whatever life threw at her, who even now could not entirely separate art from life.

The women glanced then at each other, almost but not quite exchanging wry smiles. There seemed even a certain tenuous camaraderie between them, a faint reflection of the powerful bond that had instinctively developed between Rainger and me. Without fully understanding it I welcomed it. It meant we'd finally achieved some kind of team spirit that might in the end be crucial to our survival.

Silently, we all left the car. There was a tall hedge beyond the trees and we began to creep along it, bent low, in the opposite direction to the estate car. About a hundred yards further on, we came to a gate which opened on to a rough track, wide enough to take a

tractor. We passed through the gateway and started
along the path, rapidly skirting the edge of a field
which sloped gradually down from the road. Cows,
now resting in the grass, watched us go by, the whites
of their incurious eyes gleaming in the pale light.
There was some sort of dark mass in the hollow, which
I hoped would be a spinney where we might be able to
go to ground.

'I think we're in luck,' Rainger said softly, touching
my arm.

His superlative sight had already defined what took
me another second or so – a farmhouse and, at some
distance from it, outbuildings.

Passing an elderly lorry, we crept towards the outbuildings and made a tour of them, cautiously using my
powerful car torch. The first of them was a kind of
tool-shed. Farm implements lay on the floor or stood
against walls, together with bundles of wooden posts,
fencing wire, empty sacks and rolls of heavy-duty plastic
sheeting.

In the floor itself was what seemed to be a large
trapdoor, locked into place by counter-sunk bolts.
Beyond this big square room lay a smaller room, a
built-on lean-to. This contained a work-bench, a stove,
portable gas-lamps.

Another of the buildings was a barn which housed the
tractor, with, above it, a hay-loft. Another, about the
size of a suburban garage, housed a rusting Volvo. The
last, brick-built and with a corrugated iron roof, was a
milking parlour. Trust abounded, and none of the buildings was locked, though padlocks would have presented
no particular problem to Rainger and me.

We stood in the shadow of the milking parlour.

362

'Lateral thinking time,' Rainger said. 'How many will come after us?'

'Two. They'll need men up at the road to guard our car in case we double back, others to watch the road-block, and more to search the area. I can't see them being able to spare more than two.'

'I agree. And those two will probably have orders to search and find only, and to go back for help when they think they've found us. Now – if you saw a car abandoned on the *left* side of the road which side would you search first?'

'The right. They'll think we parked on the left to make them think we're going off to the left.'

'That means we may have a little time. Now, if you were them and you came to this spot, and you suspected we were hiding, which building would you suspect we were hiding *in*?'

'The hay-loft,' Fern said quickly. 'People on the run in films *always* hide in hay-lofts.'

Rainger was grinning in the silvery light. 'That's quite true. It's as potent a message as Fairy Liquid. I'm sure they'll think that's where we'll be. On the other hand, the hay-loft *would* be a good place to hole up for the night. After all, it might take them an hour to get here. We could take it in turns to keep watch, and we'd have the advantage of anyone coming through the door. From above.'

'But we'd have to kill them,' I said, 'if we didn't want them to kill us.'

'And we need dead men down to us like we need AIDS,' he said, nodding.

'Maybe we could set something up.'

We went back to the first of the buildings, the one that

contained the tools. We looked around the littered room. I played the torch over the trapdoor, which was about nine feet long by about three wide.

I said: 'Inspection pit?'

'Got to be. If you can't mend a machine yourself you can lose a day's production.'

'Are you thinking what I'm thinking?'

'Hum the tune and I'll see if I know the words . . .'

Fifteen minutes later we were ready. The women were in the hay-loft, armed with the shotgun and the gun we'd taken from Fielding. Rainger and I sat in the little work-room attached to the building with the inspection pit, armed with the pistols we'd taken from the pretend-policemen. We were assuming that, like us, they'd examine this building first.

We sat in the light of two of the portable gas-lamps, which hung from a ceiling beam. The door of the little room was shut, but we knew from careful tests that a glimmer of light could be seen at the top and bottom of it from the barn. The door of the barn itself opened outwards, and we'd tied twine to the inner handle, taken it across the barn and beneath the door of the work-room, and Rainger now held the end of it, ready to release it if he felt the tug of the barn door being opened.

Time was playing its usual nerve-racking tricks – thirty mental minutes seemed to equal five real ones, each passing second drawing my nerves tighter, but not somehow in the right way – not in the way of a rested body gearing itself for activity. I was worried that I was getting used up, that after this long, dangerous day my body was cutting off further credit.

My eyes seemed to rest in a bed of fine sand, and I'd begun to have those minor hallucinations the brain has to make do with when not allowed to come down and have full-scale dreams.

Rainger, of course, seemed to vibrate with energy. Hyperactivity had clearly also been in his gift. For him, four hours' sleep a night was probably all it took. Apart from which, I felt he was also getting that rush in the blood from being so close to the danger his nature seemed to compel him to seek. For him, it must have been a red-letter day, made all the sweeter because it marked the end of the Daisy Edge era.

He smiled at me in the shadowy light of the gas-lamps, that engaging boyish smile that had probably never changed since his time at Beckford Boys', when he'd have led the First Eleven out to slaughter St Chad's, or swaggered across the school stage as Fletcher Christian in the Sixth Form adaptation of *Mutiny on the Bounty*, or run along a springboard to perform an exquisite swallow-dive into a sheet of glittering water. The school secretary would have known this smile very well, as she'd never forgotten it.

'How did they make the approach, Miles,' I said in a low voice, 'the heroin men?'

'With incredible circumspection. The man you saw me with at the pub on the Strand comes from an Indian trading family. They call him Ramarjee. The family firm's in Delhi, but he came over here twenty years ago to run the European end. Import-Export – he brings in things like carpets and tea and semi-precious stones, and ships out textiles – sari materials, suitings, shirtings, curtaining, anything that'll turn a rupee.

'He was doing very well, but he wanted to do a lot

better; the business gave him marvellous cover – he knew how to move things about. And he had the perfect excuse for nipping over to India every few weeks. He soon caught on that a handful of chemists in India and Pakistan were refining really top-notch heroin, and by now he knew the UK areas with a strong Asian presence.

'He came to Beckford several times to get a feel for the place, to see if he could work out a scheme for getting the stuff in. He realised from day one he needed someone in charge up there, and he started giving close attention to the execs who travelled to London a lot, such as me, because it would obviously be useful to have someone who had that kind of mobility.

'To cut a long story short, he did a great deal of homework, and he finally had me in the frame. He knew almost as much about me in the end as you do.'

He shook his head in wonder. 'All these people who have files on me – head-hunters, criminals, private investigators, Head Office . . . He was aware I was living well beyond my income, and he obviously suspected I was bored to the back teeth.

'One day I was sitting alone for once in the restaurant car of the morning Executive, and he took the seat opposite. We started chewing the fat, he told me what he did and I told him what I did, and then he says, *what* a coincidence, because he needed advice on fire-proofing carpets and could I help him. Well, I told him all we did was manufacture chemicals and sell them, but I gave him the names of two or three firms who did that kind of work.

'By this time I could tell he was bullshitting. What's

366

more, I knew he knew. We separated at King's Cross, and I thought that was that, but about a week later I got a cheque from him for five thousand pounds for "Professional Advice". Nice one. If I'd rung him and said what the hell's going on, he'd have apologised and said there'd been some absurd mistake, he'd told his PA to draw a cheque for *fifty* pounds as a little thank you for the advice. If I simply *kept* the five grand and said nothing he'd guess I was prepared to go the distance, because no respectable businessman accepts five thousand from a stranger for giving him names he could have got from a trade directory.

'So . . . I kept the cheque, and not long after, Ramarjee sidles into the restaurant car again and asks me would I like to help him with the side of his business that did drug imports . . .'

My fatigue had gradually slipped away. It was the reason I'd asked him to talk. I'd been certain it would provide the stimulation I needed, to hear that remarkable story at first hand, the one that, in a few hours, he'd be relating to a police recording machine.

He glanced at the twine held between thumb and forefinger. I wondered if our pursuers were coming this way yet, were even at this moment approaching the outbuildings. If they picked up the murmur of our voices it wouldn't matter; the whole point was that they realised there was someone in this room.

'I set up the Beckford system,' Rainger said. 'Mail. Mail by the sack-load. How easy to slip two or three ounces of scag into a newspaper container, at five thousand an ounce on the street. With decent law-abiding Pakistanis simply passing it on because they thought they were helping out countrymen who'd not sorted out permanent addresses.

'And then the bigger packages, to white householders; right number, wrong street – the one you caught Laurence up to. We pulled that one about once a fortnight. Can you believe the turnover! And practically fool-proof, even though the law suspected what was going on. They might intercept one drop in fifty, but we allowed for that in the calculations and made sure it was always the Laurences of life who were in the front line.'

'How did you get to know the people at the London end? Apart from Ramarjee . . .'

'That's a very good question, John. I don't suppose I need to tell you about the principle of insulation . . .'

'Just the one rung up . . .'

'Just the one rung up – exactly. The sharp-end Pakistanis knew Laurence; they didn't know me. Laurence knew me; he didn't know Ramarjee. I *shouldn't* have known anyone beyond Ramarjee, but Ramarjee was proud of me. His family had always been pro-British, thought our pulling out of India had been a tragedy. And now Ramarjee *employed* an Englishman, who shot and fished and knew everyone in Yorkshire worth knowing. I wasn't your average East End scum-ball, who'd worked up from scrap-metal and had a father who'd once had the privilege of being kicked senseless by Ronnie Kray in a pub lavatory. He couldn't resist showing me off to his colleagues. You realise, of course, that you can't operate in the drugs business in isolation, not if you don't want to find yourself floating face down in the Thames. You *have* to involve the other barons because it's essential to manipulate the market so it's always in the seller's favour; you can't go off at a tangent flooding the streets with the stuff. Apart from that it's almost impossible to raise investment money on the scale needed to fund big purchases without all of them tipping in. They also have a rough-and-ready insurance scheme for money lost on shipments the law gets its hands on. A kind of mini-Lloyds.' He smiled grimly. 'Only if any of the Names can't pay up they don't just make them bankrupt . . . It's a very controlled, very incestuous business at the top end.

'So . . . he started showing me off to his chums and they took to me, seemed to trust me from the start. It began to get quite dodgy in fact – one of these guys took me on one side at one stage and asked how I felt about doing a bit of business with him "that we needn't let on to the wog about".'

I could easily believe it, that hardened suspicious criminals would immediately lower their defences for Miles Rainger, instantly trust him, rely on him, want him to accept more and more responsibility, help to motivate the younger criminals who needed a role-model relevant to the complex high-tech Nineties. It would be Brit-Chem and the call to Brussels all over again, as if reflected upwards from a dark and murky pond.

'They were so chuffed with the way I'd organised the Beckford end that they were talking about promotion. They regard heroin as the second division these days, nice earner though it is – cocaine's the thing. The North American market's saturated now and they're targeting Europe, bringing it in through places like Gdynia in Poland, and moving it through countries that have little or no border control with the collapse of the USSR . . .'

I broke in: 'They actually *told* you all this?'

'My son,' he said, 'by the time I'd met them for the third time I'd begun to introduce proper business *techniques*. The trouble was, they all had *some* information about the logistics of drugs; no one had it all. They were secretive by nature, all wanting to guard their own sources and outlets, only telling each other what they had to. Just like business in the straight world, I suppose.'

He grinned. 'I got Ramarjee to talk them into a full-blown conference at one of their big houses in the Thames Valley. We took flip-charts along and an overhead projector, and I pointed out that if they pooled their knowledge and resources completely it would make them the biggest trading unit in Europe. I showed them how to draw up a three-year business-plan, and explained the principles of key-accounting and sales and expenses budgets. They loved it. The next time we met we had a full-scale brain-storming session, everything on the table, every source, every outlet, every movement. By the time we'd finished I knew everything about the drugs trade there was to know, and they voted to make me . . . wait for it . . . European director, because I could go abroad without attracting suspicion under the cover of Brit-Chem. They kept telling me I'd make the sort of money that would make a million seem like loose change. As I said, they never really grasped that money wasn't the real spur.'

For a moment I could hardly breathe with the shock. It was like knowing you'd had a substantial win on the football pools, then being sent a cheque that made it to *The Guinness Book of Records*. I'd known he had valuable names to name, or why should so many men and weapons have been shipped into North Yorkshire, but I could never have imagined he knew *everyone* in the business, would know the logistics of the tons of drugs that moved around Europe, the network by which every gram of powder hit the streets in every UK town of any size, how the illicit millions were laundered. My fatigue had disappeared without trace. It was like sunlight burning off mist, the way a new powerful determination to deliver Rainger to the police – whatever the heroin men threw at us – had forced its way through my weariness.

'Leadership, people wanting to kick me up the ladder,' he said with his ironic chuckle, 'I couldn't get away from it.'

'If you were going to be a multi-millionaire,' I said, 'why skim?'

He shrugged. 'You tell me . . .'

If he couldn't explain it adequately to himself where could I begin? He was drawn to danger, and the daily risks he already lived with had become like those drugs he handled, where an ever-increasing fix was needed to provide even an illusion of the original kick. Perhaps he'd been certain he would get away with it, even if caught, that his skilful tongue would convince them they couldn't see off a star like him, while at the same time being almost equally sure they'd make no exceptions, even for the man who could have been king.

I had read that in youth Graham Greene had once played Russian Roulette with a gun loaded with a single round, and had found my credulity severely strained, in view of the fact that he had then gone on to take great care of himself for the rest of his long life. But I could have believed it of Rainger, could have credited he'd have done it more than once to push the odds to the limit.

'If you wanted an adventurous life,' I said, 'why leave it so late?'

'When you're young you're not really sure what you want. I knew I wanted money because money gives you choices, and I *thought* I wanted the high life. I went to a fee-paying school, and some of the boys came from rich families. I'd go to their homes and there'd be these great houses standing in half a dozen acres. Horses, dogs, a garage full of cars.'

He grinned. 'There's an old Yorkshire saying – "Don't marry for money, marry where money is." So I rather restricted myself to going out with well-connected girls. I fell heavily for Fiona, who showed up at all the parties. It was only after the wedding that I discovered what you'll almost certainly have dug up.'

'The family was broke . . .'

'They'd pulled out all the stops for Fiona with what money they'd salvaged. She had her own Mini, good clothes, hair-dos, and at that stage no one knew for certain the old lad had lost his shirt.

'Anyway, we married, and I realised very soon there weren't going to be any short cuts to affluence. So I got my head down at Brit-Chem and started to get the things I wanted the hard way. It was only when it began to seem too easy, and the good life wasn't providing any of the answers . . .'

He suddenly pointed at his left hand. The twine slowly ran through his fingers, and then we heard it, the faintest creak of the barn door. I tightened my grip on the gun. I didn't want to use it but would if I had to. We sat facing the work-shop connecting door, one to each side of it. We had to accept that they might be so desperate to silence Rainger by now that they would simply shoot through the door, but we'd worked on the premise that they had to know whom they were actually shooting at – we'd made no secret of our presence, we might be farm-workers.

Time began to pass, genuine time. Not a lot, but enough to make me uneasy. I had to tell myself that if there were two heavies out there they'd need time to communicate, plan their actions, take a decision. Their brains wouldn't be the trained instruments Rainger's and mine were.

Even so, surely it couldn't be taking this long. Perhaps they'd decided to take us from a different point – from the roof or the rear of the building. Perhaps they'd already started back for help.

The time-lag was getting to Rainger now and he rasped a thumb-nail over the slight stubble on his chin. We exchanged glances, shrugged, shook our heads. The plan seemed to have misfired.

And then we heard it. It was a sound that returned me to my early childhood in the Sixties, before smokeless zones, when coalmen would dump solid fuel in the outside locker beneath the bedroom steps, a sudden heavy rushing sound followed by total silence.

Grinning again, Rainger gave me a delighted thumbs-up. We leapt to our feet, doused one light each, and swung open the door, which we'd oiled to ensure it didn't creak.

Movement and noise began in the barn's main room.

'What the frigging . . .?'

373

'Christ, I think me sodding leg's broke . . .!'
'Shit!'
'You're on me bleeding hand . . . Get your foot off me bleeding *hand*!'

The barn was wired for power and light, and there was an additional light-switch to the right of the work-shop door. I felt for it and turned on the two unshaded overhead bulbs. The deep inspection pit seemed full of writhing bodies, but there were only two. The men became still and stared up at us, blinking.

'Well, well,' Rainger said, 'how nice of you to drop in. Now place your guns and knives, et cetera, all of them, very slowly, on the edge of the pit. One wrong move and the pit becomes your grave.'

We trained our guns on a man each. They could have been clones of the pretend-policemen – powerfully built, heavy featured, hairy. They watched us in speechless fury for several seconds, and then began, as slowly as men in a space capsule, to assemble their arms. One of them seemed genuinely to have damaged a leg and lay muttering obscenities, while the other passed up the weapons.

Earlier, we'd taken up the pit-door and placed it unobtrusively against the barn wall. We'd then spread plastic sheeting over the pit, weighted it at the edges with some of the tools that stood about and then covered it with a layer of hay from the loft. To ensure the men actually walked over it and not round it, we'd artfully arranged the variety of objects in the barn so that the only place where it was possible to walk easily and quietly was in the area of the pit. It had worked – real men caught in a man-trap.

The arsenal now lay at the side of the pit – pistols

374

elongated by silencers, clips of bullets, flick-knives, coshes.

'You know,' Rainger said, as I drew them towards us with a rake, 'it makes a chap feel really wanted, the trouble they've gone to. Right, guys, make yourselves comfortable because we're going to bed you down for the night.'

'And I'm going to bed you down for good.'

It was Red Harris, standing at the open door with the attaché-case gun. As the short hairs began to prickle on my neck, I saw the aiming-spot was fixed on Rainger's heart.

'Drop the guns,' he said.

After a moment, ashen with shock, Rainger threw his gun aside. I followed suit. My mind seemed to seize up. There was nowhere else to go, no other trick we could pull in the seconds left to us. We'd lost. We'd had an incredible run, but the superior numbers had counted in the end.

Red began to smile. It was the most dreadful sight I'd ever seen. It was a wide smile, showing yellowing teeth, almost beatific. It was the smile of an achiever, of a man who'd pursued his objectives as doggedly as I'd pursued my own, and had the same endless setbacks.

He couldn't just kill us, not psychopathic Red, he had to look as if it was one of the happiest days of his life.

'Man,' he said, as if in confirmation, 'am I going to enjoy this.'

I'd expected, even then, that Rainger would launch into his easy patter after that first moment of shock, would somehow talk us through to some stage where Red could be distracted. His silence told of his awareness that he faced a total professional, and that nothing,

nothing at all, was going to distract Red from the achievement of a goal he'd worked so single-mindedly to accomplish.

He lingered with deliberate anticipation, the aiming-spot rock steady on Rainger's chest. And in the end it was because he'd allow nothing to distract him during those long seconds of gloating foreplay that made him, for perhaps the only time in his life, pay insufficient attention to his back. There was a sudden movement behind him, a kind of flurry, a confused picture in the outer darkness of someone almost whirling. Even as he became aware, and glanced rapidly behind him, some object smashed into his forehead with the sound of a cricket bat squarely hitting the ball. He crashed heavily to the barn floor. Behind him, straining for breath, her entire body seeming to vibrate with fury, teetered Mrs Rainger, holding the shotgun by its barrel like a golf-club. At her side, trembling with what seemed an identical passion, and holding a fencing-stake, stood Fern.

'Well *done*, my dear!' Rainger cried cheerfully, but even he couldn't get his voice fully under control. 'A . . . hole in one, so to speak . . .'

Relief seemed to hit me like a tidal wave – I felt my legs would give way. I leaned against the wall and sucked in air like a thirsty man gulping water. Rainger had the same uncoordinated look about him but, wary as ever, he gave a checking glance to the men lying in the pit and bent to retrieve his gun. Before he could touch it, a voice from outside said: 'Just leave that gun where it is, Mister . . .'

Two men in workshirts and bib-and-brace overalls moved forward into the light, an elderly man and another in his thirties. They both levelled shotguns.

'Lay that gun on the ground, lady,' the older man said to Mrs Rainger, 'and go across to the back of the barn. You too,' he said to Fern. 'And you men.'

We all did as we were told, and the younger man picked up the gun Mrs Rainger had laid down, as well as all the other weapons, and put them carefully in a sack.

'Now,' the older man said, 'we'll just wait here nice and peaceful for fifteen minutes, because if I'm not back in the house by then my old woman's going to ring the police.'

Twenty-Six

Rainger said: 'Rather a crowded twenty-four hours.'

We fell silent, as if all reflecting on that long day and night, packed with tension, emotion and danger. We sat now in safety, in the lofty drawing-room of Rainger's Daisy Edge house, weary, rumpled, our faces streaked with grime. I had rung the Beckford central Police Station and learned that Fenlon was on leave. Had called his house, been told he'd taken the little boy to the park and left a message for him to ring Rainger's number the moment he got back.

In the meantime, we sat and waited, our ordeal at long last over, our various lives waiting to claim us the minute the Rainger affair had received its finishing touches.

'Perhaps you'd like something to drink?' Mrs Rainger said, with the impersonal politeness of the day I'd first met her, on a burning morning in July, which now seemed as remote, despite its pin-sharp clarity, as a scene remembered from childhood. 'Tea . . . or coffee . . .?'

'To hell with that, Fiona,' Rainger said cheerily. 'I want a real drink. It could be the last for some considerable time. In fact I want champagne. Last request and all that. Hang on . . .'

He went off. He was unique. To see him working on the old farmer and his son had been a rare and wonderful experience. Speaking with that clipped and authoritative tone that came so naturally to him, he'd explained to them that he and I were high-grade secret law who had been trying to infiltrate and expose a powerful drugs ring, that the women were police officers posing as our wives, and that it was essential we got to Beckford quickly and under cover. It all sounded so far-fetched, and was so cogently put across, that it had the stamp of total veracity.

In the end they couldn't do enough for us. The old one had been in the last war and knew exactly how men in command sounded; he instinctively began to address Rainger as sir. Ignoring the foul language and protestations of the men in the pit that it was the other way about, that they were the police and we the villains, father and son helped us to tip the comatose Red into the pit too, and we bolted the trapdoor on the three of them.

The farmer's wife had then made us great mugs of sweet tea and served us with what she called oven-bottom cakes and freshly-made butter. The old farmhouse was built like a fortress, with stone walls a foot thick, stout heavy doors and shutters that could be swung across the windows, Rainger and I and the farmer's son took it in turns to guard the yards and kitchen gardens surrounding the house from the windows of the upper floor. But no one else came, and we guessed they'd either assumed the three men were still searching or, more likely, with our gathering reputation, were too scared to follow in the others' tracks without even more reinforcements. As we ate hungrily, the old man, his voice quavering with emotion, had begun to recount his experiences at Dunkirk for us, seeming to find them relevant in some obscure and tenuous way to our own situation.

At dawn, the son had covered us in a tarpaulin on the back of his lorry, and driven us over field tracks and narrow minor roads, until we joined the main highway well beyond the point where the road-block had been set up. At Helmsley we'd hired a car from a friend of his, and by nine we were in Daisy Edge Drive, where men in casual dress could be glimpsed through arched gateways loading golf-clubs and fishing tackle into car boots, and we could hear the placid chimes of a nearby church clock.

'Life goes on,' Rainger murmured. It said it all.

Our safe arrival in Beckford had been the signal for the farmers to inform the police of the men in the pit. They had my keys and would look after my Sierra until I returned in the hire-car. Their part in the story would be given to Fenlon when he contacted me. It was all over. It was finished. I'd won. I sat staring into space, trying to cope with my success, like a boxer who'd struck the winning blow, but had sustained a great many well-placed punches to his own head.

Rainger returned with two opened bottles of Krug, and one unopened, on a silver tray, their sides misting with condensation. He poured the foaming liquid into tall glasses, on which sunlight produced minute prisms from their delicate cutting, and handed them round.

For me, the first sip of it on that peaceful Sunday morning put it in the pâté de foie gras and trumpets class. It didn't produce euphoria so much as release it, the teeth-tingling euphoria of still being alive, of having got Rainger across a Yorkshire that had seemed like a county on the brink of civil war, and on to his own elegant hearthstone, ready and willing to name spectacular names. I'd had a massive professional success, I was proud of it and I was going to make the very most of it – it was unlikely there'd be another.

Mrs Rainger and Fern drank deeply too, but whatever the costly liquid produced in them it certainly wasn't euphoria. They couldn't keep their eyes from their man, who'd probably never looked more attractive, with his grime-streaked face, tousled hair and stubble of beard, his blue eyes still blazing with the high that came from just having spent what must have been the most exhilarating hours of his life. He'd been within seconds of a bullet through the heart – you didn't get a charge like that too many times in a lifetime. Isolated once more in their brooding inner worlds, their eyes followed his animated progress about the great room. I remembered a phrase by Beerbohm about a bitter freemasonry of women who loved the same man. It had certainly been there when they'd crept up behind Red, and Mrs Rainger had swung the gun-butt with a ferocity I could still scarcely believe could exist in such a dainty body, a ferocity that could only have been fuelled by an overwhelming urge to keep Rainger alive. And belonging to her.

I looked at Fern, resignation inevitably tempering my sense of triumph. The same fierce obsession with Rainger had flowered in her too – if it had ever really died – the only difference between hers and Mrs Rainger's being that the roots hadn't had time to grow so strong or run so deep.

Rainger began to sing 'Tie a Yellow Ribbon' in an unsurprisingly good deep voice as he poured more wine.

'I know it's an odd time of day,' he said, 'but I'm in quite a party mood. Can anyone do tricks or tell funny stories?'

I couldn't help smiling. Only Rainger would want to dance and skylark in the shadow of the prison door. He wasn't really wicked, he was Peter Pan. He simply could not cope with the responsibilities of the adult world, could not connect his actions in the drug trade with the human wreckage that floated in its wake, nor begin to comprehend why his light-hearted infidelities had brought his wife to the edge of serious mental disorder. Could not even think himself beyond the next hour, when the elegance of his Daisy Edge house would abruptly give way to the bare rooms and unsmiling faces of the police station. Right now, he wanted a knees-up.

But he was a man I would never be able to stop myself liking, even though I'd been brought up to despise most exactly those criminal types like him who stood well back from the consequences of their lucrative activities. I only wished I too felt in a party mood.

He was reminiscing now, as he poured yet more wine, about the times he'd gone to meet the London men in disguise. I sat, half smiling, yet with a steadily growing unease at the women's brooding silence.

'. . . must have been the actor in me, John, I loved changing my appearance – do *you* like the wigs and glasses? I'd feel I was a different man, I could get away from my boring old self. I'd sometimes take a chance and sit among men I'd known donkeys' years. Now and then one of them would give me a thoughtful look, but I'd have the tinted contact lenses in and the horn rims and the black wig and my eyebrows darkened, and I'd speak like this . . .' He gave an excellent impression of a north

European asking the way to the restaurant car in correct but over-precise English. '. . . and no one ever knew. You know, the sods would sometimes even talk about the *real* Rainger with me sitting there.' He began to laugh. 'I tell you I learnt more about the real Rainger than I really wished to know . . .'

'Milo,' Mrs Rainger said, 'you can't go to prison . . .'

Milo. It must have been the nickname used by family and close friends. And once, when Fern had slept with me, she'd called me Lymo. Which was clearly her own private inversion of Milo, to separate her from the rest, and which I had imagined to be spelt with a 'y'. The word brought back much, with alcohol speeding the images, that I no longer wished to remember.

The smile had left Rainger's face. He looked at his wife almost blankly.

'You can't go to prison, Milo. You *know* you can't . . .'

He continued to watch her uncomprehendingly. It was supposed to be cut and dried. He was a decisive man who'd made his decision and, though she'd objected bitterly at the time, he'd apparently convinced himself she'd accepted the inevitable and gone along with the idea. He'd thought it was all sorted, and now she wanted to change her mind. I suspected that the seeming capriciousness of women's minds must always have been a severe trial to him.

'My dear,' he said at last, 'I must. I don't want to go, for God's *sake*, but if I didn't my life wouldn't be worth fifty pence.'

'Miles . . .'

'But you've *seen* them,' he said, in a faintly aggrieved

tone. 'They're everywhere. If it hadn't been for you, they'd have killed me and John in the barn, and I'd not even be in a position to *go* to prison.'

'I can't . . . I can't let you go to one of those revolting places. I can't!'

She gulped the rest of her wine and put the glass down with a trembling hand.

'I must, Fiona,' he said, in that even, steely tone that I'd already learnt meant that further argument would be pointless. Because Rainger was living by a single word, a word I'd scoured my mind for to make prison seem tenable to him, a word that would gleam like a diamond against the drabness of the next years – freedom. Freedom from the heroin men, from the boredom of the chemical business, from the claustrophobia of the Daisy Edge minuet.

Freedom, above all, from Fiona Rainger.

We were well down the second bottle; Mrs Rainger distractedly picked it up, but the condensation made it slip through her fingers. Rainger, who still prowled restlessly about the hearth, caught it, filled her glass, topped up ours. This emptied it and he began to undo the wire from the third.

'You'll have us half-cut, Miles,' I said in protest, but he merely smiled and said: 'Why not?'

I was genuinely worried now, a sense of foreboding seemed to glide shark-like and menacing beneath the glittering surface of my euphoria. Because Mrs Rainger knew it too, had known from the precise moment of Rainger's own realisation that she was a major aspect of what Rainger wanted freedom from. Her grasp of the way his mind worked was the only real perception she seemed to possess.

'Miles, you *cannot* go to prison. Have you no idea – locked up in filthy cells with common criminals, no privacy, beastly food, nothing to do . . .'

He gave her a rueful smile. He knew. He knew perfectly well in another compartment of his mind, which the champagne was helping him to keep sealed, how impossibly hard it would be for a man like him to get through that stretch, however short. But right now, in the twilight hours of his comparative freedom, he merely wanted a little fun, and found it difficult to understand why anyone should want to deny him it, even his wife.

'Oh, I don't know,' he said lightly, 'I dare say they'll let me run the library or set up quality circles in mail-bag production, educated fellow like me.'

'Miles, we can give *ourselves* new identities, we can simply go, this morning. Mr Goss will help us, he's such a clever young man.'

I said gently: 'He knows too much, Mrs Rainger, about men who are drug millionaires. He'd not see the week out.'

'Fiona,' Rainger said, equally gently, 'we owe John and Fernande a debt we can never fully repay. How could we abandon them with a mess like this – a dead man at our other house, wounded men in an inspection pit, blown-up cars . . . be reasonable . . .'

I'd never heard anyone make a virtue out of a necessity with quite Rainger's appearance of unblinking sincerity.

'Miles, *please* . . .'

'Oh, shut it, you pathetic bitch.' Fern suddenly cut her off. 'The bastard's been pushing shit. Do you know what that stuff does? Do you? No, of course you don't, sat on

your fanny in your big house, year in year out. Above it
all. Well I *do* know what it does, I've *seen* what it does –
it turns kids from rat-trap broken homes into living
skeletons, who might just make it to twenty-five if they
don't catch AIDS from a dirty needle. That's what it
does, and that's why he's going inside, and if there were
any justice he'd be inside for *good*!'

They were her first words since entering the house.
Silence fell in the stately old room. She picked her glass
up and drained it as the other woman had done a few
minutes before. It had all sounded very righteous and
noble, but I'd not been taken in by a word of it. I was
certain she'd known about the heroin all along, or at the
very least that Rainger was a criminal. It was simply
jealous spite, and I wished to God Rainger hadn't
produced alcohol in such quantity, that he could have
calculated the effect it was going to have on two
exhausted women who couldn't get him off their minds.

'Miles,' Mrs Rainger said, 'I beg you to find another
way. There must be *something* we can do.'

I don't believe anything she could possibly have done
could have roused more fury in Fern than to disregard
totally what she'd said, to wait, while Fern was speaking,
with preoccupied indifference for her to finish, as if she
were an external interference you could do nothing
about, like thunder or a road-drill or a jet-plane passing
over, that held up a phone conversation. But I suspected
it was anger that the performance itself had been
ignored, not the apparently impassioned sentiments.

Fern leapt to her feet; I leapt to mine. I caught her
forearm. 'Fern,' I said, 'for Christ's sake, cool it! Can't
you see how overwrought she is . . .'

'Cool it!' she cried. 'Cool it! When you and I were

nearly killed. When we put ourselves on the line to get him and this pampered bitch back in one piece, and all she can think of is dumping the whole shitty mess on us.'

Neither Fern nor Rainger seemed to have an inkling how ill Mrs Rainger was. Her behaviour *was* monstrous, and that itself was the evidence – it was the behaviour of an unbalanced mind. It was as if they were so charged with their own powerful emotions – his vision of freedom, her embittered love for him – that there was no calm place in their minds where they could judge the poor creature for what she'd become.

'Be quiet!' Mrs Rainger suddenly cried. 'Be quiet this minute! How *dare* you! Don't you think you've done enough damage to my marriage? I *knew* . . . I've known for months, some cheap office slut . . . I don't blame *him*, he's not made of marble, I blame you, you little tart, for tempting him. He's married and he's almost forty – why couldn't you find a man your own age . . . *and* your own frightful type . . .'

I'd seen many of Fern's faces, but never one so dark and contorted. I took her by the shoulders, which were shaking as if she had some tropical disease. But I think I knew even then that overwrought as she herself was, she was giving one of the dramatic performances of her life, that though flushed and trembling with genuine emotion she was bringing to her outbursts all the skill and control of a remarkable talent not yet given its head.

'Leave it,' I said, with a coolness I had to struggle to find. '*Leave* it, Fern. No more. It's over, all of it. He's going inside and you'll never see him again. Now *leave* it . . .'

I doubt if she registered a word. '*I* tempted *him*!' she screamed, pushing me aside as if I were furniture she had to get past. '*I* tempted *him*! You want your head looking at. You're out of your tree. What kind of world do you live in? *Me* tempt *him*!'

'Oh, for heaven's sake, Fernande,' Rainger said, not so much in anger as exasperation. 'My wife flew off the handle. She didn't mean it. We've all had a difficult time. John's right, let's leave it out. I've gone wrong and I admit it and I'm going to do my time . . .'

'A *deal*!' Fern cried. 'That's what you're going to do – a deal. Well, you can talk your way out of your proper sentence, but you're not going to set me up for that bitch to throw shit at. Well, tell her the truth, *tell* her!'

'Oh, Fernande . . .'

She suddenly strode across the hearth and stood above Mrs Rainger. 'That bastard of a husband of yours,' she said, her lips inches from the other woman's face, 'prison's too good for him. I'll tell you about your precious Milo – he never stopped pestering me for sex. I *knew* he was married, and I told him to get lost a dozen times, but he wouldn't give in. And when he'd weaseled his way into my bed he told me he was going to divorce *you* and *we* were going to London to set up a model agency, and he'd help me to run it while I tried to get acting work. And do you think I'd have given a *fiddler's* if he slept with half the models as long as I was the one he wanted to live with? Only it was the usual Milo bullshit, wasn't it. Bullshit, bullshit, BULLSHIT! He'd had it off with half the women at Brit-Chem and told them all what they wanted to hear. That's his bullshit style. They took pity on me when it was over, and we all compared notes. But I'd *believed* his bullshit, you see, I'd believed it all, because that prick could make you believe green was red, and no one, *no one*, ever hurt me as badly as that bastard did. For Christ's *sake*, if he'd just wanted a *jump* I wouldn't have given a toss. What's a *jump*. But he never stopped talking about the life we'd have when he'd got shot of *you*!'

Mrs Rainger's face was as bloodless as the face of a corpse. She glanced round her with eyes that had become vacant with pain. Then she looked back at Fern's contorted features, inches from her own. Finally her eyes sought Rainger's, who stood looking deeply pained, though more, I suspected, at the ruining of his happy hour than his wife's distress, which he must have seen many times and grown accustomed to.

'Is . . . this . . . can this be true, Miles?'

'Oh, my dear,' he said, and there was something in the exasperated patience that hinted at those endless scenes that must at times have been of such ferocity as to relieve him completely, if only for a short time, of the boredom that accompanied unremitting success.

'Well, don't ask *him*!' Fern cried. 'What do you think *he'll* tell you? Just *wait*, wait till he's out of the slammer with his fancy new identity . . .'

She, too, had understood every nuance of Miles's sudden willingness, almost eagerness, to go inside. That made four of us. I forced her to turn round to me. I'd been right behind her as she'd crossed the hearth, in an attempt to shut off that stream of words that seemed to have been instinctively spat out in the best order to have the utmost impact and inflict the greatest pain, but I'd realised the only way I could silence her would have been to put my hand over her mouth, which I knew quite certainly she would then have bitten, to the bone if necessary.

'Fern,' I said quietly, 'if you say one more word, one more, I'll throw you out.'

She tore her arm free with all the deceptive strength that lay beneath the seeming fragility, and I flinched slightly from the half-expected blow to the head that I knew only too well how capable she was of delivering. But the look on my face stopped her, the look that told her I seethed with an anger that was as powerful as her own, but was completely natural and not specially fanned up for the occasion. She knew I meant exactly what I said.

'Miles,' Mrs Rainger almost whispered, 'how could you do this to me?'

Rainger's eyes met mine. He shrugged. He'd not made the remotest attempt to intervene in the dog-fight. None of it concerned him any more. Fern had managed to blow his cover completely, but as usual he'd be able to tiptoe round the debris and start afresh. In a few years he'd be a new man with a new name and in a position to start creating havoc among the women all over again. He could afford to be patient and calm.

He put a hand on her shoulder. 'Now, Fiona . . . what do these silly peccadilloes really matter? In the end it's only ever been me and you, you know that, it's fifteen years now . . .'

But giving a long low moan, like a wounded animal, she suddenly leapt to her feet and ran from the room.

'Well, Fernande, I hope you're pleased with yourself. You've put me *right* in it, haven't you?'

But he spoke with an underlay of affection, as a fond father might speak to a naughty child. Nothing really mattered too much today, he'd burnt his boats and the glorious blaze they were making was lighting his way to

391

that new life where the boring old Miles and his boring old wife and his boring old mistress would seem as if they existed in some dream difficult to reconstruct.

Fern had become very still. She'd had her almost orgasmic moment of high drama, she'd let it all hang out, she'd never delivered her lines to greater effect. But it had achieved nothing beyond the rush she'd got from the performance and she knew it. He couldn't be won back. He didn't want her, nor his wife. He didn't want anyone. All he needed now was himself. He'd tried ambition and the games the wealthy played, he'd flirted with crime – none of them had brought the fulfilment he seemed always to have sought and never found. So now he would divest himself of everything and start the search again, free of people, possessions and society. From now on I was certain he'd be rootless, using the money he'd salted away abroad to live simply, working occasionally, drifting a lot, sleeping with a woman when he got the urge, but never again letting a woman deflect him from the quest for the definitive excitement and danger. He lived at one with his perfect body, with something of the animal grace of Fern herself, and the only company he would need now until he grew old would be his own. And when he was old there'd not be the slightest problem in finding some strong, healthy and adoring woman to take care of him until he died.

'I'd better go and calm the old girl down,' he said. 'Your police chum shouldn't be long now. I suppose taking it all round the champagne was a mistake. Still, with me mistakes tend to be a way of life.'

He went off across the hall. Suddenly, we heard him shout: 'FOR GOD'S SAKE, FIONA!' and then we heard a deafening report. When I got to the kitchen I could scarcely bring myself to look at what she'd made of his head with the shotgun, discharged at point-blank range, the selfsame shotgun she'd swung like a club to knock a man senseless who was about to kill the husband she worshipped.

I heard a strangled cry from behind me and the sound of Fern's sudden retching. The stream of vomit hit my shirt-sleeved arm with a force like a jet from a pressure-hose. I took the smouldering weapon gently from Mrs Rainger and led her, as if she were a sleep-walking child, past the blood-stippled walls. The hall was suddenly filled with a peculiar physical chill and I began to tremble uncontrollably – it was the same inexplicable chill that had been there on the two previous occasions I'd entered the house, and I remembered my deep uneasiness about taking the Rainger case. It was as if the house had soaked up her unhappiness and her corrosive jealousy into its very fabric, and tried to warn me of the dreadful consequences of any involvement.

As I led her back into the drawing-room, I couldn't stop myself compulsively stroking her dark, sleek hair with my free hand. The wall-clock began placidly chiming the hour, and at that moment the phone rang.

Twenty-Seven

'There's a lot of it about, you know,' Kev said, 'drugs. My nephew, he's as straight as they come, but he knows what goes on. You can get anything on Dresden, he tells me.'

'*Apart* from women?' Tom said.

Kev laughed shortly. 'No, seriously, no kiddology. You name it, someone'll have it in your hand in five minutes – heroin, crack, Ecstasy, LSD – you just name it. There you go, squire . . .'

He put the gin and tonic before me, abstractedly rang up my money on the till. 'And it's not cheap – you're talking ten, twenty, thirty notes a throw for something you can hardly *see*. Now where do they get that kind of money from when two thirds of them are out of work? Burglary, right, mugging, right, stolen wheels. And what protection has the citizen got? When I was a kid during the war, me and my mum, we'd walk *miles* in the black-out, never no trouble. Same in the Fifties. And people were poorer then, hadn't got a penny to scratch their backsides with. You can't walk around in the dark now, not in some areas. You never *see* a bobby, not unless they're teararsing about in cars flashing like Christmas trees . . .'

'I take a big thick stick when I'm on foot at night,' Tom said. 'Pretend I've got a bit of a limp. *And* I'd use it. I wouldn't care about the consequences. No one gives a sod about the victim, so I'd make damn sure I didn't get to be one.'

'That's the way it's going, isn't it? If the politicians and the police can't protect us we'll have to start protecting ourselves. But then you get done for that, don't you, not the bad lot, *you* – remember that chap in the Tube with the ornamental sword . . .?'

I became aware of Fenlon at my side. It was the first time I'd seen him in an unofficial capacity since the killing of Rainger.

'I'm afraid you're not getting a very good press this evening,' I said lightly. 'Tom's more or less encouraging us to take arms against a sea of troubles, a very dodgy metaphor if ever there was one, bard or no bard . . .'

'Let's sit down, John.'

We took our drinks to a corner table, where diffused late-September sunlight slanted through dust-motes from one of the lancet windows. It would soon be autumn and we'd lose an hour of what little evening light was left. Leaves were already blowing across Town Hall Square from the ornamental trees. The season was an exact match for my spirits.

'We've lost everything, John,' he said heavily, at last. 'Red Harris and those other goons haven't a clue who was pulling their strings. Genuinely. They're contact-men. Not that they'd tell us if they did, not even to reduce their sentences.'

'Well at least there's no Beckford connection now,' I said bitterly. 'It died when he did.'

'They'll have someone in place overnight. They'll

jettison the mail system, but there'll be a dozen other
ways . . .'

'For Christ's *sake* Bruce,' I said, in a low, harsh voice,
'how could I know she was going to top the poor sod?'

'We've ended up with less than nothing because
they're all on their guard now. They'll never take a
chance with a talented amateur again – from now on
they'll keep it all in the family. We'll be lucky if we get
another lead this side of the millennium. And you *knew*.
The last time we were in this pub you were starting to tell
me . . .'

'And I'd just realised Fern was at risk. Where do you
think *my* priorities were? Bruce, they blew her bloody
wheels up within the *hour!*'

'So then you go to the sodding seaside without telling
anyone . . .'

'I had *decisions* to make. I was under pressure and I
thought they'd get to us before we could get it sorted
with the law . . .'

'John . . .'

'*I* talked him into it. Do you think the law would have
got two-penn'orth out of him if I'd not softened him up
first . . .'

'Good news bad news – you had him singing like
Pavarotti just before his head fell off . . .'

'Oh, *piss off!*'

'Yes, well, if you'd told us right at the start we could
have done all the things you did without all the flying
hardware. It was police work, John, *and you damn well
know it* . . .'

'And I'd not be getting all this earache, would I, if I'd
delivered the sod with his head still on. A rap on the
knuckles, that's all it would have been, not this downright

hostility from that lot down there . . .'

'That's what the police are *like*,' he said quietly. 'You *know* what they're like. Your dad *told* you what they were like . . .'

I picked up my gin with a trembling hand. 'Look, Bruce, if you'd done it your way you'd have nailed him but you'd have got nothing from him. I built up a *rapport*. There was only one thing that would make him talk and I found out what it was. He liked me and he trusted me because he knew I'd nothing to gain, except to go on living. I sold him a bill of goods.'

He was silent for some time.

'It's just you, isn't it? It's just the way you are. You've a chip on your shoulder the size of a sideboard and you just can't stop yourself being a one-man police force.'

Almost shaking with the anger that came along with the exact truth, I abruptly got to my feet and walked across the bar-parlour and out, Kev's cheery 'See you later, John' ignored. Fenlon caught up with me as I was putting the key in the lock of my car-door.

'John . . .'

'You've got some room to talk. What's bugging you is the glory you're going to lose. They'd have made you up after all this, for having access to such a sophisticated snout. *My* slogging hard work, your leg-up . . .'

The pain I'd given him equalled the pain he'd given me; we stood in the falling misty light like bare-knuckle fighters who'd battered each other to the point of mutual exhaustion.

He looked away, spoke again only after a lengthy silence. 'Do you remember Keith Moorhouse?' he said finally. 'You had a complete *file* on the guy. How old were we – twelve? You knew everything about him . . . some guy we'd picked out on the street – his age, his job, the names of his wife, his kids, his dog, where they had their holidays, you even found out he was screwing around . . .' He shook his head. 'Some guy we picked out on the street and in the end you knew things about him his wife didn't know.'

He turned back to me. 'I've never forgotten it, John. I got pissed off half-way through, but you never stopped till there were no more details to get. I've never forgotten it . . . never really been able to get it off my mind.'

He put a hand on my arm. 'I can't remember a time when we weren't friends – our mothers took us out in our push-chairs together. Let's put this lot behind us. The woman was crazy . . . it was the worst possible luck. It was a brilliant piece of work, John. I've never denied that you're the born detective, and me . . . well, I'm just good old reliable Fenlon, like my old man.'

I clasped my hand over the hand that held my arm, unable to speak for a moment. He'd never denied it because until this evening he'd never admitted it, and I knew what it must have cost him to make that admission.

I'd known Rainger about seventeen hours, and I couldn't have imagined how much I'd miss him. It wasn't missing him so much as a person, because had it all worked out I'd not have seen much of him anyway, it was missing the *idea* of him. If he'd stayed alive, we'd have met again. One day, in his new identity, he'd have re-entered my life.

'We'll keep in touch, John,' he said once, as we did our stint of guard duty at the upstairs windows of the farmhouse. 'I'll not forget you. We have a lot in common, you and me. When all this is over I'll give you a holiday. Somewhere where there's sun and water and hills.'

I'd believed him. Surrounded by people, in a structured society, we were both loners at heart, following stars so obscure as to be almost undetectable, living lives that only we ourselves could really make much sense of. Deliberately absent-minded about his other relationships, I knew he'd not forget me, we'd keep in touch, if only to meet for a few days a year at some stationary point of his endless travels. And what days they'd be, if only for the tales he'd be able to tell, of other people's wars, of latter-day Klondikes, of uninhabited islands and sailing across treacherous seas, of the ceaseless search for the definitive danger, adventure and flight. It would seem an enviably long life because I'd read that constant travel gave you an impression of getting a lot for your money.

He never mentioned his wife in terms of what he called Life After Stir, and it came to be tacitly accepted by both of us that she'd not figure in it, came to be agreed in hints and nudges that I'd help to set her up in some sort of life that would never again involve him.

As if any of it had ever been possible. I sometimes wondered if he'd been drawn to Fiona Rainger because he'd sensed the most spectacular danger of all, because his fate had been fixed when he'd married that pretty, penniless, idolising girl he'd met at the parties at the big Yorkshire houses. And I realised now how impossible it had been for him to be killed at the house on the coast or up on Goathland Moors or in the old barn. Death wasn't there. Death had made its precise long-term appointment on the day Rainger married, and though he had seemed to glimpse it several times along the way it was only because Death was travelling a parallel track, to reach its planned destination in a sunny kitchen on Daisy Edge Drive.

'Moral,' Rainger had once said, with jovial prescience, 'never confront a woman in a kitchen.'

I met Fern by chance one day in the street. We both stopped with what seemed to be the same reluctance. Her glance met mine, fell away, came back. Her smile was so brief as to be almost undetectable.

'John . . . how are you?'

I shrugged. 'So-so. And you?'

'Well enough. Are you still . . . working your twelve-hour days?'

I smiled wryly. 'If only to make up the income I've lost through interminable police interviews.'

'It must have cost you an awful lot.'

'Not just money. It's put a bit of a dent on my reputation in places where it counts. Fortunately people soon forget . . .'

She turned away; it had been an inappropriate choice of words.

'What . . .' She swallowed, and her eyes shone slightly as she turned back to me. 'How will it work out?'

'She'll never stand trial. Her mind's gone completely. And the way things are she's never going to want it back . . .'

She looked away again, gazing at passing traffic with unfocused eyes.

'Did you sort out your car?' I said. 'How do insurance companies react to blown-up cars? The third party claims must have been enormous, all those fancy motors . . .'

'I'm sorry,' she said suddenly. She dragged her gaze back to my eyes. 'I'm sorry, John. Please believe me. I'm so sorry.'

Tears glittered along her lids in the milky sunlight. 'I didn't want that, oh *God*, I never wanted that. Please believe me, *please* . . .'

She'd not wanted Laurence Fielding to die either, but her silence had helped to kill him just as her finest speech had helped to kill Rainger.

We were getting attention from passers-by. We were behind the Town Hall. There was a subway not far away that led to a sunken garden beneath a roundabout. I led her there and we sat on a bench.

'Oh *God*, John, I wish I could take it back, those things I said . . .'

She began to cry, heavy tears welling in those green eyes set fractionally too far apart, then dripping down her cheeks. I put my arm round her. She'd made me very angry, angrier than anyone had ever made me, so furious that I'd not wanted to see her again, in case I'd not be able to keep myself under control.

But time had passed, six weeks of it, and I'd come to accept how profoundly Rainger affected people, because each day I myself woke up with a sense of loss. Fern had wanted him just as desperately as Mrs Rainger, and it had been genuine emotion that had taken her over the top, even if latent skills and disciplines had enabled her to beat each word like a nail into that other woman's deranged mind.

I had come to believe in fact that Fern's love for Rainger had been stronger, more focused even, than his wife's, more somehow the real thing. Mrs Rainger had seemed to regard him almost as a possession, in the same class as the exquisite objects that filled her house, the most treasured possession of all, of course, but still somehow an object, which she was delighted for people to look at in envy and admiration, but could not bear them to touch. I suppose in a way he'd been her creation, because, though she'd brought no money to the marriage, she'd brought incredible style, and when she'd finished her tuition of that remarkable pupil he could be sent into any drawing-room and over any grouse moor, an almost identical match with any member of that old-money society she knew so well.

Fern, I felt, had fallen for the real Rainger. I'd had no difficulty in believing her when she'd screamed at his wife that he could sleep with half the models as long as it was her he wanted to live with. She herself had always used sex to get the things she wanted, just as a wealthy man used money or a salesman his gift of the gab. It was simply a tool, if not a weapon, and she could never understand people who couldn't see it in the same light. She'd wanted the man within, whom she'd not had the remotest difficulty in defining beneath the trappings, because no one she'd ever known had existed so precisely on her level of perception, had the same eternal urge for reinvention, the same ruthless instinct for an objective, the same indifference to the pain of others, the same relaxed ability to live immediately behind the cutting edge. If Mrs Rainger had insisted on exclusive rights to his body, Fern, it seemed, would have settled happily for possession of that vessel, no shallower than her own, his soul.

And Rainger had suddenly had enough, had decided that the finest luxury of all was to keep both under his own control.

'Don't blame yourself, Fern,' I said at last. 'You couldn't know she was off her head.'

'I can't help it. I *wanted* him to suffer. He'd made me suffer and I wanted her to know what he'd meant to me so she'd make *him* suffer. I knew she would . . . she was so *possessive* . . . I knew she would. I wanted him to suffer for the rest of his life. But I didn't want that. Oh God, John, I never wanted that.'

'You were past it,' I said. 'You'd not slept for twenty-four hours. And then pouring all that booze down, it would never have happened without all that alcohol on an empty stomach.'

'I loved him too much, John,' she whispered. 'You never want to hurt anyone you don't care a damn about.'

As if I hadn't known. I gazed bleakly over the enclosed garden. Even at the height of our love-making there'd never been any of the emotion I'd glimpsed the morning she'd been half asleep and thought I was Rainger – 'Oh, Lymo, darling Lymo . . .'

I'd once been on the verge of believing we might make some kind of a go of it, that I'd go to London and live with that part of her that was left over from her quest to become an actress. As if anything would have worked, however badly, with any woman who'd known Rainger. There'd been nothing Rainger could touch that didn't turn either to gold or ashes.

I took both her hands in mine. 'Don't blame yourself, Fern,' I said. 'I don't. Truly. You couldn't know you were pushing her over the edge. Miles . . . didn't, and he lived with her. It was the way things were . . . because she was who she was . . . he was who he was . . . can you understand?'

We sat for an hour in the slanting September sunlight,

404

beneath an enlarged sun that gave off little heat. I worked very hard to convince her the blame wasn't hers. She accepted it in the end because she'd detected the sincerity in my tone, a sincerity based on my own sense of guilt. Because I knew in some part of my mind, and it explained a lot of my original anger with her, that I'd tried to load the whole of it on to her. And it had been too easy.

He was dead now, and none of it would make any difference to that, but if she was to blame then so was I. And my blame was greater. It wasn't just the police case I'd ruined by not going to them sooner, it was also because of that decision that three powerfully volatile elements had been shaken together, and I'd been the catalyst that had precipitated the explosion.

'Give yourself a break, Fern.'

After a time, she nodded.

'Are you going back to London?'

'Next week. My agent's got me an audition,' she said, with a sidelong glance, 'for a 2TK.'

We both began to smile, and I remembered how we'd shouted at each other at the roadside on the night we'd taken flight from Beckford.

She began to dab her cheeks with a moistened pad she produced from her bag. I remembered my mother's near-disintegration after my father's sudden death – the hollow cheeks, the bruised-looking eyes, the weight-loss. It had lasted many weeks, had made me think at one stage I should lose her too.

Fern showed none of that disintegration, and yet I knew her love for Rainger had been equally powerful. Her face was as smooth and unlined as it had always been, the eyes as clear, the colour as healthy. She had

405

once quoted Homer at me in what now seemed a separate existence, and I felt she would have grieved for Rainger as Odysseus and his men had grieved for their lost comrades devoured by Scylla – first making a substantial supper, then satisfying their hunger and thirst, and then weeping for their dead comrades before falling heavily asleep – in that order.

I was certain she'd have wept endlessly as the classical guitar music filled her attic flat, then she would carefully have bathed her eyes to reduce the swelling, and then she would have slept that perfect unbroken sleep, where repair-work would have been continuous and totally effective.

I also felt that in a way the drama of that abandoned weeping would have appealed to her, as would, despite the guilt, the total drama of those twenty-four hours. I was suddenly quite certain that, just as Rainger's death had been pencilled in on the day he married the Forbes-Walshaw girl, Fern would, with the same inevitability, be given the acting role one day that would lead to the only fulfilment she'd ever really sought or needed.

Because her acting skills would almost certainly have gained a new dimension. She knew at first hand now how people reacted to danger and fear and death, what it was to love and lose, and to grieve. She'd never forget the impact of those powerful emotions which, combined with her training and her talent, would bring to her acting a remarkable maturity.

We began to walk back to where our paths had crossed.

'Look,' I said, 'can I ask you something – you don't need to answer if you don't want to; I'm just a detail freak. You did *know* he was in the drugs game, didn't you?'

We walked for several more steps before she spoke, in that even, unemotional tone I'd once decided was the only one that seemed to indicate she wasn't acting.

'He . . . *was* going to go to London with me. He'd made a definite promise to help me with an agency. He said that by the autumn he could invest a hundred thousand – it seemed no big deal to him . . .' She hesitated. 'I knew his wife wasn't going to give him that kind of loot, however rich she was, and I thought she *was* rich then. I knew he couldn't be making it at Brit-Chem. I've . . . been in London a long time – you pick up the vibes. There aren't many kinds of crime where you keep your hands clean and make serious money . . .

'One day . . .' she said, then broke off, blinking rapidly and touching one eyelid with the knuckle of an index-finger. 'One day the offers were suddenly off – managing my career, the agency, the money . . .'

That would have been the day he'd realised that leaving his wife for Fern would simply mean that the title deeds of ownership would pass from one to the other.

She breathed deeply, turned to face me. 'Well . . . goodbye, John . . .'

We both knew it was exactly that, that there was no point in prolonging the farewells with a last drink or meal, or promising even to have a night out together when I was next in London.

'See you at the Haymarket,' I said, trying to keep my voice light and emotion-free.

She smiled faintly, but made no attempt to deprecate the implication; perhaps she knew just as surely as I did myself what her future held.

'Good luck with your work,' she said. 'The police were awfully angry, weren't they. Will it affect your business?'

'No.' I shook my head. 'The police look after their own, even when you screw up.'

'But you're not police . . .'

'No,' I sighed, 'but they've always known I should have been.'